The Golden Door

By Alice Mitchell

With all my best wishes,

Alice Mitchell

The Golden Door – ISBN 978-1-3999-9386-9
Copyright © 2024, published by Arcanum Press Ltd.

Arcanum Press Ltd. is registered in England & Wales, company number 10704825.

The right of Alice Mitchell to be identified as the author of this work has been asserted by them in accordance with the Copyright, Design and Patents Act 1988.

All rights reserved. No part of this publication may be reproduced, stored in a retrieval system, or transmitted in any form or by any means without the prior written permission of the publisher, not be otherwise circulated in any form of binding or cover other than that it is published and without a subsequent condition being imposed on the subsequent purchase.

This novel is a work of fiction, although a great many of the historical details are factual.

Printed and bound in Dorset, England, United Kingdom or in the State of Kansas, United States of America.

Front Cover:
The 'Yorkshire' Packet Ship circa 1840
(credit – Mary Evans Picture Library).

Rear Cover:
Battle of Roanoke Island, North Carolina 1862
(credit – Mary Evans Picture Library).

Grateful thanks are extended to members of the Kansas Chapter of the Daughters of the British Empire (DBE) particularly Lynette Chastain, Lynda Krupp, Brenda Marks and Sally Helm. A special note of sincere thanks is due to Pattie Underwood of the DBE for her invaluable feedback, advice, motivation and steer.

The DBE are a non-profit American society of women of British and Commonwealth of Nations birth or ancestry. They share and promote their heritage while supporting local charities and their own senior living facilities across the United States.

We would also like to thank Ben Martin and Julie Robinson of the Kansas City branch of the English-Speaking Union in the United States (ESU-USA) for their advice, engagement, and support. For over 100 years the Kansas City branch of the ESU has continued the tradition of employing English as a shared language to inspire common bonds of friendship, development and learning.

Many thanks to Amy Brown, Kim Lovelady and Tracy Mills-Woodward for their feedback and comments. Thanks also to Eric Davis for his consultation and advice on aspects of the American Civil War.

The Daughters of the British Empire (Kansas Branch) and the English-Speaking Union - United States (Kansas City) will both receive donations from the sales of this book as will other selected historical societies and organisations linked to the American Civil War.

Author & Publisher Notice

Language and story disclaimer for
The Golden Door

This book contains language and themes that some readers may find offensive. The content is intended to present an accurate picture of the culture that immigrants encountered in the 1800s. In no way should the use of words, or phrases from that time period, that are currently unacceptable in written and spoken discourse be construed as reflecting the author's or publisher's beliefs or opinions as to what is acceptable today.

The author and publisher also believe that certain acts and behaviours depicted in *The Golden Door* are clearly not appropriate in today's world. They are included in the narrative to give readers a comprehensive understanding of time in which the action and story are set.

Finally, this book was not written to attack or diminish any group of people. The author vehemently opposes the use of hate speech or discrimination in any form.

Reader discretion is advised.

For my son Richard

"Give me your tired, your poor,
Your huddled masses yearning to breathe free,
The wretched refuse of your teeming shore.
    Send these, the homeless, tempest-tost to me,
I lift my lamp beside the golden door."

Extract from: The New Colossus
by Emma Lazarus.

Part One

The Emigrants

Chapter One

HARTLEY

1ˢᵗ June 1850

The wind is gusting in strong from the sea, bringing a light rain before it. All the creeping fog and dismal darkness of last night is gone. The ship creaks and strains to be off now that the tide is nearly full. Our sails should fill out and belly forth something grand when we pass the Mersey Bar. Oh, Mother, I am sure you will not believe me when I tell you that the name of this packet is The Yorkshire! I think that a fine omen.

I wish I could tell you all the strange sights and sounds I have seen since reaching Liverpool, but it has all crowded in so fast that I hardly know where to begin.

Last night, in the boarding-house, which was but a filthy hole (and not one I would have chosen myself), it came close to overwhelming me. A rogue who called himself an 'agent' dragged my boxes off the train and insisted I go there. I thought him helpful enough when he took me to the broker's office to book my passage, but when he began talking of exchanging my sovereigns for American dollars, I knew at once I could not trust him. I am ashamed to tell you how much I had to pay the scoundrel to regain my own baggage and have done with him. Then, when I saw this boarding house, I own I wished I was back in Bradford with only the prospect of another day's work at the draper's shop before me. I was not alone in being downcast. Indeed, there was a wretched German family down in the cellar, unaccustomed to such privation, I would say. They had spent several nights in the dark amongst the rats without even my bare boards to sleep on. Suffice it to say, the father of this family, who looked nervous and far from strong, was in tears and loath to get on the carrier's dray when it came rumbling over the wet cobbles of Great Howard Street this morning. The horses' breath was steaming in the raw dawn air. They champed and worried at their bits, tossed their noble heads, and shuffled their hooves whilst the carrier fingered his whip.

But the unfortunate man could not get on. I never felt so sorry for any man before. If it were not for his wife, they would be there yet, I fancy, for it was she who, though heavy with child, shepherded their two boys aboard, comforting them all the while. It was she who chivvied the man about seeing to their boxes and spoke firmly, though with great kindness, to her husband.

She was a sturdy figure of a woman with a plain, dark, and strongly featured face. Her cheeks still had a bloom upon them, though she was well into her thirties. I could not tell what she said to him for they spoke in German. I wish I had gone forward and taken his arm on the other side, addressing him as 'Sir' and entreating him to be calm, but something held me back. In the end, she took his hand, and he allowed her to lead him upwards. I have not seen them since we reached the dock — they are lost in the milling hordes, but I have no doubt she got him aboard the vessel. She had that stamp about her.

The quayside was packed with people, and I had all ado to keep my wits and baggage about me, though I am only a single man with nothing but my own affairs to contend with. I wonder if the families managed to keep together at all, especially the Irish, with their children. There are hundreds of them and a dreadful, emaciated set of paupers they are. Only there was one girl, Mother, in a long cloak and *a bonnet with red ties. Most of them had only ragged shawls which were poor protection against the unseasonable weather.*

But this girl was better dressed than most, though just as bedraggled and wet as all the rest. She sat, weary unto death, on her trunk with a little one asleep in her arms, though she was scarcely more than a child herself. Of a husband, there was sign of none, and, in truth, there was a general air of desertion about her. Now, you will think me fanciful, I know, my poor head addled with the oddness of the scene, but I half-reckoned she was the Madonna.

Her dress was soiled and brown, not blue. But there was something singular about the way the grey, hooded cloak draped her head and shoulders. Such beauty she had, like the Virgin in religious works of art. Her hair (what I could see of it) was long and dark, and the wind blew tendrils of it round her face.

Such a face! Young and soft as a child's, with skin like pale porcelain and brilliant blue eyes. All the others jostled and pushed round her in the mad scramble to get on the boat. I wanted to help her but there was no way of getting through the crush. Her, too, I have not seen again, though I cannot put her out of my mind. Nor have I seen the wild, Welsh fellow — a little dark runt, in my opinion, with a curiously hoarse voice and breath that stank from the night before. The fellow kept on asking me about the arrangements on board, in particular, if there would be food and where we would sleep, as if he knew not what to expect in steerage. Perhaps he doesn't. The bulk of people here seem to be ill-prepared. I showed him my 'Emigrant Voyagers Manual', the same one I purchased in Leeds last month, but made sure I kept a tight hold on it. He had no baggage and claimed it had been stolen, but I do not believe he has a ticket, and I suspect he intends to stow away.

People! Never in my life have I seen such people teeming and crying on that spray-sodden quayside. The noise and the smell of them are all around me and are most unpleasant. You may well question, Mother (as I know you do), if I am right to go, despite all I have read about America in my library books. But if only half of it is true, this hardship will be worth it. I am convinced it is a land of opportunity where even a humble man may advance himself through merit. The others feel it, too, for not everyone is a-weeping and a-wailing. Far from it! There is great excitement, and we are glad to get on the ship.

Some did not make the gangplank, so they swarmed up the ropes and the sides even as The Yorkshire pulled away. There is obviously some danger in this, and there were those who inevitably fell off into the water. However, the captain ordered a boat to follow for the express purpose of picking them up. (I am told this demonstrates he is a good man, for others would have left them to drown.)

This is the beginning of our new life! In the middle of it all, a band is playing stirring music, and those friends and relatives left behind on the quayside cheer and wave and throw their hats in the air.

We waited our turn to pass through the dock-gates into the wider river. These docks are thick with masts for mile after mile. Vast stone warehouses line the seafront, massive as cathedrals and like unto them too, with wonderful arches and colonnades. This port must surely be the greatest in the world, though my common-sense tells me New York must be bigger and better by far. Nor will there be such an ill assortment of vagabonds and rogues in attendance there, I trust.

I, for one, will not let my eyes mist up as we slip down the river. Not even for thee, Mother, for I know you are in good hands now that Jeremiah has his living as our dear, departed father intended, and I, as his second son, intend to make my way in the world. If ever a city could spur one on to do better, it is Liverpool. For much evil walks the streets, and there is squalor beyond belief despite the sea-breezes and fine municipal buildings. Every kind of vermin and criminal is here; it is full of whorehouses and gin-shops, and I imagine a murder is committed somewhere every night with no end of robberies. I cannot think how the Madonna survived untouched. (Do not judge me blasphemous for naming her such — my weak brain is fairly turned.)

But enough! We are aboard, and the Blue Peter is flying! We sail on the old Black Ball line from Liverpool, and the steam-tugs are pulling us out into the river. The open sea beckons and, with it, the United States of America. God bless you, Mother, and keep you in good health!

I hope this letter reaches you, for I have my doubts upon the matter, having entrusted it to a scurvy young fellow who blithely followed us aboard, selling razors and tobacco, sweetmeats, medicines, soap, and mirrors. There are many like him, all anxious to ply their wares till the last possible moment. He seems confident of being put ashore with the orange girls when we drop anchor awhile in the river for some account of passengers to be given. I fear, however, that he may only pocket the shilling I unwisely gave him and dispose of the letter. This is my first and last missive from this shore. My next will, I trust to God, come from a fairer and richer soil should we escape shipwreck. I remain your loving and affectionate son,
Hartley Shawcross

Chapter Two

CAITLIN

She sat at a leather-topped desk by an open window in the library, one of her uncle's books spread out before her. It was Edmund Burke's *'Reflections on the Revolution in France,'* and very long-winded she found it too. After all, it was only three years since she had learnt to read and write at all. Before that, she had only spoken the Gaelic. She had been quick enough to learn, even though her only tasks until then had been helping to plant potatoes and cabbages on her father's three acres and saving turf from the bog for their fire.

An iron corcan hung over that smoking fire for the cooking. Her mother was long dead and gone; the memory of her hazy but pictured through an eddy of steam as she took the lid off the corcan to stir the pot of vegetables. Caitlin's life had changed when her father married again and provided her with a distant and mysterious uncle, as well as a stepmother called Bridget.

At first, James remained a shadowy figure in her stepmother's past: a half-brother whom she rarely spoke of, as if she were ashamed of him, instead of it being the other way round, for it was Bridget who had been born on the wrong side of the bedclothes. Now her parents were both dead, but James knew the secret and carried on a tradition of support. He had little gratitude from Bridget, for the times she did speak of him were full of contempt and bitterness. She called him a despicable landlord, like all the other Anglo-Irish, despite any assistance he gave them.

Bridget had arrived late one night with Padraig from the horse fair at Ballakenny, both of them full of gin. She was good-looking then and at least twenty years younger than him. What business had she in marrying Caitlin's poor, feckless, labouring father? Caitlin had not, at first, understood, even when Father Francis married the couple in double quick time. It was hard to accept the sudden coming of a stranger.

They continued to live together in the low, white cottage with its one-room entered by a stable door, its thatch roof, and its stinking turf fire. Bridget behaved as if she had never known anything else though she often had a terrible frustration on her. Then, it was wise to keep out of her way, though she was sorry afterwards. Caitlin expected Padraig to chastise her, but he never did. At night, from her cold bed in the corner, Caitlin could hear sounds of urgency and relief, which she did not fully understand. It had never occurred to her that her father could provide such like. In contrast, she felt unwanted.

When the baby came, it taught Caitlin a lot. It taught her about being a mother, for Bridget took no more notice of it than she must for it to survive. It was a girl-child like herself, and Caitlin fondly imagined it growing up under her own guidance. After all, she could provide almost everything that Bridget should. Then, it fell ill and did not survive after all, teaching Caitlin about death.

That was the first time she learnt of her step-uncle's existence, for it was James who sent the canopy of white calico to cover the tiny corpse, so icy cold and hard as a doll, stretched out with sightless eyes on their table.

She knew, of course, that her own mother had died when she was still small. That entailed a lack that had been there for many years.

She often thought about her mother, imagining her beautiful and kind and made up stories about her, telling herself she wasn't truly dead at all, just imprisoned somewhere against her will.

But this death was different. She had played with this child like the doll she had never had. She had picked it up carefully and held it tightly, stroking the tiny fingers that curled round her own, thrilling to the smile that came for her. She had loved her so much. Bridget was not that grief-stricken; in fact, she seemed relieved. Padraig cried foolishly and then forgot it. Only Caitlin could not forget. The baby was dead of a fever after crying and wingeing piteously for three days. Nothing could make her come back.

It taught Caitlin the meaning of guilt. For hadn't she wished sometimes — oh, long before the baby was born, and she fell in love with it — that such a misfortune might happen? She had been afraid the child would supplant her and would take away the little affection she had. Nobody knew about this but her and God. But God would know it was all her fault. You could be sure of that.

When James came stooping under their stone lintel for the first time with a handkerchief pressed to his mouth for fear of contagion, she thought he might bring some form of God's retribution. Her fears were confirmed when she learnt he wanted to take them all away. The potatoes had failed again that year, and the land had grown awful quiet. All the dogs were gone long since and the donkeys looked like skeletons. They had not had enough to eat for a long while. Little by little, each twist of smoke from each cottage was going out. It would then fall into disrepair, or the soldiers would come to tear down the stones. Many landlords were evicting tenants.

Bridget had lost her looks with every pound of flesh that had fallen away since she came to live with Padraig. It was no wonder the baby had died. James was clearly distressed by the look of her, but she had no intention of denying herself the pleasure of laughing in his face.

Caitlin could see that Padraig, left to his own devices, would have jumped at the chance of 'going to help at the big house'. Instead, there was a lot of foolish talk from the two of them. Eventually, Caitlin, at least, should go, leaving one less mouth to feed, whilst they would stay on to exist on the Indian meal given out at the soup kitchen in the village and do what they could. There was irony aplenty in this for, as Caitlin later discovered, that maize was provided by James. But at the time, she could only think of one thing: How could they abandon her to this monster who had been spoken of so harshly by Bridget?

She was simply terrified the day she left home, not remembering that James' serious, gaunt face had smiled kindly enough at her. He had sent a trap for her, no less, when she had expected to walk, and she bounced along in it helplessly, behind the driver's back, in her dirty red petticoat with her few belongings tied up in a bundle at her feet. The waters of the lough were still, and grey under the low cloud that sat on the distant mountain, and the big house with its eaves and odd turrets seemed to lack any welcome. Bridget had not prepared her for philanthropy. It was there, nevertheless, that her education had begun.

James had explained she must learn how to speak and write in English if she were ever to 'get on'. That puzzled her — where could she get on to? But Uncle James seemed keen on the idea. Indeed, he spoke of it so constantly that she began to feel he must want rid of her, too. Yet he was kind. For he taught her himself and was pleased at her rapid progress. Nevertheless, there were days when the sun shone, and she believed him a hard and strict taskmaster.

He did not send her away, as she had thought, though he did seem at a loss what to do with her next. The trouble was that Uncle James was not married. There was a housekeeper who taught her sewing and needlework. She did take pains with it, recognizing its usefulness, though she did not enjoy it and always seemed to prick her finger on the needle.

James did not put her to work either, as she thought he might. She was glad, for learning to ride a pony was much better sport. As for any other feminine accomplishments, her uncle was powerless to instruct her there. His only available resource was to guide her through his considerable library. Hence, the dreaded Edmund Burke.

A light wind from the open window stirred the discoloured pages of the book, seeming to invite their closure, and Caitlin yawned and sighed. When she lifted her head, which was often, she could see the waters of the lough sparkling in the sunlight. The same wind that rustled the pages stirred the bright reeds at the water's edge. She longed to be out there, running free. Jesus, Mary, and Joseph, how dry all this reading was when she could barely understand its meaning! It was such a disappointment when James had laid the book so reverently before her as if it contained the secret of life itself. It was not that she did not want to please him, for she knew he had opened a whole new world, and she was thoroughly grateful to be plucked out of hardship. She was aware there was some salacious talk in the village, but he never laid a finger on her.

But he had awakened new springs for her fertile imagination. For she guessed that her solitary uncle should take her to dances and introduce her to the local gentry in general, and their sons in particular, if she were ever really to 'get on'. It was no good keeping her cooped up in a musty-smelling old library all morning instead.

Nevertheless, when she looked round the room (for at least the hundredth time that morning), her heart softened a little. At least the outer bindings of Uncle James' books were beautiful. They seemed to glow with the promise of knowledge she had not found in them. From floor to ceiling, they imparted a sense of wisdom to the peaceful room. In the grate, a fire burnt and crackled as always, despite the mildness of the spring day. It brought life to the faded red carpet and the old-fashioned furnishings that were once expensive.

She had thought this room so fine such a short space of time ago and had been amazed at the gown of soft muslin laid out for her on that first day. The housekeeper had scrubbed all the dirt off her and taken away the red petticoat to be burnt. She had brushed her unkempt, gipsy hair with such determination that Caitlin had cried out. When, at last, her hair had been combed and neatly parted, she emerged like a timid butterfly with its wings still wet, all bright and clean in the sprigged muslin. Only then had she been allowed to join her uncle in the dining room.

This room struck a new chord of terror into her heart for a table of vast proportions, large enough to seat twenty at a pinch, stretched out like a mahogany lake before her and mirrored a bewildering assortment of silver cutlery, crystal, and china. She never understood why her uncle had to sit at one end of it and she the other whilst the butler pattered deferentially between them. For, in all the three years she spent with James, he never entertained anyone other than his pastor and Father Francis (who was intended to give Caitlin instruction in her native Catholic faith). They sat in stranded silence like a pair of beached shrimps on the shore. She much preferred the warm library after dinner, where Uncle James would drink his port and sometimes talk to her, if only to explain about her reading.

Still, he had taught her much at that table. She knew how to use a knife and fork correctly now, and even which ones to use most of the time. She knew she must not gulp her drink down nor bolt her food, no matter how hungry. The food itself deserved an honourable mention, too, with meat or fish most every day. Never had she eaten so well. Once, she had imagined fondly that all these niceties would stand her in good stead at the dinner parties, which James never gave but was surely bound to resume once the famine was over.

Then what, after all, did she want with some fresh-faced, Anglo-Irish boy, still wet behind the ears? She knew now that her adopted uncle was a fine man indeed, despite his taciturn nature. This very morning, he was out as usual, visiting his tenants and seeing what he could do for them. In the first year at his house, she had sometimes accompanied him on these missions of mercy. Then the typhus and cholera became rife in the following year, and he would not let her go anymore, lest she should catch them.

He had fallen ill himself once, and Caitlin had helped nurse him through it with the frightened housekeeper. Night after night, they had sat up watching his flushed face by the light of the candle. She had wiped his brow, propped him up to persuade him to drink, and wondered fearfully if he was going to die. Except he did recover. From that moment, he became even more dear to her.

A coal dropping in the grate brought her guiltily back to Edmund Burke. But it was no good as her thoughts would keep on intruding.

Where had her uncle been all morning? She wished he wouldn't go, for he would only return with that look of painful frustration in his eyes before writing endless letters to various Members of Parliament and the like in England. To Caitlin's knowledge, the replies never brought him any joy. It made her angry when he alone seemed to have stood firm amongst the neighbouring landlords and had not turned any tenants out against their will.

Many had been urged to emigrate by the landlords — and a dreadfully poor state most of them had been in when they were sent away. Caitlin doubted if so many poor had managed to survive in the whole of Ireland as in this little corner of the country, and that was due to her uncle's intervention, even if his peers thought him a fool.

At last, she heard horses' hooves on the gravel outside. She sat up and went straight back to her reading, anxious to impress him. Then came the familiar sound of his voice and his step in the hall. When he entered, she saw that his riding boots and coat were muddied, and his long, thin face looked very tired. He stood with his back to the fire and looked at her in silence for such a long time that she became nervous. She wished he would sit down so she could sit at his feet while he talked as she sometimes did.

"You look awful tired."

"Dear child!"

It annoyed her now when he addressed her in that way, though she had thought nothing of it once. She was not a child any longer. She was nearly eighteen. He turned away from her and went to pour whiskey from the decanter that was always placed on a corner table. He did not add water. She watched his abnormally long and thin fingers cradle the glass, twisting the honey-coloured liquor this way and that reflectively before tossing it back. He refilled the glass immediately, and she knew this as a familiar symptom of his distress. He ate little these days but drank more and more, it seemed.

Aware she could not help, she viewed the back of his head with growing disquiet. His hair was streaked with grey, though he was not yet forty. Yet, she fancied he had somehow always been old. His shoulders were gathered so that he stooped slightly like many tall men. Something in the set of them today hinted of especial despair. She moved towards him, wishing she could curl up at his feet as they sat and talked. But his next words pulled her up short.

"How would you like to go to America?"

"With you?" She thought that might very well be fine and couldn't smother a small exclamation of delight.

"No, my dear child! With your father and Bridget and their new baby. To New York. To live."

"You're sending me away?" She tried not to sound reproachful, but her mind leapt involuntarily to that conclusion.

"I must. I can't see anything else left for you here."

It was not to last then. She had once suspected as much. Lately, she had thought differently. Now, it appeared she had been wrong. James had plucked her out of poverty like picking a wayside flower on an impulse. But the flower had withered and might as well be thrown away. She said the first thing that came into her head.

"But it's such a long way. You said it wasn't right for people to emigrate without thinking about it." The echo of his words came out without any conscious cleverness.

"You must never believe that everything I have told you is right," he said quietly.

"But you were right. I know it!"

She was surprised by the vehemence of his reply. "No, you don't know. You know nothing yet. I have failed you," he admitted, clenching his fists at his side. "In every way."

"Uncle, you mustn't say that. It isn't true!"

He took the trembling hand she held out to him. "Bless you, Caitlin!"

"Please don't send me away. Even if you think it's for the best. We will get through this terrible time."

"You don't understand. Come and sit down whilst I explain." He drew her over to the settle and made her do as he asked, still clutching her timid hand. She knew that his next words would set the seal on her life and wished fervently she could be sitting by the window again with nothing more to worry about aside from Edmund Burke.

"The potatoes have been better this year," she said. "Praise God, the famine is over."

"Yes, but I must sell the land."

"Sell the land?" The idea awed her. "But it is your land."

James shook his head wryly. "Oh no, it isn't. Not really. The land belongs to no one, as it has demonstrated most cruelly these past few years. I was merely its custodian for a while." He sighed as if to imply he had not even served it well in that capacity. "I had to raise more and more cash. I had to speculate, rashly as it turns out. Last year, I financed a particular venture involving a sea voyage, and the ship sank, taking the rest of my capital with it. Now I am finished, and I must sell the estate to survive. The new laws make it easier. I am not alone in my misfortune, you see. Many other landlords are similarly placed."

She stared at him dumbly. It was a shock to realize that his resources and power were finite.

"There's nothing left, Caitlin. We cannot go on here." He chafed her hands in his large, cold ones. "I am sorry. As I say, I have failed you."

She could not express what she felt. It did not seem possible that all of this, the solid stone of the ivy-covered house around her, the gravel driveway, the horses in the stables, her own dear pony that she loved amongst them, and even the waters of the lough could dissolve away. Then how could she go to America? The question filled James with a momentary eagerness. He had enough left to pay their passage it seemed.

"I know a good Irishwoman in New York. Constance Regan is her name. She will take you in. And Padraig, I hope, will get a job and pull himself up, for he is neither stupid nor lazy. I have always known that."

Caitlin looked away. More letters. Endless letters to uncaring people. Only this time, it appeared he had been answered.

"But what about you? Will you not come with us?"

"In time, maybe. Not yet. I have much to see to here with the sale. Oh, Caitlin, little one, do not look so doubtful! I know I have long been against the idea of emigration. Nevertheless, I now think the time has come, and the Lord knows there is nothing else — ***nothing***." His face slipped into shadow again, and he had to struggle to regain an appearance of brightness. "I shall book your passage in advance on the best packet I can find. I have sent others — in increasing numbers, I confess, of late. It may well be a new and better life after all if they can only get there. You will start out strong and well, so there should be nothing to fear. I could have been mistaken all along!"

Caitlin was dismayed to find that tears were running down her cheeks.

"My poor child. I should have spoken before! It is the suddenness of the shock."

"'Tis not that," she sobbed.

"Then what is it, Caitlin?"

"'Tis because I may never see you again."

"Does that worry you so much, little one? It will not. And it isn't so. We will meet again," he said. "In New York harbour, or up the Hudson River, or even in Boston."

At last, she smiled. They were all just names to her then. But she took comfort in the thought that Uncle James would know all about them if anyone did.

Chapter Three

CAITLIN

It was barely a month later when James took the reconstituted family, which Father Francis himself had blessed, to the cattle-boat at Cork. In the interim, Caitlin had allowed herself to become excited at all the preparations, most of which involved the refurbishing of their wardrobes, for James was determined to send them all (and Caitlin in particular) to New York in decent style. It seemed such a pleasant prospect now to a girl of eighteen, and she couldn't think why she had allowed herself to become so upset about it.

When James saw the steamer that was to take them to Liverpool, with its cattle pens on deck, he quailed visibly. He had failed to secure them a cabin as he had intended, for there were none to be had.

"Oh, Caitlin," he said, suddenly deterred by the reality of what he had planned for them. "What have I done?"

His face was so grief-stricken she couldn't bear not to comfort him. "We'll be all right," she said lightly. "I know we will. You'll see."

Padraig and Bridget were busy seeing to their boxes and so the two of them stood alone together for those last few moments, with Caitlin holding her parents' new child once more. She was aware of the importance of the moment but could not hold onto it like the child. Already, the memories were fading: her father's cottage seemed a lifetime ago, and even the waters of the lough under the mountain and the details of James' house would soon slide into the past. The pony she had wept over would be sold at the next horse fair with the rest of the horses, and soon, she would find it difficult to remember its face.

Her uncle was here for a few final seconds, and she strove to appear brave for him. It was easy enough in her ignorance. She held onto him with her one free arm. Afterwards, she would remember the feel of his long, slender fingers through her grey travelling cloak. They pressed desperately into her back, and she was keenly aware of the brush of his beard against her cheek as he kissed her goodbye.

"Forgive me, Caitlin," he pleaded. "Forgive me for everything."

"There now," she responded cheerfully, confident still, as if he had really prepared her for everything the world might have to throw. "Sure, and there's nothing to forgive! Kiss little Maeve now, too. We'll be fine, praise God! And we'll all meet again in New York City. Don't be too long. Remember, you promised."

He assured her he would not and that she would never leave his thoughts.

Then Padraig and Bridget were among them again, and there were more formal farewells. Padraig at least wrung his brother-in-law's hand heartily in his gratitude. Bridget merely turned an unforgiving cheek to be kissed.

Caitlin kept her spirits up until they were herded onto the deck of the steamer like the cattle it was intended to carry. She had never thought there would be so many people. All of Ireland seemed to be leaving. She saw the clouds lowering out to sea and fell silent. It wasn't the idea of the crossing that troubled her, for she was still ignorant enough about that. More important was the knowledge that she had lost sight of James' dark head and tall shoulders in the crowd below. He was gone, and her eyes were brimming with tears.

She wished she had said more to make him stay, persuading him to leave the sale in the hands of others, for she deluded herself that she had that power. She wished she had thanked him more. Once, she had half believed that one day, he would marry her — though he had never given her any indication of that. She saw no reason why not in her daydreams. From fear to an imagined romance had not been such a large step down the road.

The crossing was an ordeal the like of which Caitlin had never imagined. She knew the sound of the wind in darkness as it whipped down the mountain and moaned about the white cottage and the big, turreted house on the lough side. Often enough, she had heard it on a stormy night. But out here, on the open sea, the wind was like a live thing, a being determined to wreak as much havoc as it possibly could. It screamed and wailed like a banshee as if enraged that any boat should dare put out in the teeth of its almighty blowing. Caitlin was terrified at the look of the sea, for great black walls of water rose to crash upon the deck of the steamer, which was soon awash.

They were all sick as the boat plunged and rolled continually. Worse, far worse, was the cold. Huddling together around the funnel, under the tarpaulins they had been hastily given, in no way kept it out. Caitlin's body shook along with the boat, and her teeth chattered. James had given her an umbrella, but her fingers were too numb to hold it, and the wind would only have snatched it away. The rain lashing the deck stung her cheeks like a thousand arrows. Bridget appeared to be senseless in Padraig's arms.

Caitlin was afraid for the child, who was alarmingly quiet. She placed the babe against her body, in the little warmth that was left under her cloak and next to her gown. She sat with her knees hunched up and her back against Padraig's. Two men she didn't even know huddled against her on either side, clasping various members of their own families. An old woman, left to her own devices, had passed out at Caitlin's feet. Her face was white and pinched, and Caitlin hoped fervently she was not dead but had neither the courage nor strength to push away the outstretched arm flung across her feet. The edge of the tarpaulin flapped against her cheek, and the water continued to dash in round her feet. She shivered and vomited again, becoming even more drenched as she shook uncontrollably. Over the black deck, she could dimly see countless other miserably huddled shapes.

Towards morning, she slept fitfully, nodding off despite her attempts to stay conscious, only to wake a few seconds later with a start and the awful dread that she might have let the baby go, that it might have rolled away from her in a bundle of rags, over the decks and into the sea. It became a recurrent nightmare so that she cried out repeatedly as she woke in a frenzy at the anguish of her loss. Then she would feel the infant stir beneath her cloak and would weep with relief only to drift off again and waken with a fresh, unspeakable terror, certain this time that she had let the child go. Morning came at last with clouds of vast grey movement spitting rain from a sky the colour of lead.

The steamer still reared and bucked like an unbroken stallion and threatened to sink in the troughs between the waves. Oh God, if there was a God above those clouds, how could he make them suffer so? She knew her thoughts were blasphemous but didn't care.

The long, grey day passed, seeming as if it would never end, though the sea grew slighter in time. There was no food or drink, but everyone was too ill to care. Then, towards another evening, the wind which had borne them on manically dropped as suddenly as it had arisen, and they were left to coast in gently to a new shore — not yet the Promised Land, but Liverpool Bay. They took a river pilot on board.

Bridget woke at last, though she had an awful pallor on her. Her hair was wild and matted, and her clothes soiled and wet. Caitlin supposed she looked every bit as bad as her stepmother, who now took the baby. Incredibly, the child seemed well enough. But the old woman who had fallen at Caitlin's feet was indeed found to be dead. She moved away instinctively. She could feel no emotion, no empathy at all within. If she had been told this would happen before boarding, she would have been shocked and distressed. Now, it was just a harsh fact, and she was glad when two men carried the frozen body away.

She heard the mournful tolling of a bell buoy close at hand through the low mist that covered the water. It was only there to warn ships off a dangerous part of the channel, but it sounded as if it were knelling for more dead. Caitlin burst into tears, not for the old woman, but because she suddenly felt so frightened.

"Don't cry, child," Padraig tried to comfort her. "We're safe now. 'Tis nearly over. Look! You can just see the first of the docks and other ships. Jesus, 'tis a forest of masts all right! We're nearly in Liverpool. 'Tis nearly over, child. 'Tis nearly over."

They quartered in Liverpool for several days, glad of the chance to recover with the luxury of dry clothes rescued from their baggage. James had arranged for a reputable agent to meet them and take them to one of the better boarding houses, where they ate tolerably well. None of them seemed to have suffered any lasting ill effects from the crossing at first, and Caitlin's spirits returned. Even the baby remained miraculously unharmed.

But then Padraig fell ill. It started innocently enough with a disinclination to eat and an inability to throw off the shivering that had afflicted them all aboard. Then he came down with a raging fever and talked a lot of nonsense in his bed. It passed, and he was lucid again but couldn't eat. It was Bridget who panicked.

"Eat, man, will you?" she cried. "The Yorkshire sails in two days!"

He tried, but the effect was disastrous.

"God, they'll think you have the cholera!" Bridget said. "We have to pass a medical before they take us on board. They'll never let you on!"

"I don't have the cholera, woman! Don't talk daft! My stomach's just not ready for food."

"You're in no fit state to travel further, that's for sure."

Caitlin, sitting at the other end of the room, looked doubtfully at her father. It was true; he was very weak. But what on earth would they do if they didn't sail on The Yorkshire?

"We don't have to go," Bridget went on as if reading her stepdaughter's mind. "We can keep this room here for the moment, though 'tis dear enough. When you're better, you'll surely be able to find a job in Liverpool. Caitlin, too."

Caitlin's heart sank. England? She didn't want to live in England.

"Don't you want to go?" asked Padraig slowly, a new light dawning in his eye. Bridget turned abruptly from his side and pretended to busy herself with folding the clothes in their open box.

"I'm not sure," she said. "It's an awful long way. And what does James know about it, after all?"

Caitlin interrupted for the first time. "We'll be undercover on The Yorkshire in a proper berth, and there's food on the ship. It won't be like the cattle boat."

"Aye, so they tell us. But how do we know it's true? Maybe James just wants to be rid of the lot of us. Yes, you too, Caitlin! He wasn't after coming himself, was he?" Bridget countered.

Caitlin flushed angrily, but it was Padraig who intervened. "Your half-brother has done the decent t'ing by us, Bridget! You know he has. Don't go putting him down again! An' what about the ticket? Isn't it all booked and paid for — on the very best ship he could find?"

"Caitlin can take the ticket if she's still desperate to go," Bridget said.

Father and daughter looked at each other in silence, and Caitlin dropped her eyes in embarrassment.

"What do you mean?" asked Padraig. "Is she to go on her own? I'll not be having that."

"She'll be met in New York by Constance Regan. She'll be all right. She's young and she wants to go. Maybe she'll marry an American with all these new airs and graces she's got now. America is for the young, I fancy. We're too old to change our ways."

"But on her *own*!" Padraig repeated. "All that way when she's little more than a child! And we may never see her again! She lost her poor mother when she was a babby. Is she to lose us now, too?"

But Bridget was having none of this. "Caitlin wasn't a child when I married you, Padraig! She has been three years with James since. She's a woman! Look at her with the child, will you!"

Padraig looked, and Caitlin flushed up to her temples. It was true. She dandled Maeve expertly on her knee. Her experience with Bridget's former child had not been wasted. She looked pretty as a picture with her bright, blue eyes cast modestly downwards, even though her long, dark hair had grown wild and unkempt again. The picture pulled at his heartstrings, for she was still his own little girl — no longer ragged and barefoot but refined and matured by James, like the wine in their landlord's cellar. Still, he wondered if Bridget had been right all along when she had said Caitlin ought not to go to the big house. He stirred uncomfortably and raised himself on one elbow, the better to see her.

"What do you say, Caitlin?" he asked. "T'ink hard now! Do you want to go?"

"Uncle James intended for us to go to New York," said Caitlin stubbornly. "He intends to follow us there. That's all I know, and I think a man like him is bound to be right."

"He certainly intended for **her** to go," Bridget put in with some asperity of tongue. Caitlin wished she would stop speaking about her as if she wasn't there.

"Where's the harm in that, woman?" Padraig flared up again in defence of his daughter.

"If you don't know, I can't tell you!"

"He didn't intend for her to go alone."

"She needn't be alone. She can take the babby."

"For God's sake, woman, how can she manage a child as well?"

"Caitlin is good at looking after babbies. She'll manage. Girls do. The child is weaned. And I expect Mrs Regan will have plenty of servants to help. She'll sort out a better life for the child."

Padraig moaned and fell back on his bed, defeated. "I could understand you not caring much for the first one. But this is Maeve, and you said she was mine! Are we to lose all our chillun, then? I don't understand you, woman." He began to cry.

"It's God's will," said Bridget flatly and turned away with another barb, "It's precious little you saw of Caitlin anyway when she was at James's. So don't act the devoted father with me."

Padraig groaned again, but Caitlin, though shocked at first, suddenly realized the truth about what Bridget was saying. It might be the truth for the wrong reasons, but it was the truth no less for that. The child was now over a year old and had been lucky to survive that long. Of course, she would be better off in America, away from Ireland. Unnatural though it was, at least Bridget recognized she was no fit mother — not for a dog nor a cat, and certainly not for a human child. Caitlin knew that. Suddenly, she wanted to take her half-sister away. She wanted it more than anything she had ever wanted, except perhaps James. She swallowed her spleen and decided it was time to speak up.

"Bridget is right, Father. Of course, I shall look after Maeve. America will give us both a better chance in life. Only I wish I could persuade you to come too."

Padraig looked at his wife despairingly, but she kept her back turned and went on folding clothes. He sighed. "Sure, and you're a good girl, Caitlin, to care about your old father no matter what's been said and done." The tears continued to roll down his weather-beaten face, and he let himself sink back into the pillow in his sentimentality. "But Bridget's right. I am weak and still poorly. Maybe the doctor 'ud stop us all going on board if he saw the likes of me. And I'll not spoil your chances, Caitlin. I'll stay right here in Liverpool with Bridget."

"But what will you do?"

"What she says. Get a job. On the docks, maybe, when I'm well enough. There must be plenty of unloadin' to do with all these big ships coming in. We'll make out right enough. We might even get enough together to go back to old Ireland when times is better."

Caitlin saw the way it was going with him. "But then you could come over to America with James when he comes out," she pointed out. "I'll write and tell him how things have turned out." Maybe everything would fall into place, and she felt more cheerful. "You must take all the money. I won't be needing much, what with the ship's rations and that. I'll just take the ticket."

"Just promise me, colleen," said Padraig tearfully. "That when you're a rich lady married to some American ' fella from Boston, you'll spare a thought for your poor, old daddy and come and visit us."

Caitlin planted a kiss firmly on his forehead. "We'll be back together again before then," she said, smiling. "You wait and see! Uncle James will manage it all."

So it was that Caitlin came to be sitting alone on the quayside, on top of her box, with an infant clutched tightly in her arms, which everyone assumed was hers, and with such a sad look in her eyes. She had held up well until now but suddenly felt lost and vulnerable.

We have to be brave," she whispered to little Maeve. "James would have wanted us to be brave."

Only James hadn't known how soon they would be deserted. If he had, thought Caitlin, he would surely have come with us. Bridget and Padraig had not even come down to see them off, and that hurt. Of course, Padraig was still not entirely well after his fever, but he was well on the way to recovery. Bridget's fears turned out to be groundless anyway.

For hours, Caitlin had queued outside the small office that was no more than a shack on the dockside to see the doctor. She began to think she would drop where she stood, so tired was she of nursing an energetic fractious child with one arm and pulling her box along behind her with the other. When she did eventually reach the head of the queue, and it was her turn, she learned that the medical examination was nothing but a farce.

All the doctor said was, "What's your name? Put out your tongue! Are you well?" All without drawing breath.

He was stamping the ticket the same instant the words were coming out of his mouth, and he barely glanced at her. A hundred Padraigs would have got through if they'd lied. Of that, she was certain.

"And he never looked at you at all!" she murmured to the dark, downy head, now thankfully asleep on her shoulder. "Did he now? You could have had the typhus and the cholera and the pox all rolled into one for all the notice he took!"

It was too late to tell Padraig that. She wasn't even sure it would have made a difference. Not when Bridget didn't want to go. Bridget didn't want her around. That was clear. Well, Caitlin wasn't going to shed any tears over that. It was Padraig's weak acquiescence in the plan that hurt her, despite his sentimentality. Of course, knowing him as she did, she could have predicted it. Still, he had once been the most important person in her life, and it hurt that he hadn't come to see her off. She had to acknowledge that James had taken his place these last three years, and maybe she hadn't visited the low, whitewashed cottage as often as she should have. But she had always meant to.

Perhaps she was being selfish. Bridget had told her often enough she was. Only it wasn't easy to be brave at this moment. There were too many strangers on the quayside, jostling and shouting and making a fearful racket. She knew well enough that they were mostly O'Reillys and O'Rourkes, Flanagans, Dohertys, O'Connors, and the like and knew as well as she did the low white cottages in the wet green land where death had sat for so long like a great black crow. But they were strangers to her now. My own people, she thought! Because of James, they all seemed like foreigners because she was different now.

If only he were here, everything would be all right! She would have felt excited without any anxiety over how she was going to get a child she did not want to wake onto the boat, as well as a heavy box, when there was only one of her. Tears pricked her eyelids, but she held them back, telling herself off. It was no good worrying. She would get on the ship and secure a berth. She had a ticket, and they would survive and, in time, reach America. Best be patient and sit and wait while the crowd dies down. Best not to think of Padraig and Bridget, nor even of James.

She shivered slightly in the wind and hitched the hood of her cloak further forward over her bonnet and the dark, rebellious hair that was escaping. The gay red ties of her bonnet flapped in the wind. In this attitude, she was seen by Hartley Shawcross, though she remained unaware of it.

Chapter Four

ROSA

In the cold and damp cellar of the boarding house in Liverpool, many miles from home, Rosa Kleist had a dream. She knew it was a dream, for she could still feel the hardness of the floor in her sleep and the way the cold gnawed at her body. She was aware too of the odd moans from many other restless sleepers and was conscious that Friedrich and the children huddled close beside her so that, if any one of them woke, she must too.

All these threatened to disturb the images that flickered behind her eyes. They would then fade, and once again, she was back in Frankfurt in another May with the black, red, and gold flags of a liberal Germany streaming from every public building and every bell in every bell tower ringing in unison with the swelling cheers of the crowd. Even the trees were decked out in a new glorious green, and the splendid weather was with them. There were no barricades, no bloodshed, nor wild and undisciplined riots. The first elected members of the new Parliament were processing to the Paulskirche in the centre of the city for the opening session. Perhaps the franchise had not been universal or entirely fair, but it was a beginning for democracy. Rosa's own husband no less, was one of four artisans amongst the newly elected members.

Although she had just been standing in the gaily decked streets, she found herself — with the ease of movement common to all dreams — in the public gallery inside the Paulskirche. Packed though it was, she saw the beaming face of her father turn towards her reassuringly.

They clasped each other's hands somehow over the crowd, and her father's voice rang in her ear:

"You see, Rosa! We were right. There is nothing to fear. This revolution will work!"

It was as clear as if it was yesterday and not two years ago that this happened. Only it ought not to be so cold.

Rosa stirred and moved closer to Friedrich's back on account of the cold. Down below, in the imposing circular body of the great church, stood a dais where there had once been an altar and a pulpit to God.

"For the sake of the people, Rosa," said her father's voice. "For the sake of the people, the crosses are torn down."

Each member of the Parliament took his place. Rosa wondered why her father, with his superior learning and wisdom, was not among them. But he had singled out Friedrich as a more fitting representative of the Jewish people of Frankfurt through his trade as a bespoke tailor. She noticed her husband's collar was not as white and starched as it should have been and woke with tears on her face as the cold intruded again.

All was well. Friedrich was there with her, and he was still sleeping. Rosa wiped the tears away angrily with her hand. It was no good feeling guilty over her sensitive husband. If she allowed it in, she might crumble just as he had done, and she must not. She held the fate of all of them in her hands: Friedrich, the two boys, the child yet unborn, and herself. She couldn't rely on Friedrich anymore. But it didn't matter. She was the strong one. She would get them all to America. Still, she couldn't help letting her mind's eye dwell a little on the past for the last time.

In particular, she remembered the first time Friedrich had come to their house in that respectable part of the city where they lived in genteel poverty. Late at night, he had come, crossing Romer Square and hurrying past the huge shadow of the cathedral, down the narrow, dark streets of half-timbered houses to knock at their door. She had let him in, though he had never been before, for it was the right kind of knock, and the whispered password was answered correctly. In the passage, he had divested himself of his outer clothing with some embarrassment. His was the most handsome face — finely boned, sensitive, even lively then, though unaccountably shy, with a neat, black beard framing his mouth. It made her painfully conscious of her own plain, dull face, for she knew she was no great beauty.

She did not dream then that he could ever look at her with more than kindness. She led him to the inner room where the curtains were drawn tight against the prying eyes of the night and faces flushed with firelight turned uncertainly to welcome the new member. Rosa stayed, though she did not often do so, for they bored her and made her impatient with their constant talk of revolution, which she believed would never come to fruition.

The newcomer's connection with the group was tenuous. Rosa's father was a schoolmaster at the local gymnasium and knew many of the university professors who, in turn, associated with artists, writers, and poets who were politically inclined. But Friedrich Kleist had made her father a suit of clothes, for he was a fine tailor, as well as being a seeker after truth. She wished now that he had remained one. For her father had been delighted to discover his true cast, so Friedrich had no need to fear the quality of his welcome. They needed his kind to carry the banner.

Rosa no longer questioned which banner: it was merely the insignia of a new Germany, united in freedom, for the people. It had nothing to do with the anarchists. Later, she began to doubt that, but at the time, she trusted her father implicitly. He was a liberal of the best kind, and he had brought her up in the same way, and she naturally agreed the world ought to change for the better, even though she couldn't see any likelihood that it would. The old order and the old ways seemed too strong. Rosa was not unintelligent by any means but was practical to a fault and saw no point in grieving unnecessarily over matters she had no power over.

Friedrich was different. He was an idealist, a sensitive dreamer, a private poet with whom she fell in love, and he needed her protection. Rosa sighed. Yet she wouldn't have him any different, only happier if that were possible. In America, she believed it would be — not at first, perhaps, but eventually when they had settled down. She could have done without the extra burden of this third child coming, but it was no real hardship. She believed everything would be possible in America, and it was this thought that sustained her in the cold and the darkness.

Chapter Five

OWAIN

Although he had never been to Liverpool before, Owain felt safe in its streets for the first time since he had fled the mine. He took a room and spent his last money on food and drink. These actions implied a kind of freedom, but he knew he was still a hunted man, and his thoughts of the last few days had never gotten him farther than this.

After a while, he grew tired of the noise and heat of the overcrowded taproom and turned out to walk the streets. It was almost dark on a misty summer evening, but the city did not sleep. The drink that Owain imagined would anaesthetize his sorrow and blur his thoughts was working the very opposite effect. As he stumbled along narrow alleys and cobbled streets, he felt they were more real than he, and in the dark, he was beset by a series of lurid and threatening images. A man with a stovepipe hat and a nose like Punch followed him persistently, overtaking now and again to gesticulate. He acted out a pantomime to indicate some item of immense worth and value, cupped in his hands that he would show to Owain in a secret place if only he would follow. Drunken country boy though he was, Owain recognized the trick and kept shaking his head vigorously in reply. It was a long while before he could get rid of the fellow.

At every street corner lay a disfigured beggar with a hat or a tin box held out for alms. Some of the older ones wore dirty placards around their necks, claiming they had lost an arm or a leg at Waterloo. Painted ladies draped themselves around the lampposts, sporting their wares in the soft circles of gaslight. They leered at Owain as he walked by. Other women, scarcely more respectable, worked eagerly over piles of rubbish in the street. There were plenty of ragged boys and girls, too, despite the late hour, with an eye out for a carelessly bulging pocket or an errand to be run for a coin or two. Most scampered barefoot through the muck on the road. A haze of smoke and the sounds of singing or raucous laughter issued from a gin shop or a spirit vault every hundred yards or so.

 Owain went on telling himself he had escaped. But he had brought his own hell with him into this terrible place. He plunged into the side streets, which were relatively deserted and dimly lit. For some time, he walked on senselessly until he was thoroughly lost. Then, his path ended in a foul-smelling court between tall rows of tenement buildings. He would have to turn back. He blundered into the main street again, only to lose his way once more. Was there no end to this city's miserable quarters? Yet he knew, if he climbed the hill like he had done this morning, he would see rows of fine terraced houses, with steps and iron railings and polished, brass bellpulls which servants would come running to answer. Was there no end to all the injustices, meanness and poverty in the world? He felt this great sprawling city would never be free of it. But what right had he to criticize? He knew he no longer had the right even to exist.

 The streets now all seemed to lead downwards, and he followed them again without thinking. The low-lying fog off the river crept into them the further he went until he found himself wading knee-high through a thin mist. You could see it moving slowly under the streetlamps, oozing inexorably up the hill. In the darkness, the forest of masts which marked out the docks was invisible. But Owain could smell the river and knew it was near. He seemed to have come round in a circle.

He was very tired now and sunk into a dark corner by some barrels. Further down the street was the brightly lit opening of yet another gin shop and the distant sound of voices. In despair, he bent his head to his knees and wished he might die. Why hadn't he stayed in Blaenau like a man to die? But he knew the answer. He had been too afraid. Now, he only had a shilling or two left in his pocket, and he could not find his way back to 'The Hope and Anchor' where he had planned to board the night; he had neither hope nor refuge anymore. He might as well sit here till he died.

Yet Owain, though weary and totally downcast, was a good deal too strong to die just yet. When he raised his head and stared miserably at the brick wall opposite, he saw a poster that had been pasted there. By the diffuse light of the gas burner nearby, he could see a picture of a ship and some words. With the unfailing curiosity of mankind, he struggled to read it. It said:

THE BLACK BALL LINE OF PACKETS
To sail punctually on her regular day,
The first of June,
The celebrated packet ship, The Yorkshire
Commanded by Capt. Shearman
At 1058 tons per register.

The Yorkshire is, on all hands, allowed to be the finest and fastest of the numerous packets sailing between this port and NEW YORK, and her accommodations for second cabin and steerage passengers will be much superior on this voyage to what they have hitherto been, much greater space being allotted to each. Her commander has invariably made remarkably quick passages and his kindness and attention to passengers have secured for him a lasting reputation.

For terms of passage, apply to: *J & W ROBINSON*, *48, WATERLOO ROAD, LIVERPOOL*

Owain had seen many such advertisements pasted up in the streets, along with incitements to young men to join the army or navy. None had been couched in quite such glowing terms or with the same confidence, however. Would it be possible for him to make a new start in a new country?

It was a long way from North Wales, but he could not go back, and he did not think he could bear to stay in Liverpool, even if he found a job. He knew the place would go on dragging him down.

The new resolution strengthened in his mind, but he grimaced. He had no money. He had spent his last few shillings on gin to keep out the cold. Then he remembered he had seen many pawnbrokers' signs in these streets as well as the gilded grapes of the spirit vaults. He still had an old watch, and it was a good one — given to him by his mother, Elen. It had belonged to his grandfather, and it didn't work, but it looked most fine. Almost a gentleman, his grandfather had been. Well, he could pawn that, and, with luck, it might pay his fare to America. He took it out and turned it over in his hands. It was his last link with Elen. Her dear face seemed to smile up at him and his eyes filled with tears.

It was a hard thing to do. He knew that when he left Liverpool, he might never come back. He had heard a man speak about emigration once in Chapel. He couldn't remember his name now. But there was even an Emigration Society in Tal-y-sarn. Men went out alone to become rich and sent back money for their relatives to join them.

Perhaps one day, he might be able to write a letter to Elen and the others, asking them to join him in America. He could not pretend to have cleared his name, but they might find solace in hearing from him and knowing he was doing well.

In his imagination, he saw himself as the owner of a fine farm (you could buy land aplenty and cheap in America, he seemed to remember — and own it forever), showing his family around his livestock. Would that not help a little to reinstate him in Elen's eyes? His hand closed around the watch. It was only an object, not a person. He made his decision.

Part Two

The Voyage

Chapter One

Forewarned by her experience aboard the steamer, Caitlin got herself and the child below decks as soon as she was able to board The Yorkshire. There was an air of general pandemonium about that she recognized. Already, most of the berths seemed to have been taken. She was relieved to secure a lower one that was empty and laid Maeve gently down on the berth to stake her claim whilst getting out blankets from her box. Mercifully, the child had not woken. In the end, she had not fared too badly as one of the sailors, a rough and unlikely-looking tar, had taken pity on her and helped her aboard and down the hatch with the heavy box she struggled with. When he smiled, he showed a mouth full of rotten teeth, and he rolled his eyes at her lasciviously. She felt relieved when he said he was needed back on deck and tried to ignore the broad wink he gave her, though she thanked him kindly enough.

Gratefully, she manoeuvred her box until it came flush up to the end of the berth. Then she placed the blankets as best she could without disturbing the child and lay down next to her, exhausted, closing her eyes to gather her thoughts.

Underneath the berth, Owain tried to breathe as quietly as possible. There was precious little room between the planks on which Caitlin lay and the floor. Owain, who had been curled up, stretched out his legs tentatively and felt them come to rest on the hard edge of Caitlin's box. To either side of him, a fold of grey blanket curtained him off from view. Behind his head, he could feel the timber of the ship's hull. His makeshift hiding place had improved with the occupation of the berth above, but the boards seemed terribly close. Owain was not good in confined spaces. He had to quell the panic, which reminded him of his feelings when going into the mine.

He had no choice other than to hide. Although he had pawned his watch, he had not got much for it. He knew he had been duped, but every pawnbroker gave him the same answer, that it was of little worth not being gold, and he was desperate. Then, in the last shop, he had met a sailor from The Yorkshire who was pawning a fine-looking knife in order to buy tobacco. Owain was complaining to the old proprietor that he still didn't have enough to pay his passage when the sailor took his arm and offered to help. Apparently, it was easy to stow away — there was so much hustle and bustle while passengers were boarding. If Owain would risk it, this jolly-looking tar would meet him aboard and show him the best places to hide — for a small fee, of course. There was plenty of food aboard, and as soon as they were in America, he would find work and board quickly. He had no need of extra money. Far better to buy a second-hand coat and hat from this excellent fellow, than waste it on buying an unnecessary ticket. Why, people did it all the time, and once out at sea, there was nothing anyone could do about it! It certainly wasn't worth the bother of a captain troubling himself over it. At worst, he might have to work his passage to get food. The main problem was in securing a good hiding place to lie low until they were out of the harbour, and he was fortunate there in finding someone who could advise him so well in the matter! The couple of sovereigns Owain had received so recently and at such cost changed hands, and he did indeed buy a coat and hat as well as the invaluable aid of the mariner.

Nevertheless, Owain wasn't able to find his new friend when he got aboard. When he finally did see him, hauling on a rope, the man scowled and said something about all the barrels being full. Evidently, he would have to take his chances where he could. He was shown brusquely down between decks and left to get on with it. The sailor said no one looked underneath the berths, hence Owain's choice of a place, but he didn't trust the man anymore and feared it was little better than a trap. Suppose he was found and sent back? It would be the gallows then, for sure! How could he have fallen prey to such an ill-conceived plan after all he had been through? He tried to calm himself. Perhaps it would be easy enough to stay concealed until it was too late. Surely the sailor would not have had the cheek to take his money otherwise. Working one's passage wouldn't be so bad — if only they didn't find him too soon and send him back.

So Owain lay shaking with fear, whilst above Caitlin was at last able to change the baby's napkin, though she could not wash out the wet one she had removed. Perhaps later, when they got their ration of water. Three quarts a day, like it said on the ticket, didn't sound like much. Still, she didn't need to wash her face and hands as long as she had water to drink, and Maeve was well cared for. It was only for — what had James told her — sixteen days at best and a month at the worst? She must hope for the best. At least there was going to be shelter from the elements and biscuits, oatmeal, rice, tea, and sugar.

≈

Up in the first-class cabins, The Honourable Miss Caroline Cholmondeley pressed the pomander she had bought from an orange girl against her nose and inhaled its perfume. She knew the conditions of her cabin were luxurious in comparison with steerage. She had a chair as well as a bunk — fixed to the floor though it might be. She also had a basin to be ill in if required. The door and walls of her coop were made from the finest mahogany, and there was a boy to call for water and tea and anything else she might require. She also had an invitation to dine at the captain's table, where there would doubtless be plenty of meat and fine wines.

It was apparent to her nonetheless that her heart was beating faster than usual, though she would not let her resolve weaken. It was merely the slightest nervousness consequent on embarkation. She would kneel to pray.

Only her face revealed that she had been born to some station in life, her father being a Baron, for her travelling gown was simple and, though the skirt was full, it did not attain the ridiculous proportions of the crinoline which were so fashionable. Her hair was neatly pulled back and braided, and, though still young, she had taken to a cap which she wore with lappets. Her eyes reflected the calm simplicity and sobriety of her clothes.

As she prayed, she thanked God for the blessing of her freedom, for she had been left relatively alone in the world since the death of her parents, with a small inheritance that was hers alone.

She did not give thanks in any spirit of self-congratulation, for this extraordinary woman (so recently released from the tyranny of her father by his death) had turned her back on all her suitors and the fripperies of an elegant house in town. She travelled alone with her maid, Alice, whom she had seen as comfortably installed in a second-class cabin and was bound for the New York Association for the

Improvement of the Condition of the Poor, with whom she had corresponded before offering her services. If they proved not to need her, she had some vague idea of seeking out the North American Indians and bringing those who had not been destroyed and driven out by President George Washington into the lap of God.

≈

On deck, Captain Shearman stood on the bridge as the tugs, one before and one at either side, bore The Yorkshire out into the middle of the river. The pilot stood ready by the helmsman. Unfurling canvas flapped noisily above them, and every rope and line were manned. The captain, who was an intelligent and courteous man, if somewhat melancholy in aspect, felt that exuberant lift to his spirits that always came to him when leaving shore. Then he turned to survey the lower decks, and immediately, his enthusiasm was quenched by the sight of the emigrants taking their last look at their native land.

Inevitably, they made him feel like a slave trader, although every one of them had been anxious to come aboard, and there were many signs of gaiety. Yet there seemed no end to them, no halting this interminable flow. With every trip, there were more, and although The Yorkshire was unquestionably one of the better packets afloat, he knew there was no avoiding the suffering entailed in steerage on their crossing. He could only hope for a fair wind and a speedy passage. He was proud of his vessel and its reputation. Yet there was only so much one could do.

He knew, for instance, that the ship's surgeon had been carried aboard drunk again and was worse than useless. Then, whilst he trusted his first and second officers implicitly, he was not happy with the general standard of the able seamen engaged this time and would have preferred a little less surliness mixed with the hard efficiency of the purser. The cook, though amiable enough, was clearly nothing but a scheming, scurrilous rogue. Now, as if his own conscience weren't enough to bear, he discovered he had a crusading lady aboard plus an extremely difficult first-class passenger named Andrew Tyrrell, with a flaming red beard and a temper to match.

Still, the lift of The Yorkshire cheered him as always. She was well-corked and rode the water superbly. He loved and respected her even though she did not always obey his will, much like a wayward woman. He thought of her as a fine and patient lady, especially when battling her way through a storm, showing her mettle and undaunted spirits — a kind of Honourable Miss Cholmondeley of the sea, in fact.

The crying of seagulls overtook the cheers of the emigrants, who fell silent as they passed down the river. They were now ready to drop anchor again and take a roll call of all the passengers. Captain Shearman gave the order for the search party to get all passengers with tickets on the quarter deck so that they could be checked. In the meantime, every nook, cranny, and quarter below would be scoured and searched.

≈

Caitlin screamed. She had dropped some small thing as she was getting ready to obey the purser's gruffly shouted command to go above to be counted. It had rolled underneath her berth. When she knelt to retrieve it, her hand had encountered — not empty space, as she had imagined — but soft and yielding human flesh.

"I 'ope it's not a rat you've found," said a fellow traveller on passing by. But no one took much notice. The purser was calling out names thick and fast, and everyone was pushing forward, straining to hear their own and get up the hatchway in time.

Caitlin sank down to her knees and tried to summon the courage to look underneath her berth. Then a hand grasped hers and wouldn't let go, crushing her fingers.

"Come out! Whoever you are!" Her mouth was dry, but her words sounded brave enough. Surely, nothing could happen to her here. In reply, the hand tugged urgently at hers, and there was a mutter she couldn't hear. She bent her head down in exasperation and looked under the bunk. A pair of very frightened dark eyes met her own.

"You'll kindly let go of my hand!" Her words were severe but not that loud, and she could smell the man's fear.

"Please," he whispered, not releasing her hand. "Please, keep quiet, and don't give me away! I won't trouble you or hurt you, I swear! But they'll send me to the gallows if they find me here."

The gallows! Did they hang stowaways in England, then? For it was clear that was whom she'd caught. Caitlin supposed it was possible.

"Don't be an eejit! They're bound to find you there," she said. It was true. Already, a search party was at the other end of the steerage with storm lanterns and sticks, poking into corners, opening boxes, and upturning barrels. She could hear their coarse voices and laughter as if they savoured the task.

"Will you let go of my hand, or I'll scream again and bring them running!"

Her hand was released, but she thought she heard a sob.

"Why didn't you buy a ticket, like everyone else?" she demanded.

"I had no money, see. The accent was unfamiliar to her, though understandable enough.

"Then you shouldn't have come." She was cross at him for choosing her berth to hide under amongst all these others.

"I had to come. There's nothing else left for me now. I can't go back. They'd hang me!"

"What's all this talk of hanging? And how do you think you're going to stay hidden, with them pushing dirty great poles under all the berths?"

The voice groaned. "He said it wouldn't be like that! And I gave him all the money I had!"

"Who did?"

"The sailor who brought me aboard."

"Then you'd better come out straightaway if he knows you're in here. For you've been swindled for sure!"

Caitlin had seen enough of Liverpool in her short stay to be convinced of this. There was a sigh, and the fold of the blanket was pushed away by an arm attached to the hand. The fingernails and the sleeve of the jacket were ingrained with dirt, and Caitlin shrank back instinctively, fearing some desperate, hard-bitten face.

Slowly, Owain rolled out and sat up. She almost laughed. The coat and hat he had purchased from the pawnbroker did nothing to improve his appearance. Overall, he was only a little man — barely a few years older than herself — with dark, curly hair and a small beard and moustache. There were tears in his deep, brown eyes that reminded her of some large and gentle dog.

"I suppose you had reason enough to hide away," she said, a little kindlier.

Owain hung his head. "You must tell the search party you found me. Otherwise, they might think you helped me aboard."

"What about the hanging?" Caitlin answered pertly.

"I deserve it. There is no escape."

Caitlin frowned. They could hang a man for little enough, God knows. But he was scarcely more than a boy, and there was something in his face that touched her. She couldn't think he'd done anything terribly wrong, and she knew she had the power to save him.

"Get up!" she said. "You're a bit dirty to be a fella' of mine, I don't mind telling you. But it can't be helped. Here is my child to hold. Her name is Maeve, and mine is Caitlin. You can have my ticket and claim to be Padraig Murphy, my husband. We can say we left your sister, Bridget, behind in Liverpool as she was too afraid to come. There's some truth in that anyway." On she went, explaining the reversal to him. When she bethought herself later about what she had done, she would cross herself hastily and say (as if to Father Francis), "God forgive me! But I didn't know I was going to be emigrating to America, did I?" For now, she was too busy disentangling her hand from Owain's clutch to think of aught else.

"I'll make it up to you, somehow," he promised. "I swear I will. And I'll be no trouble to you. I'll look after you as best I can. You'll see."

"Don't drop the child, then!"

"Hey, you!" A seaman appeared round the corner of the next berth. "What are you two still doing here?"

"Sure, and we didn't want to disturb the babby until we had to," said Caitlin quickly. It was fine what a marvellous liar she had become.

"Where's your ticket?"

She showed it, and he perused it quickly.

"Padraig Murphy? Your name's sure to have been called out afore now. Get up that hatchway darned quick if you don't want to lose your passage."

Behind the head and shoulders of the man, Owain recognized the face of the sailor who had taken his sovereigns. His mouth had dropped open in surprise at the apparent domesticity of the scene. Owain also caught a secondary light of fury in his eye and wondered if the seamen were paid some kind of reward for rooting out stowaways.

Meekly, he followed his saviour on deck, marvelling still at his good fortune and shouldering the softly awkward, unexpected burden of an infant.

≈

"Rosa," whispered Friedrich Kleist urgently. "Rosa, wake up!" His wife opened her eyes wearily. She had only just managed to drop off into a doze in which the movements of the ship were if not eliminated, at least partially removed.

"What is it, Friedrich?" He clutched her hand and stared around him, his eyes trying to burn a passage through the darkness that clothed steerage.

"They're battening down the hatches. They're doing it to keep us in!"

Rosa raised herself on one elbow and felt her head swim along with the ship's movement, which was now marked. The children were asleep, and most other folks were trying to sleep, too. Rosa still wore her dress for she felt quite unable to remove it amongst so many. The chaotic conditions of boarding had put paid to any idea of segregation of the sexes and families, and single people were jumbled up together. So, Rosa had merely undone the hook and eyes behind. She had to admit she could hear hammering from the direction of the hatch.

"I expect they're doing it to keep us safe," she said. "The sea is quite rough now."

"No, Rosa." Friedrich increased the pressure on her arm. "They'll not let us out. They mean to keep us here, trapped like rats in the dark until we reach America, if we ever do!"

"I'm sure that's not so, Friedrich. There's probably a storm coming. No doubt they want to make sure no one is foolish enough to go on deck."

"How do we know where they're taking us?" Friedrich demanded, raising his voice. "How do we know what their plans are? They are against us simple folk. They have us in their power!"

Someone shouted at him to hold his damned foreign tongue, and there was a chorus of groaning approval. Rosa sat up and placed her arms round his shoulders comfortingly.

"No, Friedrich. You are mistaken, liebchen! You mustn't worry about it anymore. Come, lie down with me, or else you'll waken the children." She made him do as she asked and stroked his bearded cheek gently. But his muscles were tense, and his body would not relax. "When the storm is over, we will be allowed on deck again."

"I cannot bear the darkness, Rosa, or the bodies."

"I know, mein liebchen, I know. And this nausea is so wearisome. But it will all pass. We must think of America and hold together. Hush now!" Still, his body remained tight and tense and lonely in the darkness.

"We should not have left Frankfurt," was all he said.

Chapter Two

4th June

Before ever I set foot on The Yorkshire, my intention was to keep a full and accurate journal for your eyes, Mother, so that you might gain some insight into the way of life aboard this vessel, which is the fastest of the packet ships (I am led to believe) that flies the flag of the Black Ball line. Yet here I am, on my fourth day out, with never a putting of pen to paper until now. I had believed that such a journal would be instructive, as no doubt it is, and would not only inform but entertain if I might be skilful enough to describe the antics of my fellow voyagers. Now that I know better, I shall never allow you to read it, although I have addressed it to you through force of habit.

On the days already unremarked, it was too rough to have the inkwell out for everything loose was sliding about first one way and then the other, causing great confusion and inevitably some minor injuries as we are packed in so tightly together, with such a mess of paraphernalia belonging to each person. But it wasn't the lack of a quill that floored me. Hardly had we gained the Irish sea than I, Hartley Shawcross, who had never imagined himself to be such a weakling, realized with horror that he was going to be seasick, and the physic bought in Liverpool for a whole half crown was completely useless.

As my first thought was to take a turn on deck, where I imagined the freshness of the sea air might stem my nausea and blow it away, I made my way with some difficulty to the hatch, attracting ill-mannered curses at every step from my fellow sufferers. When I reached my goal, you may understand with what dismay I saw that it was in the very throes of being battened down! The mariner entrusted with the task — a very hard-bitten fellow — was unnecessarily surly, in my opinion, and hooted with laughter when he learnt the nature of my request. When I protested, he was short in telling me it was the captain's orders for the safety of all below — especially such idiots as myself. On calmer reflection, I can see that he was right, and I was as naive as the greenest 'landlubber' could be, but his arrogance infuriated me at the time. Oh, but the sound of those bolts being hammered home was harsh on my ears as the very last chink of daylight disappeared!

There was nothing for it but to clamber and claw my way back, hanging on to this berth and that, gauging the distance between them as best I could and ending up in several outraged laps on the way, for the roll of the ship had undeniably worsened. Subsequently, I lay in my own berth and did not stir. Did not stir indeed! My choice of words is ironic. I certainly did not wish to stir but could hardly avoid being pitched out of my bunk at times. The ship reared up on each wave and hung there for an instant. I gritted my teeth and braced my stomach but there was no avoiding that yawning drop downwards into the chasm that waited below. In the trough of the waves, we rolled unsteadily from side to side before the next heave upwards and the next pitch down and the next, for there is no end to it.

I tried desperately not to be sick but soon ended up emptying my stomach ingloriously into my chamber pot, having had the foresight to remove it from my baggage earlier. I regret to say that the pot was promptly jerked out of my hands the next instant by a particularly sharp lurch to one side, and it smashed on the floor where it dropped, spilling its vile contents onto the planks. Here, its shards rolled about with several like companions, all similarly filled. The most unconducive odours now arose, as you might imagine in our airless state, all serving to make me retch again uncontrollably. Even when my guts were empty, I could not stop the fearful spasms.

When I put my hands down to the boards, I found them wet already as four or five inches of seawater had poured in somehow, despite the battening down and the bilge pumps. The air, as I mentioned before, was quickly foul. It was very dark, for all the candles and lanterns had been doused through fear of fire. But that darkness was alive; the timbers that encased me in this watery coffin were continually creaking and groaning, as well they might. Can you imagine the answering moan of nigh upon six hundred souls cooped up down here in such abysmal conditions? Words cannot describe its unearthliness. It was as if we were in hell, and I do not use the term lightly. I hope I shall never live to hear such a sound again. If I could have stopped my ears, I would, but I was too much in extremis to do aught but cling onto my berth, bathed in sweat, whilst the timbers shrieked and the ship did its damnedest to turn over.

But now, at last, the storm has abated, and the world steadied. The whole of the steerage stinks with the smell of vomit and ordure but one tries to ignore it somehow. We are allowed on deck to cook at last, having subsisted on water and ship's biscuits till now. I felt weak as a mewling kitten when I let my legs gingerly hang down, and I have three days stubble on my chin, though Tim, an Irish lad who has been forced to share my berth, assures me this is not so, as we have only been two full days at sea. He may be correct, but it seems twice that, at least. I was too ill to be bothered about writing of Tim before. But he seems to have become a fixture in my life despite any intention of mine.

He is full of high spirits now and shouting cheek to the family of four above, who answer back in like vein.

He says he is fourteen but looks much younger, and he is an orphan, a real jackanapes who already knows everyone's business except his own. I fear for him when we reach America as he is all alone in the world, without any plans and with no friends or relations to meet him. That is why I let him share my berth. Yet his plight does not seem to cast him down one whit. He just takes out a mouth organ and, screwing up his densely freckled nose, begins to play a merry tune whenever I mention the subject of his future.

I own I was none too pleased when I saw he had to muscle in amongst my baggage or sleep on the floor; it seemed outrageous after paying three pounds and ten shillings that there should not be adequate berths for everyone and not at all what I had been led to expect. Yet now I am almost glad of the young rascal. He is not unkind in his way, so I cannot but think that God may, after all, look kindly on him.

I have been on deck, as Tim urged me to do, saying he could see land on the horizon. But it was only the receding coast of Ireland: a fact which, when conveyed to the passengers, cast the Irish contingent down into the doldrums, as the more ignorant amongst them had believed it must be America already. Still, I felt sorry for Tim as he fixed his eye on that grey strip, little more than a line now between land and sea. He said that now he was back where he had started and, although he tried to say it cheerfully, he had a manful struggle on his hands.

For myself, I felt overwhelmed as I leaned against the rail and looked around underneath the flapping canvas. In dropping, the wind had veered round so it was now directly before us, and the vessel had to tack this way and that, making precious little progress at all. It was grand to feel the cold air blow on one's face and to taste the salt where one licked one's lips. Yet it was fearful too to gaze over the waves, clutching onto the moving rail. I was astounded by the sea and the sky — their sheer size was beyond belief. I felt as if I had never seen them before and certainly never thought they were so vast. Both were watery grey and on the shift. It was hard not to dwell on the possibility of drowning when the ocean impressed itself upon us in this way. The Yorkshire, so large and sturdy in dock, must seem like a mere blob under a microscope to any God now.

I had hoped to stretch my legs, but there was little chance of that. Although The Yorkshire has a fine deck space in all, we find we are confined to a small part of it. A line is painted over which we must not cross lest we trespass on the preserves of the cabin passengers.

There were so many from steerage queuing to cook this morning that the situation was impossible, and I felt unable to stand for long, leaning first one way and then the other. I was more thirsty than hungry anyway.

But Tim offered to wait in line and cook the provisions for us both if we might share them. I suspect he is anxious to procure a little more than his fair share, but it does not worry me over much if he is willing to do battle on the galley range! So, I thanked him heartily and sought my berth once more.

The stench was renewed as I descended the hatchway, but at least the lamps may now be lit, and I can endeavour to apply myself once more to this journal, as my *'Emigrant Voyagers' Manual'* advises, to occupy the mind and keep from bad habits. Most of my sex are sitting idle and unshaven on their chests, smoking clay pipes and creating a suffocating vapour in the air. Still, anything is preferable to the human foetor.

I forgot to say, though now it concerns me much, that most of the privies on deck were swept away in the storm, and those that are left are already filthy with the doors ripped off. I can see that I shall soon be reduced to asking Tim if I might use his chamber pot if he has one, having broken my own. These must be emptied over the side. It is dreadful to endure all this embarrassment. Dear God, if I had known the truth of this voyage, I think I should never have found the courage to come!

I am amazed at how quickly I have taken to the young lad as a companion and how grateful I feel toward him; nay, how reliant I have become on him in truth. It is due to our extraordinary situation, for it appears that man must have society above all else. All over steerage, I see other strange friendships breaking out and there is a deal of conversation going on between those who would surely never give each other the time of day ashore.

I am mortified to acknowledge that Tim appears to be better at survival than my own poor self as if he were the man and I the boy. As I said before, he soon knows everything there is to be known. Perhaps folk tell him things because he is a boy. He catches the eye, too, with his curly, bright red hair. It was Tim who told me that more than a dozen stowaways were rooted out before we left the Mersey estuary. He made an amusing tale of it, with his account of men stuffed into barrels being upended in no uncertain manner by the sailors. The miscreants were all sent back in irons before we put out to the open sea. I wager that the scurrilous Welshman I met on the quayside was amongst them.

≈

For the first time since he had left home, Owain felt happy. To be sure, he, too, had felt his skin crawl at the sound of the battening down. He hated darkness and was terrified by the behaviour of the ship. But he was not ill or, at least, not as ill as Caitlin was, and where he would have once let his fears overwhelm him in the stinking darkness, he was able to put them aside in the face of his duty to ensure her welfare. It was as if he had been deliberately spared to look after this woman and child. The more he thought about it, the more convinced he became. This must be his last chance for salvation. God had sent him on the voyage with this purpose, and that meant he was no longer damned. It was his means of redemption, and he felt his heart spill over with joy.

On deck he had stood tongue-tied whilst she showed the ticket and answered questions. It would not have done to bring out his Welsh accent against her Irish one. But he had tried to shelter her from the rain with her umbrella and shyly stolen secret glances at her face. He thought she was an angel. Her face was fitted to the role of saviour, though her speech could be flippant enough.

Back in the berth, he could see she felt awkward with him, embarrassed now that her bravery was done, so he sat on the floor, leaning back against the foot of her bunk, and told her quietly about his life in the slate quarry, how he had hated it and how he had run away. He wanted to tell her more, to tell all of it, to lay out his burden in confession and be rid of it. But he knew that wouldn't be wise. It was too large a burden and would only frighten her. So, he just told her about running away.

In her turn, she told him about Ireland and the famine, her parents, and James. Except she didn't say James was a relative and a landlord. In moments, he somehow became a kindly older husband who had sent her and their child on ahead and was saving up the money to pay for his own passage. It seemed such a little lie, wish fulfilment as it was, and she told herself it was only wise to protect her unmarried state under these circumstances.

Owain sat at the foot of the bunk, on the hard boards, like a faithful hound on guard and wouldn't let any disreputable sailor nor passenger touch her or intend to do her any harm. He kept his own eyes averted when she self-consciously unhooked her gown and unlaced herself at night, though her modesty at being seen in her chemise was soon swept away with the first ravages of seasickness.

Owain brought her water and held it to her lips, wiping her sweating face and trembling hands, covering her with blankets, and begging her not to be afraid when she thought the ship might capsize. He took the baby and cared for it as gently and carefully as she did herself. By the time the storm was over, she trusted him and called out to him whenever she felt wretched again. He made no move to take advantage of their situation, and she felt safe with him.

≈

The sea did not respect cabin passengers any more than it did those in steerage, someone having omitted to inform the elements that they had paid considerably more for their passage. One of the first to fall ill was Mr Andrew Tyrrell, of the flaming beard and short temper. He lost no time in demanding the ship's surgeon, being unaccustomed to discomfort of any kind. When the good doctor eventually appeared, his gait was rolling with rather more than the swell of the ship, and his breath was heavy with spirits. Nevertheless, he ordered saltwater drinks and a mustard poultice to the stomach, both of which made Mr Tyrrell feel very much worse but effectively silenced him from further complaint. The only thing that brought him the slightest grain of comfort in his distress was the thought of how much money he would make in America, by fair means or foul, and the satisfying knowledge that he had escaped his gambling debtors back home.

≈

The Honourable Miss Cholmondeley, on the other hand, sought to control her sickness with prayer. When this failed, she succumbed willingly to laudanum and lay as prostrate as Tyrrell. She knew better than to bother the surgeon with her malady, even though she had never, in her whole life, felt so dreadful. At least she had the comfort of a basin and sink, and she even had her maid Alice, whom she dispatched back to her own cabin with medicine as soon as she saw the colour of her face.

Miss Cholmondeley tried to imagine what it must be like in steerage and gave up with a shudder. As soon as she could, she must get the captain's permission to go down there and see if she could provide any help. She was not in the least daunted by the magnitude of this task, for she had brought a plentiful supply of herbal tea, in which she placed the greatest faith.

≈

7ᵗʰ June

Three days after the storm, the weather continues fair. We seem to be making better progress now. However, we must tack about interminably, with all the canvas fluttering, to gain as much advantage as possible from the headwind. But at least we are not thrown back by every wave.

I have been doing my best to exercise on deck, despite the restrictions, and even had a little expedition some third of a way up the rigging to the first crossbar. What a dizzying task it must be to climb to the very top of the main mast! The morning sparkled with light, and, at last, the sea appeared blue with flecks of cream foam edging the waters that had been cut in two by our vessel. What a grand wake we leave behind us, spreading out over the sea and yet how insignificant when one remembers the vastness of the ocean as a whole! This thought still terrifies me, though I enjoyed my excursion. I saw the curved backs of porpoises jumping out of the water like flying fish. Mr Banks, the purser, soon caught me at it, however, and bawled at me to come down, so I was left in no doubt that this was a transgression. I feigned ignorance, and he threatened to keep a sharp eye upon me in the future.

Afterwards, I stood at the rail and filled my lungs with good, clean, fresh air whilst I was able. It is intoxicating after the rankness below. The horizon appears curved in the distance as if we might indeed turn round and over it, as they say.

I saw Captain Shearman on the bridge, his legs firmly planted against the swell. He was looking rather grim as usual, though the emigrants were entertaining themselves below by dancing to the music of some lively fiddles. Tim has been in great demand with his mouth organ.

We are beginning to get a kind of rhythm into our day. At eight o'clock, we are served our coffee and ship's biscuits, though served is hardly the right word. There is a great deal of roughness and slopping about it. The coffee itself is indescribably awful and, as well as being bitter and nasty, often varies strangely in colour. Yesterday morning it was perfectly green! Drinking it from a tin mug scarcely improves the flavour. At the same time, we are doled out our daily ration of water and oatmeal (as if we *were* horses to eat that stuff) and, if it is the beginning of the week, molasses, and flour or sometimes rice and potatoes. Then, we must make shift to turn these into some palatable mess.

It is a problem knowing when to queue for the galley range on deck, for if it is done too early in the day, we may well feel sated early on but hungry later. If we delay, we run the risk of never getting to the galley at all, as the cook is very rude about dousing the fire when the hour is getting late.

Tim continues to be my 'manservant' and my saviour, for he is not averse to queuing all day long and gleaning all the gossip while he is about it. He can hold his own in a fight for the stove, too. I could wish he did not burn the rice so often, but he does his best, and I cannot complain. I opened that nice piece of smoked ham, which you cured for me, Mother. I have been saving it since we sailed until I could bear the plain fodder they give us no longer. But when I retrieved it from my baggage today — imagine my despair — It was full of maggots, and I had to throw it away!

As Tim is so very much about the steerage and the deck, I asked him, as casually as I could, if he had seen anything of a young Irish girl travelling alone with her baby. I described the Madonna to him in such cool terms as I could muster. But he says there is no one of that description on her own, to his knowledge, though plenty with husbands. Perhaps I was mistaken about her abandonment, or perhaps she could not board. The Welshman must surely have been thrown off with the stowaways. Maybe he was one of the two in barrels of flour that nigh on suffocated, according to Tim.

I saw the unfortunate German family again, however, and raised my hat to the sturdy hausfrau, who recognized me and inclined her head politely. They are billeted nearby. The children, two boys of six and nine or thereabouts, are attractive, plucky, and well-kept. But, oh dear, how wild and unkempt her poor husband looks and how his eyes stare! I do not think he is sufficiently robust to stand the rigours of this voyage.

After some exercise and our luncheon, I apply myself to my journal until teatime comes round. Thereafter, I am afraid I smoke and play a few hands of cards with my neighbours. I know you would not approve. In other circumstances, I would not either, though I always retire before I lose too much money. But there is so little to do, and one needs some distraction from the endless creaking of timbers and the constant rising and falling motion. Anyway, the stakes are not high — anyone with any real money is anxious to keep it for the New World. On Sundays, I forgo the diversion altogether. There is little enough to mark that day off from the others, though there are a couple of chaplains aboard, and prayers are said at various times on deck. At ten, the order is given for all lights to be extinguished below, and the surly Banks comes round with several assistants to make sure it is done. Any candle left burning is confiscated immediately. I do not complain about that, for there is no doubt the risk of fire is terribly real. Then the darkness (though not silence) claims us, and we must make shift to sleep as best we may. I talk to Tim to begin with but soon find my eyelids drooping, though I do not sleep soundly all night. Even in our dreams, the ship is all around us.

Chapter Three

8th June

During the night we had a serious disturbance. I awoke to find the most dreadful racket going on about a dozen berths away on our side of the ship. A candle had been lit, and there was a man shouting and fighting with others who strove to put it out. There are those who have brought strong drink aboard and we have had some brawling at night before now. But this was different — the assailants of the man sought only to avert a calamity. The owner of the candle was ranting and raving at them unintelligibly. He cowered in a corner and was obviously panic-stricken. A woman's voice was raised, too, and I thought it sounded familiar. Then I realized it was my worthy German lady and the 'madman' — for such he appeared to be, kicking and flailing out at everything in sight — was her poor, distressed husband, unable to bear the confinement of the night any longer. More candles were lit to throw light on the scene, and I dispatched Tim to alert the watch, for I feared for the man's safety.

The sight the candles lit showed nothing alarming. Indeed, if one had neither a sense of smell nor much imagination, one might have thought it all warm and safe with the close timbers of the ship bathed in the cosy glow of candlelight. Women and children huddled low in their bunks or peeped out nervously over blankets whilst the madman shrank back, as terrified as his own weeping children. Some fellow, braver than the rest, stepped forward to try to calm him, but this only rendered him more panic-stricken than before and renewed his senseless shouting and lashing out. He seemed to believe all the eyes in the dark were against him. Perhaps his wife could have reassured him, but she was held back in the arms of a determined saviour. Then Tim returned with the men of the watch, and the inevitable conclusion was that the mad German was overpowered and taken away in irons, which made him take to screaming terribly. Everyone returned to bed, but not to sleep, for we all felt shaken by the experience. Sorry for the man, of course, yet sorely frightened at what might have happened and glad he had been removed somewhere he could no longer disturb us, where we would forget about him if we could, make no bones about that.

We heard later that, when he had been shackled fully, the ship's surgeon was called and made a thorough examination from a distance of at least twenty paces. He ordered a heavy sedative dose of some opiate to be given, but Herr Kleist, for that is his name, would have none of it and spat out the little they managed to force through his lips as if it were poison. No doubt he believes it is. In the end, they left him to go on ranting till he was exhausted.

Now they say he sits quietly with his head in his hands, doing and saying nothing and leaving the food and water they bring him untouched. If this goes on, he will surely die. His wife has been allowed to see him but did not take the children for fear they would be more upset than they already are.

Of course, he was in a weak state before he ever came aboard, as I, for one, can testify. Most are saying it is the voyage that drove him mad. All of which helps Frau Kleist and her two children not at all. Poor woman! She looks as if her worst fears have been realized but is determined not to sob her heart out and merely to get through each day by attending to the manifold needs of her little ones. I should have spoken to her last night with some words of comfort, for most of the emigrants will have nothing to do with her now. But it was the first time I had seen a lunatic at close quarters, and I own, I found it disturbing.

Still, I have sent her a note (via Tim) to express my concern and condolences and to proffer our services if we can ease her trouble in any small way. Of course, we cannot, and they are mere words, but they are meant kindly. I half expected her not to understand, but it appears she is an educated woman who knew well enough the purpose of the message. She thanked Tim in precise, heavily accented English, which Tim parodied good and proper to me later. Sometimes, that boy needs a good box on the ears. He will come to no good in New York, I fear. Anyway, the good woman smiled warmly when she saw me later and thanked me herself, most correctly. I was dismayed to remember and embarrassed to see, though she conceals it well with her full gowns, that she is very heavy with child, and I cannot think how she will manage in the new country alone.

≈

There was a sharp tap at Captain Shearman's door, and the very next moment, before he had time to call out, the Hon. Miss Cholmondeley entered in full sail. The captain was taken aback. He was sitting with his frock coat off and his shirt and waistcoat unbuttoned, smoking a Havana cigar, and had an open bottle of bourbon, from which he had been imbibing moderately, in front of him. He was not accustomed to having his sanctum invaded in this manner, and certainly not by a female passenger.

Miss Cholmondeley's eye took in the unbuttoned shirt, the cigar, and especially the bottle of bourbon. She sank, unabashed and uninvited, into the nearest chair and launched her attack forthwith:

"Captain Shearman, I believe you have had a man in irons for over 48 hours!" It was an accusation. Miss Cholmondeley continued, with two pink spots burning in her cheeks. "What is more, he is now calm and quiet. In fact, he is terribly withdrawn and little wonder considering his treatment."

"I am astounded that you have any knowledge of this. Have you seen the man?"

"No, but I have ears, Captain, and I have spoken to the man's wife. She is sore and distressed because he will not eat."

"I believe that is correct."

"Then he will die sooner or later, and it is a scandal. He was a man of some note in his own country."

"What would you have me do, dear lady? We cannot force him to eat".

"Why, you must set him free, of course, and return him to his family! Then he may eat, given the tender ministrations of his wife."

Captain Shearman sighed. "How little you know of the world! I trust I speak with respect, madam. But do you imagine his companions in steerage will welcome him back with open arms? If so, I'm afraid you're very much mistaken."

"Nevertheless, with equal respect, Captain, it is your place to give the orders and surely not to give way before the uneducated and prejudiced."

The captain smiled wryly. "Then you must leave me to exercise that right when the time is appropriate, Miss Cholmondeley. Amongst those persons whose class is prevalent in the steerage, I fear an ill-judged decision could incite a riot. It is a difficult enough matter having such persons aboard in large numbers without seeming to put them in any additional jeopardy."

"But the man is now harmless!"

"We cannot be sure of that, dear lady."

"Has he been seen again by the surgeon?"

"I think not but will seek his advice. Perhaps it is time to remove the shackles."

Miss Cholmondeley sensed a partial victory and decided to press her advantage. "Another matter, captain. The emigrants are complaining that they are not getting their full weekly ration of flour or even of oatmeal."

"The cargo was badly stowed, and it took a while to sort out supplies. That I know, and Mr Banks is not as solicitous as he might be. But this week should see those matters corrected."

He wondered how she knew. It was impossible to imagine a lady of her refinement and sensitivity descending between decks. Only she must have done so unless she had accosted these people on deck during her daily exercise. He had no doubt her motives were honourable and fine. At home, he guessed she was one of those gentlewomen who spent their time knitting vests and making shirts for the poor in the parish. He had heard of such charitable works. Nevertheless, championing the cause of a confirmed lunatic was rather more serious.

"Is there anything else?" he asked as she made no move to leave.

"Well, there is the matter of the privies." The pink spots burnt a little higher. "They are intolerable!"

"Again?"

She nodded sternly.

"I am sorry about the doors. The storm swept them away. And I am aware they are a poor makeshift at best and too few. But the biggest problem is that most of these people do not know how to use a water closet! It has been reported to me that they are continually choked up by meat, bones and the like. Still, I will see what I can do and get the men to hose them down regularly."

Miss Cholmondeley inclined her head. "And you won't forget that poor German in irons?"

"Is he German?"

"Yes, and Jewish, so therefore not much liked."

"I won't forget him."

"Thank you, Captain."

Having obtained these assurances, she deemed it prudent to withdraw. When she had gone, Captain Shearman sighed heavily and poured himself another drink, rather more generous than the last. He felt he had been patronizing. After all, the woman had shown pluck to tackle him, and she had right on her side. But what could he do, more than he already did, to alleviate the sufferings of so many? It was useless to tell a crusading lady of Miss Cholmondeley's worth that The Yorkshire was one of the best packets of that class afloat. She would only think him immodest and casting about for an excuse if he said he knew for a fact that some of the treatment meted out to emigrants aboard The Washington, say, amounted to sheer cruelty. He finished his drink, did up his buttons, and put on his coat. It would be better to find the ship's surgeon before sundown, for he would be useless thereafter.

≈

11th June

It gives me some pleasure to report that Herr Kleist is back in the bosom of his family or at least in their berth. True, he looks sorely shaken and lies in bed all day, never bothering to get up, not even to wash. But he accepts all the messes of food his good wife gives him on a spoon.

I find, to my surprise, that Frau Kleist speaks most tolerable English and is able to read the language. She came to thank me again this morning for all my enquiries. Apparently, her husband was released on the captain's orders, though the ship's surgeon swore he would have him committed to the hospital on Staten Island at the slightest hint of any further trouble.

Frau Kleist has promised to keep him in order. There was a deal of grumbling around steerage at first when they saw him returned and some talk about 'mad Jews,' but now no one takes any more notice, seeing as he is apt to lie there motionless.

However, no one, apart from myself, talks to Frau Kleist anymore and gives the family a wide berth. So, she has begun to confide in me. She told me, with the most amazing calmness, that her husband and her father had both played an active part in the revolution which swept Germany two years ago. It had been planned for a long time — so long that Frau Kleist herself had not believed it would happen. But when it did — in the spring of 1848 — it was carried out with breathtaking ease, and the expected resistance did not materialize. Only in Berlin was there significant bloodshed, and even there, the king was so anxious to conciliate that he rode the streets in black, red, and gold, the colours of the revolution, and had collection boxes put up for alms for all those injured on the barricades.

It seems the German princes were sorely afraid. Louis Philippe had been overthrown in France that February, and the spectre of a French-style revolution weighed heavily upon them. So, elections were held, and Friedrich, as she calls her husband, was elected as one of the Members of Parliament in the first National Assembly. I found it extraordinary sitting and listening to the tale told by this sturdy little hausfrau.

"You would not think it now," she said to me sadly. "But Friedrich was a fine young man then, noble and courageous, despite his lowly origins, and hono*u*rable too — ja, honourable to a fault."

Then things began to go wrong. She could not clearly tell me why. But it seemed the well-intentioned liberals had unleashed a small but radical band of anarchists among themselves.

The King of Prussia (who was still in control of the army) took it upon himself to drive the Danes out of South Jutland, and the new Parliament made the mistake of supporting him to begin with. It became difficult to maintain law and order and even more difficult to find out who instigated the riots, which occurred when the Parliament changed its mind. Troops were called in, and the army opened fire on the people, this time in the name of the democratic government instead of the kings and princes of old.

That day, Herr Kleist came home in stunned disbelief, for that was not what he had intended at all. The Parliament, he said to his wife, is by the people and for the people. How, then, could such a thing happen? He began to blame himself from that moment on, though there were others far more guilty. I listened with interest as Frau Kleist went on.

There were other troubles that came thick and fast, interminable squabbles over new frontiers amongst them, for Germany apparently is a land of racial minorities. It does not exist in any other way. The Kleists were German Jews, but Friedrich had been forced to undergo a Christian baptism before they could marry in Frankfurt some years before when there had been 'enough Jewish marriages' already that year.

Frau Kleist's eyes misted over, and she blushed as she told me that.

It had severed Friedrich from his own family. He had done it for her, and she was sorry for it. Still, they had enjoyed a happy and tranquil marriage before the revolution.

Further riots came when the King of Prussia refused the crown Parliament offered him, saying it had come 'from the gutter.' There was to be no stability. Worst of all, their Prince, who was an Austrian delegate to the Assembly, was murdered in Frankfurt. The militia was called out again from the garrison. The shreds of the new Parliament struggled on but never regained the respect they once had.

In June 1849, the Parliament was disbanded by troops. A counter-revolution began, and all the respectable burghers of Frankfurt were relieved. It was time that share prices rose again after all. Frau Kleist said this without any bitterness. The feeling was general, she explained. The old order was back in power. A new Germany would emerge — a nationalist Germany in the end, and decidedly not a liberal one. That had failed, and Friedrich could neither forgive nor forget his part in it.

There were reprisals. Lasalle, a prominent leader of the revolution, was sent to prison. Someone called Robert Blum was executed in Austria despite his pleas for diplomatic immunity. Others met similar fates. It was all Rosa Kleist could do to stop Friedrich from rushing out into Romer Square and shouting for them to come and take him, too, for the strain had made him ill, and he was no longer fully in control of himself.

Rosa conferred with her father. There was no need for instant flight. Friedrich was not as important as he thought he was. But perhaps it would be better to leave the country. Rosa's father was safe enough in the gymnasium as he had always kept a low profile. But it was obvious that Friedrich would lose all his custom as a tailor. Sensible Frankfurters would not want their suits to be made by a failed revolutionary. So, they decided to emigrate and sadly began to prepare.

They lived in Rotterdam for the best part of a year, delaying their departure for Hull until Herr Kleist was well enough to travel further to Liverpool by rail. Despite this, there was little improvement, and Rosa became convinced they needed to get to America urgently to begin a completely new life. Now, she fears this is a mistake, although she is sure she can nurse him back to health once off the ship. I agree and do my utmost to encourage the poor woman.

But Staten Island is a long way off yet. I asked the first mate if we were anywhere near it this morning, and he shook his head and laughed. We go on very much as usual, about twelve knots, I believe, with the waters mercifully quiet. My stomach is still not well settled. I am heartily sick of the porridge young Tim cooks for us. It is not his fault, but my spirits sank even lower when the first mate told us, on further questioning, that, by his estimations, we were not over halfway there yet! I feel very out of sorts, and there is another reason I must confess.

For I saw her this morning — the little Madonna. She is berthed at the opposite end of steerage and turned her blue eyes upon me for the merest instant as I passed by, restless and desirous of exercise as usual. When I told Tim, he laughed and said she had a husband all right and one who scarcely ever left her side, so devoted did he appear. Stupidly, I felt utter disappointment at this news, though I should have been glad for her. I'm sure I don't know what I was expecting, but I can no longer entertain any pleasant fantasies concerning her in my mind, and I feel the loss of that acutely, almost as if I had really gained and lost her.

I have resolved to play no more cards as I lost again last night to the fella' from Cork who plays the concertina. I am determined instead to read in the hope of improving my mind. Jeremiah was wise to send me from home with a copy of the Bible. Tim thinks I have taken up some thought of being a parson in the New World. I cannot be bothered to disillusion him, though he is mistaken. How heavily the days hang at sea! It seems like years since I stood in the streets of Bradford and weighed my lot.

I have not entirely forgotten them. In winter, there always seemed to be that thick pall of rain over the town, blotting out the hills. Unhealthy streams of water dribbled down the gutters, and the mill girls hurried along in their pattens, lifting their skirts with one hand and clutching their plaid shawls with the other. I remember the bustle at the beginning of each factory shift, the horses straining and slipping on the steep streets, the smell of their piled droppings in the damp air, the news-sellers shouting themselves hoarse with the first evening edition, and the lamplighters about their rounds early on the short, dark days.

I remember the Wool Exchange and the offices where small and insignificant men bent their heads and scratched their quills on paper. It was a mild fancy of mine that some of them never went home and would certainly never die but crumble away to dust in a corner behind their ledgers. And I was no better off as a mere draper's assistant. Until that day, I borrowed the book from the library, which burnt its way into my heart with its stirring words, every one of which I can recall.

'The United States of America covers a vast amount of territory. It encompasses wide, open spaces, magnificent forests, and ancient ranges of mountains. Truly, the scale of the land cannot be fully appreciated by one who has never crossed the Atlantic. Agriculturally speaking, the land is rich and plentiful, although largely untilled due to the smallness of the population. Nor is there a lack of fine cities, all growing daily in their prosperity through commerce...'

How many times thereafter I read that again! How I struggled in my heart to ignore it and to exercise prudence and caution! But I did not want to stay a draper's assistant forever. So slowly, the words worked their magic upon me until I could resist them no more.

This voyage is only the forerunner. Every dreary day spent tossing here will be well spent soon. I must not lose my fortitude now. I am, at last, on my way to America, where dreams can come true.

Chapter Four

"There he is!" Owain turned sharply, with all the fear he thought he'd left behind him. He found himself looking into the scornful face of the seaman he had paid to get aboard. He was not alone. Two others flanked him. One of them held a spare end of rope in his hand and kept on whacking it against his dirty trousers, grinning all the while as if he expected some amusement.

"We want a word with you," said the man in the middle. He appealed to his friends, jerking a thumb at Owain. "Thought he could stow away and get away with it!"

They murmured their feigned outrage.

"That was the arrangement, see," said Owain staunchly. "I paid you for it, though I received little help!"

"Paid for it, did he?" jeered the mariner. "S'es he! The little Welsh rat! Don't he know no crewman of Captain Shearman's ever takes a bribe?"

His companions laughed, and when Owain turned round in disgust, he found his way barred by two more seamen, both of whom held ropes. It was obvious something unpleasant was on the way, but it was useless to struggle against five. His fear suddenly ebbed away. Carefully, he set down the bowl of cooked rice and treacle he had been carrying to Caitlin. He had avoided punishment for a long time. If it had to come, it was a relief it should come now. He would not struggle but accept it as his due.

He felt his arms pinioned swiftly from behind. Then, he was dragged along the deck into the waist of the ship to be lashed to the main mast. He could see the purser and the second mate upon the fo'c'sle in the distance, but a rag was stuffed into his mouth to stop him from crying out. Whether or not the officers saw him, he could not tell; only he fancied they did, for they both turned their backs and walked deliberately away.

"When did you say you give me this money?" snarled the first seaman. He took the gag out of Owain's mouth temporarily to enable him to reply.

"In Liverpool. At the pawnbrokers." He felt his lower lip split open at the force of the blow which followed.

"Jesus Christ! I'll rope-end you for that foul lie!"

The blows rained down until he began to feel dizzy and felt warm blood running down from his nose into his mouth.

"Where? Where did you say?" roared his tormentor. "And when?"

"I never gave you any money," Owain muttered.

"Louder, you filthy liar, louder."

"I never gave you any money. I was mistaken. It must have been somebody else."

The gag was pushed back into his mouth. Meanwhile, it had been soaked in something vile, and the taste of it made him retch. Yet he bit hard into it at the next stinging blow.

"There's a good one for lying to all these respectable gen'lemen. God damn you and blast your soul to hell!"

Through a haze, Owain saw a knot of bystanders had gathered around the seamen. But no one moved to intervene.

"Let's make sure you remember the truth in future, eh?"

There was a rumble of approval from the onlookers, and someone hooted with laughter as he saw what was being prepared. Owain's clothes were ripped off, and one of the seamen slopped a pail of foul-smelling grease over him. It was in his face, his eyes, and his mouth, and he struggled despite himself as the whiff of excrement mingled with blood choked his breath.

Another seaman set to with a knife, grabbing handfuls of his hair and hacking it off, close enough to his scalp to leave the cut ends sticking up unevenly, like a savage. There was a roar of laughter and encouragement. Someone else took a cut-throat to him, claiming his whiskers needed 'a tidying up', and abruptly and not without a nick or two, he found that half his new stubbly beard and moustache were gone.

Another pailful was thrown over him, and this time, it was tar, black and sticky, which they proceeded to slap up and down his body. Shrieks of approval and laughter surrounded him. But then another cry went up.

"Look sharp! Cap'n's coming aft!"

Within seconds, both spectators and seamen had melted away. Owain realized the ropes that bound him had been cut, but he was too dazed and blinded to do more than sink to his knees and crawl around feebly looking for his bowl, quite forgetting in his degradation and misery that he had been dragged a good twenty feet up deck from the place where he had put it down.

"Mr Banks!" The voice above him was cold with anger. "Bring this man a bucket of hot water and his clothes."

"The men claim he is a stowaway, sir."

"I said bring him some hot water!"

"Yessir."

"I suppose you don't know who did this?" His voice crackled with fatigue.

"No, sir."

"You're a damned liar, Mr Banks!"

"Yessir."

"Get this man cleaned up."

"Is he to work his passage then, sir?"

"He's already done so."

"Beggin' your pardon, sir?"

"Clean up the poor devil and let him be! If it happens again, I'll have you personally keel-hauled."

"Yessir. Right away, sir."

≈

Caitlin was horrified when she saw Owain. Although he had done a fair job of washing himself, his hair stuck up at right angles, and he lacked a razor to finish off the work done on his whiskers. His face was swelling up, and his nose and lip were still bloodied. Despite his toilet, he still stank, and his clothes were hanging in tatters.

"Jesus! Look at your face!" she cried. "Mercy, Owain! Whatever's happened to you?"

"I've been getting myself tarred and feathered."

Once, at the county fair, Caitlin remembered a woman who had been accused of loose behaviour and got herself tarred and feathered. It was a long time ago — she was but a child — but she still remembered those revolting scenes and shuddered.

"In God's name, why? Who would do such a thing? They should be flogged whoever it was."

Owain shrugged. He felt humiliated and angry yet had no desire to make too much of it. "I deserved it," he said, bleakly.

Caitlin stared at him.

"But who was it?"

"The seaman who took all my money off me in Liverpool, like the baby I was. I think your kindness robbed him of the bounty he might have got for rooting me out as a stowaway."

"Then you surely deserved no such thing! How can you say that? That eye looks awful sore. Let me bathe your face!"

"Don't bother yourself about it. I've already washed, and there's nothing else to be done."

Still, Caitlin wrung out a piece of old cloth in cold water from their ration and pressed it to his eye. He flinched but told her it felt easier.

"Sure, and you're going to have some wonderful bruises! You'd better take off that shirt, and I'll try to mend it as best I can. It won't be easy! Why in heaven's name did you come away with no money and not even a change of clothes to your back?"

Owain hesitated. Underneath her peevish interrogation, he felt all this sympathy was wrong.

"Caitlin, you don't understand. I killed a man. I'm a murderer, see. A murderer!" His voice was low, but she heard him all right. Her hands froze on his shirt. There! It was out. In the sudden rush of emotion, his legs shook, and he had to sit down. He hid his face in his hands as he saw fear flit across her own.

"I've got my life to thank you for, not just the passage out. But it was under false pretences. I'll go if you want. Of course, I can see you wouldn't want me to stay."

There was no answer. She was too shocked. Of course, she was bound to be terrified. But he had needed to say it. "I never meant to bother you. I'll go." And he picked up his coat and hat, his only possessions, to suit the action to the words.

"Go? Where can you go? We're in the middle of the ocean!"

"I mean, I won't trouble you any longer. I'll find a corner. Maybe I'll go to the captain." But he knew, even as he said it, he wouldn't. He didn't have the courage. Shamefaced and silent, he left her.

He hung his head over the rail in anguish and watched the dark purple water churn below. Wouldn't it be easier to let his body slip into the waves? Would it be so very painful to drown? But he had been brought up in the Welsh chapels and was too afraid of what might follow. 'Thy sin shall find thee out.' In a little while, he felt a light touch on his arm and turned to see Caitlin.

"Come," she said calmly. "Let's walk." He let her guide him along the deck.

"Where is the child?" he asked, for he had grown quite fond of the babbling little girl and knew that since she had learnt to toddle a little, Caitlin worried about losing her.

"It's all right. She's quite safe. I left her with the woman next to us," Caitlin hesitated. "Owain, I cannot believe you are a very evil man. Not when I think of the way you handle Maeve and the way you've tenderly cared for us both. There must have been some good reason why you killed. You are not a murderer."

You don't know," he said wretchedly. "You know nothing about me! I killed the under-manager at the mine because he was bullying a friend of mine who was old and sick and had to leave..."

"There you are then. I knew there had to be a reason!"

"But that's too easy, Caitlin. Much too easily said. There was more to it than that. You'd have to understand about the mine."

Caitlin led him around one of the lifeboats so that they were sheltered from the wind. Then tell me," she said. "You owe me that."

Chapter Five

The trouble with Owain was that he was different. Elen had always known it from his earliest days and feared for him. Other sons of small Welsh hill farmers and shepherds bore adversity with patience like their fathers and remained obedient to authority, whether that of parents, landlord, or chapel. But Owain, though far from being a bad boy, had an instinctive and keen sense of injustice that would never be denied. He could not wait for time to put matters right, neither for himself nor others.

It would not have mattered so much, perhaps, had he been a great big, muscular fellow able to command respect. But he was not. He was small and dark with an angry eye. As a child, he always came home to Fedwr Gog the worse for some fight with a boy much older than himself. Elen knew he would continue getting into trouble — often for the right reason — but what good, as she had once said despairingly to his father, was any of that?

Still, she was proud of him. He was understandable to her in a way that the sturdy, reliable Rhys and placid, hard-working Tomas were not. She knew it was wrong to have favourites amongst her sons. But how could she help it when Owain sorely needed a champion? Sometimes, Elen thought that only she would remain loyal to him in the whole wide world. However, their world was far from wide. It consisted of these hills with their scattered farms, bounded by the great peaks of Eryri to the west and the upper reaches of the Conway Valley to the north. The main coaching road between London and Holyhead ran at the head of the valley. But no-one Elen knew had been to either of these places. To the east lay the Marches of England, and to the south, the hills of central Wales.

Over this last year, a new slate mine had opened at Blaenau, five miles away as the crow flies, and the boys had gone to work there, driven by the promise of higher wages and the unsteady nature of hireling labour round about. Elen could scarcely conceive of a different land across the sea to the west and indeed hardly believed that one existed, though she had heard tell of it.

≈

It is the blackest of nights in the slate quarry. Outside, it is day, and cloud shadows chase sunlight over the hills. The sun even shines now and then on the great black slag heaps, beginning to tower over the town. But in the depths of the slate quarry, it is always night, black and impenetrable. Water drips from the ceiling, and it is intensely cold. Owain should be used to it by now. Yet he could never resist a shiver at the chill nor overcome the feeling of dread that comes over him when he enters the tunnel leading to the mine.

He remembers the first time — a little over a year ago now — when he joined his brothers so uncertainly, with a spare candle tucked into his cap, his bread in a tin box, and a billy can for tea under one arm. It was every bit as bad as he had expected.

Tomas and Rhys had convinced him that the mine was the place to be. More certain than tending sheep and grubbing about on the land could ever be. You soon got used to the dark, and the men were a decent lot. The work was hard, but in a good chamber, you could earn well by the end of the month. Owain didn't see it this way. Nor did he ever seem to get a good chamber.

It was not that he minded chipping away at the rock for hours with a long, metal rod to drill a hole for gunpowder and fuse. It was tedious work, true enough, but you could get a mind-numbing rhythm into it after a while. You got so that you hardly noticed the ache in your arms and the ringing in your head. Nor was he afraid of being roped up with a chain round his thigh whilst he worked the upper reaches of the chamber with both hands free. He had scrambled up enough precipitous slopes with his brothers, and being small meant he was nimble. There were three quarrymen besides himself in the chamber and a fourth man to labour. Together, they made a partnership and were indeed a cheerful enough group.

Only Owain cannot overcome his dread at being inside the mountain. He is always afraid his candle will sputter out (as it often does), and he will have to fumble to relight it. Candlelight at home in Fedwr Gog is supplemented by firelight from the hearth and the range where Elen's face glows as she ladles out food. Even outside the cottage, it is never totally dark, as the sky is usually lighter and more alive than the inky hills. Often, there are stars wheeling on their way, or the clouds gather back from a big, white moon. On summer nights especially, the dawn is quick to come. But down here, there is no relief, and the darkness dwarfs each tiny candle-point, turning Owain and the others into pygmies from a strange land.

He sticks his candle into its lump of clay on a ledge and tries to get on with his work. Not in silence, for there is little enough of that. The rods ring on stone, and, at intervals, the low thunder of explosions can be heard from other caverns, followed by the rumble of wagons carrying slate to the surface. They blast their own chamber and return to find it full of smoke and rubble. It takes a long time for it to settle, and they cannot afford to wait. Owain's eyes are used to the smoky atmosphere now, but he always has a cough. Sometimes, the larger slabs of slate have not been completely freed by the explosion, and they have to be levered off the rock face with a crowbar. There is some danger in this. In the sweat of exertion, Owain forgets where he is. It is when he pauses in his work that the feeling of being buried returns. It is especially there in the caban when he takes his break.

The caban serves all the chambers on their level and provides a welcome respite with its kettle steaming over the fire. The tea is marvellous healing to a dry mouth and parched throat. There is the chance of a quick clay pipe and plenty of other fellows to talk to. Indeed, the hut is often the centre of a surprising amount of discussion and debate — and sometimes even singing if there is an eisteddfod approaching.

Only then, someone tells how young Dai got his hat blown off this morning and was lucky his head didn't go with it, all on account of being too hasty, see, and not using the special brass rod to pack down the explosive in its hole as he ought. Dai is a bit of a character, and the way the story is told, with much embellishment, causes considerable mirth.

Owain sits alone and sweats despite the cold. His skin begins to crawl as he feels, through the thin walls of the caban, the great press of rock that is the mountain bearing down on him. He wipes the tea off his moustache nervously and disturbs a layer of grey dust. Sometimes, he feels he cannot breathe at all and that he must escape into clean air. He must take a firm grip on himself then to stop the roaring in his ears.

He never tells any of the others how he feels, not even Huw, his opposite number and partner in his own chamber. Huw is the kindest of men, old before his time but generally cheerful and whistling. He took Owain under his wing from the start. They are both small, but Huw gives the impression of having shrunk into his clothes and continuing to do so. His bony nose dominates a lean face full of shadows and hollows. Owain wonders if he will look like that in another twenty years.

Huw senses some of his distress as he never makes jokes to Owain about the mine. The nearest Owain gets to mentioning his feelings is when he asks Huw what the work was like at Penrhyn quarry over the other side of Snowdon. Huw used to work there, but his wife's relatives brought him to Ffestiniog. Penrhyn was an open mine, though hardly less dusty for that.

"Here, the slate's too damn stubborn and deeply angled into the rock for open quarrying. It's a different colour too ... grey instead of purple. But I reckon the job's much the same otherwise."

Owain wonders if he would be better off working Penrhyn, but it is a long way there, and he doesn't want to leave Fedwr Gog. The year advances wearily. In the winter, it is still dark outside at seven when they enter the mine and dark again when they leave at four. There seems no end to drudgery, then. Yet now that spring has come, it is worse; the sudden return of warm fresh air and the brilliance of the light are hard to leave.

Owain hikes back over the moorland tracks, and each moment spent crossing the open expanse of hills seems precious. He thinks he cannot bear to be shut up in the earth again for one more day. He must see the sky and live on the hills. There is fullness in his heart when he drops down at last into the lee of a small wood and sees their cottage nestling white in an evening sun: Fedwr Gog. It is but a poor and rough place in truth, yet a quality of peace descends on him each time he arrives at his journey's end.

So, he always treks home now that the lighter weather has come, unlike Rhys and Tomas, who board the week in Blaenau.

Once home, he takes water from the range to the tub in the washhouse, for Elen will not allow him in her clean, scoured kitchen otherwise, caked in slate dust as he is. Whilst he washes, his younger sister, Mair, comes and prattles on to him, trailing the head of her old rag doll through the farmyard mud. Later, he will eat before Elen's winking black range. At night, he sleeps on a clean straw mattress in the loft above the byre, and the warm, comforting smell of animal dung is all around him.

When it is the lambing season, tired though he is, he will get up in the night to take a lamp round the flock with Madoc to check that all is well with the pregnant ewes. He envies his father, although Madoc does not own the sheep and hires himself out to others. Maybe, when his father has grown old and infirm, he can take his place; Tomas and Rhys seem determined to stay on as quarrymen. Only Madoc is tough and far from infirm, and Owain feels shame in anticipating his father's demise. If only he could earn the good money his brothers speak of, then he might, in time, save enough to take a smallholding and build it up with his own small flock. Then, one day, he could even be the master of Fedwr Gog.

He often dreams of this in the night, stretched out on the wooden bench seat before the fire with the cat. Secretly, he watches Elen's face in the glow of the flames as her deft needle flashes in and out. She is never entirely idle, although she exudes the presence of calm. Owain likes it best when they are alone together like this, with Mair already in bed and Madoc out in the fields, for he is selfish and has no wish to share her. Given the chance, Owain will choose a good Welsh wife like Elen, though her face is lined, and her waist and figure thickened.

He does not speak to her of the quarry though she often asks him about it. When he must, he uses optimistic phrases borrowed from his brothers, but she is not deceived. Sometimes, she will tell him of his father's hardships with a frown, as if to say that no life is easy and never has been. She always receives the money he brings home graciously, with more than a little guilt, knowing his unhappiness, and sees that he has the best of the mutton stew and fat bacon to eat. When he talks of his future plans, as he is sometimes emboldened to do, she merely nods and smiles uncertainly.

"I shan't be at the quarry forever, Mother," he says with determination.

"No," she replies. "Certainly, you will not be there forever."

But, at the end of each month, Owain sees his chamber's bargain with the quarry manager fall short. Even in a good month, his wages only amount to a few miserable shillings a week. He can see the logic of being paid for slate actually brought up. Yet, lumbered with a difficult chamber, it does not seem fair to have worked so hard for so little return. Had they not been forced to pay for the same amount of gelignite, the same number of fuses and candles, and clay as the more fortunate? Had they not worked the same hours each day? One month, he is driven to complain to the under-manager: a sleek, well-fed man apportioning the wages out in his dust-slaked surface hut.

"We should be moved further on into the quarry," he says, mildly enough, though his heart is beating rapidly. "That chamber's no good. It's all worked out, and we ought to try somewhere else."

The undermanager looks at him hard, disbelief growing in his small, cold eyes. A welter of broken blood vessels on his plump cheeks begins to dilate.

"We'll tell you where to drill, boyo. There's plenty of good slate left in that chamber yet."

"Not enough to pay us a decent wage." Owain will not be put down so easily.

The under manager rises to his feet and draws himself up to his full height, which is not remarkable. Nevertheless, his expression is withering in its contempt.

"Have to work harder for it then, boyo," he says. "won't we?"

Huw glances at his friend's flushed and angry face as they leave the shed.

"You ought not to have spoken up, Owain."

"But it's true!" Huw sighs.

"I know, my boy, I know. But you won't do yourself any good, see. You'll just go getting into trouble. The under-manager is only doing his job. When he goes to Chapel on a Sunday in Ffestiniog, his conscience is all square. He doesn't 'ave to give us anymore. Your complainin'll only mark you down as one to watch, in his eyes..."

Huw breaks off coughing and has to lean against an empty slate wagon for support. When he regains his breath, it comes rasping painfully against his ribs. He has not been too good of late, and Owain knows it. When he puts his hand on the older man's arm, he can feel the sinews tight and tense under his grip.

"You're not well, Huw. You should be at home."

"No, no, I'm all right, boy." Huw recovers himself slowly. "The chest's not been too good. The wife's been sick, too. It'll pass."

"You've lost a lot of weight recently."

"Oh well, I've always been a sparrow, like yourself. I'll be fine."

Only Huw is far from fine. The very next week, he coughs up some blood in the chamber, and Owain insists on taking him home. Huw rents a small cottage in Blaenau Ffestiniog, under the shadow of one of the slag heaps, and it is Owain's first visit there. It is a cold afternoon for spring, with the wind buffeting the narrow, bleak streets. Despite this, there is no fire in the hearth. Huw's tired wife rises to greet them. Instead of remonstrating with her, as Owain expects, Huw explains shamefacedly that he tells her to save the coal till nightfall. There is mould growing on the walls and a nasty odour about the place. Five dirty children are playing on the doorstep or in the street.

"It isn't Nan's fault," Huw says quickly, indicating the untidy, unclean room. "Everything's been too much lately with us all being ill. And we seem to keep on going down."

Owain leaves promptly so as not to cause further embarrassment, but the knowledge of Huw's conditions stays with him.

Over the next month, his friend's health continues to worsen. Huw seems to be shrivelling away like a dry, old leaf. He is easily breathless and cannot load the slabs of slate onto the wagon anymore. Nor is he safe up on the face, for the height makes his head spin. He continues to drill low down, but his efforts are feeble. Owain works like a Trojan to try and make up. Even so, it is obvious their quota for the month is going to be low.

"You should be at home, man," says Gwilym Roberts, one of the others. "You need a good rest to get your strength back."

"I can't," gasps Huw. "We got to 'ave money. And I can't go on letting you three chip in for me either, like last time I was off. I know I'm letting you all down. I don't know what to do for the best."

"Could you not get work on a farm?" Owain suggested. "The fresh air might put you right. Breathing in all this dust can't be helping."

Huw shook his head sadly. "I couldn't manage the hills. Not anymore. I reckon I'm not much use anywhere." And his eyes misted over in the darkness. "I want to keep on 'ere if I can, to keep Nan and the kids out of the workhouse. But I know it's not been fair. If you say so, I'll go."

They held a conference in the caban. It had gotten that bad. But everyone agreed — Huw was the one who had to decide when to go, and not his partners. Until then, they must carry him as best they could. That was the only humane thing to do. After all, they knew it could happen to any one of them.

Afterwards, Huw turned gratefully but sheepishly to Owain, "I'm not sure Gwilym Roberts thought that was the best decision, Owain. And if you agree with him, it doesn't matter what the rest say. It affects you more than most. If you want me to go, Owain, I'll go."

Owain shook his head. "You'll not go," he said fiercely. "I shan't let you."

"It means you have to work so hard, boy."

"I don't mind work." Owain forces a joke about it never harming anyone, which isn't in the least bit funny. Huw smiles sadly.

At the end of April, their quota is predictably low. However, Owain keeps his mouth clamped shut, to the under-manager's surprise. In 'The

Miners' Arms' afterwards, Gwilym Roberts is not as reticent when Huw has gone home.

"It can't go on," he says. "Not month after month."

"That's not what we decided in the caban," Owain points out.

"They don't have to work with him, Owain! What one can put up with for a while ain't the same as putting up with it forever," his partner, Davies, agrees. "We got kids too, Owain. And you know how little we're taking home."

Owain remains stubborn and silent.

"It's not that we're not sorry for him," said Roberts. "We all are. But he's not getting better, see. He's dying, man, and the family are all consumptive. He's not doing himself or anyone else any good dragging himself to work."

"One day, he'll drop on the job," adds Davies. "And then I'm afraid that family's going to 'ave to go into the workhouse anyway."

Roberts nods, but Owain springs to his feet, clattering his chair over on the floor behind him in his emotion. The publican's wife, who has been rattling the coals in the grate, looks at him with disapproval as Owain downs the rest of his pint in one go.

"If he drops, he'll drop where he wants to drop. He's my partner, and he'll leave when he has to, or it'll be over my dead body!" Owain leaves them impetuously without looking back.

Gwilym and Davies are left alone to shake their heads despairingly at the rashness of youth. Outside, Owain covers the first few miles to Fedwr Gog almost without realizing it. He is out of breath by the time he reaches the top of the moor, but his anger still smoulders. In his heart, he knows that Roberts and Davies are right and, what is more, that Huw himself would be the first to admit it. But he cannot lie down and accept it. What will happen to Huw and his family if they go into the workhouse? Huw would die alone and apart from the rest of them, that's for sure.

Chapter Six

Springtime — always late in the coming — is truly breaking now, and the mountains seem fresh and new, bathed in light. Only today, the view gives Owain no solace, no peace at all. He sees only boulders and grass and sloping screes, barren and timeless under a blank sky. There is no answer here nor in the whole world. No answer and no care. None at all. His rage flares up again but merely bounces off the mountain slope as if he had thrown a tiny, insignificant pebble.

It is a green May afternoon outside but night in the slate quarry as always. The chamber is black and cold and thick with dust. Owain works hard, in desperation and in discomfort as always. Huw has been attempting to man the crane but has had his position taken over by the labourer. He sags against the timber tripod in exhaustion. He is very nearly done for and knows it, yet his spirit will not lie down and die. The candles bob and flicker in a sudden draught of air, and the backdrop of rock rears up behind into darkness.

Suddenly, the undermanager is there. He looks around in silence for a moment or two, pulling his jacket closer around his belly against the cold. He says nothing but watches. Eventually, he calls Huw over. Owain, stranded on the rock face, is still sharp enough to see what is happening below. Hurriedly, he abandons his work and leapfrogs down the face.

"Huw Jones," the under manager is saying. "You have to go. Your work is way below standard. You are dismissed."

Owain lands on his feet beside them out of the darkness with a clatter of stones, and the under-manager looks up and frowns. He is telling Huw he is sorry, but Owain thinks he can see satisfaction in those small, mean eyes and certainly a self-righteous pleasure. Huw is beginning to explain, and even wildly, to promise a better performance when Owain butts in.

"He can't go! There's nothing else he can do. We decided he shouldn't."

The under manager gives Owain an unpleasant sneer. "We? And who might 'we' be?"

"The caban."

"The caban!" The under manager does not trouble to disguise his scorn. He sucks in his soft, fat cheeks with a dismissive popping sound. "I have spoken to the manager," he says. "And the manager has spoken to the owner himself. Huw Jones must go. He is officially dismissed." How good it was to have authority on your side! He added, somewhat pompously, "For his own sake."

Huw crumpled back against the tripod and began to weep. Small though the candles are, they throw grotesque shadows of each figure against the nearest slate wall. The other men have stopped work and are watching.

The under manager is put out by the tears and lays a stern hand on Huw's arm. "Come on, boyo," he says roughly. "You've had your chances. Save all that for the bloody Poor Council."

Owain angrily divests himself of his rope. "Leave him alone! I'll take him."

"Get on with your own work, man."

Huw nods helplessly and motions Owain to be silent. There is nothing further to be done. In the darkness behind them, Owain sees a stranger, a new man, all ready with an extra candle in his cap and a rod in his hand. He is strongly muscled and healthy.

In the meantime, Huw collects his bread tin and his billy can for the last time whilst the under-manager waits imperiously. When the sick man stops to say a word of farewell to his partners, he marches forward and propels him roughly away.

Even then, it might have been all right. In a moment or two, Owain would have turned back to the rock face, refusing to look at the newcomer and not wanting to speak to him, taking the anger inside out on the stone.

Then Huw is seized with a bout of coughing. It racks his shrunken body, and the cavern echoes with it. He reels back weakly against the under-manager as he coughs again. When he raises his head, there is a small cob of green phlegm on the under-manager's coat sleeve. The fat man curses and cuffs Huw sharply away as if he were a dog. Somebody laughs, and Huw winces at a second blow and stumbles on his hands and knees onto the floor.

It is then that the fuse inside Owain's brain blows; there is an explosion somewhere beneath their feet, and everything crowds in together — the tons of rock, the eternal blackness, the huge candle shadow of the under-manager like a fat, self-satisfied slug on the wall, certain of his salvation despite Huw's cringing despair.

Owain bellows in pain as his head implodes and launches forward. He is only small, but he is fit and stronger now than when he first entered the mine. He forgets he is holding a crowbar. But he thwacks it down again and again as startled faces freeze in horror.

The under manager's arms are thrown up desperately over his face. Someone screams, but it sounds a long way away to Owain, who rains down blow after blow. He feels a wild heat inside at the orgy of attack. He cannot stop, though the screaming is ghastly. He goes on, and nobody can stop him nor even get close. Then, slowly, the redness in front of his eyes clears; he realizes the sticky, wet mess on the crowbar in his hands is not slime but blood. Even more slowly, he becomes aware that the fat, soft shape on the floor is the carcass of the under-manager with his head stoved in.

Owain is trembling all over, even before the fear rushes in. All around him, stark, hollow faces stare in the candlelight.

"Oh my God..." whispers Huw hoarsely from the floor, shocked into speech. "My boy! What have you done?"

If it were an Irish community, they would have crossed themselves in terror at the devil unleashed. As it is, they can only stare numbly and invoke God in impotent silence.

Owain lets the crowbar drop and it falls with a clang at his feet. He wipes his hands on his trousers without thinking and leaves bloodstains. He does not know what to say or do. He cannot believe it is his own self standing there. Then Gwilym Roberts pushes forward out of the shadows.

"Go," he says harshly. "Go quickly, while you can. Look here, run, will you, man? We'll say you got away before we knew what was happening. But we can't keep this quiet for long! Go on, damn you! And for Jesus Christ's sake, never come back!" It is said with distaste, but he gives Owain a shove which galvanizes him into action. He turns and runs, and no one makes a move to stop him. The dripping tunnels are dark but temporarily deserted. His footsteps pound in his own ears.

At last, light bursts upon him and hurts his eyes. Two quarrymen engaged in surface work pass by and stare at the wild expression on his face. He forces his legs to walk, telling himself that no one out here knows yet. He must try to think clearly.

His first instinct is to run straight to Fedwr Gog. But that would be no good. They would send men after him there. Maybe dogs in packs. And though he could stay hidden in the hills for a long time, how would he survive? The town is abhorrent to him with its certainty of people. He cannot expect to be shielded there. The quickest way out must be the railway.

Yes, the railway! At the quarry sidings, he cowers behind a shed like a cornered animal and waits, with some vague notion of hiding in one of the wagons coupled up for the long descent to Dinas station and on towards the coast at Porthmadoc. Yet, even in his fevered state, he can see this is impractical. Each wagon is tightly packed with bundles of split slate, wafer thin and neatly cut to size by the surface-men. There is no room, even in the dandy wagon at the back where the horses ride, ready to haul the empty trucks back up the line.

What is more, he sees that each fifth wagon is to carry a brakeman in accordance with company regulations. He trembles but does not give up. Instead, he goes down the path to the river, which runs past the depot and the crossing on the other side of Dinas. There, he might lie up till dark on the hillside and then follow the empty track to the sea. It is his only chance.

Darkness falls at last and brings rain. The hunted man crouches behind a boulder on the hillside. To his right, a mountain stream tumbles over rocks on its way down to the river on the narrow floor of the valley. He had reached this very spot hours ago and washed his hands in the stream.

The stains on his trousers have dried to two sticky brown marks, which he cannot get rid of, but he has thrust his head under the waterfall to clear it and get rid of the slate dust. Now he sits hunched with his head on his knees, his hands over them, and shakes.

He has rent his world apart, and he knows it. I, Owain Griffith, have killed a man. Not in self-defence. Not because there was no other way out. But in a frenzy of passion and rage. Not only because of Huw but in a blind hatred of this world. I can never go home again.

By now, the men will have been able to track him down, beaten roughly on the door, and given an incredulous Elen and Madoc the news. They could not have imagined any such thing when they saw him off this morning. Now, they will never be able to hold up their heads in Chapel again. The Griffith family! He hears excited, shocked whispers under the roof already in the chattering of the stream. "Owain Griffith is a murderer, see! We always said there was something wrong with him..."

Atonement! The stern visage of the Sunday school minister who tried to teach him the rudiments of reading and writing swims before his eyes, along with the grim Chapel and gravestones in the mist and the rain.

"Christ died for our sins, see. Thy sin shall find thee out."

The cloud that rolls down the hill envelops him gleefully, and the darkness appears to know its own. It is damp and miserable, but he feels neither wet nor cold. When he lifts his head and thrusts his back against the hard rock, he seems to be endowed with supernatural powers. Every splash of the waterfall, every sound on the hillside, and every rustle in the undergrowth of the still-distant valley stands out. So alert have his senses become. He can feel the rolling movement of the mist over the hill. With his wits about him like this, he won't be caught and should surely escape! He must convince himself that he has merely squashed a fat rat against the floor of the quarry. He must! For he has looked into the chasm of his own soul and seen only madness waiting there.

He heard the last slate train with its long line of clanking wagons pass over an hour ago when the light was just fading. It was searched as he knew it would be, with raised voices and sticks and torches. Now, the line is clear. He plunges down the hillside. The track is shining and empty in the rain. His escape has begun.

≈

Caitlin sat and listened in perfect silence for a long time. At first, she had been won over by Owain's description of his family and countryside. It reminded her of what she felt on the loughside on a sunny day, looking back at James' house. Then, she had shuddered in sympathy when he spoke of what he felt about the mine. Although she was accustomed to seeing privation in Ireland, God knows, the tears still stood in her eyes for poor Huw. Only when Owain reached the climax of his tale, the words of understanding she had prepared all along faded. She could not deny that she was frightened. She could see why he had done it, but oh, how she wished he had not!

His eyes became cold and hard even now as he recounted his thoughts and emotions on that wet and lonely mountainside. It was true that he had experienced revulsion, but Caitlin didn't think it was the same as remorse. He still hated the fat under-manager, and though he regretted his crime, it was clear he would have done it again.

Now, he was looking at her, wanting her to say something comforting.

"You got to the coast, then?" It was all she could manage.

"Yes, to Porthmadoc. It's a busy little port, but I had to be careful. Most of the ships are slate ships. I had to lie low and wait. At last, I persuaded the captain of a small ketch to take me to Liverpool."

"And there you decided to emigrate?"

"Yes."

"To begin again?"

Owain nodded and bowed his head sheepishly. It astonished her that he could still show such human emotions, after the terrible thing he had done.

"I expect you think I'm a coward for not giving myself up?"

"No," said Caitlin. "It's not that. I'm sure no one wants to give themselves up to ... "

"Certain death and damnation?"

"That's what all this talk of hanging was about."

"So, what should I do, Caitlin?"

The question troubled her. "I think you should find a priest and tell him what you told me." She was thinking of Father Francis, of course.

"You're my priest, Caitlin."

"Oh no, I cannot be that! You see…I cannot forgive you in that way, no matter how much I might wish to do. Only a priest can absolve as God does." Her Catholic teaching was coming out, but Owain did not understand that.

"Do you believe it is possible to be absolved?"

"Yes, of course I do. God hates the sin but loves the sinner. In the new land, you must do all the good that you can so that, in time, God may forgive you."

"That is what I wanted to know."

For almost the first time, she saw him smile. It made him look even more boyish, which she felt was incongruous, as she was still very shaken.

"But perhaps you don't want me near you anymore? I would understand that," he said.

Caitlin's heart was beating in her ears, telling her she did not want him at all despite his usefulness. But she thought she knew what Father Francis would have said.

"No," she said. "I will not turn you away now. Though I wish, maybe, you hadn't told me."

"Look at the clouds," she said with an unsteady voice, changing the subject. "We are going to run into another storm ahead."

Chapter Seven

14th June

A wretched time we've had of it again, having run into more rough seas! The first mate says he's hardly ever seen the like of it before in the summer on the Atlantic and that he is sorry to say this will not be a record-breaking passage as the headwinds have been so strong.

I cannot imagine the sea having seasons. To me, it is only fair, bad, or worse! It is such a different place to shore, being governed by different rules and laws and language. I cannot imagine it ever being worse than this, though I suppose, when the hurricanes of autumn blow, it must be. How thankful I am that I did not embark at that time of year!

Needless to say, I have been extremely sick again, as have most others. The steerage was quickly as foul as ever. Then, to compound my misery, when I awoke this morning, I found myself lousy. I haven't the least doubt that I picked up the dratted things from Tim, who, in his turn, got them from the Irish above. Tim was quite unconcerned at the discovery and teased my dismay. I confess I have always had a horror of such things — oh, irrational if you like, but fervent; I could have wept.

I have put 14th June at the beginning of this entry, but I am no longer sure of the date. One miserable day blends into another, full of discomfort and privation. We have been battened down again because of the seas. It is like being in a vast prison. No wonder poor Herr Kleist lies in his bunk with lifeless eyes and is convinced this voyage will last forever or, at the very least, terminate in a slave colony. Still, he keeps his terrors to himself now, though the rest of us are in such a sorry state (except for Tim, of course) that I think we should be ready to believe him now. My guts ache as if I had been kicked in the stomach.

≈

15th June

Feeling much better today. Frau Kleist has been exceedingly kind in letting me drink some of their own coffee as I was still too weak to face the cook's evil brew. What an admirable woman she is: everything is packed so methodically in her trunk, and she seems to have brought all manner of useful things. Day after day, she keeps her spirits up for the children, though she must long for the end of this voyage more than anyone, as it seems clear that is the only way her husband may be brought to his senses.

We have been let out again and have been able to promenade our paltry bit of deck. The wind has come round at last — to the port side, I believe — and we are racing ahead for the first time. At least fifteen knots now, I should say.

The only blot on the horizon, so to speak, is that I have discovered there were two deaths in this last storm. Tim tells me a mariner was lost from the rigging, pitched into the sea (poor soul), by a fault in his foothold.

I suppose this is liable to happen on any crossing; it is understandable enough. They say he never came up again.

But the other death was one of our own number, a young emigrant woman in steerage who took ill a few days ago. Amongst so many —

from suckling babes to drooling old women — it is perhaps natural for one to die during the course of so many days. Yet we are all afraid this young woman may have had the cholera. The sailors are afraid, too, because no one would handle the body until the captain forced them. Even then, she was thrown into the sea as quickly as possible, without a shroud to cover her or a stone to weigh her down, as is only decent and usual. The captain did say some prayers, but her method of dispatch was not as it should have been. Neither were the chaplains aboard in any great hurry to expedite the order of service.

Such is the fear that the shadow of this illness exerts over us.

≈

17th June

Another death and two more have been badly taken. There can be no doubt of it now; we are a ship of death. The surgeon has declared it is not cholera, but the diagnosis matters little, I fear, to those the Grim Reaper has already struck down in the prime of their life.

There is some panic in the steerage. Those nearest to the patients have been erecting barricades in a foolish attempt to protect themselves. Still, one cannot rightly blame them when one is sitting at the other end of the boat. Nevertheless, Captain Shearman ordered them taken down. To soften this indictment, he also ordered the steerage to be scrubbed down, though, of course, one cannot exchange the badness in the air. Still, it seems to me he is trying to do his best. The action was not popular, as you can imagine. It fell to the seamen just finishing the second watch and had to be done before they fell exhausted into their bunks. All other hands were required on deck to constantly alter sail, there being such a fine, stiff breeze come round now. Some of the emigrants helped, but most refused out of fear of contamination.

I am afraid the sick have seen little of the surgeon, and the man is now said to be no more than a drunken apothecary and a quack. He probably knows nothing of cholera anyway. But with my own eyes, I have seen a gentlewoman, in every sense of the word, come down from her cabin above to administer some medicines and give comfort to the desperate creatures who are ill. Tim says she is a lady who regularly undertakes missionary work amongst the poor, and her name is the Honourable Miss Cholmondeley. She is such a petite and pale little thing, very plainly dressed after the manner of a governess or seamstress rather than a lady from an aristocratic family. She seems insensible of any risk to her own person and has been right through steerage from one end to the other, dispensing comfort and concern, especially to those with the old or very young amongst them. I have heard the roughest of men speak kindly of her, and it is whispered that she has done it in defiance of Captain Shearman. Doubtless, the poor captain was anxious for her safety.

She spent some time talking to Frau Kleist, who has not been feeling so good these last few days. She is not sick but bothered with the burden of the growing child.

≈

19th June

There are three new cases, all from the same section of steerage, but no more deaths and one is said to be recovering. Perhaps the doctor is not as bad as we have thought him — or is merely less drunk now — as he has suggested to the captain that it might be of benefit to quarantine the sick and their families.

So, they have been removed to some dark and distant corner where the cargo is stored below, and only Miss Cholmondeley and the surgeon may visit. The feeling amongst most of us is one of relief. Cardplaying and music-making, both of which had been subdued by the aura of sickness, have broken out again. Some are saying the illness is only a trifling ague, dangerous only to the elderly, infants, and the infirm. It may be we were wrong to panic. But I confess I still feel uneasy, for all of us must be pretty weak after the storms and our poor diet. I know I am.

≈

20th June

One new case today who has also been removed with his family. Still, the illness seems to be petering out. If it had been cholera, I suppose there would have been far more cases by now. It has been rumoured there have been more deaths, and we have not been told about them to keep us calm, but rumour will say anything when people are afraid. I hope I am not too critical, as I have certainly felt my own bowels turn to water at the thought of an untimely death. The idea of it happening before ever the new land was gained is such a cruel one!

I also have the advantage of Tim's inside knowledge. He has become quite a favourite among the crew and enjoys small confidences. There has only been one more death, and that was a septuagenarian who had much ill health before he ever came aboard. The others are recovering, and it appears that the illness has been curtailed by the action of the medical man who was right after all. Captain Shearman had the crewmen who refused to handle these last bodies flogged. Tim says he was much criticized by Miss Cholmondeley for this and there was a heated altercation. It is a shame that the captain and this fine lady make such sparring partners as I do declare that each, in their own way, is responsible for the only shining lights in all the darkness and distress of this voyage.

Tim thinks he may try to join a whaler when we reach New York. I reminded him of the fate of the mariner who fell from the topmast, but he shrugged it off and said the remainder of the crew had often remarked upon the man's carelessness. It seems to me to be a horrid life for a boy who now claims to be fifteen but is probably less. I cannot deny his sea legs are better than mine, however, and he does have the sort of cheeky personality which is not easily cast down. The sailors seem to like his mouth organ and have taught him some shanties. He spends a lot of time in the fo'c'sle now and is rarely thrown out as we would be. Sometimes, he comes back with a quarter for some tasks or other well done, or maybe a chew of American tobacco, which he sits and masticates with great determination, though I can see he dislikes the taste. He has learnt some terrible oaths and is also practising his spitting and showing a vast improvement in range. I have banned these accomplishments, in which he takes so much pride, from my vicinity.

I cannot imagine why I did not throw him out of my berth when I discovered the lice. But, since we both changed our clothes and made a separate bundle of the old ones, which Tim flung into the sea, there have been no further irritations so far. Tim is immensely proud of his new outfit, which he bought for a song from one of the cabin lads who had outgrown it. He is sporting bell-bottom trousers, a striped shirt that is several sizes too large, and a shrunken monkey jacket. What with his bare feet and the plug of 'baccy' plus a dirty red scarf round his neck, from which he will not part, he looks the very picture of an old tar. All he needs is a hat, which he will doubtless obtain in New York, and maybe some boots for wet nights and the growth of a few whiskers.

I cannot deter him, but I fear for him because he is so cheerful and willing. The innocence of the child comes out in his open, freckled face when he is asleep. He is too beautiful then, with his red curls, for his own good. Perhaps I have let him stay with me to avoid him taking up any less savoury attachment. But, then again, there is no doubt that he has been helpful to me, and I have treated him like a manservant. So much for fine motives! I know well enough, too, that he is a devious bastard (for I am sure he was a bastard before he was orphaned and ran away from the workhouse), and I will give him my knife and some money when we leave the ship before he has had the chance to steal them.

When we leave the ship! Will that day ever come? I think I am a different person now than when I came aboard. Wretched though I have been, I know I am a little better for the disappearance of that brash, young, self-confident fellow who selfishly joined ship in Liverpool.

The voyage has not been wasted because of those whom I have met or discovered. But I wish it were safely over.

The good Frau Kleist now suffers dreadfully from backache, as if she had not enough worries.

Chapter Eight

"If we ever get out of this alive," said Caitlin, who had been sorely frightened at the cases of sickness aboard. "What shall you do in New York?"

They sat in the constant twilight between decks, surrounded by the reek of oil lamps, the flicker of candles against the dark, and the everlasting creak of timbers. Maeve, whom Caitlin had been so concerned about because of the fevers, had been a shade fretful this evening but had finally dropped asleep, lulled by the rhythm of the ship. She didn't seem to get seasick when it was rough and had prospered so far, despite Caitlin's anxieties.

Caitlin was curled up on the other end of the bunk but wasn't ready for sleep yet. Owain, as usual, sat on the floor with his back against the bed. She was no longer as frightened of him, for familiarity had blunted the shock of his story. Still, she didn't like to think about it and was a little more reticent with him. But she needed conversation tonight.

"I don't know," said Owain. "I'll go to a place where they tell you about jobs."

"What kind of job will you do?"

"Anything but mining. I daresay there are plenty of miners needed in America, but I'll not go below ground again. I know a bit about blasting, though. Maybe they'll find a use for me with that. But it'll only be till I save up some money. I want a farm, and the land's supposed to be cheap, isn't it?" Caitlin shrugged.

"I don't know. Maybe it is out west. Won't you be afraid, though, of savages and things?"

"I'm not afraid of anything now. When I've built up my own farm, I'll write to my mother and father and ask them to join me. Rhys and Tomas too, if they want to. I've got a little sister as well."

"Will you not write to them before then?"

"No. Not till I can write them of some good."

"But they'll be so worried about you!"

"I can't help that. At least they'll know I got away. And maybe they won't want to know me."

Caitlin digested this in silence before speaking. "It seems hard."

"What will you do anyway with no one to take care of you and the child?"

"Oh, but I will have ..."

"I know you're not married, Caitlin."

Caitlin blushed. "How did you know?"

Owain struggled with his embarrassment. "You haven't nursed the child," he said finally. "Not once. She's eaten what we've eaten, though I'd have thought she'd been better with mother's milk. Then there's no ring, though I suppose you might have hidden that for safety's sake."

"No," said Caitlin, feeling rather ashamed. "You're right. I did lie. Maeve is my stepsister, though I love her as my own. I thought it was best to lie, coming onto a ship with everyone so close together like this."

Owain nodded. "So, there's no James about to follow you?" he asked. "I'm glad."

"Oh yes, there is," Caitlin corrected him hastily. "Only he's my uncle. And he's sending me to a friend of his in New York — a Mrs Constance Regan and her family. So, you see, I'll be well taken care of."

"That's good," Owain said. "May I come and see you ... make sure you're alright?"

"Oh." Caitlin hardly knew what to say.

"I'd like to see you right," Owain insisted. "After all you've done for me. Don't worry! I won't come until I look respectable."

"That's kind of you," Caitlin said stiffly. "But I'm sure I'll be fine." She had meant to say no but could see that Owain would not take a refusal. Well, where would be the harm in it? She should be glad someone cared.

"Alright," she added. "You may come to see me. I'll give you the address."

$$\approx$$

25th June

No new cases of fever for five days. May God be praised! He hasn't deserted us after all. Everyone now says the surgeon is a capital fellow. It is obvious he is making light of the matter because no man, woman, or child has any desire to spend a month's quarantine in the harbour when we get to New York. So, his somewhat unreliable word is accepted happily by all, seeing it is what we want to believe. Even Captain Shearman, of whom I have spoken of warmly, takes his word in good faith. Tim tells me (though it may be one of the crew's wilder stories) that a certain Mr Andrew Tyrrell in first class gave the surgeon a sizeable backhander to make his medical report more favourable. Miss Cholmondeley is of an alternative persuasion and says the ship came off very lightly indeed due to the captain's excellent management of the crisis. Dear, kind lady though she is, I fear she will disappear overboard before we dock if she does not temper her opinion!

No sooner had we come out of one calamity, however, than we were straightaway thrown into another. At the hour of day, I would normally consider a suitable time for lunch, but is now signified by eight bells marking the end of the third watch, I was manfully swallowing one of Tim's very hasty puddings, trying to make believe it was roast suckling pig or ox when The Yorkshire suddenly lurched to port, without any warning, and made a rapid change of course.

When I had picked myself up and scraped the oatmeal off my nearest neighbour with a humble apology, I joined in the general rush up the hatchway to see what was amiss.

On deck, we were assured there was no cause for alarm. The fella' in the crow's nest must have been nodding off, for the helmsman had suddenly caught sight of an iceberg advancing to the starboard side and done the prudent thing by changing course abruptly. The mates gave repeated assurance that there was no longer any danger. Indeed, the iceberg seemed to our untutored eyes a long way off. But I have read of how their greater bulk lies below the water and understand they are a menace to shipping lines in this part of the world.

Tim and I hung over the rail and watched it awhile. It looked like a great, white cliff of marble on the horizon, appearing ominously out of the sea. An eerie sight, and I thanked God we were not drifting through some vast fog as we might so easily have been. It seems, despite everything, we are a blessedly lucky ship. Captain Shearman ordered an extra tot of rum all round for the crew and put two men to the helm, though there were no clouds banking up ahead, and the sea was slight.

≈

28th June

There is little to report since the incident of the iceberg. We go on very much as usual. Slowly but steadily now. I have been reduced to reading my *'Emigrant Voyager's Manual'* over again for the hundredth time. But I threw it away in the end with disgust, for it was really very silly. How on earth can we play foolish word games when the majority of steerage cannot read or write and are only interested in liquor and cards? How can I try my skill at carving models from meat bones when we are given no meat? I have tried the exercises mentioned on deck to keep fit, but I am weary of their inadequacy; my muscles seem to have wasted away from too much sickness and too little good food. I really cannot imagine that the well-meaning person who wrote this book has ever been to sea!

Oh well, I confess I am exceptionally low today and cannot even be bothered with this useless journal, which no one will read. I cannot help but remember (if I am correct with my dates, which I may not be) that it will very soon be feast time at home when all of us shut up shop for that blessed week's holiday. How I long to take a picnic up on the moors as we used to. To climb the crags above Ilkley whilst our waggon waits below, to feel the wind blowing through our hair, blessedly free from salt. I hope that you are well, Mother and that Jeremiah may have mellowed, like old wine, now he has his living. I miss you both, and I miss the hills and dales of the real Yorkshire around our town.

For almost a month, I have seen only the crests and troughs of waves and succumbed to their giddying motion. I have given up asking questions of our first mate, for I do not think even he knows when we may be expected to make land. I try to think about why I came and how even this interminable month will soon be over, but we are still lost souls on the vast sea, though the fever, in its own impatience, seems to have winged on and left us.

≈

1st July

Nothing happened, though Tim claims he saw the spout of a whale. The boy is a lost cause.

≈

4th July

It is the Americans' Independence Day, and the crew are celebrating. Well, I suppose we are almost Americans now, though I certainly don't feel like one. But we had a celebration, too. The captain ordered the cook to give one and all a fair portion of salt pork. I have never tasted anything so wonderful in all my life. Only the Kleists would not eat it. They believe pork is unclean. It seems such a shame. I had a little too much beer to drink, but it did me good.

≈

6th July

May God in heaven be praised! We have sighted land at last. Merely a narrow strip on the horizon, but a green line and definitely land. It appears we have been blown too far north and must now tack back down the coastline to reach New York. Maybe three or four more days, the purser says. This is our surly friend, Banks, whose demeanour has not improved one jot on the voyage, yet I swear I could have kissed him! There is much merriment, although the steerage now stinks again like a pigsty.

$$\approx$$

7th July

Rosa Kleist has been delivered safely of a child. As if the infant knew that land was in sight! We are all delighted, though the poor woman had a hard time of it. The ship's surgeon refused to attend, declaring that normal births were none of his business. Miss Cholmondeley, bless her heart, found a midwife somewhere in steerage, and together, they looked after her as well as they could. They rigged up a poor screen of blankets and dosed her with laudanum, but the poor woman still suffered and lost all the remnants of her dignity. Or maybe not, for even the blackest, dirtiest Irish peasant seemed to understand the miracle in hand. At length, the child was delivered — a girl (being acceptable enough after two boys), and all is well. Frau Kleist looks quite changed. Although not a slight woman by any means, she looks younger, almost girlish in the candlelight, and her face is much thinner. Even Herr Kleist has been shaken out of his stupor to some extent and is ordered around rather cleverly by the older children. I fear the woman will not be able to rest for long, however.

Many of the crude peasant women (who would not speak to her before) have given some small thing — a warm shawl, a baby's bonnet, or maybe an extra ounce of tea. It gives my heart hope to see it from such unwashed, uneducated, and primitive folk.

I had nothing to give except my Bible, which I did before I remembered they were a Jewish family and only believed in the Old Testament. In painful embarrassment, I stammered and stuttered my apologies, assuring Frau Kleist no insult was intended. She smiled at me kindly and said it didn't matter at all. Her father had always brought her up to be tolerant, and the book would remind her of the circumstances of this voyage, fraught with difficulty but also visited by many kindnesses. She has named the child Rachel. Although tiny now, it seems she will be as strong as her mother, for she took well to the breast and is thriving. She puts me in mind of that other baby carried aboard by the Madonna. I wonder how different or similar these daughters' lives will be in this brave new world?

≈

8th July

The steerage is being scrubbed down and sanded for the last time. Every man, woman, and child lend a hand, and there is no shirking, for we are, at last, almost there! The strip of green land is closer and more substantial now. How delectable those green forests appear!

Here and there, white wooden houses with green jalousie blinds peep out of the foliage as if to wink at us. How neat and clean and bright they are! This sight, so long denied, compensates for everything.

I drank my last bottle of beer after the scrubbing down and drying of the timbers with pans of hot coal from the galley and made my bed up for the last time. Tomorrow, we will ditch our blankets and bedding overboard, along with all the rest of our rubbish, so as to appear shipshape for our inspection. I cannot believe it. I really cannot believe I am here at last and am far too excited to sleep.

≈

Caitlin found thoughts of Mrs Regan looming large in her mind. What had been an abstract idea from thousands of miles away was now threatening to materialize in the flesh. What would she be like? Would she be kind? How would she treat her? There was a daughter, too, not far off her own age, as well as a Mr Regan. That was encouraging, and Caitlin longed to make friends with the girl. But she was a little afraid, too.

"Oh, I do hope they like me!" she sighed aloud.

Owain smiled at her. "Of course, they will."

Without a doubt, she must look her best. She rummaged through her trunk to find her smartest dress. It was one that James had made for her, in green velvet with a matching cape and bonnet. She shook out the crushed folds. It would still suit her, even though she had lost weight on the voyage, and she would put her hair up as well as she could without a maid to help her. Owain watched her every movement.

"If you don't like it there," he said quietly. "I'll come for you and take you away."

Caitlin went pink. "Sure, and I expect I'll be fine," she said quickly. "It's just getting the meeting over and done with. That's all I'm worried about."

≈

10th July

It is the most glorious morning, as if it were the first day of creation! To the right of us is Long Island, and to the left, the state of New Jersey, as we approach New York.

The pilot has come aboard. Now we have arrived opposite Staten Island. What a great number of windows the houses have! They evidently have no window tax as we do in England. The customs house officers boarded us at eight and were shortly followed by a doctor. We all had to pass along in front of him as our names were called. All below were examined, the surgeon spoken with, and the ship was pronounced healthy. So, it will be allowed to pass. You may imagine the spontaneous cheer that arose from our throats! A first-class passenger with a great red beard bribed the customs officers to take him ashore with them directly, being unable to stand the waiting any longer.

Everyone else is on deck now, watching as we enter New York harbour. What a busy place it is, with steamboats passing and repassing in front of us, ferrying goods and persons between the island of Manhattan and the mainland. We follow in their wake in a more stately fashion. The waters are blue, the sky is clear, and the air delightfully warm in the bay. It brings a great lump to my throat, and my vision is blurred from sheer emotion.

We pass an old fort surrounded by trees at the tip of the island, which I am told is called the 'Battery.' But there are no gunners to stop us and no restraints to the entry of The Yorkshire. Slowly, we move into the East River. On land, there appear to be many buildings, some of which are very tall, being four or five levels high. I can see many church spires and patches of smoke here and there. I am glad to think it is a religious city. Everything seems to move and buzz most industriously.

Closer now, and I see, to my surprise, the docks are not as grand as Liverpool, being only a collection of wooden piers and shacks. Still, they are a fine sight to our sore eyes as we dock. I shall remember this day forever. We are here in the United States of America, here at last, in the land of freedom and opportunity! It is almost beyond belief. And so here ends the journal of Hartley Shawcross.

Part Three

The Door Opens

Chapter One

Constance Regan did not enjoy being in town so late in the season. Already it was hot and sultry and seemed an effort to breathe. By August, she knew she would feel as limp as a wrung-out rag. But what concerned her more was the fact that all fashionable people were out of town now, on the quieter shores of New Jersey, Long Island, Connecticut and Maine. Thaddeus Regan's resources had enabled them to move to a smarter address, and the matter was, therefore, of some concern to her. Not for herself. She was, on the whole, a sensible woman but for her daughter, an only child, now at the dangerously ripe age of twenty-three. She wanted her Polly to escape the taint of three words: Irish, Catholic, and immigrant. In short, she wanted her to marry well into one of the 'old' New York families or, at the very least, to choose a husband who was native-born and wealthy. A Bostonian connection was the most likely as Thaddeus' sister lived in Boston and that was where, at this very moment, they should be, having been invited to Polly's aunt's house.

Then James had pleaded so eloquently in his letter for this 'little waif' he had plucked from disaster and at one time, in her youth, Constance Regan had been very fond of him.

Polly herself was excited over the girl's arrival, and Constance supposed she would make a pleasant companion for her solitary daughter as long as her manners were not too rough. There lay the rub. It was difficult to decide what to do with her until she had been seen. She might be better suited as a domestic servant. She was not prepared to lodge the rest of the family beyond a day or two, hoping they would find suitable lodgings and that Padraig Murphy would likewise find employment. If not, it would be Tinkersville for them.

She tilted her handsome face back to take full advantage of the little air the buggy displaced as the sweating horse went spanking along.

"What number pier did Papa say again?" she asked Polly, who sat beside her. "Number 32, Mamma. Oh, Mamma, I feel so excited! And I guess Caitlin will be nervous."

"More nervous than us, I guess."

As usual, Constance felt irritated by her daughter's ingenuosity. Such frankness might be disarming, but it lacked sophistication. To compound this grievous fault, Polly was not pretty. She lacked both height and daintiness in addition to what her mother considered maturity, although an essential goodness shone out of her sweet face. Not for the first time, Mrs Regan was struck by an awful thought: supposing, just supposing this Caitlin Murphy should outshine her own daughter in looks if not manners? After all, James had educated the girl herself and might have succeeded in putting a false shine upon her. Wracked with anxiety, Constance fanned away at the extra heat which had arisen in her face. Unaware of her mother's discomposure, Polly was prattling on:

"We've been expecting them for so many days now. I can hardly believe The Yorkshire is docking today at last! Oh, Mamma, can you remember what it felt like to see America for the first time?"

Constance grimaced. The tenement smell from the Lower East Side, with its close association with noxious industrial enterprises, was already assailing her nostrils and bringing back those distant memories.

"I guess I was excited," she admitted, "though I was but a child. I was frightened too when I saw where we had to end up. You mustn't forget, Polly, that my father had lost all his money. We lived in a shanty town not unlike Tinkersville to begin with, though it wasn't for long. It was terrible."

"We won't let the Murphys do that, will we, Mamma?"

There was no answer, but Mrs Regan's confession of her earlier status in life altered her mood. Truly, it had been dreadful. She had no right to look down on Padraig Murphy even if he did come straight from the bogs. No right at all. It wasn't until she married Thaddeus that she began to rise in status.

"Well," she said briskly. "Here we are at last!"

Telling the driver to wait, she alighted with her daughter, and they rustled along South Street in the lightest of summer petticoats and silken dresses.

≈

Meanwhile, Caitlin sank down, perspiring and exhausted, on her box, which Owain had brought off the ship for her. She had never expected it to be so hot. The air had hit her with its wall of heat as soon as she came off The Yorkshire. The green velvet, although it was her best gown, was a terrible mistake. Owain held his greatcoat and hat over one arm and was still sweating in his shirtsleeves.

"Caitlin," he asked anxiously, looking at her pink face. " Are you going to be all right?"

She nodded and tried to recover herself by smoothing out the folds of her dress. The skirt was so full and heavy it dragged her down, and the waist was so tightly laced she could scarcely breathe. She wore an ermine-trimmed cape and bonnet to match, and Owain thought she looked very fine. But her pulse had begun to race, and she felt a little dizzy when she stood up. To add to her misery, as she sat there upon the box, she heard the scornful laughter and jeers of a gang of rowdy American youths passing by.

"Yah!" they taunted her. "**Greenhorn**! Look at the stupid greenhorn!" They passed on by, rolling and clutching at their sides as if fit to burst.

It was too much, and Caitlin began to cry. She had wanted so badly to present a good impression to Mrs Regan and her American cousins ... to show them that she had style and refinement and was not a poor, Irish greenhorn after all! Now that she realized her folly, she felt utterly defeated.

"Don't cry, Caitlin," Owain begged. "It's a bit hot but you look wonderful, see, and the Regans will know you couldn't tell it would be so hot!" He managed to find a rag in his pocket, which had once been a neckerchief, and mopped her tears away. The action would have been outrageous once, but after the boat journey with all its hours of suffering spent together it was no longer.

"Here," and he lifted little Maeve onto her lap. The child chuckled and beat at her wet cheeks with tiny hands that did not understand. Caitlin hid her head gratefully in the child's dark curls and succeeded in knocking her bonnet askew.

"You're going to be all right now, Caitlin. You are. Your well-off friends'll take care of you, see. The voyage is over, and it'll all have been worth it." He took the baby from her and into his own arms, giving her a kiss and hug as she squirmed against him. It was suddenly hard to say goodbye.

"I'll be off now, then."

"Oh, but won't you stay and see the Regans?"

"No, I think not. It'll be better if I don't ... if *they* don't see you with a wretch like me."

"You're not a wretch, Owain. You must remember that. Please be good and take care!"

He nodded and straightened himself as if strengthened by her concern. "Goodbye then. And good luck."

"Goodbye, Owain, and good luck to you! I shan't forget you, but see you do good, now!"

He was stung suddenly by his old fear of being apprehended and slipped away, melting into the crowd while she was speaking. It was a disorganized, enthusiastic crowd milling around rather aimlessly, looking for relatives, friends, lifts, and even runners to direct them elsewhere — so lost did they feel. Owain turned back once at the end of the street, overhung by bowsprits and figureheads and furled masts. She was still there, though hidden by the crowd. In a sudden rush of recklessness, he waved both arms violently in the air, hoping she could see him still, though he couldn't see her. Then he yelled at the top of his voice.

"*Caitlin*! I'll come back for you one day. I *will*!" Passers-by stared at him, but he no longer felt foolish as he turned again and was gone.

≈

"Oh my!" said Mrs Regan. She had made many fruitless enquiries to Irish families with a grown-up daughter amongst them. But now, at last, she was faced with Caitlin in all her emerald finery.

"Caitlin Murphy? Is that really you and the child, Maeve? I believe it has to be. You must be powerful hot!"

Caitlin cast her eyes downwards in embarrassment and remembered too late she had forgotten to straighten her headgear.

"A little, Ma'am," she said sheepishly, trying to adjust her bonnet without anyone noticing. "Yes, I am Caitlin Murphy, and this is Maeve."

Constance Regan was not as old as she had imagined. She was certainly a mature woman with a strong face, greying hair, and a statuesque bearing. Even in her fine lilac silk, which was so much more suitable for New York's summer months, her marble bosom made the material seem overstuffed. The bodice was braided by a jet-black fringe of beads, which trembled as she breathed in and out. Her eyes were youthful and sharp, and her appearance, not unattractive.

Next to her stood a fair-haired, rather plain young woman in an inoffensive pale blue stripe. This must be her daughter. Caitlin saw at once, when their eyes met, that she was kind and revised her first impression of plainness when the girl smiled and exclaimed in delight over Maeve, who, in her turn, was laughing and showing off as if she, at any rate, had nothing in the world to trouble her now they had got here.

"My daughter, Polly," said Mrs Regan. "Hello!" Caitlin inclined her head stiffly in case she should be less than formal.

"But where are your parents, my dear?" asked Mrs Regan, who was trying not to think how pretty this young girl was with her pale Irish complexion, her dark hair, and unusually blue eyes. She looked around to see if they were struggling elsewhere with their baggage.

"They did not come," said Caitlin quietly. "They stayed in Liverpool." "You mean you came *alone*?" Constance exclaimed whilst Polly's eyes grew positively round in astonishment. "All the way across the Atlantic? In steerage!?"

"The people on the boat were very kind to us," Caitlin said. "I was afraid, yes, sometimes very much so, but we were really quite fortunate."

"And why didn't your parents come?"

"My father was ill. He feared the doctor would not let him aboard. My stepmother stayed with him. But she wanted to send the child as she hoped you would be kind enough to take her in, too, and settle us somehow." Caitlin blushed. "But Uncle James will join us soon, and I am sure he will have some plans as to what is to become of us ..." She faltered in her speech, for her head had begun to spin again, and the figure of her benefactress was receding into a blur whilst the ground had begun to rotate. "I'm sorry ... I must ... sit ... down." She collapsed onto her trunk.

Constance uttered another exclamation and bade Polly remove Caitlin's warm cape. Then, leaving her daughter administering such aid as she could muster, she returned to the waiting carriage to summon the driver to help them aboard.

The Regans lived at No. 24. Union Square Place, between the 15th and 16th Streets, to the east of Union Square. Caitlin could scarcely assemble the horde of impressions that rushed upon her on the way there. She still felt ill from the heat so that the images recurring before her eyes seemed to race up and blaze upon her nerves. The streets were straight and wide but were choked with buggies, waggons, and cabs whilst people and even pigs roamed freely amongst them. Everywhere was a vast hive of activity, with some buildings being knocked down whilst others were taking their place. The dust and noise were immense. Polly told her that all the long 'avenues,' as she called them, were intersected by streets at regular intervals, and they were all numbered, so it was quite easy to find one's way around.

Once they had left the Lower East Side of the dock area behind, the five-storied tenements gave way to rows of smaller brownstone houses, all reached by flights of stone steps up from the streets. There were stores, too, displaying their wares in the window and advertising the relative merits of their goods on placards. There were also many churches, the spires of which they had seen from the boat. Everything seemed to co-exist willy-nilly, with no order or harmony about it, and the thoroughfares were lively with peddlers, newsboys, runners, streetwalkers, and pickpockets. Now and again, Caitlin caught a glimpse of a leafy square, which seemed to promise welcome relief in the form of shade and quiet.

When they reached the upper sections of Broadway (for that is what Polly now called the avenue), the more elegant of the townhouses and the more stylish of the hotels began to establish their supremacy. At last, they trotted into Union Square, and Caitlin let out her breath in relief as she saw it was well-leafed. There were actually green trees set out at regular intervals within railings in the centre of the square. There were fine gates leading into and intersecting paths across what amounted to a small park, with a fountain in the middle gushing three separate streams of clear water. Caitlin had never seen such formally tamed greenery before, and something of the sort must have reflected on her face.

"What do you think of it?" asked Polly eagerly. "Do you like it? The fountain was built to celebrate our Croton water."

"What?" Caitlin was bewildered. Surely water was water, wasn't it, from a stream or a well?

"From the reservoir," Mrs Regan explained, though Caitlin was no wiser. "Come, we are almost there."

The carriage drew up in one of the streets leading off the square before a bow-fronted house, four storeys high, set in a row with its identically smart neighbours. 'We know what we are about,' they seemed to say. 'No vulgar differences are tolerated here.' There was the same stone flight of steps leading up to the front door and the glimpse of a concealed basement down below, behind iron railings. A splendid marble floor to the entrance floor was revealed when the door was opened with a flourish by a black-faced manservant.

Inside, a sombre mahogany staircase ascended to the upper reaches of the house. On the walls was an embossed, gilt-covered wallpaper of a curling design. A bronze statuette appeared to take flight above a bowl, which Caitlin learnt later was intended to receive visiting cards. A heavy clock ticked on a dark, heavy sideboard, and an aspidistra sprouted elegance from an ornate jardiniere. Caitlin passed timidly through double doors into the premier room. This was, without any doubt, an expensive house.

Even the hall had not prepared her for the surprise of the drawing room, and she let out an involuntary gasp. She was used to the sober restraint of James's bachelor house, grand but rather dark, faded, and tired. This could not have been more different; the ceiling was painted with artistic woodland scenes, the frieze appeared to be gold, and more brightly coloured paintings were suspended from it. Long drapes were tied back with tassels to reveal net curtains at the windows, and the gas burners were enclosed in crystal wall brackets that wept pendant glass. All the furniture had something in common with Mrs Regan's upper parts, being over-upholstered, whilst every chair, cover, and object that could be fringed was fringed, and, similarly, every wooden whatnot was loaded with bric-a-brac. Ebonized wooden cabinets and papier mâché tables were present in profusion yet there was scarcely room to put anything down.

Caitlin sank down into a chair gratefully and took off her bonnet. Her hair fell untidily. She had not done a good job of putting it up on the ship and felt like crying again. A servant appeared to whisk Maeve away, and Mrs Regan gave the manservant in the hall orders about Caitlin's box. For the moment, she was left alone with Polly, who had already pronounced her 'a dear' to her mother.

"It must all seem very strange to you," this gentle girl said sympathetically.

Caitlin found herself speaking naturally for the first time since they had met. "Sure, it is ... 'tis all harder than I thought it would be."

Polly stepped forward impulsively with her hands outstretched, and Caitlin took them gratefully.

"I hope you'll be happy here with us," Polly said, with a warm pressure of her fingertips, "I know you'll feel much better in a day or two."

"Thank you so much."

Then, a chorus of carriage clocks chimed the hour. Mrs Regan joined them, and tea was ordered.

Caitlin was almost too tired and overwrought to drink it. She had begun to worry, too, if Maeve was all right with her strange nurse.

Constance saw she was ill at ease and suggested that she retire to rest for a while, bathe, and change. That sounded so good after six long weeks at sea that Caitlin gave in gratefully and allowed herself to be shown upstairs into a room which was unbelievably and blessedly her own.

Chapter Two

It took Hartley less than five minutes to realize there were as many runners, spongers, and general hangers-on at the South Street seaport as in Liverpool. It was especially easy to identify the runners as they all wore the same checked trousers and fancy waistcoats like a uniform and dangled fat cigars from their mouths. They all wore official badges on their lapels, so it appeared they were licensed swindlers, but Hartley was not going to be taken in again. He brushed them off and selected the most honest-looking face among the many cabdrivers drawn up alongside the quay, asking to be taken to 'decent lodgings' and calling at a bank on the way where he might change his money.

The driver turned out to be another emigrant or 'immigrant' as he must now learn to describe themselves. He was a friendly Irishman who had been here two years.

"I always come down here when an emigrant ship comes in," he said, having pumped Hartley's hand up and down several times. "I've seen so many of 'em fleeced good and proper. I was taken in well enough meself when I came, till the back of me didn't know where the front was coming from. Now, rooms are awful expensive in New York, 'tis a fact. I'll take ye to a daicent boarding house all right, but ye might not be wantin' to stay there too long."

"That'll be fine for the moment," said Hartley. "I appreciate your honesty. But it'll give me a chance to catch my breath, as it were. What are jobs like here?"

"There's plenty a-navvying required," said his new friend. "Buildin' of pavements and houses and railroads. Only you don't look like the sort of fella' to be wielding a pickaxe and shovel to me."

Hartley laughed. "Indeed, I am not," he replied proudly.

"Plenty of farms goin' out West if you've gotta bit of money put by. Only I'm after thinkin' 'tis best to take your time over that and make sure ye know what ye're lettin' yourself in for ... I've seen some come back awful dispirited. There's always a few places goin' for farm hands upstate in daicent land. But they generally take better to a married couple ... that way, they get two workers for the price of one."

"I'm not married, I'm afraid," said Hartley, ruefully. He had never felt it a disadvantage before but how good it would have been to have had the little Madonna beside him now!

"Sure, and that's a shame." The Irishman laid his whip lightly on the back of the unwilling horse to quicken its gait. "What trade would you be after followin', now?"

"I was a draper's assistant back in England, and I did the books for them."

"A man of letters, eh? I don't know about that. They's always needing navvies. But I expect ye'll find somethin'." "I like Americky," he added after a pause. "I've heard plenty of moanin' and groanin' from them who wished they'd never come though they wouldn't let on to the folks back home. But I like it. When I came here, I was starvin', really starvin', you know, back in the old country. There's plenty of food here and money to pay for it if you're willing to work. What more can you ask for?"

He told Hartley he had been helped to find employment through the Irish Emigration Society, and he thought there must be an English one, too, though he didn't know where it was.

Hartley thanked the good fellow for his advice. He found the boarding house was at least clean and his room adequate, although it was going to cost him eight dollars a month. Meals were taken communally in great haste and with much gusto at an enormous table in a room overwhelmed by a central stove. Hartley hadn't realized before how hungry he was, but that lunchtime, he tasted real food again with as much soup and rolls of bread and chicken, and pork and pies, and doughnuts and coffee as he could manage.

After lunch, he presented himself at a Court of Record to register his arrival and pay the head tax necessary to stay in the state of New York. In return, he was given a dated certificate, which he placed carefully in an inner pocket of his frockcoat. In five years' time, he could present it as proof of the required residence for naturalization.

Although it was extremely hot, Hartley could not resist wandering round the streets in a glazed kind of happiness, staring at first one thing, then another. The city was much bigger than he had expected — that much he had seen from The Yorkshire — and it was also busier: gloriously, temptingly, excitingly overcrowded with people of all kinds of faces, rushing places instead of merely going there. A constant clip-clopping of hooves and jingling of harnesses rang in his ears as the loaded wagons and carts passed by. He felt like taking off his top hat and throwing it up to the bright, burning sun with a shriek of joy or swarming up one of the gas lamps singing. Although, being Hartley, he did nothing of the kind.

Instead, he found Broadway and sauntered along like a swell with his hands in his pockets, looking in shop windows. And what shop windows they were! Most of the establishments on this thoroughfare handsomely displayed fancy luxury goods. He could have bought a pair of fine French calf boots for $1.50! Or he could have had his likeness captured in the Daguerrian Rooms for $1. That really tempted him, thinking of the folks back home, but he thought he should perhaps wait until he looked more 'American'. He lost count of the number of eating places and hotels. And who on earth would want or be able to afford a solid gold birdcage? Certainly, no one in Bradford!

Off Broadway, he found more conventional shops such as tailors and milliners and dry goods stores, liquor sellers by the hundred, and everything, in fact, that anyone could ever want. In one of the smaller stores, he made his first purchase. It was a copy of a paper-bound booklet entitled *'The Wealth and Biography of the Wealthy Citizens of New York'*. This was an alphabetical list of the most prominent capitalists in the city ... those with estimated fortunes of at least $100,000. He stood and pored over it for a long time, regardless of passers-by knocking his elbows as he read. It filled him with delightful optimism. Look! Here on the very first page was Adams John (of Irish descent) in the dry goods business, $300,000! And here was Astor John Jacob, born in Heidelberg, a steerage emigrant who had beaten skins in Gold St., New York, and then made $25,000,000 in the fur trade! Hartley's imagination ran riot: '*Shawcross Hartley, born in Bradford, England, a steerage emigrant, now a shipping magnate, $3,000,000*' ... he could almost see it leaping up at him from the page!

"No, I'm sorry," said the man at the Labor Exchange. "I don't think there's anybody wanting a draper's hand or a clerk today ... there's nuthin'...no, nuthin'."

"What do you mean?" asked Hartley, brought down to earth with a bump. "There's nothing?"

"Nuthin's nuthin', boy! Don't you understand plain English? I guess you'd better come back in a day or two." He spat his tobacco juice contemptuously into a spittoon by the side of his desk.

Hartley continued to go every day with as little result. On the fifth day, when he was beginning to feel desperate, the man looked at him sharply over his glasses.

"Office clerk and bookkeeper required at Mr Elmer James, Merchant Shipper. Clean, bright, and willing. Must write a good hand. Can you write a good hand, boy?"

Hartley assured him he could.

"Then you'd better go on up and see if the manager likes you."

The office manager, von Blumen, was a spare, stooping individual with a permanently anxious expression that hardened into suspicion as he glanced at Hartley over his spectacles. He would not have been out of place at the Wool Exchange in Bradford. He tested Hartley's mental arithmetic and then watched him copy out a sample sheet in his best handwriting.

"You know about trade, boy?" he asked doubtfully.

"I know a lot about the wool trade," Hartley answered truthfully. "I suppose you don't have a great call for that over here, but tobacco and timber and furs and any commodity...I reckon I know the principles involved, and I'm keen to learn."

"All right," said von Blumen, somewhat grudgingly. "I like the cut of your jib, boy, and you just might be of some use to me. I said might, mind! You're hired. Ten dollars a month."

"Ten dollars?"

"Yep ... take it or leave it."

"I'll take it." It didn't sound very much and he would certainly need to move his lodgings, but he was in.

"Start tomorrow."

"Tomorrow!" Hartley hurried away on lighter feet. However, after several inquiries, he soon found out that all rooms in tenements were at a premium and mostly sub-let by the letters. Feeling cast down again, as he had developed an understandable aversion to the idea of sharing after steerage, he turned out into the streets — this time on the East Side — and wondered what was best to do.

It was then that he was fortunate enough to run into Frau Kleist hurrying back from a baker's shop. She hailed him like a long-lost friend and insisted on taking him to show how much better Friedrich had been since leaving the ship. They had managed to rent two first-floor rooms (in America, this was on street level), which were not quite as miserable as their neighbours. One room was going to be Friedrich's shop, and the other one was for themselves. But the rent was high, and they had considered sub-letting until Friedrich found his feet. She wondered if Hartley would be interested. They really didn't want to be overrun by another family — that would make life impossible for Friedrich, but a young working gentleman of good character would be ideal. It would be such a comfort to know it was someone they could trust. Would Herr Shawcross think $5 a month too much to ask? No, he certainly would not and confessed the arrangement would get him out of a 'spot'. Herr Kleist need not worry; he would be off early every day now he had secured a job, so the shop room would be entirely vacant during the day for commercial use. He didn't have many belongings and would ensure what he had was always tidied away properly. This pleased Frau Kleist so much that she now said he must call her Rosa and bore him off for coffee and some funny little cakes, which were quite delicious.

Friedrich Kleist was indeed much improved ... a little on the quiet side perhaps, but at least his thin and nervously handsome face registered expression and emotions. He seemed to approve of Rosa's suggestion and shook Hartley's hand warmly many times.

Looking round, Hartley was amazed to see how Rosa had transformed their poor living quarters into something more homely in such a short interval. The place looked clean and well-scrubbed and was set out neatly with various mementoes from home. The beds were covered with colourful quilts and pushed away into one corner of the room. The baby, Rachel, slept peacefully in a low cradle on a rocker.

Frau Kleist (for Hartley found it difficult to call her Rosa all at once) said that the young boys were out selling newspapers, and she was not at all happy with this, though they had both insisted on doing something of that sort, like the little men they were. Did Hartley think they would be all right? They were together, of course, but she would feel better if she could get them into some kind of school. Hartley said he was sure they would come to no harm ... they were such bright, sensible boys and no doubt wanted to help as much as they could, which was to their credit.

"Have you seen Tim?" Rosa went on, pressing more cakes upon him. He confessed he had not since they had finally parted at the Court of Record, but he had left his address with the boy in case he needed a friend. He must leave a message at the boarding house now as to his whereabouts.

"He was intent on joining a whaler."

Rosa made a face. Her colour was slowly coming back, and the gesture made her appear less stiff, formal and much younger.

"The poor boy!" she said. "That must be a horrid life. I do not think I could get on another boat at this moment, no matter how much you paid me!" Hartley agreed.

"But Tim has his sea legs. He seems to let all hardships wash over him and wants excitement and adventure. He was a cheerful lad and knew how to wheedle his way along with the sailors."

Rosa shook her head. "I can't help thinking it's a bad life for a boy. There were some very rough and coarse men in that crew, and we had a fair captain, I think. There must be others who are not so good."

Hartley agreed again. It was very pleasant to sit here drinking Frau Kleist's coffee, eating her cakes, and agreeing with everything she said — especially when the subject of conversation was known to them both. For the first time since leaving ship, Hartley realized he had been lonely. The prospect of having these familiar, friendly souls as neighbours was distinctly encouraging.

"You want a new suit for your job?" asked Rosa suddenly. "Friedrich will make you one! Very cheap for you. But it will have been made by the best tailor in New York!"

Hartley was not certain he could afford it. "Well ... erm ... that would be grand," he said uncertainly.

"Friedrich!" Rosa's face looked flushed and happy. "Let us open some wine. We can celebrate, ja? Your first order!" She looked at

Hartley with a big apology in her eyes, and he realized at once that she was trying to keep her husband's spirits raised.

"You need not pay till you are sure you can," she whispered, under cover of Friedrich finding and uncorking the wine.

Hartley blushed. "Not a bit of it!" he whispered energetically back. "I am sure it will stand me in good stead."

The wine was brought and duly poured.

"Mmm," said Hartley appreciatively. "That is good."

"Good German wine," Rosa told him. "You will have some more ... ja?"

Hartley allowed his glass to be topped up, then rose to his feet and toasted Friedrich.

"To the best tailor in New York," he said.

Chapter Three

Caitlin found her new home delightful in many respects. It was comfortable to the point of luxury and cleanly polished, thankfully not by her, with food arriving at regular intervals. Mrs Regan engaged a full-time nurse for Maeve, and Caitlin found herself a new and charming companion in Polly. Still, she felt uneasy, and the reason for that lay in Mrs Regan. It was not that she was unkind, though she was naturally critical of the way Caitlin spoke, dressed and behaved. She had agreed that Caitlin should stay with them as a guest, at least for the present, and would be a pleasant companion for Polly. But Caitlin knew, in her heart of hearts, that Constance Regan had, almost immediately, taken a dislike to her. At first, she thought she must be imagining it. But whenever Polly or her father — an open, jovial type of man — addressed the slightest remark to her personally, she felt Mrs Regan's eye rest upon her coldly when she answered. What could it be? Had she been unwilling to accept James' foundling? Was it too great an imposition by the friend of her youth? Yet James had been so pleased with her response and emphasized the woman's generosity.

Caitlin was left with only one alternative — that she had somehow created this antipathy herself. For some reason, she was disliked, just as she had been by Bridget. Only Bridget had been jealous. Surely there was no reason why Mrs Regan should be? It puzzled and troubled her, though she tried to shake it off. Anyway, the arrangement was only temporary; when James came, he would take her away, and they would set up home somewhere else. She did not question how on earth her uncle would achieve this with his straitened finances. It was enough that he had said he would come.

Then, one morning, the maid came into the sitting room of No. 24, Union Square Place, bearing a letter.

"There's a note arrived for Miss Murphy," she announced. Polly and Caitlin were both crouching on the floor, laughing at and encouraging the antics of Maeve in play. Caitlin struggled to her feet with a high colour in her face. "For me? But I don't know anyone in New York."

"Who left it, Adie?" asked Polly.

"He wouldn't leave his name, Miss. I asked him to wait, but he said no, he couldn't do that, and hurried away. A young man and an immigrant, I'd say."

Caitlin took the scrap of paper, lacking even an envelope, off the silver tray Adie proffered, and Polly dismissed the maid. She scanned the poorly written message quickly, her hand at her throat.

"It's Owain," she said in some embarrassment. "Of course. He said he'd let me know."

"Let you know what, dearest?"

"How he was getting on. It's a young man I met on the boat. I can't tell you exactly how, but I helped him, and he was ever so grateful and took good care of us ..."

Polly was interested but did not pry. "That's like you, Cait," she said. In the space of days, the girls had become good friends. "What does he say?"

"He's found a job working on the railways, laying track and blasting tunnels, I think that says. Yes, that will be it. He says the work sounds hard, but he's used to that, and the pay is good. Only it's a long way off, upstate, and over to the west, and he doesn't think he'll make it back to New York for some time. He wanted me to know and wishes me well."

"Don't tell Mamma," said Polly darkly.

"Would she not approve?"

"Possibly not, but she's much more likely to have you married off to him in the twinkling of an eye!"

"Oh, Polly!"

"It's true. I'm afraid I'm a great disappointment to Mamma. I fail to attract any suitors for my hand, and if any do hover near, I fail to show the requisite amount of interest. She's become very worried about me." Caitlin laughed, though she could see Polly was serious underneath the banter.

"Don't you want to get married, then?"

"No, I don't think I do. At least, I haven't met anyone I'd ever want to marry. What is more, I doubt if I will. Poor Mamma! It's no wonder she's concerned."

"But you wouldn't want to remain a spinster all your life, surely?"

"Why not? I think I'd make a good one! I only wish to be useful in some way. If I don't marry, then I can do exactly what I want to without anyone making a fuss. I could work with the poor. I went down to the New York Association for the Poor one day to offer my services, but Mamma found out and forbade me to go again. She was horrified. I feel it's what I'm meant to do, but Mamma doesn't understand." Caitlin thought about it.

"I've never met anyone so good before ... except perhaps Uncle James. I think he'd understand."

"I'm looking forward very much to meeting him! Though I'm not good, Caitlin. Far from it! That's why I need to improve myself. Mamma refuses to discuss it, and I know it tortures her, yet I can't be, refuse to be, the young lady she so desperately wants me to be!"

"Sure, and that's nonsense!" said Caitlin, quite forgetting Mrs Regan had told her not to say 'sure' all the time because it sounded so Irish. "You're only the goodest person I've ever met! I wish Uncle James would hurry up and come and sort us all out!"

"He'll be a marvellous man if he can sort out my mother," said Polly wryly. But she leant over and gave Caitlin a kiss on the cheek. "You're a tonic to me, Caitlin. I do love you! But you'll see what I mean in time about Mamma. We're left blessedly in peace for now as everyone is out of town, but it won't last."

Caitlin received her embrace gladly. "And you're a good, true friend! I'd feel very strange here without you, and I'm so happy you don't dislike me!"

"Why should I do that?"

"I don't know. But some people do, and I thought you'd be different, you know ... all high and mighty ..."

"Like Mamma wants me to be, in fact?"

"Yes, I suppose so!"

They both laughed at that and took Maeve back upstairs to the nursery for her lunch, singing to her on the way.

≈

However, a second letter had been delivered to the Regans' house that morning, and it was one which caused Constance Regan considerable distress. For a long time, she sat in her boudoir with the letter from Ireland in front of her on the dressing table. She shed a few tears, then brushed them angrily away, sitting lost in thought. At last, she rose, tucking the letter into her gown, and swished downstairs into the drawing room, where she rang the bell and asked Adie to summon Miss Caitlin and her daughter at once.

They came, leaving Maeve alone with her nurse. The nurse was kind, but Caitlin still felt a little reluctant about the arrangement, having had sole charge of the child for several weeks now. Of course, it was wonderful to have her own room again, so close to Polly's. However, she still felt unsure of herself as its tenant and kept on thinking she should be up in the servants' quarters, next to the nursery, where she could hear Maeve if she cried out in the night and needed a comforting, familiar face. The generous provision of the nurse had alarmed her. It was as if she was no longer considered good enough to be entrusted with the care of her half-sister. She was still thinking of this when they entered the drawing room.

Mrs Regan stood by the fireplace, elegant and regal as always in grey silk. She held a letter in her hand, and her bosom heaved slightly. The room was shuttered, and the drapes firmly closed against the heat outside. Caitlin found it rather oppressive, for the light was not good, and the room was filled with the uncomfortable movement of clocks.

"What is it, Mamma?" asked Polly quickly, sensing her mother's distress.

"I have news from Ireland ..."

"A letter from James!" exclaimed Caitlin eagerly.

"No, Caitlin. You must learn not to interrupt."

"I'm sorry, Mrs Regan."

"It is a letter from Father Francis ... the pastor of your parish, I gather."

"Father Francis?" Caitlin forgot the admonition in her surprise. "But why from him?"

Constance sighed. "My dear, you must prepare yourself for a great shock."

Caitlin's heart beat a little faster at this, as anyone's would. "What is it? Is it my father?"

"No. Father Francis has no news of them. Your letter telling him of your arrival will not have reached James yet. In fact, it will never reach him at all."

"What do you mean?" asked Caitlin, thoroughly frightened.

"My poor child ... there is no easy way to break such news. I feel quite distraught myself."

"Tell her quickly, Mamma," said Polly with sudden insight.

"It appears that your step-uncle returned to Ballakenny after seeing you off on the boat and shot himself through the head with his revolver. He died instantly, of course."

Polly let out her breath, which she had been holding, sharply, but Caitlin stood transfixed on the spot. The colour slowly drained from her face.

"James?" she said. "My Uncle James? He's dead?"

"Yes, my dear. I'm afraid so."

Caitlin began to tremble all over. "Oh no," she said. "It can't be true, it can't possibly be true! Not my James! Not like that. There must be some mistake!"

"I'm afraid not. See, perhaps you'd better read it for yourself." Mrs Regan handed the letter over, and Caitlin stared at it. She could see the words, but they didn't make any sense. Just that awful phrase: 'shot himself in the head'. It had happened in the library. The minute he got home. He had gone straight there from the boat. Knowing what he would do? Her knees gave way underneath her, and she sank onto the rich patterned carpet in bewilderment, clutching the letter with one tearing sob.

"Polly!" said Mrs Regan brusquely. "Ring for some brandy."

"Yes, Mamma!" But Polly did better than that. She flew to get it herself.

Caitlin felt Mrs Regan's stiff arms around her, helping her to her feet and into an armchair. Her voice seemed to come from a distance.

"I am sorry, my dear," she said, "I know it's a terrible thing to hear."

"But he promised me!"

"Promised you what, dearest?" asked Polly, who was back already and kneeling before Caitlin to put it to her unwilling lips.

"That he would come ... he would follow! Oh, I should never have come alone. We should never have left him!"

Polly, her gentle eyes full of tears, looked at her mother.

"No," said Mrs Regan. "You must not think of that, Caitlin. James was most anxious you should come. He must have felt he had given you a new life and that doubtless gave him relief. It must have been hard for him. For a man to be financially ruined is a great disgrace."

Caitlin choked on the brandy and pushed it away. Polly wiped her lips.

"But I said goodbye to him at the boat, and he smiled and said he would soon be here. I can't believe he went straight back home and did such a terrible thing!"

She began to moan and rock herself to and fro.

"Adie!" Mrs Regan addressed the maid she had rung for who had just appeared. "Take Miss Caitlin to her room and put her to bed."

"I will go and sit with her, Mamma."

Polly and the maid helped Caitlin, now wailing, from the room. Constance Regan stooped and picked up the crumpled letter from the floor. To tell the truth, she was a little unprepared for the extravagance of Caitlin's grief. She had reckoned her tougher than that. Shrewdly, she saw the reason. Not 'my James,' she had said. The girl had obviously hero worshipped her uncle initially because of his kindness and care for her, no doubt, but in the end, through infatuation. Constance grimaced. It was easy enough to believe once she thought of it. James could be very personable in his way or had been. It was unlikely he was aware of the change he had wrought in the girl. Whether James had really intended to do this, he had now left her, Constance Regan, with a major problem ... two problems, in fact.

However, the way ahead for the little one seemed clearer. She had already made some plans about that. No, it was Caitlin who troubled her, this young nymph of a girl with her striking, wilful looks and a spirit to match. For it was obvious that Polly had already taken her to her heart, in her naivety, and would be determined they should not part now.

"What am I supposed to do?" she muttered to herself angrily, pacing up and down. "What am I supposed to do with her, James? What plans did you have for her? Oh, useless to query that! None at all! That is evident. Did you think I would take to her at once because of the affection we once had? Perhaps you believed Thaddeus to be more successful than he really is, and I suppose that is my fault for all my heartless boasting ...! One wilful daughter is worrisome enough, but two will be quite impossible! And she would have to be so pretty, that she outshines my own child! I can already see Thaddeus looking foolishly at her in his cups!"

But then James had known nothing of this. She had made him believe she was happy for years, even though she could have had James once but refused him, knowing that he was a hopeless idealist. So, James had gone on believing her lies ... how like him! How like him, too, to have clung to his own memory of her as a woman who was pure and good throughout. The bitter, angry tears came again, and this time, she did not brush them away.

Caitlin passed through the many stages of grief that summer. At first, she could not believe it had happened and requested to see the letter several times. She sat down to write to Father Francis but could find nothing to say. She felt there must be more to it than had been said. Something must have happened on the way back from Cork. There must be something that Father Francis had withheld. It was such a sin to shoot yourself.

She felt guilty because she had not been there. She was the sole person (she thought) that might have prevented the fatal act. Yet she had allowed herself to be sent away, quite happily, when he had needed her most! How could she have been so blind? She could not bear to think of their parting on the quayside in detail. No doubt, men shot themselves every day in the despair of financial ruin. But she could not believe it had happened to James when he was so wise.

Polly procured sedatives from her mother, which enabled Caitlin to sleep for a few nights. Except then, she would wake early as their effect wore off and lie awake in the growing dawn with tears on her face, listening for the first sounds from this foreign house in this strange land. There was no one else she truly belonged with now. Her father had gone. James was dead. Even Owain had left New York. There was no one who remained, and Mrs Regan would find her a tiresome burden. Only Polly seemed to be her friend, but she was new and untried.

She scarcely noticed how Polly did indeed care for her. It was not enough. She needed someone of her own and a place to belong. She wept angrily now in self-pity. How could he have shot himself? How *could* he? In the library with her image before him? How could he have deserted her when he had promised? What had he promised? He had promised to be with her in spirit until they were reunited. He had deceived her. She beat her fists against the wall until Polly came rushing in alarm.

Then she really cried — hot, bitter tears that tore her heart asunder. Polly held her close and took the brunt of the anguished blows. She wanted him back. There was no one she would ever love so much. That was surely impossible.

"I know, I know," murmured the faithful Polly. "But it will pass, my darling! Little by little, it will not hurt so much. Every night, I pray that you may be given strength ... God never sends us anything without giving us the strength to bear it. Let me read to you a little. It will make you feel calmer."

She read to her from various religious works, though Caitlin did not hear the words. Polly does not know, she thought. Polly is good, but she has never felt love for a man, and perhaps she never will. She is self-contained and close to God. She needs no one else. But I cannot be like that. She does not know how I feel — me,

Caitlin Murphy — the little Irish bogtrotter with all her wickedness and selfishness, her longings and desires. How could she? She does not know what it is like to feel abandoned.

Even so, she was gradually quietened. Something of Polly's blessing must have entered her soul after all. Eventually, she began to feel resigned, though it was a bitter and hard resignation that hurt. She became unnaturally dull and lethargic, taking up sewing and needlepoint when encouraged to do so because it occupied her hands. She insisted on wearing mourning clothes, although Mrs Regan pointed out that it was not necessary here. She devoted herself to Maeve's welfare as well as she could. In short, she was determined to suffer, and suffer she did.

Chapter Four

The summer passed quietly, bereft of all society, but Caitlin had no wish to go out. A turn around Union Square was the most she would submit to. She felt incapable of pondering her own future. Although she felt a burden on the Regan family, she could do nothing about it. She was content to live quietly with them in this state of self-imposed martyrdom.

So, it came as another shock when Constance Regan chose one afternoon, about six weeks after they had learnt of James' death, to speak to her about Maeve. They were sitting in the drawing room with the blinds and drapes drawn against the heat as usual. Even though the summer oozed and choked its way in, it was nearly over…already the weather was fresher at the beginning and end of each day, and the first patter of invitations for the approaching social season had begun to fall on the Regans' mat.

In Constance's mind, Caitlin's grief had been seemingly under the circumstances for a while, but it was now time for it to end. She had two belles to launch in New York City in the coming year. Chastening though it would be if Caitlin were to receive an offer before Polly, she knew it would be the only long-term solution to her problem. She had other plans for Maeve, and these had now come to a convenient and suitable fruition.

"Very pretty, my dear," she said in response to Polly's repertoire on the piano. "But take a rest awhile. I want to speak with Caitlin."

Caitlin's head was bent over her needlework with blank eyes. She raised her head when Mrs Regan spoke, though without any suspicion or foreboding. Maeve was taking her afternoon nap upstairs.

"I do believe I've come to a highly satisfactory arrangement about the child," said Constance. "I think your stepmother would be more than satisfied, and I hope you will approve, too, my dear."

Caitlin's needle was arrested with its point in mid-air. She looked at her benefactress in wonder. "What do you mean?"

"About Maeve. I have come to an arrangement with the most ideal family."

"I don't understand."

"Adoption, my dear. A new start in life. That is what your stepmother wanted, is it not? I am afraid Thaddeus and I are much too old to consider, and you can't be expected to look after a child forever. A young woman who should be out enjoying herself. It would spoil your chances, my dear!"

Polly dropped some of her sheet music and bent down to pick it up in a fluster.

"Mrs Regan, I don't understand. What have you done?" Caitlin protested.

"Mamma, I think --"

"Don't think, Polly! It doesn't suit you. Shush now while I tell Caitlin. I know this excellent family, my dear, well, a couple to be exact. A childless couple. They live upstate in Rochester and Mr Hooper is an extraordinarily rich man. He owns several of the flour mills there and has shares in the canal. Mr Edgar J. Hooper. See here, I have a likeness of him." She opened a little box lined with blue velvet and took out a daguerreotype framed in brass.

"He looks old," said Caitlin.

"Oh no, not old, dear. In the prime of life! A little portly, perhaps. But not much older than your Uncle James was. His wife is a deal younger, though something of an invalid. They have never been able to have children of their own and would dearly love to take Maeve as theirs. It's a wonderful opportunity for her. She'll have everything she could possibly want. They're such good, kind, **wealthy** people. See, here is a sketch of their house." She passed it across triumphantly. It was a grand Georgian-style mansion with creeper and classical columns around the door. Caitlin held the drawing with a trembling hand.

"So, will he want me to go with her?"

"Oh dear, no! They only want a child. They'll have a nurse and a nanny, and a governess, too, in time. I think it's greatly to your advantage to stay in New York." Mrs Regan was wise enough not to mention suitors in marriage.

Caitlin swallowed. "Is it a long way?" she asked faintly.

"Why no, dear. It's still in New York State!"

Polly felt constrained to intervene at this point. "Mamma! I fancy that, to Caitlin, it will seem an awfully long way. It's as great a distance as two or three Irelands. One must travel up the Hudson by boat for two or three days and then the canal. And in winter ..."

"In winter, what?" asked Caitlin, alarmed.

"Oh, in winter, it snows a great deal," Mrs Regan shrugged. "As it often does here. But it is a lovely place, Caitlin. By the shore of Lake Ontario. And I do assure you they are the best of people! Why, the railroad will soon be built, and then you can go and visit her in comfort, yourself!"

A single hot tear rolled down Caitlin's face and onto her work. "Please don't send her away," she said.

"Now, Caitlin," Mrs Regan said firmly. "You're not thinking sensibly. What do you expect me to do? Of course, you'll miss her. Why, we'll all miss her for a while. But you mustn't be so selfish. Just think of the life she'll have and the joy she'll bring to Mr and Mrs Hooper!" There it was again: that awful word — selfish.

"But she's my sister!"

"Half-sister, Caitlin." Constance Regan shut her workbasket with a snap. "You brought her here at her mother's request to be resettled, didn't you, now? It seems hard to you at present, I can see, but it is in the child's best interests. In time, you'll see that."

"Are the Hoopers really kind? Do you know them well?"

"Of course." Mrs Regan did not qualify which question she was answering in particular, seeming to think her reply should suffice for both. Neither did she mention that a large amount of money had changed hands.

"Mamma, perhaps it's too soon —" began Polly again.

"I do wish you'd be quiet, Polly," her mother rounded on her crossly. "We don't want to know all your details about geography and such like. I don't know where you get these things from. I'm sure I never knew them at your age and never wanted to! A woman can be far too clever for her own good!" She took out her spectacles and placed them irritably on her nose. "Well, Caitlin, what do you say?"

Caitlin wilted. "I expect you're right. If you think it's for the best..."

"I do, my dear, I do."

"Then she must go." Caitlin bent her head low over her sewing and shortly excused herself from the room, saying she was tired and would take a rest before dinner.

Polly began to play the piano again, but her fingers transmitted anger to the keys, and the tune became increasingly discordant. She stopped abruptly. "Mamma!"

"Yes, Polly?"

"Don't you understand how difficult it is for Caitlin to give Maeve up?"

"Not really." Mrs Regan was unrepentant. "Neither will you if you consider the facts a little more. Maeve is not, so we trust, Caitlin's own child. She never saw her until she rejoined her family to emigrate. Her whole life centred around James."

"Yes, but now he is gone ... and so cruelly. She has no one else left and has become very attached to the little one."

"She has a home and friends through our bounty, my dear. That is more than a great many Irish immigrants have! Otherwise, she would have been condemned to Tinkersville and the very worst kind of trade for a woman! And another thing — this mourning over her uncle, don't you find it a little unhealthy that it should be so prolonged?"

"No," said Polly, "I don't. She loved him dearly."

"Ah yes, but your loving and her loving are quite different!"

"That is very cynical of you, Mamma!"

"Perhaps. But I knew James. And why do you think she had such a passion for him?"

"He was a good man."

"He was the *only* man, my dear. Quite handsome and definitely superior to her own father, although almost as old as him. I guess

Caitlin didn't see much of society in James' house. She hasn't had the chance to meet normal young men. She's never really enjoyed herself, and it's time she did. And I need your help, Polly."

"Mine?"

"Yes. Now the fall's coming, I want you to take her to parties, and we'll go to the theatre and the opera again. The O'Briens will be back soon. I know you object to Cornelius and Seamus rather strongly, but don't you think one of them might do for Caitlin?"

"No, Mamma, I do not!" said Polly coldly. "They haven't a thought in their heads other than making money and spending it!"

"I don't see why you think that's such a crime! And Caitlin is rather fetching, you know! Don't be surprised if she ends up with more than one beau! I think she'll soon forget all this dreary mourning when she's seen a touch or two of society here. Why don't you take her shopping, my dear? Take her to Ladies' Mile, show her the lace room at Stewart's, get her to try on a new bonnet, and order stuff for a new gown. Get her interested in normal life again. It's no help to her that your nose is stuck in a book all day long."

Polly considered this and sighed in resignation. "Perhaps you're right, Mamma. It might cheer her up. I'll try if you think it will help. Only not the O'Briens! You know quite well that they trifle with young ladies' affections. It would be terrible to see Caitlin hurt by them."

"Forget I ever mentioned them!" said Mrs Regan hastily. "I know they wouldn't do for you with all your funny sensibilities. But you're a deal too fastidious. I just wondered if they might suit Caitlin with all their fresh, Irish ways, and their father is such a well-known banker now. Still, there are lots of others. We might even meet some new families this season. We might even get invited to Fifth Avenue —"

"Yes, Mamma," said Polly firmly, to cut off the way the conversation was trending. "I do know what you mean, and I promise I'll do my best…for Caitlin."

"And for yourself too, my dear, I hope!" Polly ignored this.

"But how is Papa going to pay for all this socializing and elegant new finery?"

"Really, Polly! One doesn't talk about such things. You know that quite well. Papa's work in the city does not concern us!"

"Doesn't it, Mamma? Only Papa looks so old and tired and careworn sometimes! Not a bit as if he is enjoying his successes, any more than his failures."

Constance's bosom bristled at this. "He will manage, never fear! And please don't let me down by any more of your ridiculous ... philanthropic talk…you know what I mean! I really cannot cope with that as well as everything else now." An angry red flush of emotion spread from Mrs Regan's powdered cheeks to her proud neck and bosom at the thought of these matters. Polly saw it with more than a little sadness but bent her head and tried hard to be dutiful.

It seemed to Caitlin she had a great weight on her shoulders that evening as she sought cooler air in Union Square. Sometimes, she felt as if she must have fresh air after a day in the house and came here alone before it grew dark. It was her own fault because Polly often suggested a drive or a walk, but the heat and her depression of spirits caused her such lassitude and lack of enthusiasm that she almost always turned the proposal down until it was too late. Only tonight, she had to see the trees again and the dying light in the sky above.

She was so unused to living in a city. Not that it could be said she was living in it when she had hardly ventured out of the square, and the thousand lights of the place were passing her by. Quietly, her footsteps tended towards the fountain, and she sat down on one of the seats nearby — a small black shadow in the last of the evening sun. She thought about losing Maeve and cried some more. She had never imagined Mrs Regan would seek this separation. Her first instinct was to write to Mr Edgar J. Hooper and plead for a situation. But then how badly Mrs Regan would think of her! No doubt she was right, and the Hoopers would not wish to be reminded of Maeve's origins by seeing Caitlin's Irish face every day. They had not asked for her, so it was clear she was unwanted.

She brushed away her tears. Why did she always have to be so dependent? If only it were possible for a woman to make her own way in the world! In this, she understood something of Polly's frustrations.

A man passed before her, raising his hat politely, and walked on a little way. Then he stopped and turned as if to come back and Caitlin was consumed with embarrassment. She had the feeling she had seen him somewhere before, but that seemed unlikely. If only he would turn and walk on. Instead, he walked towards her and stood a little apart, obviously anxious to speak but uncertain how to begin. Caitlin saw that he was a young man with fair, curling hair, the slightest of side-whiskers and a pleasant face with eyes that were rather serious. He was well-dressed, and she knew instinctively that he was not the sort of man to be alarmed by. Still, she wished he would go away, but as he did not, she decided to speak first. She was not, after all, naturally shy. It was only sorrow that had cast her down lately, and if she did not speak soon, it appeared he would be waylaid for the next half hour, wondering how to begin to talk to her.

"Good evening," she said flatly.

Hartley blushed but appeared pleased. "Erm ... good evening! It's very pleasant."

"Yes," even more flatly.

"Forgive me ... but I think I have seen you before."

"Oh, I doubt it! I am but lately arrived in New York."

"But so am I! From England?"

"No, Ireland." She corrected him.

"Of course. We had many Irish on our ship ... The Yorkshire."

"Yes, that was my ship."

"Then we must have seen each other."

"I don't remember it. But then I was in steerage and not a cabin passenger."

"And so was I! "Hartley smiled. "I have bought a new suit since then."

Caitlin also smiled briefly. He had such an agreeable smile it was impossible to do otherwise.

"Why don't you sit down for a while?" Hartley did so with alacrity.

"Mr ...?"

"Shawcross - Hartley Shawcross."

"Mr Shawcross," he said, extending his hand.

"And you are Mrs ...?"

"Miss Caitlin Murphy."

"Oh, I see!"

"You thought I was married?"

"No, no, I just had the impression you were not travelling alone. I must have been mistaken."

How tactful you are, thought Caitlin! "My little half-sister was with me."

"Ah, that must have been it!" The mention of Maeve made Caitlin downcast again, and she fell silent.

"It was quite a voyage," said Hartley meditatively.

"Yes, it was. And where have you been staying since you arrived?"

"In a street not far from here, with friends of my uncle. In the house of a Mr Thaddeus Regan, a businessman. Do you know him?"

"No," said Hartley, amused, though in a kindly way at her innocence, for, of course, the question was absurd. "I know hardly anyone yet!"

"Neither do I."

Their eyes met for the first time, and the grey solemnity of Hartley's eyes impinged upon her. A fresh wind came through the square and played in a healing fashion on her wet face.

"You must excuse me," said Hartley. "I am sure it is not a delicate thing to say ... but you seem very unhappy! Can I help in any way?"

Caitlin immediately dropped her eyes. "No," she said. "You cannot. It's nothing ... that is, I have suffered a severe loss since coming here ... of someone back home."

"I am very sorry," said Hartley, and he meant it, though his heart was bounding and the blood rushing to his head.

"I haven't begun to know New York as yet. I was so excited about coming here, and now it means nothing to me. But what about you, Mr Shawcross? How have you fared so far?"

"Oh, pretty well, I suppose. I have a position, and I lodge with a kind German family I met on the boat. Still ...."

"Yes?"

"Well, I own, I am a little disappointed in my situation. It does not seem that different from the one back home. It's going to take many more years than I thought to make my way. Of course, it was foolish of me to ever think otherwise! I know better now, and I am not really cast down. No, not a bit of it! But I do feel ... well, a little homesick at times, I suppose."

"Homesick," said Caitlin meditatively. "Oh yes, I know what you mean." Despite her preoccupations, she found herself liking this honest young man. But the air was cooling rapidly, and she could not prevent a sudden shiver.

"You are cold," said Hartley protectively.

"Yes, a little. I fear I must go in." Caitlin stood up. "I came out without thinking of the necessity for a shawl. The days are still so hot ..."

She realized, in fact, that she had been so distracted she had even come out without her bonnet! What must he think of her? But he didn't seem to notice that as he stood up courteously.

" ... though freshening daily," he said with typical English persistence on the topic of weather. "Permit me to escort you home. It grows dark." She allowed him to take her arm.

"You are very fortunate to live here," said Hartley.

"I suppose I am."

"Did you know that only Madison Square Garden and Fifth Avenue are more fashionable these days?"

Caitlin shook her head a little impatiently. "I know nothing of that," she said.

He saw he had made a mistake and cursed himself for it. Now, she would think he was a mere social climber. But, by the time they reached No. 24 Union Square Place, she seemed to have forgotten all about it.

"Would you like to come in?" she asked him uncertainly as they paused before the steps.

"No," said Hartley. "That is ... I don't know if it would be acceptable to your hostess. I know so little of New York society."

"So do I," and Caitlin laughed. "We have much in common, Mr Shawcross." She gave him her hand.

"It would appear so," he said gravely, with more than a little wonder in his heart at his good fortune, and he pressed her hand gently against his own fingertips. It felt soft and yielding.

"I will wish you goodnight then," said Caitlin. "Perhaps you may like to call some other time when we are more certain of New York and its ways!"

He pressed her hand warmly again in reply and watched her alight the steps and ring the bell. A servant admitted her, and the door was closed. She was gone, but Hartley stood there in a trance.

At last, he made his way back to the busy thoroughfares whilst treading on air. He had found her! The meeting seemed unreal now but had actually happened with an immediacy about it that had driven all else from his mind. He had found his Madonna, and though she was sadder still, she was well-cared for and safe. How beautiful she had looked in her sombre black apparel, how gleaming her dark hair, how pale her skin, and blue her eyes! What is more, he had been mistaken all along ... she was not married! It was not that he hoped exactly. She seemed too far above him for that. But he was sensible that, against all the odds, he had unexpectedly made her his friend. They had a bond, a connection, and he exulted in the fact that she would now recognize him again, inadequate though his speeches had been.

He seemed to fly over the streets. You may well wonder what he was doing there anyway, so far from his own environs. But the truth was that he did indeed feel somewhat disappointed with his lot so far at the merchants, though he would not have admitted it for the world in his letters home. It was good to return to a meal with the Kleists, but he did not feel he should sit with them all night, nor did he want to shut himself up alone in his hot room. So, he had taken to wandering the streets much as he had in his first days here for evening air and exercise but also to raise his spirits and indulge in his dreams.

Invariably, his steps took him towards the upper reaches of Broadway to Union Square, Madison Square and Fifth Avenue for he delighted in seeing the houses of the prosperous not that far away from his own mean lodgings. In his imagination, he already owned one. Many were the times he had been to Union Square before without knowing of the Madonna's existence there! He had not been searching for her because he had believed her gone forever. Caitlin! He repeated the name interminably, in every possible kind of inflexion and manner. It had suddenly become the most wonderful name in the universe. Now, he would return every night to gaze at her windows without yet daring to call.

Chapter Five

Although Hartley claimed to know no one in New York, he was, in fact, on the brink of forming his first friendship. He rarely saw the elevated personage of Elmer James, Shipping Merchant, but the man had a son, Ralph, who also worked in the offices under von Blumen. No doubt he had a share in his father's business, or one promised, but he was apparently learning from the floor up, just like Hartley. He was of a similar age and often called out a greeting, which surprised Hartley, who was used to a rigid class barrier between employer and employee. Naturally, he replied, and they exchanged a few words.

One evening in September, when the city was starting to cool down, Ralph accompanied him out of the office and into the street.

"Ready for a beer?" he asked Hartley in an obviously friendly fashion.

"Definitely!"

"Let's find a bar then."

"When does this city start to cool down?" Hartley asked him over the drinks.

"Well, from now onwards," answered Ralph. "October, well, October can be pretty fine, I guess, but the nights get a real nip in them. By November, winter'll start to set in. December and January will be darned cold! This city gets so cold in January, you wouldn't believe it! You'd better get yourself some furs!"

Hartley laughed.

"How're you settling now, Hartley?" Ralph seemed genuinely concerned and Hartley found himself warming to him.

"Fair enough. It's becoming better. But it's a shock at first ... all this ..." He indicated the street outside with its constant tumult and motion.

"I guess it is. You're a good worker, though. You don't make mistakes. You'll get on."

"Do you think so?" asked Hartley eagerly. "I know I could do more if I got the chance."

"You will. Von Blumen's a shrewd man. He'll begin to give you more responsibility soon. You'll see."

"I hope so."

"Are you happy with where you live?"

"Yes, it's fine. I've been lucky there."

"Good. I see you're starting to get into American politics, too." Ralph nodded his head at the newspaper Hartley carried under his arm.

"Well, I'm trying to learn as much as I can. You all talk about it all of the time!"

Ralph grinned. "Maybe it's because it hasn't been going on as long as yours. I don't know."

Hartley unfolded the paper thoughtfully. "This Fugitive Slave Act that's just been passed ... it seems to have caused quite a storm."

"It sure has. It's a compromise ... to keep the South happy ... but a lot of New Yorkers and New Englanders don't like it."

"Do many slaves run away, then?"

"Sure do. At least, they try to."

"Do they come here? I haven't seen that many Negroes in New York."

"No, not that many. But have you ever heard of something called the Underground Railroad?"

"No. What is it?"

"It's a kind of trail — a chain of safe houses for fugitive slaves run by the abolitionists. Mostly ends in Rochester, upstate from here. They ship them out to British North America across the lake. That way, they're sure of getting their freedom. Still, I guess they only save a few hundred every year. That's what this act's about, aiming to put off the active abolitionists by making it an offence to shield or help a runaway slave and punishing it with a fine. It won't make any difference, of course, because the abolitionists are radicals, and some of them are real wealthy. But it makes the North seem less receptive."

Hartley was listening with interest. "How many slaves are there in the South?"

"Oh, I don't know, two, maybe three million, I reckon."

"Two or three million! Even now, they don't ship them in any longer?"

"No, that's been illegal for over forty years. But they've had a couple of centuries to breed, and the South's a big place. They sure need them to run the plantations."

"I can understand that. But why can't they be free and do the same work?" Ralph considered.

"I think," he said. "The plantation owners are afraid of that. They feel they need to keep them down to have control. Some of them think that's the way God intended the Negro to be, anyway."

"You don't think that, surely?"

"No, of course not. That can't be right. I'm not much of a religious man and certainly not for justifying what's wrong. But I sure as hell wouldn't know what to do about it either if I was a Southerner! I'm not an abolitionist ... I'm a businessman. I happen to work in the North, and

I think our way is better. But they say it's a different country down there. They say a lot of the plantation owners treat their slaves real well, and maybe they do. I've never been, and I don't suppose I ever will. What concerns me and a lot of other Northerners is that it doesn't bode well for the Union to have two parts of it on a collision course. You'll hear some folks up here talking as if the Southern states are an enemy, and maybe they're half right. It don't fit in too well with America, the land of freedom and opportunity."

"No, it doesn't. But the British aren't that aware of this ... I must admit, I'd never really thought about it before I came here. It's such a long way away."

"And you need that cotton!"

"Yes, we certainly do."

"Hey, what's all this 'we' business? You sound as if you're going back next week!"

Hartley flushed uncomfortably, but Ralph laughed and slapped him on the shoulder. "I'm only joking," he said. "It takes time to be American. Are you going to stay and renounce your Queen Victoria in five years?"

"Yes," said Hartley with determination. "I am."

Ralph nodded. "I admire you," he said. "You know that? It's true. I didn't have to decide a darned thing. My grandaddy made the decision for me. He was a Scot. You didn't know that, did you?"

Hartley shook his head.

"I've seen you looking at me, kinda' shy and uncertain, because you think I'm a native-born American," Ralph went on, good-humouredly. "Well, it's true ... but there ain't that much difference between us, you see. So, you don't want to go on thinking there is."

"Thank you, it's good to know that."

"Want another drink?"

"No, I ought to go. But thanks, Mr James."

"Mr James! Who's he? You better call me Ralph if you want to be an American! Perhaps I didn't explain well enough. You're as good as me, Hartley Shawcross! That's why my granddaddy came and why you've come too."

"Well, thank you," said Hartley again, feeling pleased but embarrassed. "Er ... Ralph, there's something I'd like to ask you. It's about etiquette."

"Go on!"

"There's a girl I met on the boat over here who's living with an American family off Union Square. I saw her again yesterday, and she asked me to call sometime ..."

Ralph grinned again.

"Only I'd have to go in the evening. I don't know if that would be considered acceptable."

"Sure, it would if she asked you. They might be out, of course. But you can always keep on trying. I might even come with you if she's pretty! Anyway, I think you need my help if you're ever going to stop acting so darned proper English!"

When Hartley reached his lodgings that evening, he knew straight away that something was wrong. The pieces of cut-out cloth, the needles and thread, the tape measure, and the scissors, all usually tidied away by now, remained scattered around his room. When he entered the Kleists' room, there was no sign of the boys or their father. Frau Kleist, who was clattering around with pans and dishes, was obviously upset whilst the baby lay crying in its cradle, ignored.

When Rosa caught sight of Hartley, she put down her kitchenware and picked up the infant to hush her.

"Here you are, as I knew you would be!" she exclaimed. "And no dinner ready, no room tidied or nothing!"

Hartley assured her that didn't matter but was curious, all the same. "Where is Herr Kleist?" he asked.

Rosa sniffed and shrugged her shoulders as if she were not in the least bit concerned, which, of course, she was. "He's gone out. I have sent the boys to find him."

"But what is wrong?"

"He says he makes a few cheap clothes from a little cheap cloth all day. He is not used to it. The people round here can't afford more. They want second hand clothes. I say let us buy in second hand clothes and make the alterations. He says is he, Friedrich Kleist, a fine bespoke tailor, to do nothing all day but take in the odd seam here and raise a hem there like a common seamstress? He says we must move to Broadway, where the real tailors are. But how can we afford that before we make money here?"

Hartley sympathized but could do little beyond endorsing Rosa's commonsense. "Everyone must learn to walk before they can run," he agreed. "Even in America."

Frau Kleist nodded, but the agreement gave her no satisfaction. However, at that moment, the boys returned with their father, who certainly looked very miserable. Nevertheless, he apologized to Rosa and went away sheepishly to clear Hartley's room. Hartley sensed that Rosa would get her way over the second hand clothes.

The following morning, when Hartley arrived at work, von Blumen called him up to his office. At first, Hartley was alarmed in case his work should be criticized but was relieved to find that it was nothing of the kind. The manager was going down to the wharves later in the morning to see a shipment that had arrived and wished to take the diligent Hartley along to record certain matters. Hartley strove hard to overcome his elation. Already, it seemed as if Ralph's predictions might, after all, be destined to come true.

≈

Thaddeus Regan arrived home on the evening of September 18th feeling depressed. He had also, in theory, deplored the passing of the Fugitive Slave Act, which he read about in the morning's papers. But, to tell the truth, he was far too worried about his business concerns to give this more than a second or two's thought. Most of his money was tied up in real estate in lots that he had bought above the present northern boundaries of the city. It was a fine investment long term, but it required a deal of patience to hang onto it in the short term. Consequently, he found himself short of cash unless his daily speculations in buying and selling turned out well. Today, they had not.

Arriving home after such an uncomfortable day, he took himself straight away into his personal den, his smoking room, and study, where he did not run the risk of bumping into Constance nor any other member of his family. They were to dine out after the opera, and that would be time enough to talk. He hated the opera but recognized its social necessity.

He saw the pile of bills on his desk but decided to ignore them, pouring himself a huge drink and lighting a cigar instead. There were still bills to be paid for the furnishings of the house, and now, here was

Constance, encouraging expenditure of another kind on dresses and hats and other women's fripperies for the new season. It was of no use protesting. Constance would only claim these items, although regrettable, were essential if they were to do well for Polly, and now he supposed Caitlin as well. It was not that he begrudged either of them. It was merely inconvenient at the present.

He must ask Constance again for the money she had evidently received from Hooper but had so far withheld. He had not even been allowed to know the amount, and Connie claimed it was only to cover expenses incurred.

Polly must be married soon ... she had been a worry for far too long as it was. As for Caitlin, Thaddeus was aware of his wife's feelings but felt them to be unjustified. Thank goodness she had decided to make the best of it. It would not have been to his liking to have a Cinderella in the house, however attractive, and there was no doubt the little Irish girl was that. The very thought of her made him feel lascivious.

He poured another drink but spilt most of it down his full, greying beard as he raised it to his lips. Cursing himself and the world in general, he mopped at his bushy hairs with a large, greasy handkerchief. His hands were shaking, and to control them, he took another gulp. It steadied him, and, screwing in an eyeglass, he took up some of his papers with an attempt at a new resolve.

Upstairs, Polly was helping Caitlin prepare for the evening ahead. For the first time, Caitlin was out of mourning and dressed in a white muslin gown that looked beautiful on her in its simplicity. But her face in the looking glass did not smile, for Maeve had left that morning with her nurse on her way to the Hoopers in Rochester.

"I think you must try this pearl and jet circlet of mine to break up the neckline," Polly was saying.

Caitlin submitted like a child, but her eyes were full of tears. "Oh, Polly," she said miserably. "Must I go?"

"Yes, dearest, I think you must. I am sure you will enjoy the opera, and it will do you good and take your mind off your cares."

"But I keep on thinking of Maeve on that boat. Will she be asleep yet? Will she understand I have left her and why? Will she cry?"

"She will understand none of those things," said Polly soothingly. "And she will be quite happy because her nurse is with her."

"But what about tomorrow? And the day after that? What will she think when she arrives at the Hoopers? Oh, I wish I had never let her go!"

Polly let her sob for a while with an arm about her shoulders. "Caitlin, dearest, don't cry! She will settle and is too young to remember how this happened. And in the springtime, we will go and visit her and be glad to see how happy she is."

"She will have forgotten me by then!"

"No, not so soon."

"Am I very selfish, Polly?"

"No, of course not! Just unhappy and I feel for you!"

Caitlin raised her head and looked at her pale reflection in the dressing table mirror.

"I wish I hadn't come to America," she said. Then, a moment later, "Oh Polly, I'm sorry! I don't mean to be ungrateful. Not when you are so kind."

Polly shook her head sadly. "I know. You cannot help it. Mamma has not handled things well."

"But she meant only for the best," Caitlin countered bravely.

"Yes."

"You were right about the necklace." Caitlin's hand strayed to her throat. "You are so good to me; Polly and I do love you so."

The girls embraced and cried some more together, then made swift to repair the damage as best they might.

When they appeared together downstairs, Caitlin was more collected, though her face remained wan and strained. But her hair shone black and glossy in the gaslight, and her deep blue eyes were so enhanced by the white gown that Thaddeus Regan involuntarily caught his breath. He could not help noticing how delicate was the curve of her bare, white arms and neck. Nor could Mrs Regan fail to notice the effect that Caitlin wrought upon him. She saw it with a certain amount of resignation but also with foreboding. Polly was wearing blue — her favourite colour — but it really did nothing for her, as she was so fair-skinned. Constance's lips pressed firmly against each other, and she drew up her bosom higher.

They had ordered a carriage to drive to the Opera House, which was in Astor Place. Polly arranged a rug sympathetically over Caitlin's knees, though she didn't feel cold. She stared out at the streets which were growing dark but, if anything, appeared even more frenetic. How long had she been hidden away from them? One month? Two? It must surely be at least two. She felt confused by the bustle and almost afraid. She wasn't thinking about the opera nor the Regans, nor even of Maeve. It was James' spirit that haunted her as they drove along, constantly slowing or swerving or being brought to a halt by the press of the city traffic. This is what he had wanted. This was the kind of outing he had planned for her, perhaps even imagined with pleasure as he considered her entry into well-off New York society.

Then the buggy turned into Astor Place, and the sight of the Opera House with its classical columns lit up by gas burners made her gasp in pleasure after all. Thaddeus gave her his arm solicitously as she alighted.

Not only had Caitlin never been to the opera before, but she had also never seen any drama played out on a stage. At first, the auditorium with its crowded rows of seats bewildered her with its babel of noise. But when the lights went out, and the curtain rose on another world, she was entranced. She didn't understand a word of what the performers were singing. But the story was clear to her nevertheless, and being necessarily tragic made her weep silently. She had never experienced nor even conceived of anything so wonderful.

In the interval, they met the O'Briens, amongst others. Cornelius and Seamus were both good-looking young men in a large, careless kind of way, and both had identical shocks of Irish red hair. They were friendly and attentive, but Caitlin thought them rather stupid. She was anxious to get back to her seat for the second half to see what would happen, and the only face that floated into her mind all the while was that of her dear, dead James.

Yet afterwards, at a lavish supper at Delmonico's, she felt alive for the first time in weeks despite all the easy tears which had flowed for the stage drama.

"Did you enjoy it, Caitlin?" asked Polly anxiously, for she had sensed the tears in the dark.

"Oh yes!" said Caitlin. "To be sure I did! It was wonderful. If only I could sing like that!"

"You'd like to go again?" asked Thaddeus, pleased.

"Oh yes, I would look forward to that, sir! Thank you. And thank you so much for all you're doing for me. You're truly kind."

Thaddeus patted her hand in what he meant to be a paternal fashion. "It's a pleasure, my dear. The least we could do."

Constance smiled, too, albeit a little drily. "Polly," she asked. "Have you anything to tell?"

"Yes, Mamma," said Polly with resignation. " We are invited to a house party at the O'Briens in four days' time."

"I am glad. It will be an excellent opportunity for Caitlin to meet everyone. And for you, of course, too, my dear."

In fact, the next few weeks were a whirl of parties and gaiety for Caitlin proved as popular as Constance had suspected, and Cornelius O'Brien seemed smitten with her. Life was very pleasant on the surface, but Caitlin was living in a dream world that failed to stir her deeply. Cornelius' interest was not returned, though she treated him kindly enough. She was unaware of flirting and artful conversation, though she saw it all around her. Anything she said was direct and spontaneous, just as it had always been. But, because she felt deeply unsure of herself, she tried not to say too much despite many attempts to draw her out. This had the unfortunate effect of making her seem enigmatic when she was not, and the invitations continued to flood in for the moment.

Polly was shrewd. She knew, of course that the invitations were really for Caitlin, though addressed to them both, and didn't mind a bit. She also knew Caitlin had been sized up status-wise and been found wanting. Her looks were her passport to the drawing-rooms of New York, and even the desired invitations to Fifth Avenue were forthcoming. But it could not last in the hypocrisy of those drawing rooms — not for a penniless steerage emigrant from Ireland.

To her relief, she saw that Caitlin was not swept off her feet by it all. Mrs Regan, however, was delighted. She obviously entertained high hopes of marrying Caitlin off comfortably by the end of the season, and if it were to be to Cornelius, she at least would by no means object. The fact that Caitlin herself appeared more astute reassured Polly. She did not understand why her mother, whose own marriage she knew to be unhappy, could contemplate a similar life for anyone else.

On one of their now rare evenings in, the bell rang yet again to announce visitors. No doubt it would be Cornelius O'Brien again! Mrs Regan smiled and made herself scarce. Thaddeus was out somewhere, so the two girls were left alone in the drawing room — Caitlin with her self-imposed needlework on her knees and Polly at the piano. But when Adie came in, she proffered the card of an unknown Mr Ralph James, whom she said was accompanied by another young gentleman called Mr Hartley Shawcross.

"I don't think we know them, Adie," Polly said, puzzled.

Caitlin looked up from her sewing. "Mr Shawcross," she said meditatively. "Yes, I think I do. I met him in the square, Polly. I'm sure it was very wrong of me, but he came over on The Yorkshire too, you see, and I think I said he might call. Oh dear, your mamma will not like it, will she? I am sorry."

"Never mind, Caitlin. I will explain to her. Adie, let the gentlemen in."

Adie did not look too aghast, so Polly surmised that at least the callers must appear respectable. She hoped nonetheless that they had no ulterior motives in tracking down Caitlin, having found out she was staying with a well-to-do family off Union Square. Then, she felt ashamed of her suspicions when they were brought in.

For some unaccountable reason, Mr Hartley Shawcross seemed painfully shy, if not actually struck dumb. It was obviously a relief to him to be able to introduce his friend Mr James, who was a deal more confident, to help him out. Polly divined very quickly that what he really wanted to do was to have a quiet conversation with Caitlin, so she and Ralph James, who seemed equally cognizant, began their own friendly dialogue despite not knowing each other previously. It was not as arduous as Polly expected, for Ralph was easy to talk to and naturally likeable.

"You appear better," Hartley said to Caitlin, his tongue cleaving uncomfortably to the roof of his mouth. "Since we last met."

Caitlin smiled. "Do I? I suppose I am ... a little."

"You are out of mourning."

"To others, perhaps. I shall never be entirely free of it in myself."

Hartley knew he must change the subject and quickly, too, for this beginning was not exactly auspicious and he blamed himself for bringing up the worst possible topic of conversation.

"Have you seen anything else of this fair city, now?"

"Yes, I own I have. I have been to the opera, which was ... oh, quite wonderful! ... and I have been kindly invited to various persons' homes." "I am glad to hear it!"

"But tell me, Mr Shawcross, do you still think this is a fair city?"

"Not always. Perhaps my remark was ill-judged. But it does have great vitality. It is alive and throbbing, and it still encourages me. It begins to feel a part of me."

"Ah!" Caitlin prejudged him. "I think you are settling a little better now then. Am I right?"

Hartley nodded and smiled.

"I am glad," she said and meant it, for she had empathized with his loneliness that evening they had first met. "I see you have found a friend, too!" She motioned to Ralph.

"Yes." Hartley was proud now. "Ralph is a capital fellow, is he not? He is the son of my employer. Can you believe that? I am a mere clerk, but he does not let that stand in the way of friendship. That is the American way, apparently. It would not have been the same in England."

Caitlin remembered all the letters that James had written to England in vain and decided that would certainly be true. She had never been there, of course — apart from her passage through Liverpool — but believed she probably would have hated England.

"I am glad you are feeling happier," she repeated, for to tell the truth, she could not think of anything else to say, but did not want to appear haughty and unfriendly before this eager young man. "Tell me, have you seen anyone else from our boat?"

"I lodge with a German family that were on the Yorkshire."

"Oh yes, I remember now, you told me. How are they?"

"Struggling a little. He is a bespoke tailor. But they cannot afford very grand premises. So, they do not have grand customers either. Herr Kleist is not a strong man and is much cast down at present. He was ..." Hartley broke off. Perhaps Caitlin did not know about the chaining up of a man on board The Yorkshire? She had been berthed at the other end of the boat. It would not be right to tell her.

"He was what ...?"

"Quite an important man once in his own country. One of the liberal revolutionaries."

"Oh." Caitlin didn't know anything about that. The only image it stirred was a vague memory of reading about France and its revolution one morning by an open window in a library.

"He finds his life here quite different," continued Hartley. "But his wife is a good, strong woman and will see him through. Then there was a young lad from your own country that I met. He was a fifteen-year-old orphan who was entirely alone. He joined a whaler, and I've not seen him since. But I would dearly love to know how he is faring."

"Oh yes!" said Caitlin. "How brave he must be! I wonder if his parents died in the famine. 'Tis the likely thing, you know. How hard it was on everyone."

Her eyes filled with tears as she said this, and she bent hurriedly to her work again so he should not see. She supposed she ought to tell him what had happened to Maeve, if not James. He must be wondering. But she could not bring herself to.

"How industrious you are!" said Hartley gently.

"Oh, it is only plain work. Nothing fancy or complicated. I hate it to tell the truth, but it occupies my hands and my mind."

She raised her eyes and found Hartley's grey ones looking seriously into her own with a sympathetic expression. *He* **understands**, she thought, and for one mad moment, wanted to fling herself weeping upon him and tell him how unhappy she was and ask him to take her away. Then she recovered herself. How absurd! She had been weeping so much of late. But this young man, though almost a stranger, was so tender in his approach that she felt confused. He looked at her as Owain had sometimes looked, but surely that must be her imagination?

"And you?" he asked. "Have you seen anyone from the boat?"

"Oh no. At least, there has been a letter. From a young Welshman aboard. Oh dear, you must not tell anyone, but he was a stowaway, and I sheltered him by letting him lay claim to the ticket made out for my father, who stayed in Liverpool."

"Indeed?" said Hartley. She blushed. Now, he would believe here to be a forward hussy, and no wonder in those cramped and awful conditions! "And what did the letter say?" Hartley yearned to know the worst.

"Oh, only that he has gone to work on the railroads upstate. I do not expect to see him again. He was a rough sort of young man."

"Ah!" Hartley recovered his good humour.

At that point, Mrs Regan entered and was severely surprised to find the visitors were unknown to her. She recovered herself when Polly explained, especially when Mr Ralph James was introduced, and made fresh attempts to be sociable. But it put an end to all private conversation. Hartley and Ralph soon said they must take their leave, which they did after Polly made them promise to call again.

It was the first of many visits. Frost nipped the leaves on the trees in Union Square into brightness shortly before they fell, and in time, the first snow fell. For a little while, the city was blanketed beautifully in white, and all sounds were muffled. Then the snow shovellers got to work, and the horsecars pounded the streets into dirty slush. The social life of the season swung on with visits to the theatre and the opera, house parties and card parties, and musical evenings. Throughout it all, Ralph and Hartley, although on the fringes of these social activities, came and went like two constant planets in a shower of flashing meteorites, sometimes invited and sometimes not, but always assured of a welcome from Polly. Hartley felt he was flying high into an impossible dream, but he didn't care as long as he could continue to see Caitlin and have her lay her hand on his, occasionally turning her eyes toward him.

One evening, after such a visit, when the girls were preparing for bed and brushing their hair together, Caitlin began to quiz Polly.

"Polly, do you like Ralph James?"

"Very much. He's intelligent and level-headed."

"As much as he likes you?"

"Ah!" said Polly, suddenly understanding the question, putting down her hairbrush. "I value him as a friend, Caitlin. But not in the way you mean. Anyway, he isn't interested in me in that way."

"You think not? He's very attentive."

"Oh, Cait, that's just his way! He would be surprised if he could hear you. He comes to keep his friend company and perhaps for a little diversion and conversation. But Hartley is the one who is serious ... about you!"

"I had not thought it," said Caitlin with a stiffness worthy of Mrs Regan. "Hartley is serious about everything. Especially about making his way in the world. I guess Hartley's God does not approve of merrymaking but only of making money."

"Oh, no!" cried Polly. "Cait, you are quite wrong! Hartley is terribly unsure of himself, so he can, at times, seem pompous. He does want very badly to elevate himself, that is true. But his heart is good, despite that. I think he is a little too hesitant and needs a push where other matters are concerned. Perhaps one day, you will unwittingly give him what he needs."

"What a strange idea!" said Caitlin. "I had not thought of it like that. He *is* a kind boy but too much of a stuffed shirt for me!"

Polly looked at her sharply. She sensed an added sophistication that had crept up on Caitlin through all those social engagements. Was that the case? Or was it merely Caitlin's repressed youth and gaiety emerging at long last? She mustn't be too hard on her.

Still, she could not help but say, "Caitlin, how can you? Hartley is worth twice as much as anyone else you have met in New York, and so is Ralph!"

"Perhaps. And your mother does approve heartily of Ralph!"

Polly sighed. "I'm sure Ralph would make a good and devoted husband. But as I told you before, I have no wish to marry."

"It's a shame."

"So is your opinion of Hartley!"

Caitlin became mischievous. "You seem to think a lot of Hartley! Perhaps you'd like to marry him?"

Polly was cross now. "To tell you the truth, if I were forced to marry, I would just as soon have Hartley Shawcross or Ralph James as anyone else. Far better than an O'Brien! Or worse! But the question doesn't arise. I'm not the marrying kind. Something will always make me hang back. But you're not like that."

"Oh, no?" said Caitlin, "I'm not allowed to have reservations, then?"

"Of course you are! Caitlin, whatever has got into you tonight?"

"Sure, and it's the devil! Didn't you know? But I suppose you're right. I do need someone to take care of me. Only not a Hartley Shawcross! I shan't marry for love, though. That died with James!"

Polly picked up Caitlin's hairbrush and began to smooth out her black locks thoughtfully. "You're far too young to say such a thing. So much of life is before you. I know you loved James. But he's gone, and time will heal. He wasn't even suitable for you. I hate to see you deceiving yourself. You're not giving yourself, nor Hartley, a chance. Can't you give him even a little love?"

It was Caitlin who was angry now. "You don't know anything about it!" she cried. "You who've never been in love. What do you know?"

Polly fell quiet so Caitlin could see she'd hurt her and burst into tears.

"I'm sorry, Polly!" she cried. "I'm so confused. Please forgive me for speaking to you like that!"

They were in each other's arms in a moment. "Me too," said Polly, humbly." I spoke out of turn, too."

They parted the best of friends again, but Polly was left with much to worry her, whilst Caitlin, unconvinced, decided she must try to foster Polly's own relationship with Hartley or Ralph if she could.

Chapter Six

A few days before Christmas, Hartley walked home from the shipping offices as usual. It was bitterly cold, just as Ralph had told him it would be. The streets were still full of life, but figures muffled up to their ears hurried past with a renewed necessity to keep on the move, and the pedlars stamped their feet and shifted about restlessly to keep their blood flowing. It was getting dark, and the gas was already lit. Inevitably, Hartley thought of Christmas in Bradford and had to stifle a small stab of regret. He had much to be grateful for now that his first six months in America were drawing to a close. For he had already achieved a small promotion in his office work, and von Blumen continued to teach him many things. Life was comfortable if lowly at the Kleists, and above all, he had become a friend of Ralph James, Polly Regan and Caitlin. He had a small dinner to look forward to in the next few days at the Regan's. And, of course, he was in love.

As he turned his street corner, smiling to himself at all this, a slight figure muffled up and cloaked against the wintry air, staggered into his side and bounced off again like an India rubber ball.

"Hey!" shouted Hartley. "Watch where you're going, can't you?" But his spirits were too high to sound over-censorious. The youth, for such it must be from his lack of height, made a mock bow and disappeared round the corner into a flurry of snowflakes that had begun to tumble down.

It was not until Hartley reached for his key, realizing that Herr Kleist had shut up shop early, that he discovered with anguish that his wallet was gone and his newly collected pay with it. There was no one in sight now. The street had emptied miraculously as if in a dream. Only the new snow continued to fall like shoals of tiny silver fishes under the streetlamps. Sick at heart and cursing himself for a fool, he turned his attention to opening the Kleists' door. After a struggle with gloves and pockets with stiff, numb fingers, he had the key in the lock when the sound of low laughter from behind disturbed him again. Swinging around, he saw the muffled form of the person who had charged into him intentionally, as he now realized. But he gasped as he saw the creature extend a hand with his wallet in it.

"Are ye looking for this?" a far-off but strangely familiar voice asked playfully.

Hartley nodded, mystified.

"Too bad, Mr Shawcross. Y'oughta be more careful and not be after mooning along!"

Hartley grabbed the wallet and began checking inside to see if the money was still there, which, incredibly, it was. Then he realized his tormentor had not bolted, and catching him by the shoulder, he propelled him roughly into the shop.

"Explain yourself!" Hartley demanded. "Before I call the police! What sort of a trick were you playing?"

Friedrich Kleist looked up from his stitching in surprise and, uncrossing his legs, rose to his feet and brought the lamp over as the spry figure calmly unwound layers of scarves from his face, like one dirty bandage after another.

Hartley exclaimed in loud astonishment. "Tim!" he cried with genuine joy. "It's Tim! Well, I never! Little Tim O'Reilly home from the whalers." He clapped Tim on the back in relief.

As Tim laughed and nodded, Hartley dispatched Herr Kleist to fetch his wife so that she might see the miraculous arrival. Then, whilst they were alone, he spoke in a more serious undertone.

"But stay, Tim! You shouldn't have done that! You shouldn't have taken my wallet!"

"Twas only a joke!" The impish face of the boy grinned up at him, though Hartley fancied something had changed ... some of the innocence was gone, and his mouth was a little harder and grimmer around the lips.

"Tell me the truth, Tim. That's not how you earn your living now, is it?"

"Sure, and 'tis not!" Tim was scornful. "But there's plenty of lads too young to go to sea who do! So let it teach you a lesson, Mr Hartley Shawcross, not to keep your valuables in the pockets of your outer clothing like the great big babby you are!"

"I shall never do so again, you young rascal!" Although Hartley's tone was good-humoured again, he still felt uncertain. If he had to state an opinion, he would have said that Tim had behaved like a professional pickpocket rather than an amateur. He hadn't felt his wallet go. But perhaps he was merely being sensitive because his pride had been bruised.

Then Rosa and the boys were amongst them, all exclaiming in delight and asking Tim far more questions than he could possibly answer at once. Of course, he would stay over Christmas. He could sleep on some bedding on Hartley's floor. It would be a palace after the ship's quarters! Of course, Mr Shawcross wouldn't mind. Rosa would set another place for dinner at once.

He regaled them with stories over the meal until the dark eyes of the little Kleist boys grew perfectly round with wonder and admiration. All summer and autumn, he had been on the whalers as a cabin boy, and he had tales to tell of wild and stormy seas, of hard men and bloody battles with harpoons and nets that sometimes resulted in the landing of whales big enough to overturn any ship with a flick of their tail. Much of this Hartley put down to Irish exaggeration and the natural desire to impress his old companions back on land. Yet, no doubt some of it was true. At any rate, when Rosa asked if he would be going back, his reply was revealing. No, he admitted. It was a grand life for a boy and had made a man of him. He'd recommend it to anyone with a taste for the adventurous life of the sea. There was nothing like it. But perhaps after a few months one did begin to long for other things. It was hard and cold and always wet. He fancied a bit of shore life now to spend the money he'd earned.

Hartley met Rosa's eye above Tim's red, curly head, and she gave him an almost imperceptible nod. He smiled. Rosa was not deceived, and neither was he. Let the lad swagger and run on as much as he liked.

Friedrich was somewhat bemused. Like so many things about their voyage, he had almost forgotten Tim, which was not surprising and, indeed, perhaps a blessing.

"Will you stay on to get work in New York?" asked Rosa as she cleared the dishes.

But no, that wasn't for Tim either. After his experience in the street, Hartley was relieved to hear it. Tim had decided to join one of the canal boats on the Erie. After the whalers, it would be an easier, gentler way of life, and he would be able to come back and visit New York whenever he felt like it.

Later on, in Hartley's room, Tim produced a bottle of whisky from his belongings, and over the shared drink, he indicated a willingness to talk some more about his future.

"I've got something to show you," he said. "You're one of the few honest men on God's earth, I reckon, and I want your advice on what to do with it." Carefully, he unwrapped a small bundle of cloth, and Hartley heard the unmistakable clink of coins against each other. "Count them," said Tim proudly. Hartley moved the candle closer to see.

"They're Dutch florins."

"Yes. It's still good money, though, isn't it?"

"Of course. I don't know exactly how much in dollars, but it's a considerable sum." Hartley fell into an uncomfortable silence.

"Well?" Tim prompted him.

"That isn't your pay from the whalers. You could never have earned that as a cabin boy, nor even a regular seaman."

"I'd be going back again if it was."

"Did you steal it, Tim?"

Tim laughed. "Cross my heart, no! I must ha' given you a terrible shock back there in the street."

"Then how did you get it?"

"One of the sailors gave it to me."

"He *gave* it to you?"

"Sure, and that's what I said! Afore he died, you see, in secret like. He'd gotten awful fond of me. Took a real fancy to me. He liked young boys, you see. A lot."

Hartley was silent for a long time. He was not at all happy about this. "All right," he said eventually. "It's your money, so you claim."

"Honestly gained, Mr Shawcross. I swear it."

"Then I don't wish to know anymore."

Tim thrust it back into the bundle and tied it up again. "What I want to know," he said, "is what to do with it. I thought it'd maybe be enough to buy a canal boat of my own."

Hartley considered. "No doubt it would be."

"So, do you think that would be the best thing?"

"It depends."

"God bless your carefulness, Mr Shawcross! But what do you mean by that?"

"If your main ambition is to own your own boat and be master of it, then it seems like a good idea. But what about the future, Tim? Once the railroad is built, the canal won't carry the same amount of cargo and certainly not passengers. Get yourself a job on the canal but invest this money in something else ... a railroad company perhaps ... then you'll have it to fall back on. It's too much to squander. The ... fortune ... of having it come your way will not happen again, I hope."

Tim grinned at him, well-satisfied with the advice and unabashed at the implied disapproval. "I knew you were the right man to ask! You talk good sense. Will you see to it for me? I don't mind giving you a share or two for the good advice."

"Of course, I'll fix it up for you, Tim. But I shan't take anything from you. It's your money, and it wouldn't be right. And I'm afraid I don't like the way I think it fell to you."

Tim shrugged. "Suit yourself. But have another tot then."

Hartley accepted, still feeling uneasy. He did not feel comfortable with this new Tim. The old Tim had been a rascal certainly, cheeky, and pert, yet not as worldly-wise as he made out. There was no doubt who this new Tim was. It seemed as if he was the first casualty of America, though Hartley knew that was unfair. The boy had been in no-man's land, out on the wildest waters of life and not a part of any country. He wished he could have stopped him from going on the whalers, even though it had brought him this fortune.

"So," Tim said, lighting up a clay pipe. "How goes it with you, Mr Shawcross?"

Hartley told him briefly, though he did not mention Caitlin. For some reason he was unsure of, he preferred to keep that knowledge to himself.

"Well done. A man like you should go far."

Hartley would have liked to agree with this judgement, yet he read a line of doubt in Tim's older mouth. Confound it! The boy didn't know all the answers.

"I see you're still tied to the good Frau Kleist's apron strings," Tim carried on. This remark stung Hartley to the quick.

"Nothing wrong with that," he countered a little too sharply. "It made good sense to share rooms with New York prices the way they are. Anyway, she's an excellent landlady."

"To be sure she is." Tim puffed smoke into his face. "Well, I guess I'll be turning in now. It's a mercy to be able to sleep all night, I can tell you." The pipe and the candle were both put out, and they lay in the dark. Tim was soon off, snoring lightly on the floor, but Hartley lay awake for a long time, annoyed with himself and with Tim. Change was all very well if it was for good. Only sometimes, it was not.

Chapter Seven

When Hartley arrived ten minutes early at the Regans, Caitlin was still dressing but Polly received him in the drawing-room. He apologized bashfully for his lack of expertise in arriving at the given time and did not add he had been walking round Union Square for the last half-hour. Polly however was not the person to make him feel awkward or embarrassed, and she soon put him at his ease with a few well-chosen questions as to his welfare and business concerns. He could not help but like Polly — no-one could — and soon he was speaking freely, telling her about Tim's reappearance and some of his anxieties about the boy. Polly tended to the view that regular employment would soon settle him down and keep him out of trouble. But then she always persisted in thinking the best of people.

Ralph arrived punctually - as the very clocks were striking the half-hour. He had brought a pretty nosegay of artificial flowers for both girls and Hartley felt his own small gift for Caitlin take root in his pocket, with the sudden embarrassment of realizing he had nothing for Polly. How could he have been so thoughtless? His neck went hot with shame. Perhaps Caitlin would not like his trinket anyway. He realized he could not give it to her now, and this, in its way, was a relief.

A trickle of other guests arrived. They were to be a small party of twelve, most of them friends of the senior Regans and Hartley felt very sensible of the honour Polly had done them in the invitation. It seemed that he and Ralph were special friends. He was grateful that the noisy O'Briens were not there. As he watched Ralph being agreeable to Polly, he reflected that Ralph had every right to pursue young ladies with his prospects whereas he, Hartley, with an uncertain future and no capital, certainly had not. He admired Ralph's easy manner and natural confidence with a twinge of jealousy. Ralph was not handsome in a conventional way but his slim body and face, framed by wavy, brown hair, carried a seal of likeability in its friendliness.

The Regans' drawing-room was now crowded with bright crinolines like overblown flowers amongst the sombre frockcoats and starched white shirtfronts of the men and was full of the buzz of idle chatter. Mrs Regan was there, smiling overall like a benevolent but stately goddess, and so, belatedly, was Thaddeus. But where was Caitlin? Then at last the door opened and she entered. Hartley was struck dumb with admiration.

Standing there, a pale and perfect figure with a tiny waist he could have encircled with his two hands, dressed in shot pink silk off the shoulder, her beauty impaled him. Her shoulders were remarkably formed, and her black hair shone like silk itself. Only her eyes looked strained and held a suspicion of dampness. Why wasn't she happy? Hartley longed to know and to assuage that pain. In a moment, he was by her side, moving as though the drawing-room were empty and as if the rest of the world did not exist.

But Ralph and Polly were there too and although Caitlin rested her eyes in a friendly way on his and returned his greeting, it was Ralph's flowers she exclaimed over, and she left Hartley with Polly. She had never done such a thing before nor given any intimation that she preferred Ralph to him. Polly followed his eyes sympathetically.

"You love her very much, don't you?" she asked in a low voice. Hartley recovered himself and allowed Polly to lead him into a quiet corner.

"Is it so obvious?"

"It is to me."

"Will you help me, Polly?"

"In any way I can."

Hartley sighed. "But I cannot speak to her," he said. "I have nothing to offer."

"Caitlin might expect far less than you imagine. She was used to little enough before she came here, and she needs someone's love very badly. Though she needs to grow up some more to recognize when love is worthy."

"She always seems so unhappy."

"It is because she lost all those dear to her back home, her parents, her guardian and uncle, her half-sister. Especially the uncle. But it will pass ... if only Mamma will give her time."

"Mrs Regan is impatient with her?"

"I had not meant to speak of it. But sometimes, I think she makes Caitlin feel ill at ease. Please do not mention it to anyone else."

"Of course not. Tell me, would I be permitted to send you both a small gift in my gratitude for your befriending us?"

"Yes, Hartley, of course. But send it to Caitlin, not to me! Come, we go into supper, and I shall contrive so you sit next to her."

However, Caitlin was capable of contrivance, too, and managed to seat Hartley next to Polly whilst she sat opposite with Ralph. It hardly mattered - they had all become quite intimate with one another, but Hartley was hurt to see it and did not understand why.

During the meal, Caitlin seemed very pensive and fell silent for long periods. Then Hartley remembered what Polly had said about her losing all her dear ones and needing time to recover. But he felt there was something else troubling her tonight. Once and once only, he managed to stir their old feeling of comradeship and light her face up like a glowing candle. He had been talking about the hardships of life at sea and how wonderful it had been to hear real birdsong again on landing instead of all the gulls' mournful cries.

"Ah, yes!" said Caitlin. "I remember that. But the birdsong here is not like it is in the old country. Do you remember, Mr Shawcross? How I miss it, for in the city, although there are birds, they seem to be drowned out by other noises and cannot be heard singing as loudly or sweetly as in the country."

Then she relapsed into silence again. She knew she was scarcely being sociable. But she was full of a new inner discord. On her way downstairs, she had chanced to pause for a moment on the landing to secure an awkward brooch, when a voice had hailed her through an open door. She was startled until she realized she had stopped outside the room that Thaddeus Regan used as his study. She had entered it innocently.

"Did you need anything, Mr Regan?" She believed her relations with her benefactor were excellent and always attended to what he said in the manner of a respectful daughter or niece. He never made her feel a burden in the way that Mrs Regan did. Her livelihood depended upon him in the end, and she was grateful for it. He had replaced James as her guardian. There, of course, the comparison ended. He did not look nor speak like James, nor was he anything like the same kind of man. Indeed, he was often over-hearty and coarse, though generally kind enough. But tonight, his big face was flushed and bloated. He sat at his desk in evening dress but was surrounded by a mess of papers and a half-empty bottle of whisky whilst the room stank of cigars.

"Come in, Caitlin. Close the door for a moment." She did as he asked.

The room was small and redolent with dark colours and masculinity. Oppressively so, thought Caitlin, who had never seen it before.

"I need to be reminded ..." Thaddeus said, his eyes fixed on her bare shoulders and neck. "How pretty you look in that pink dress!"

"Do I remind you of someone, Sir," asked Caitlin nervously.

Thaddeus rose to his feet and made his way heavily toward her. She realized with a sense of alarm that he was very drunk. He walked all the way around her to study her from every angle. Then he came so close that she could smell the liquor on his breath. His skin under the bristling beard and side whiskers was very red. She drew back, but he stepped nearer.

"Don't move! I want to see you close."

"I'm sorry, sir, but I'm afraid you'll crush my skirt."

Taking no notice, he went on. "You remind me of what I work for, Caitlin." She coloured up with deep embarrassment.

"No, no ... there's no need to blush and posture and apologize! You needn't be afraid. Don't you know I would rather work to keep you pretty than for that stiff bitch and her saintly daughter downstairs? I would, you know ..."

Caitlin's cheeks flamed. These were terrible words, unbelievably awful.

Thaddeus put out his hand and touched her cheek. She dared not move. "I don't ask for much, Caitlin, believe me. Just the odd word, the merest gesture, the constant sight of you...an occasional kiss." His enormous face floated nearer.

"Just one, Caitlin. Just one." His breath was in her face, his wet, blubbering lips close to her own. They pressed down on her. She pushed him away, trembling with fright. He reeled against his desk and scattered some papers to the floor, looking angry and surprised.

"Sir," said Caitlin, her voice and body shaking. "You forget yourself!"

But he mocked her. "You too, my little Irish emigré from the bogs, you too!"

Her temper flared then. "I am here because I had no choice!" she cried. "Believe me, I have been grateful. But I shall leave tomorrow."

Thaddeus pulled himself together. "Come now," he said. "Perhaps too much has been said. How can you go out onto the streets with no money and no home? I would never allow it. Now I know I have overstepped the mark. Forgive me, and I promise it shall not happen again. Let us speak no more of it." He would have comforted her had she let him, but she took herself out of the room with a sob and a fetching symphony of ruffled pink silk and layered petticoats.

She could not go downstairs directly. Instead, she sought the privacy of her own room and flung herself on the bed. She could not believe what Thaddeus had done, nor what he wanted to do! Was it merely the madness of an unguarded moment? No, she didn't think so. How could he? She took deep breaths.

When the first storm of her anger was vented, she went and sat before her dressing table, pulled out all the pins that secured her hair, and looked in the mirror. Had she the power to drive men to this kind of behaviour then? It was a formidable thought. But she didn't want it. It made her position in this house very precarious indeed. Well, she would not go down. Let them come to find her and see what was wrong. What would Mrs Regan say then? Nevertheless, her composure crumbled when she thought of Polly. How would she feel? Sadly, she began to repair the damage done to her hair.

But she must leave this house. If not tomorrow, then soon. Somehow, she must earn her own living. She did not think she could bear to look Constance Regan in the eye again. Yet how could she explain, and what could she do? She thought of James, and a flood of new tears came. Oh, if only he had known, he would never have sent her here! He had told her she knew nothing of the world, and she now saw he was right.

It was some time before she felt ready to go downstairs as she must. Composed at last but shaken, she made the journey bravely and this time was undisturbed. She remembered she had determined to leave Hartley alone with Polly as often as she could and set about the task, thereby unconsciously spurning poor Hartley and it was in such a turbulent mood that she sat down to dinner.

≈

The following day, there was a special delivery at No. 24, Union Square Place, for the Misses Murphy and Regan. The young ladies had been sitting in the morning room, idly discussing the supper party of the night before. Or at least Polly was. Caitlin seemed rather preoccupied. But Polly put this down to Caitlin's habitual lowness of mood in the mornings. She felt the evening had been a singular success and knew as surely as if she had been told that this delivery was Hartley's tentatively proffered gift. It was an oddly shaped parcel and, once opened, began to trill, and sing. Polly clapped her hands together and laughed with delight.

"It's a canary!" she said. "A canary in such a pretty birdcage from Hartley. Do look, Caitlin."

"How typical of a man," said Caitlin, who was still thinking of Thaddeus. "To want to imprison such a pretty thing."

"Oh, Cait!" cried Polly. "Don't say that. Do look!"

Caitlin grudgingly came over to examine their gift.

"Don't you like it, Cait?" asked Polly enthusiastically.

"Yes, it is very pretty. But I should like to free it from its cage."

"No! You must not. It is a tropical bird and quite tame. It would never survive in New York."

"I suppose not," said Caitlin.

"Well, then, don't you think it's wonderful?"

"I suppose so. But how typical of Hartley to send a bird in a cage."

"It's like his love for you," said Polly quietly. "He can't set it free by expressing it yet. And have you forgotten why he sent it?"

"Why?" asked Caitlin miserably.

"Don't you remember your conversation about the birdsong and how much you missed it?"

"Oh yes, of course." For a moment, Caitlin was touched. "I remember now. Yes, it was kind of him. But only a stuffed shirt would send a bird in a cage." She was half joking, but Polly was cross with her.

"Very well, Miss Murphy," she said. "You can be as deprecating as you like. But I predict the day will come when you need Hartley Shawcross and will be glad if you are fortunate enough to have him!"

≈

Christmas at the Kleists was surprisingly pleasant for Hartley. He had not imagined they would even note its passing being Jewish. But Rosa, like her father before her, although Jewish by birth, was very much in touch with the world and its ways and did not want to disappoint Hartley. She decorated the house with greenery and lit more candles than they needed. Everyone was dressed in their best, and though the table was full of Jewish delicacies and sweetmeats, Rosa had also cooked a small goose.

Best of all, Friedrich Kleist seemed to come alive. Hartley had always found it difficult to talk to him before. It was not that he didn't want to, although he had to confess that the memory of that wild night on the ship still lingered at the back of his mind. But Friedrich seemed to live in a world of his own. He did not start conversations, and although he answered questions and addressed himself to idle remarks, it could hardly be said that he continued them either. Still, the second hand side of the shop was doing well now, and he had bought Rosa an old pianoforte, which was delivered a day or two ago and fitted into their room somehow.

With a little encouragement, she played for them — at first stumblingly, but then with greater confidence — German melodies and lullabies, then some Bach, Beethoven and Mozart. They all sat in a circle and listened, warm from the heat of the stove and replete with food and wine, as Rosa's plump arms and fingers hesitated, then rippled over the keyboard.

Friedrich, who had earlier uncorked the wine and served at the table, having played games all morning with the children, listened with a glow on his face as if to say, "Ah yes, this is what life is about." Afterwards, he talked to Hartley over cigars about art, music, and science and showed an amazing breadth of knowledge and depth of understanding. No wonder the poor man found it difficult to address himself to the drudgery of alterations on second-hand clothing every day. When Hartley raised his head, he caught Rosa looking at them both with a flush on her face and a new light in her eyes. ***You see,*** it said triumphantly, ***you see now how this man can be!***

Later, Ralph called in, as he had promised he would, and had them all laughing and gay again in minutes. He duly admired the piano and made Rosa play again for him. Then they found some tunes that Rosa could play, and he could sing them, and they made a very entertaining evening of it. Ralph sang well and had a fine tenor voice. Little by little, the others were tempted to join in, and they became quite merry and toasted their new life in America several times.

It was late when Ralph finally left, and they all turned in. The children had been nodding their heads for ages but were determined to stay awake. Hartley and Tim left the Kleists to their own affairs and repaired to their own room, which looked more like a draper's shop every day. Hartley wondered if it was time to move on. He must be an inconvenience to the Kleists now that they were settling down, although he knew his money was a great help.

Perhaps after Tim had gone to the canal boats, he should think about it though it was pleasant to feel like part of the family.

He wondered if he should ever have one of his own. In his breast pocket, he had a note from Caitlin, at least from Caitlin and Polly, though he knew it was Polly's hand which had written it, thanking him for his delightful gift. He fingered it with regret.

Tim, possibly inspired by the evening's entertainment, was playing a melancholy air on his old mouth organ.

"What do you hope for most in America, Tim?" asked Hartley, taking off his boots.

But Tim was not given to reflections of that nature. He merely shrugged and carried on with his playing. When he had finished, and Hartley thought he had forgotten all about the question, he wiped his mouth organ and finally spoke.

"Freedom, I guess. To do what I want when I want with no one tellin' me what to do."

"Is that all?"

"I reckon."

"Don't you want to be a rich man, too?" asked Hartley, remembering the railroad shares.

"Maybe. That might be part of it."

"And what about girls, Tim? Don't you fancy one of your own someday?"

"Girls?" asked Tim, as if Hartley had mentioned another species. "I don't have much use for girls. They boss you around too much before you know where you are."

"Is that why you don't like Frau Kleist?"

"She has you all doing what she wants you to do."

"But it's what we want to do too."

"Maybe now, but not for always."

"Then that will change, and so will you, young man! You must admit you enjoyed having someone to cook your goose and bank up your stove and sing with you tonight."

"The secret is," said Tim solemnly, as if speaking to one much his junior. "In and out quick, before they start thinkin' it's permanent."

"Is that your advice to me then, Tim?" asked Hartley with a wry smile. But his companion was already asleep.

≈

Far, far away in the Northern Woods, Owain ate venison alone over a fire in a dugout. Outside, the world was silent, white, and still. Though not without life, for under the frost-stiffened branches of maple and spruce, there lay a tangle of tracks in the snow. That way had been field mice, rabbits, foxes, and deer. But Owain was on his own regarding humankind and was strangely content.

He had suffered the railroad all summer and much of the autumn, too. The work was hard, right enough, and sometimes dangerous, but he never complained. All his wages were saved. He earned a reputation for being a reserved young man who never drank, nor gambled, nor had any kind of fun. He did not want to become involved with them. They were a rough lot. If he was to earn money for his farm out west, he must stay out of trouble.

Sometimes, during a work break, his eyes would dwell on the distant hills. Not grand peaks but old, rounded mountains covered with trees. The Adirondacks, he heard they were called. They reminded him a little of Wales. Then, one day in early November, when the colours of autumn (such as he had never seen before) were all spent, and the leaves were off the trees, an odd thing happened. The branches of the maple had gone black, and the evergreens were slowly darkening too, whilst the mountains themselves suddenly appeared much closer, every fold and crevice thrown into relief. Owain saw the blue-grey peaks as if for the first time and knew he had to go there. It was as simple as that.

Getting there was a little more difficult. Firstly, he travelled back up the railhead towards Albany, then up to Glen Falls on Lake George. From there he got the stage to Warrensburg and North Creek. Then, finally, a buckboard wagon took him to Indian Lake Village. The ride over deeply rutted tracks jolted and jarred every muscle and bone in his body, but it was worth it, for he was now in the heart of the wilderness. Already, winter's coming was shown by a bladed wind across the lakes and snow flurries against grey skies.

In the store, he met Old Pete, a French-Canadian trapper who knew the woods like the back of his hand. It was he who showed him around, taught him how to survive, and set traps. The beavers were all gone now, but there were still marten, foxes, deer, and even bears. In the spring, he could take his hides down to the towns, and they would fetch a good price. In the meantime, he had to learn how to live. Old Pete was a good teacher but valued his privacy. He showed Owain trails, camps, and dugouts that others had left.

In the summer, this place could get real crowded with folks awantin' to fish or hunt deer and teams of lumberjacks coming in for the timber. But in the winter, well, that was a different story. Pete didn't mind taking him around for a few weeks to show him the ropes, but after that, he'd be strictly on his own. Maybe they might run into each other once in a while, and maybe not. But the store would have all the essentials he needed: rifle, shot, traps and wire for snares, axes and twine, oil, and furs. Food was to be had in the wild if you knew where to look for it.

Owain liked it. He knew that work would probably stop soon on the railhead anyway due to heavy snow. He had considered going back to New York to shovel city sidewalks and avenues like most of the others. That would have meant he could see Caitlin again. But then Pete told him one good bearskin would fetch eight to ten dollars at least. Why, that meant two of them would be well over a whole month's pay tracklaying! It seemed to make a whole lot of sense to stay here if he could stand the ice-cold and the loneliness and survive. For some reason, he revelled in it. He felt in touch with the earth at last. He still thought of Caitlin and the farm; the two had become inextricably mixed in his mind by now. But these lay in the future as an eventual goal.

Once kitted out in warm clothing, the snow and the ice seemed no problem. It was a fiercely white, crystalline world of beauty, bare and clean. There was no rest as good as that after being out on the trail all day. Better by far than breaking his back for the railroad foreman. He soon grew to know his new world and to love it. Of course, it would take a lifetime to know it completely like Old Pete did, but he had made a good start.

There was one other new skill he had to learn up here and now it began to come easy. This was how to kill: systematically and without anger, how to think his way into the head of the prey and hunt it down without mercy. Owain was a good learner. He did a lot of killing that winter.

Part Four

Troubles

Chapter One

It was the spring of 1851 when Cornelius O'Brien made his offer. For some time, the O'Brien brothers had been paying special court to the Regan household. The day before, Caitlin and Polly had enjoyed a drive out of the city in welcoming mild weather. Encouraged no doubt by the leafing out of trees, Cornelius had sought to hold Caitlin's hand. When she withdrew it, he chided her for her cruelty, so she let it be with a little shrug. She couldn't see it would do any harm and was enjoying herself after being trapped inside all winter long.

The waters of the Hudson shone blue in the distance, and all the greenery was pleasant to the eye. Seamus O'Brien was going to West Point soon to start the military training he had decided was for him. He couldn't wait. But his brother Cornelius was joining his father's bank. So, there wouldn't be many more days like these. It made Caitlin feel more friendly than usual.

Nevertheless, it came as something of a shock when she was called down to the drawing room the following morning by Constance Regan and saw Cornelius there, beaming all over his face, with his hat respectfully in his hand. Mrs Regan was beaming even more.

"I will withdraw, my dears," she said. "As I know that Cornelius wishes to see you alone, but I shall be close at hand if you need me for anything ..."

When she had gone, Cornelius spread his hands a little and laughed. "Well, dearest, after that, I am sure you can guess what I have to say!"

Dearest! Why was he calling her that? He never had before. Only Polly did that. She sat down and tried not to frown but said nothing, suddenly wary.

"I guess I've surprised you a little, after all?"

"You might have, to be sure, if you'd only say what you mean!"

Cornelius laughed again, not without good nature. "Why, I've come to ask for your hand in marriage." Caitlin was astonished and rose in agitated fashion.

"Oh, I know what you're going to say! I guess Polly's told you that I'm one for the ladies and not the marrying kind. Maybe that's how I used to be. It's good for a man to sew a few wild oats. But now I'll have a reg'lar income in joining the bank, it's kinda time to settle down, raise a family and all. And I sure can't think of a prettier girl I'd rather do it with!"

Caitlin saw that he was serious and knew she must treat him seriously in return. But it was no good. However convenient the match might be, she couldn't accept. Her heart wouldn't let her. She looked steadily at the marble clock on the mantelpiece, which kept perfect time as if it were really a Parisian piece and not an American fake.

Then, she began firmly, "Cornelius, I do like you."

"That's all I need to know! "

"No, it isn't! I do like you, but I don't think, in fact, I am quite sure I could never love you. It would never do."

He looked disappointed but not completely downcast. "You want to think about it? It's come in a bit of a rush, maybe."

"No, no. I have thought about it. I always make my mind up firmly before I speak. I cannot marry you."

"Maybe you didn't oughta make your mind up so fast," Cornelius pointed out. He was beginning to feel a little disgruntled as he had expected her to leap at the opportunity. "I can provide you with a steady income, as I said, a real nice home and some status as my wife".

"I know that, Cornelius, and I do appreciate the honour. But it's not enough."

"Not enough! You talking about love again? There's plenty of folks who get married without that. Most all of them, I'd say. It ain't like these novels women read. Love grows afterward."

She knew he was right. There would be advantages, not least of which would be her escape from the Regans. But when it came to it, she couldn't exchange one set of chains for another for the rest of her life.

"May I speak to you again about it?"

"No, Cornelius. I wish you wouldn't."

So, he took his hat and departed, much chastened by the result of the interview but not, as she noted wryly, entirely broken hearted. It confirmed her in her decision. She fled up to Polly's room to avoid Mrs Regan. Polly answered her knock and immediately read the news in her face.

"He's asked you!" she declared.

Caitlin nodded.

"And you refused him, of course?"

"Bless you, Polly!" Caitlin heaved a great sigh of relief. "I did, too. But your mother will be furious."

"Yes, but never you mind. It isn't her who'd be marrying him!"

"But I suppose it would have been a good match. Oh dear, what is she going to say?"

"Come now, Caitlin, you followed your heart and not your head?"

"I did."

"Then you have nothing to be ashamed of. It is true you would have been comfortably off for the rest of your life. But shall I tell you what would have happened? Within a couple of years, he would have several mistresses, and you would not be happy despite all your comforts. Come, let us face Mamma together to tell her the terrible news!"

But Mrs Regan had already heard it from young Mr O'Brien himself on the way out. Although she was generally made of sterner stuff, she retired to the morning room and resorted to smelling salts. When Polly and Caitlin entered, she looked up with an injured sniff.

"Well, Caitlin, what on earth do you have to say for yourself?"

"I'm sorry, Mrs Regan."

"Sorry! I should think you are after all I've done for you, introducing you to the best circles, taking you here, there, and everywhere; fitting you out, speaking generously of you, accepting you as my own daughter ...." She was more than furious; she was beside herself. Caitlin winced at each condemnatory phrase. Polly was more robust, however.

"Mamma, Caitlin does not love Mr O'Brien, and that is that. It has nothing to do with what we may or may not have done for her. I am sure she is not ungrateful and did not mean to distress you. But it really can't be helped!"

"And indeed, I am very grateful to you, Mrs Regan."

Constance was not mollified. "I think you should consider the matter some more. It would have been a brilliant match for you. I would have approved it even for Polly. You will never get such a chance again. Never. Do you understand? You have nothing, after all."

Caitlin flinched and bent her head at the angry words.

"You must have given him a deal of encouragement, too, for him to make you such an offer."

"Indeed, she did not, Mamma. I can vouch for that. They never had any private interviews or anything of that nature. Cornelius O'Brien is always over-sure of himself. It will do him good if he is more careful over such matters in the future."

"I cannot think what to do now," said poor Mrs Regan. "Did you say he could speak to you again on the matter?"

Caitlin shook her head. "I asked him not to."

"Then what can we do?"

"Why must we do anything, Mamma? There is nothing to be done."

Caitlin could see the difficulty. She cleared her throat. "Mrs Regan, I am truly sorry. I know I must be a worry to you and a burden, no doubt. But I cannot marry Cornelius O'Brien. It would not make me happy."

"Happy," repeated Mrs Regan bitterly. "You girls are so short-sighted with your talk of 'happiness'. You understand nothing of the world. Who is happy?"

" I have no wish to be a burden on you forever," Caitlin added with more determination. "I can see how difficult it must be for you. I wonder if I could take up some form of employment?"

Mrs Regan sniffed again. She was not impressed. "Employment, my child? What could you do? You do not have the education for a governess. I cannot possibly send you into service or out on the streets as a common shopgirl after introducing you to society. Whatever would our friends say?"

"I thought perhaps I could sew."

Mrs Regan thought it over. "It's not such a bad idea," she said suddenly.

"Mamma!"

"Naturally, I'm not thinking of some smelly little shop, Polly. But there is Madame Arlott. Perhaps I could speak to her, and she could train Caitlin as her assistant."

Madame Arlott was the mantua maker or dressmaker who called in at the Regans before the beginning of each new season to suggest alterations and improvements and make up new gowns. She was a highly competent lady who had her own thriving business and was in great demand, being accepted into the most gracious of households, almost as a friend.

Mrs Regan began to feel more enthusiastic. Caitlin might well build up her own fashionable clientele once trained to Madame Arlott's requirements. It might be the making of her. Indeed, it would open more doors, not less. She could become a respected confidante of the New York ladies, and there was no doubt she would marry eventually, with her good looks — not quite as well as the O'Briens perhaps — but she could not expect that now. If this was what the girl preferred, why then no one could blame Constance Regan for that. There was no doubt it would be easier to marry Polly with Caitlin off the social scene.

"Yes," said Mrs Regan, assimilating all these points in an instant, "I could speak to Madame if you wished it, my dear."

"I think I do."

"Very well. Of course, you are welcome to remain in this house as part of the family for the time being. But I see no reason why you should not earn your own keep in a genteel profession if you have a mind to it and no taste for another kind of life. To tell the truth, it would help matters somewhat ...."

"Then I must do the same," cried Polly immediately. "How much better it would be!"

"Don't be ridiculous, my dear!"

" I could give piano lessons or drawing lessons!"

"No," said Mrs Regan, firmly. "I have not entirely given up hope of you yet, Polly, despite your lack of savoir-faire. Now you must leave me, girls! You have made me quite exhausted, and I have plans to make."

That night, Caitlin sat before the mirror of her dressing table for a long time, brushing her hair and staring at her reflection.

"I know I have done right," she said to herself. Now, she could hold up her head with some pride before Thaddeus Regan and Cornelius O'Brien. It was only natural that, inside of her, there should flutter some misgivings.

≈

Madame Arlott was not French though she endeavoured to sound as if she was. Neither was there a Monsieur Arlott, so far as Caitlin could tell. Her name lent a certain chic to her business and authorized her to talk about the latest European fashions with apparent confidence.

She was a small, dark woman who always wore black to perpetuate the myth and had polished talons for fingernails. She might have been considered handsome by some, but her features, though regular, were a trifle sharp and her eyes cold, whilst her mouth generally bristled with pins.

She agreed to take on Caitlin as her assistant in deference to Mrs Regan's wishes, not without conveying the impression that she made this a great exception to her general rules and reiterating she could not promise, "ow it would turn out." But she assured Mrs Regan she would train Miss Murphy up to the highest standards if the girl showed any aptitude and left Constance well satisfied. Madame Arlott had an impressive batch of clients from Broadway to Fifth Avenue and was excellent at her work. She kept her promise by taking Caitlin with her to measure the well-stuffed bosoms and tightly laced waists of families old and new alike, their only common factor being the material success reflected in their addresses.

The first two weeks passed pleasantly enough. Caitlin was determined to try her hardest to be a good pupil. Madame Arlott respected Mrs Regan, or at any rate respected her custom, and was resolved to be encouraging. Only at first, Caitlin did no real work at all. She accompanied Madame Arlott on her daily rounds visiting this house and that, taking tea with the ladies concerned, listening to their interminable needs, and looking at whatever length of unsuitable material they had bought at Stewarts'. She admired Madame Arlott's tact, watched her swathe and pin, nodding her precise, dark head as if she knew exactly what the young or old lady in question wanted. Sometimes, she would produce fashion drawings, and everyone would pore over them at great length. There was always a great deal of discussion, and decisions seemed almost impossible to make — indeed, they would not have been made at all without Madame Arlott's guidance and strength of character. Of course, skirts must be full and ever fuller in accordance with the fashion, necessitating great hoops and wads of underwear. The shape of sleeves was a trifle more difficult whilst, when it came to considerations of trimming and lace and borders, full rein could be given to a lady's flights of fancy.

Caitlin tried her hardest to pay attention and give due weight and gravity to each tiny matter, but she could not help feeling in her heart that these elegant ladies had far too little to do. This was surely not what the world was about. She supposed these peccadilloes were reasonable anxieties for each young unmarried lady in view of the fact they must look their best to gain a husband, but for the dowagers to prevaricate and ponder as much as they did seem plain cussed.

For the first time, she began to appreciate Polly's views and became aware of how much her friend had influenced her for the better. Of course, she was vainer than Polly and had definite ideas about style herself of late, but she would not have had the patience or the silliness to agonize in such overwhelming detail as these customers. Could she ever learn to be as forbearing and patient as Madame Arlott appeared to be?

After these tedious processes, enlivened only by the gossip of the day, the dressmaker would bear away the material to her workshop and pore over measurements and drawings, making sketches of her own on paper before cutting out the precious cloth. This was a skilful matter. Caitlin watched and felt daunted. Her own sewing was rudimentary in contrast and lacked creativity. Clearly, she had a lot to learn. The pieces of cloth would then go into the workshop, where girls of various grades made up the garment in its various stages, ready for Madame Arlott to add the final touches.

"I am afraid you 'ave to start with the others soon," said Madame Arlott. "Little by little, you must learn to do everything. You 'ave to know it all, and start at the 'ow you say, the bottom? "

Caitlin duly and literally started at the bottom. The lowliest task was hemming, which was also the most time-consuming. Madame Arlott's workshop was a big contrast to the elegant salons they had visited. Here, girls worked long hours for a pittance in a poorly lit, inadequately ventilated room half the size of most drawing rooms. There never was such a cruel fashion as the crinoline, thought Caitlin despairingly, not for those who wore them, but for those who sat sewing by hand and had to hem yard upon yard of material which must be bolstered by five layers of petticoats beneath, all equally voluminous. Her first week in the workshop left her much chastened with aching eyes and sore fingers.

She reminded herself this was only the lowliest task. She had to start here but would surely not be long at it. Madame took a special interest in her, thanks to Mrs Regan. Soon, she would be able to do more interesting work. At least she was earning her own keep. But when she received her wages at the end of the interminable week, she thought with disappointment how little it really was.

≈

For the Kleists, it was moving day again. Every day in New York was moving day, if not on and up, then on and out. For the Kleists, it was scarcely into Broadway but out of the Lower East Side into a new shop, with a couple of rooms above and their name painted on the door.

Hartley was moving, too, but not with the Kleists. It was time for him to go his own way, and he had chosen a room in a seemingly respectable boarding house in a better area. More expensive, of course, but more fitting for a young man who was going places. Still, it wasn't the same, and he couldn't help but feel a little sad.

Rosa was full of optimism as they piled their belongings onto the hired cart. Hartley was helping Friedrich who seemed uncertain now, though he had wanted this move and worked hard for it. It meant he might get some real tailoring at last. The boys were excited at the thought of their new home where they would have more space. Little Rachel toddled about without any concern, getting in everyone's way. She was growing into a pretty little girl with a sunny nature, and everyone loved her, including Hartley.

"Ayup!" he said, catching her out of the way of the feet of the oldest boy, Johann, who was staggering under the weight of a pile of blankets towards the cart. Hartley took her to see the horse who was snuffling in his nosebag but raised his solemn head to inspect the newcomer with patient eyes and nostrils that snorted and quivered and blew bits of hay at her. She shrieked with delight and felt his strong nose tentatively.

At last, they were ready, and Hartley gave Rachel up into Rosa's lap next to the driver. He walked behind with Friedrich whilst the boys rode atop the cart, holding onto chairs and table legs as they rocked and swayed through the noisy, crowded streets, complete with boxes and beds and Rosa's piano, pots, and pans, and what seemed like a vast amount of clothing and material. Hartley stayed to help until they had unloaded at the other end and then bade his farewell with mixed feelings. They all stood round him in a tight little circle that was suddenly solemn. Friedrich clasped his hand and clapped him on the shoulder in a heartfelt manner, and Rosa made him promise to come and visit them often.

"Especially if they do not feed you well at this boarding-house," she said. She seemed to have formed a profound distrust and suspicion of the place already. "Our door will always be open to you!"

Hartley thanked her warmly and felt a little embarrassed at her answering embrace. Then, quickly, before he could show any inappropriate emotion, he left them to sort out their new home.

≈

Caitlin spent a quiet, sweaty summer hemming petticoats and skirts in Madame Arlott's workshop. She had begun to hate the place. It was so close, airless, and shut away from the outside world. The chairs were hard and there was no room to move about with all the material and thread, scissors, tapes, needles, and pins everywhere. She soon found out she was not as good at sewing as she had imagined. To do a little mending and simple needlepoint was one thing; to hem yard upon yard of slippery silk or muslin for hour after hour was quite another. She was not as quick or nimble as the other girls, and if she tried to be, she often went wrong and ended up with perverse tucks in the material, which would not disappear and, therefore, had to come out.

She could have borne it better had the other girls been more friendly, but they were rather hard on her, immediately sensing she was supposed to be Madame's special protégée. She couldn't really blame them when they toiled away without any such hope of promotion. They knew that she came from a superior home and resented it, though she had never shown any superiority. Mostly, they ignored her.

Madame Arlott seemed to have forgotten about Caitlin, too. There were no more social visits together. Occasionally, Madame would whisk in to look over the work in progress. She would stand awhile and tut-tut over Caitlin's efforts. Sometimes, she would pick it up with her bright fingernails and feel the stitching. Then it would be, "Thees and thees and thees, is no good! You must do again."

It was a vast relief to return to No. 24, Union Square Place, at the end of the day, where she could see Polly and sometimes Hartley and Ralph. Except she could not tell them how miserable she felt. It would have distressed Polly, and she was sure that Hartley and Ralph had to wade through many boring figures and invoices during their days of bookkeeping and accounting, so it would seem churlish to complain.

There were no more parties, although Caitlin would have been too tired to go. Still, she found she missed them. She was not inclined to sew in the evening now, but Polly provided her with books to read, books that she was surprised to find were very much easier to understand than James' had ever been.

Sometimes, she thought about Maeve with tears in her eyes, but now she knew that Constance Regan had been right. In her heart, she envied her little half-sister. If only she had been a bit younger, then perhaps Mr Hooper might have taken her too. She was so tired of New York. At least Maeve was safe and hopefully happy. She was sure the child would have forgotten her by now. There was no suggestion of a visit by Mrs Regan, and Caitlin resigned herself to the fact that she would never see her again. She had at least done her best for the little girl. That was all she could do. But it left an emptiness in her heart.

Chapter Two

Another Christmas came and went, and once again, the New Year brought bitter cold. Madame Arlott's workshop was heated by a giant central stove — so common in America — but the tall pipe must have had a defective flue, for the room was very stuffy, and the fumes made Caitlin's head ache. She had graduated from hemming to taking in and letting out tucks and trimming bonnets with tiny ruches all over, but this was equally tedious and difficult in the poor light. She was still nowhere near as good as the other girls, though she liked to think she was improving. She longed for the end of each day when she could step out into the darkness and the icy wind and take the streetcar back to Union Square.

There, she would wearily climb the stairs into her own room, where the fire was always lit in the grate by hands other than hers and stretch out on the soft bed for a while before dressing for dinner. Sometimes, she would read one of the books that Polly had lent her. At the moment, she was especially anxious to get back to one of these, though it made her cry. She was not alone. The book was Harriet Beecher Stowe's *'Uncle Tom's Cabin'*, and all over America, women were thrilled by the story of poor Eliza's escape, feeling compassion for Uncle Tom and weeping at little Eva's death. It hurt Caitlin to read about the black women being parted from their children. Could this really be going on in America? But then, hadn't Mrs Regan, albeit for the best, sold Maeve to Mr Hooper in effect? The story was touching, and she knew that poor Uncle Tom was going to die far away from his cabin at the hands of his cruel master, yet read on desperate that Mas'r George should find him and save him in time.

This particular evening, she hurried back to Union Square Place with that story on her mind. She turned into the road and trudged up the steps of No. 24. She had her own key, so there was no need for her to ring for a servant. The warm, gaslit gloom of the hall received her, and she sighed with relief. Taking off her cloak, gloves, and bonnet, she blew on her stiff, frozen fingers to warm them and changed her button boots for house shoes.

The house was quiet with the semblance of emptiness, though she knew the servants would be in the back or under the stairs somewhere. Polly and her mother were nowhere to be seen, and Thaddeus Regan would hardly be back from the city yet. She felt she had the house almost to herself.

Caitlin mounted the stairs softly, the carpet deadening her footsteps. The door of Thaddeus' study was ajar, but she thought nothing of it. Reaching her own room, she closed the door thankfully. A pain throbbed behind her eyes, and the back of her neck felt intolerably sore. She collapsed gratefully onto the bed, still in her plain brown seamstress dress.

What a haven this room was, soft and warm from firelight and lamplight, the world of the street shut out by heavy drapes. The servants had lit her an oil lamp for there was no gas at the top of the house. The furniture was far simpler than the style Mrs Regan generally favoured, being plainer and utilitarian. But the bedding was luxurious, and the wallpaper a pretty coffee print, matched by the fabric around her little dressing table. Caitlin surveyed the room with content and closed her eyes. No workshop until tomorrow. This was her private place.

At James' house, she had often felt lonely in her own room, being unaccustomed to having one. Now, she had learnt it was a privilege and truly felt it to be so. Sometimes, in bad dreams, on restless nights, she would fancy she was on the ship again, crowded by hundreds of others, and the relief when she woke and found it was not so was immense. She almost dozed off, forgetting her book, lulled by the warmth and the peace.

Then, something sounded an alert in her brain, and she was wide awake. It was the sound of heavy footsteps followed by the draught of the door opening. Turning her head, she saw Thaddeus Regan in the doorway. She could see he had been drinking heavily. His face was bright red. He closed the door behind him swiftly, and she sat up with her heart beating fast.

His eyes rested on hers, and she knew what he had come for. In an instant, her cherished private room had become a prison.

"Mr Regan! Whatever is the matter?"

For answer, he lurched over to the bed at the same moment that Caitlin sprang to her feet. She was not quick enough. He caught her wrists, flinging her back down roughly, and his black eyes bored into hers.

"Now!" he said. "I have you! I have waited. I have waited a long time, my little bog girl!"

He half fell on top of her, and one of his arms was across her throat. Pressing his lips against her face, he began to kiss her. Caitlin tried to scream but choked instead. His thick lips and beard were soaked in spirits. She could hardly breathe. She struggled like a trapped animal.

Then he raised himself and tore at the buttons of her dress. She bit his hand, and he swore. All thought of him as her benefactor had gone. He had become a monster who managed to open her bodice and tore at her camisole, plunging in his big, rough hand to maul her breasts. She lay quiet, gathering her strength, and felt sick. Then, as he got one leg over her, she began to fight and kick with a concerted effort. They rolled onto the floor together, knocking the oil lamp over with them.

She fought like a wild cat and, because he was slow and clumsy with drink, found herself suddenly free. Staggering to her feet, she tore her skirt from his grasping hand and ran for the door.

He raised an arm in desperation. But she took no notice. She was through the door in a moment and, picking up her skirts, hurled herself downstairs, gasping and sobbing uncontrollably.

On the floor of her room, Thaddeus Regan tried to raise himself and found, to his surprise, that he could not. The arm he had flung out dropped uselessly to his side. He couldn't feel it anymore and the leg on the same side had likewise become a dead weight. Puzzled, he managed to twist and turn himself over but could not get up. A horrible sight met his eyes.

The oil lamp knocked over in their struggle had spilt on the carpet. The flames had caught and were working their way slowly but persistently across to the window and its drapes. He lunged for the lamp but had no hope of reaching it. All his power had gone. Now, one of the drapes caught and flared upwards.

Terrified, he tried to shout to raise the alarm. His mouth formed the shape, and he took a breath to holler, but only a small, strangulated sound came gurgling out. He was dumb as well as paralysed and could only lie there stricken as he watched the leafy print of the wallpaper next to the window brown and curl.

Caitlin, meanwhile, had almost thrown herself down two flights of stairs. In the hallway, she came face to face with Mrs Regan and Polly, who had just come in and were shaking wet snow from their capes and bonnets. They stood astonished as she burst upon them with her bodice all in disarray.

"Caitlin!"

"Mrs Regan, I must leave this house! I cannot bear it anymore. I will not! I must go!

The two women stared at her.

"But, dearest, whatever for?" cried Polly in distress.

The sight of her anxious face calmed Caitlin a little, and she faltered. How could she tell them why? Then, as ever, Mrs Regan proved herself mistress of the situation.

"Run along, Polly," she said. "Caitlin and I must talk," and she shepherded Caitlin into the drawing room, closing the door firmly behind them. For once, Caitlin was glad of Polly's absence. It made what she had to say easier. Mrs Regan bade her sit down and cover herself up but showed no surprise.

"Do you want some salts?" she asked sharply, seeing the girl was still trembling.

Caitlin shook her head.

"Then you will tell me exactly what has happened."

Caitlin's tongue failed her. How could she explain when Mrs Regan held herself so proudly? She stood like an empress in blue satin on the hearthrug, every grey hair in place with one hand across her bosom as if to keep all emotions firmly in their place. She was no fool and suspected the truth, though she could not let her mask slip just yet.

"You say you must leave," she said coldly. "I agree it may be for the best. But you must do me the courtesy of telling me why."

Caitlin swallowed hard. "It's Mr Regan," she said.

"Is he home?"

"Yes. And has he been drinking?"

"Yes, very much so. I don't suppose he knows what he is doing ..."

"Oh, he knows," Constance said bitterly. "He knows well enough. He has made advances before, hasn't he?"

"Yes." This was quietly spoken.

"Speak up, girl!"

"Yes!" Caitlin's face burnt crimson. She dreaded Mrs Regan saying it was all her fault.

"He attempted to molest you this evening, then?"

"Yes."

"Did he succeed?"

"No, but it was very unpleasant. I could not say so before Polly."

"Well, it seems we must send you away then."

Mrs Regan turned away and was silent for what seemed like an eternity. Then she spoke, "I appreciate your discretion," she said. "I really do. You see how difficult it is for me. I am terribly sorry that you should have had to endure this."

Caitlin raised her head. "Thank you!" she said, much humbled. "I thought you would not believe me."

"I am not a fool, my dear," Mrs Regan said wearily. "It is not the first time, though it's usually the chambermaids. Still, I have feared it.

You must not be too harsh. Thaddeus has been losing money and drinking heavily. It releases a demon in him."

She was very matter of fact, though it must have cost her dearly to say all of this. "We will arrange different accommodation for you. Naturally, I shall continue to help you in any way I can, and no doubt Polly will want to keep in touch. But it is for the best. You see, I cannot guarantee it will not happen again. I shall think of something to tell Polly. She should not know the truth."

"I understand," said Caitlin. "And I'm truly sorry." She was, and grateful too for Mrs Regan's largesse, wanting to say as much, but not knowing how to begin. If only she could have embraced this noble woman and thanked her, but that seemed out of the question.

"Well, it's no good crying over spilt milk," said Constance flatly. "I do wish, though, you might have married Cornelius O'Brien."

Caitlin remembered how cynically Mrs Regan had spoken of happiness then and felt for her. Her fear disappeared, and, in a moment, she might have gone up to her and put her arms around the stiff neck in tears. That moment never came.

Instead, the door was flung open, and Polly almost fell in. From the look on her face, Caitlin thought she must have discovered the truth about her father, but the reality was different.

"Mamma! The house is on fire!"

At once, Caitlin remembered the oil lamp. Too late. Only why hadn't Thaddeus picked it up and done something to stomp out the flames?

They ran into the hall. Thick smoke was pouring down the stairs. The bronze statuette continued to leap into the air with a disastrous lack of concern, but the aspidistra was wilting in the heat.

Constance took charge of the situation. "Polly, rouse the servants! We must get everyone out."

She hesitated, then plunged bravely up the stairs, Caitlin following, but they were both driven back by the smoke. Constance took hold of her arm. She shuddered once, then turned staunchly.

"Come, we can do no more. We must leave the house! Get your cloak and boots." Constance demanded.

Caitlin felt like sobbing despite her revulsion for the man upstairs. Something dreadful must have happened. Perhaps he had passed out. Now, he would be burning.

The night air came as a welcome shock. They stood helpless whilst the frightened servants hurried out and gathered in the street.

Neighbours flung open windows and shouted their concern. Many of them joined their huddled group, crunching over the snow with angry, alarmed voices, fearful for their own homes. Then came the frenzied clanging of a bell, and a fire engine clattered into the street, drawn by a team of galloping, sweating horses, rolling their eyes and scattering froth and foam from their mouths. Fire laddies leapt off the vehicle and pulled out a hose from the tank on wheels, the great steam boiler pumping noisily. They levelled the spray at the upper levels of the house, where flames were bursting and leaping out of the windows. No. 24, Union Square Place would surely be burnt to the ground. The best the firemen could do was prevent the blaze from spreading to the rest of the terrace.

Caitlin tugged frantically at Mrs Regan's arm. "Polly! Where's Polly? She should be here."

"She will be here in a moment."

"But all the servants are out!"

"She will be here."

Caitlin broke away for she could see that Mrs Regan was dazed. She darted up the steps and in at the front door. The hall was now full of smoke, and the stairs had collapsed. Oh, please, God, Polly hadn't gone up there! Why should she when she didn't know her father was in the house? But where was she?

Then, through the fog, a figure appeared from the morning room, stumbling and coughing with eyes streaming from the smoke. It was Polly, and in her hands, she held the cage with the canary that Hartley had given them. Caitlin cried her name and, seizing her arm, pulled her out of the hall and down the steps into the street. They were followed by a crash as the hall ceiling fell in.

"Polly!" she yelled. "How could you? How could you put yourself in such danger? For a bird! You must be mad!"

Polly was shaken and could not speak for a while. When she did, she croaked feebly but unrepentantly. "I couldn't leave it to die! You had forgotten it, but I knew you would be sad when you remembered it was left in the morning room. We couldn't leave it ... it didn't deserve to die. It was so frightened."

The bird did seem to be distracted, fluttering wildly around its cage.

Caitlin embraced her friend tightly. "You silly girl!" she sobbed. "You nearly didn't get out!"

Then she remembered Polly did not know about her father and fell silent. The orange flames spiralled up to the black sky, showering sparks down on the street. Thaddeus Regan could not have survived. It was his funeral pyre.

Chapter Three

The morning after the fire, the three women met at breakfast in the modest dining room of a newly opened hotel in Union Square. The servants had all disappeared the previous evening in various states of shock back to the places they had come from after ascertaining where Mrs Regan was staying. Outside was the sombre dawn of another winter's day. Inside, the mood was equally bleak.

During the night, Mrs Regan told Polly about her father. Not the full version as Caitlin had given it to her, but an abbreviated account of the constant downward trend in his affairs and his resorting to the bottle. Poor man, he must have knocked over an oil lamp, perhaps whilst reaching clumsily for another drink, and been too far gone to control the ensuing blaze quickly enough. The smoke must have rapidly overcome him.

"We should have heard him," Polly had said, but there was no answer to that from any of them.

Constance sat dry-eyed and tight-lipped, sipping her morning tea as if it were some nasty medicine that must be taken. Caitlin was totally subdued.

As soon as it was properly light, they went to see what could be salvaged from the house. The answer was absolutely nothing. From a distance, the building did not seem too irreparably damaged. It had lost its roof, and part of the upper storey was crumbling away, but the ground floor was still intact from the outside. Then, as they drew nearer, they realized that the whole edifice was nothing but a blackened and empty shell. Walls still stood, but inside floors and ceilings were gone, and there was nothing but stinking piles of smouldering rubbish. Here and there, a piece of scorched wallpaper survived on an upright wall, but that was all. The drawing room was a mass of twisted metal and charred wood. There was a long silence as Polly moved forward to support her mother.

"Come, Mamma, let us go back. There is nothing to be gained by being here."

Back at the hotel, Constance. Regan rallied, but it was a poor version of her former proud voice that spoke.

"Well, that is that. We must visit Mr Regan's lawyer who will advise us what is to be done. I suppose we must pay off the servants if we can."

Here, Caitlin left them, for it was already past the time when she should have been at the workshop. The acrimonious smell of fire in her nostrils went with her.

All day, she sat and sewed with a heavy heart. If only Thaddeus Regan had not come home early! If only she had been braver and stayed in the room to retrieve the oil lamp and put out the flames! But how could she have known Thaddeus would not or could not do that? At the time, she had been in terrible danger, but now the Regans had lost everything. She tried to comfort herself by thinking that Thaddeus would have left them well provided for.

For herself, the way ahead seemed painfully clear. She must continue in the employ of Madame Arlott and lodge in the smallest of hotels, living carefully within her modest means. She had wanted independence or said she did. Well, now she had got it, and most unpleasant the prospect seemed. Her comfortable life as a favoured protected emigré was over. Not only must she join the working masses, but she had nothing apart from the clothes she stood up in, less even than when she had arrived in America.

She supposed it was fitting that her working clothes had been saved. How ironic it was that her fortunes had turned again. It reminded her of some child's board game in which an unlucky throw of the dice resulted in swift reversals. She must try not to mind about her green velvet, her pink silk, the white ballgown and other garments. Much good they had done her! She wouldn't need them now anyway. She wondered if Hartley would mind if she sold the canary to buy more clothing. Distracted by such thoughts, she pricked her finger and cursed silently.

By the time she reached the hotel in the evening she was in a fever of impatience to find out what the Regans had discovered that day. Anxiously, she hurried into the small, public sitting room. Polly was sitting there alone before a roaring fire, her feet upon the fender. She looked pensive but jumped up and smiled bravely on seeing Caitlin and came forward to kiss her.

"How cold your hands are!" Polly exclaimed. "Come closer to the fire."

Caitlin shuddered, but Polly didn't seem to realize what she had said. She wished she could tell Polly the truth and unburden herself, but she knew it would be unfair. Besides, it was wrong to talk ill of the dead.

"Where is Mrs Regan?" she asked.

"Mamma is lying down in her room."

"Oh dear, is she well?"

"I think so. She's very calm. But this has hit her hard. We have nothing left from the house at all, and now it appears that Pappa was not insured. For myself, I don't mind so much, but for Mamma, it must seem like the end of the world."

"What will you do?"

"Well, the house has to be knocked down before it can be rebuilt. We will get no compensation of any kind, but we can at least sell the plot. Mamma was right about Pappa's finances, I'm afraid. It appears he has very few bankable assets left. There are some pieces of land in the area above the railroad depot. Mr Brogan, Pappa's lawyer, advises us to hold on to those as long as we can because they should appreciate in value and provide some surety for our future. He will invest it for us wisely, although the whole will only generate a modest income to live on, even with the sale of the plot."

"But where will you live?"

"Mamma thinks there is only one course of action. I don't like it a bit, but I have to agree. I can't see anything else to do. She will write to Pappa's sister in Boston and ask her to take us in for my sake. We will be very poor relations, existing mainly on her charity, and knowing Aunt Sophia, I don't think she will let us forget that."

"So, you will leave New York?" said Caitlin.

"I wish I didn't have to! I don't want to go and would rather stay here and get myself a job like you. But Mamma won't hear of it, and she says she cannot possibly ask Aunt Sophia for you, too. What a blessing it is that you are settled at Madame Arlott's."

"Yes," said Caitlin, feeling it was far from a blessing, "I must try not to mind you going."

"If it wasn't for Mamma, I would stay. But I can't leave her now."

Caitlin saw the truth of this and both girls stared with melancholy into the fire.

"You must come and visit me," said Polly. "I shall positively twist Aunt Sophie's arm."

Caitlin sighed. "If I can," she said, privately thinking that she was the very last person Mrs Regan would wish to see.

"Hartley came round to call," said Polly after a while. "He was sorry not to be able to stop and see you but will come again. He couldn't stay but sent you his most concerned and dearest wishes. He was so worried about us all when he heard about the fire. I guess he was pleased to hear the canary had survived."

"I must feed it," said Caitlin guiltily. "Before dinner," and she withdrew her toes from the fender.

"I did it for you," said Polly, "when I saw Madame Arlott was going to keep you late, and I cleaned the cage as well. I hope you didn't mind me going into your room".

Caitlin laughed. "Sure, and you're a daft one to think I'd mind! It isn't as if I have many private possessions now, is it?"

"No, I suppose not," and Polly smiled too. "Me neither! In a way, it's liberating."

"No, it's not," Caitlin said glumly. "It forces us into doing what we don't want to do."

"Caitlin, will you promise me something?"

"Anything, if I can,"

"Please be nice to Hartley after I've gone. It makes me glad to think you will have at least one true friend."

However, the Regans could not depart straightaway. First, all the important letters had to be sent to Aunt Sophia in Boston, and a favourable reply was awaited. Then there was Thaddeus' funeral to arrange... Caitlin had no desire to attend but knew she could hardly avoid it. What she had discovered about Thaddeus must be put to the back of her mind as she needed to support the emotionally shaken Mrs Regan and Polly. She should also remember that he had been her benefactor. It crossed her mind that she was rather like a bad penny being passed on from hand to hand. Death and disaster seemed to follow her everywhere. It was a depressing thought.

There was nothing about the day of the funeral to redeem it. A freezing wind whipped through the long streets and tore round the corners of each block with an icy blast. The sky was grey and banked with clouds that threatened more snow. The horses with their black plumes slipped and strained on the frostbitten ground as they pulled the black-trimmed sled carrying the coffin. At any moment, Caitlin expected it to slide off into the mounds of snow packed up at the side of the road. She imagined the lid being thrown off and a blackened Thaddeus Regan rising from the dead to accuse her. It was a horrid image, and she was glad when they reached the church, and she could endeavour to put it behind her. The Latin Mass brought some comfort, though she barely understood it.

She saw Hartley and Ralph at the back of the church and was glad they had come. The O'Briens were there, too, but although Cornelius passed his condolences on to Constance and Polly, he never once looked at Caitlin. *I am not sorry,* she thought with spirit. What was wrong then would be wrong now.

By the time they reached the cemetery, there was something of a blizzard blowing, and it was into a black hole surrounded by whirling snow that Thaddeus Regan was laid to rest, somewhat hurriedly, it must be confessed, for the priest began to accelerate his pace through the order of prayer. There was no soil to throw on the coffin after it had been lowered into the grave — only wet handfuls of snow. *Forgive him, Lord,* thought Caitlin, *and forgive me too, the Unwitting Servant of Thy Wrath.*

The women returned to their carriage, and the mourners dispersed, melting into the snowfall as if they had never been. They slid and swayed back to the hotel in Union Square in silence.

For Constance Regan, it was the end of an era, almost the end of life itself as she knew it. She had not loved him, but everything that he entailed had gone with him, and her status as a wealthy married woman had disappeared overnight. She had aged into a dowager who felt she had little function left in life to fulfil, and that reflection was most bitter. All her fine possessions, her drawing room, her servants, and her home had gone, crumbled into ashes. With it went her respect, her pride, and her independence. For what, she wondered, had her life been about? What was the good of it all now that it all lay in ashes? Only Polly was left to her, and she must devote the rest of her days to promoting her interests.

It had been a bad day for them all when she had accepted Caitlin into the family. She did not blame the girl personally. What had happened was clearly Thaddeus' fault, but she would be relieved never to see her again. When they reached the hotel, Mrs Regan retired directly to her room. Polly offered her company but was declined. The two younger women were left together to warm themselves by the fire.

"Mamma is sadly crushed," said Polly. "She held up magnificently whilst the practicalities were being sorted, but now, well, she seems to have collapsed. Life is going to seem dreadfully hard for her, and I shall have to try not to cross swords with her again."

Caitlin looked at her with concern. "But what about you, Polly?"

"Oh, I shall be fine. I feel downcast now, but God will raise me up again. Everything has a purpose."

"Do you really think so?"

"Yes, I am sure of it."

"I don't have a purpose," said Caitlin sadly, in a small voice. "I just cause trouble wherever I go. It's always been like that."

"Oh, Caitlin, you mustn't think that. It's not right. It's hard for you to see now, but..."

"Your mother blames me for what has happened."

"No, she doesn't. Why should she?"

Caitlin didn't say anything, and Polly gently took her hand.

"Cait, I know what my father was like! Mamma thinks I don't, but of course I do. I know why we had to send so many chambermaids away. I guess he approached you that night of the fire, and you ran away frightened. I didn't think of it at the time, only afterwards when I remembered how you looked in the hall with your clothes, all dishevelled. What happened after that was an accident. It certainly wasn't your fault."

Caitlin was astonished. "But you loved him?"

"He was my father," said Polly simply.

Caitlin struggled with conflicting emotions.

"I still feel like a bad omen," she said, eventually.

"You mustn't. That's just superstitious nonsense!"

"Oh, Polly, I do hope so! I'm going to miss you so much when you go to Boston!"

The expected missive arrived in due course. Disagreeable Aunt Sophia might be, but she knew where her duty lay. There would be a home of sorts for Polly and her mother in Boston. So, as soon as the last snow had melted and Spring was on its way, preparations were made for their departure.

"You realize, of course," said Mrs Regan to Caitlin, correct unto the last. "That we cannot take you with us. If it were my decision, it would be different. But I could not expect Sophia to take on extra burdens outside the family."

Caitlin bowed her head.

"I had not expected it," she said.

"No, well, at least you are well placed with Madame Arlott," Mrs Regan continued. "She will keep an eye on you. I am sure you now see how wise it was for the child to go to the Hoopers."

"Yes, ma'am."

Hartley came round to see them off, and Caitlin felt glad she was not left entirely alone in the square as the carriage drove away. She was not to know that Polly had extracted a promise from him to look after her or how willingly he had agreed. Farewells were emotional between the three friends.

"You must both write," Polly insisted, "and I shall too, every week. There will be lots to tell each other."

Then it was time, and Polly had to mount the steps of the waiting buggy with suspiciously bright eyes and settle her skirts down beside her mother. She waved all the way until they had left the square far behind, but Mrs Regan sat staunchly facing the future, never once looking back.

"I shall miss her so," said Caitlin, swallowing an enormous lump in her throat. It would not do to cry in front of Hartley, though she wished she could tell him how her heart felt broken by all that had happened since she had come to America.

"So shall I," said Hartley sincerely. "But your loss will be greater, I am sure." He picked up her new carpetbag with a few possessions inside and the canary's cage in his other hand. "Shall we go?"

She was moving to a modest establishment, a boarding house further downtown, and he was going to escort her there. She nodded regretfully, and they set off together down the street.

Chapter Four

That summer was good for the Kleists' shop, for business improved with the new premises. Rosa still ran the second-hand clothes with Friedrich's help but had started to add other relevant goods such as belts, cravats, and gloves. At last, Friedrich himself was moderately busy and gaining a reputation for quality and good value.

"We have an assistant," Rosa told Hartley proudly when he called in one warm evening. "Come and see."

Hartley allowed himself to be led into the shop, expecting to see a young man or woman sitting sewing. Instead, he saw a black device with a handle and poised needle and a treadle underneath the table.

"Why!" said Hartley, surprised. "Is it a sewing machine?"

Rosa nodded, pleased at his reaction. "We are very modern now, yes?"

"Yes indeed. And what do you think of it, Herr Kleist?"

He shrugged his shoulders. "It has its limitations, but it is useful, yes."

"He didn't want to get one," said Rosa. "But they will be in all the tailors' shops sooner or later, and now that he has it, he agrees it is good." Friedrich opened his mouth to protest, but Rosa butted in. "Come now.... let Hartley take you out for a drink. You have worked long enough. I will clear up the mess and start dinner. You will eat with us, Hartley?"

"I should be glad to."

He felt less sure that Herr Kleist wanted to go for a drink with him, knowing well enough that he made no attempts to socialize with others, but they both meekly obeyed Frau Kleist and repaired to a local bar.

"Well," said Hartley, raising his glass. "Here's to your business. It seems to be coming along fine now."

Friedrich thanked him. "It is better, certainly."

"And what do you really think of this new-fangled machine?"

"It is a useful aid. No more. But Rosa insisted we have one, though we can scarcely afford it. Still, she is right. It will change the trade. Work will be done more easily without as much skill."

"You don't approve of that."

"The world is changing," was all Friedrich would say.

"Don't you think that is a good thing?"

"It may be, and it may not be. The Americans will find out first. You can be sure of that."

"You don't approve of all their energy, all that hustle?" Friedrich considered.

"It sounds childish, perhaps. But no, I don't. The New World lacks caution. It rushes in. Rosa would like me to be like that, too. But I cannot, not anymore, and I sometimes wonder where it will all end."

It was Hartley's turn to think. "Another three years, and you will become an American too."

"Perhaps. You will apply for citizenship then?"

"Oh yes."

"You will have to renounce your Queen Victoria."

"I know. But I can't see myself going back."

"So, is America treating you well, Mr Shawcross?"

"I have another promotion," said Hartley proudly.

"I am glad to hear it."

"Yes, I am now secretary to Elmer James."

"That sounds most impressive!"

"Well, it's not quite as good as it sounds. I would rather have von Blumen's job as office manager! I reckon I could do better than him now. But it will be good experience for me, and it is a regular post. Ralph's father isn't a bad sort. Still the pay is only as much as the Chief Clerk's."

"Nevertheless," said Friedrich, "I think you will be getting married soon. We must celebrate."

Hartley blushed. Naturally, it was his dearest wish to marry Caitlin if she would have him, but the obstacles in his path seemed enormous.

"I can hardly afford such a step yet, sir," he said, respectful as always to Herr Kleist.

"But I thought there was a young lady from Ireland with whom you are acquainted, and I suspect you are very fond of her."

"There is," stammered Hartley. "And I am very fond of her. Yet I hardly know if she'd have me on such a wage."

"Then you must ask her! Women are often surprising creatures and say yes when they should say no. Ask her and ask her soon before someone else does."

Herr Kleist was not in the habit of proffering advice. Indeed, he had hardly said so many words together at one time to Hartley in the whole of their acquaintance, barring that first Christmas when they had all been a little drunk. So, Hartley endeavoured to take him seriously though he could not help thinking that Friedrich was now urging him to forget caution despite his earlier opinions.

"But I must be able to offer her more," he said. "Perhaps in another two or three years, I may."

Friedrich shook his head. "It is a shame she has lost her parents," he said. "Often, the father is able to be generous to start with."

"I do not think Caitlin's father could have been that, sir. They were extremely poor. Until lately, she has been living on charity, and you know what tragedy befell her benefactor's family."

"Ah yes, I had forgotten. Then perhaps she will expect less."

"But deserves more, sir. Anyway, I fear she will not have me now when she is all alone for that very reason. She is proud despite her origins."

"You know best I suppose," said Herr Kleist. "But don't leave it too long. Think about it. Let us go for a walk. It is too hot in here."

Outside they threaded their way through the streets and made their way down to the shoreline — never far distant in this city — in the hope of gaining some refreshing breeze from the sea. Another emigrant ship was disembarking.

"Look at them," said Friedrich, his face grown a little sadder. "Still, they come, as we did. You know they are talking of making Castle Garden into a centre to receive them now?" "I had heard something of the sort. That would be useful," said Hartley. "How glad I am that we have two years' experience under our belts now!"

"Still, they come," said Friedrich, as if he had not heard Hartley. "And for what? Pouring into this city, which is already bursting with the bad side of life. Sometimes, I feel we cannot breathe. Sometimes, I long for our simple German countryside and the old streets of Frankfurt. The children, they have forgotten it already, and Rosa, she is always so busy she forgets. I do not, I often come down here to think of it. I am too old to forget."

"I am sure Rosa does not forget," said Hartley kindly. "Not really. Do you ever talk about it together?"

"Not now," said Friedrich. "It makes her impatient. You see, Rosa does not mind the loss of what we fought for. She never really did. Her concerns are more domestic. She will be a true American."

Hartley was unsure what to say to this, so he said nothing, though he privately thought there must be other 'forty-eighters' in this city who had thrown themselves into new causes and new fights. Only Friedrich had lost heart. He felt deeply sorry for him but did not know what to do or say.

"Of course, she is a good woman," Friedrich remarked as an afterthought.

"Oh, an excellent woman!"

"Yes. More capable than I. No, no, do not protest. I am not blind to my faults. Yes, she is most capable. In fact, I sometimes think ...." His thoughts were left trailing in the air and Hartley felt uneasy.

Then Friedrich seemed to pull himself together: "Come, we must go home. She will be waiting. You know, I often forget what time it is these days. I must be growing old, ja?"

Hartley pooh-poohed this suggestion.

"I am glad we had this talk," said Friedrich with unexpected warmth. "We must go out again. It is good to talk. I cannot talk to Rosa anymore. She treats me like a child."

This intimate piece of information embarrassed Hartley more than he cared to say, but he felt an outreach of the tailor's loneliness and promised himself that he would seek further opportunities to discuss with Herr Kleist.

However, although Hartley had good intentions, he did not have the means of putting them into operation for some time. His new post kept him working late and then the pull of seeing Caitlin, who also needed his support, was strong.

Poor Caitlin! How she suffered, or thought she did, since the Regans left New York. Her boarding house was much less comfortable than the hotel, bordering indeed on squalor, but it was all she could afford. In addition, after Mrs Regan's departure, Madame Arlott's attitude toward her had hardened, and so there were no more attempts to teach her the rudimentary skills of dressmaking. She was relegated instead to the endless rituals of hemming and ruching and trimming in the stuffy workshop all day long, and she knew she would never be a fashionable mantua maker now.

One Sunday afternoon, whilst walking with Hartley in Madison Square Garden, Caitlin became especially pensive and depressed. The full blasting heat of summer was upon the city. Caitlin shaded herself under a black umbrella, (no pretty parasols being affordable now) and Hartley wondered if they had walked too far, for they had walked up to the reservoir and along Forty-Second Street to see how the work on the magnificent Crystal Palace was coming along. Caitlin seemed exhausted, and she leant upon his arm freely. The normal pallor of her face had given way to a bright flush.

"Come," said Hartley with concern. "Let us sit down under the trees."

They found a seat, and Caitlin abandoned the umbrella, closing it up wearily.

"Have you heard from Polly?" Hartley began.

"Yes, a week ago."

"Is she finding life with Aunt Sophia tedious?"

"No, not now — far from it. Of course, Aunt Sophia is tedious, and so is Polly's mamma, by all accounts. But she has met some ladies in Boston whom she finds most intelligent," Caitlin paused and repeated the words with emphasis. *"Most intelligent."* To tell the truth, she felt a little hurt at this communication concerning Polly's new friends. She felt as if she might have been lacking in that department herself, though it was doubtless not Polly's intention to imply this.

"She has become an abolitionist and a supporter of, well, women's rights, as she puts it, and spends an awful lot of time at meetings."

Hartley raised his eyebrows and laughed, but it was not an unkind laugh. "Yes, that is Polly exactly! Dear me, how vexed Mrs Regan will be!"

"Yes," said Caitlin with some satisfaction. "Polly says she's been busy at lectures and bazaars and money-raising functions for these causes, so she hasn't had much time lately to write to you. But she promises she will soon and sends you her best love."

Hartley blushed perceptibly at this, and Caitlin noticed it.

"Have you written back?"

"Not yet." Caitlin added, with considerable pathos, "I have nothing to tell her."

There was a short silence during which she struggled with her emotions. The green leaves of the trees above them stirred in a welcome breeze, the fountain water continued to splash merrily, and they could hear the pleasant chinking of horses' harness from cabs drawn up at the edge of the square. It was a beautiful day, but Caitlin felt wretchedly apart from it.

"Oh, Hartley!" she burst out at last. "I shall go mad if I stay at Madame Arlott's much longer!"

Hartley saw how distressed she was and pressed her hand with his own. She allowed the gesture as she would have done that from a brother.

"Is there no sign of advancement yet?"

"None, and never will be. I am back at the dreariest of tasks. It is my own fault, I know, for I lack aptitude. It was all a terrible mistake, and now I sit and sew the most wearisome articles all day long and even in my sleep at night. My back aches, my arms ache, my neck and eyes ache and, Hartley, I am so bored! But how can I say this to Polly? How can I be so ungrateful for her mother's arrangements? Yet I am never out of doors unless it is on a Sunday with you. I never meet anyone now. I have no friends but you. I must do something else!"

Hartley considered. "Why not let me speak to the Kleists? They may well need an assistant. The atmosphere there would be better, I am sure."

"Oh no," said Caitlin quickly. "Herr Kleist would soon find fault with me. Madame is always picking up 'thees' and 'that' and saying it is no good. I could not bear it if Herr Kleist thought the same and was too polite to mention it. No, I am not suited for this kind of work!"

Hartley knitted his forehead in thought. Across the way, two black-skirted figures were pushing perambulators of cane across the park.

"Of course, you would not like to go into service, but have you ever thought of becoming a nanny in a good family? You were so fond of your little stepsister."

"I have thought of it. I have even looked at advertisements in the papers for such posts. Do you know what they say?"

"No."

"No Irish need apply!"

"Oh. Really?"

"God forbid that the smart infants of New York should grow up with an Irish brogue!" Her tone was bitter. "But I thought I could become a shopgirl, at Stewart's perhaps."

"Oh! Really?"

"What is wrong with that?"

"It is just that a shopgirl is not quite as genteel as a seamstress or a nanny."

"A seamstress has little opportunity to be anything else seeing as she is shut up all day!" retorted Caitlin. She felt hurt by his attitude and showed her anger by tearing off her bonnet and flinging it to the ground.

Hartley picked it up. "Why did you do that?"

"Why do we have to wear bonnets when it is so hot? Why wear them at all? Look at the stupid things with their tucks and their trimmings! What is wrong with bare heads and decent, honest hair? Why do we have to pin our hair up and pretend it is not so long? Why do we have to wear such ridiculous skirts that hamper us from moving about so that we could not run if we wanted to?"

Polly, with her new-found allegiances, might well have said, "Hear, hear!"

But Hartley was astonished. "Run?" he repeated in amazement. "Why should you want to run?"

"I don't know! Why shouldn't I? Do you know that Polly says there is a young woman upstate who wears bloomers and is ridiculed for it?"

"Bloomers?" Hartley swallowed. He was shocked.

"Yes, bloomers! What is so bad about that? Why must women never be able to do what they want?" Caitlin rose tempestuously to her feet. "I shall become a shopgirl, Hartley, I shall! Better that than a maid who is black all day from cleaning grates or a lady of ill repute."

Hartley was amazed she even knew about such matters.

"And if you no longer wish to speak to me when I am a shopgirl, then so be it!" And she charged off down the path as fast as her legs, or more particularly her skirts, would carry her.

"Caitlin, wait!" Hartley grabbed her umbrella, gloves and bonnet and followed her. This was not at all what he had expected from their téte-a-téte. The afternoon had started so pleasantly, and he had felt so tender towards her when they first sat down that he found Herr Kleist's advice on his mind. Now, it had all gone wrong, and he hardly knew why. He did not know how to deal with Caitlin like this. Still, his instinct told him not to let her go. She was easy to overtake, and he found she was sobbing.

"Oh, Caitlin," he said. "Forgive me!" though he did not know exactly what he had done. His hand was upon her arm when she swung round. He thought at first, she meant to strike him in the impotence of her anger, but instead, she crumpled into his arms and sobbed some more. He was overcome by the sweet scent of her hair against his face and the sensation of her light body pressed against his.

"If you are to be a shopgirl in Stewart's," he said, gravely teasing. "It will be terribly bad for me, for I shall be in there buying every day!"

At this she laughed, though she struck him after all, upon the chest, however gently. He caught her hand and stilled it with a kiss. Now was the time, *now* in this intimate moment. Only he hesitated.

"I wish you would wait," he said. " Before making a hasty decision. Do you know that shop assistants earn very little money?"

"It isn't merely the money."

"I know. But I must think what is best for you."

"You must not tell Polly how unhappy I am, on any account," she said, withdrawing her hand. "It is impossible for me to join them."

"What about Maeve's Mr Hooper of Rochester? Could he not help you out?"

"I have thought of it. Sometimes I have even sat myself down to write him a letter. But I cannot. I would have to set aside all my pride to beg him, and I could not bear to be turned down or turned out again. Better to be a shopgirl, for I lack the education for anything else."

Hartley persisted. "Just stay with Madame a little longer," he asked. "And I will try to find you something better."

"Very well. But I cannot wait too long, Hartley."

"You know I would take you away from it forever if I could. But I cannot just yet, though the time will come. Would you let me, Caitlin?"

Did he mean what she thought he meant? Caitlin was perplexed. If he did, why not say it more clearly? No, such stirring proposals were not Hartley's way. Besides, it was Polly whom he respected and admired surely, not her, the poor little Irish bogtrotter. What could she give him? She was plagued with self-doubt.

"Hartley," she said. "You are my dearest friend! My only friend!"

He averted his eyes. She had meant it to be encouragement of sorts, but he took it otherwise. Surely it was a denial to speak, no matter how warmly, of love. He gave her the bonnet quietly and she put it on, tucking away her dark curls under its rim and feeling rather ashamed. I must wait, thought Hartley. Time alone can change affairs between us. I must not force her to love me.

He gave her his arm, and she took it as naturally as ever, relieved that his seriousness was over.

"I thought," he said, " that next Saturday evening, we might go to Wallack's and see *Uncle Tom's Cabin*. Should you like that?"

"Oh yes, that would be wonderful! How good of you to cheer me up!" Now, there was something she might like to do, to go on the stage and hang respectability once and for all! But she couldn't sing or dance and hadn't the slightest notion how one was to start.

"Come then. Let's go and buy some lemonade. I'm thirsty with all this talking," Hartley said.

Caitlin felt her spirits lifting by the time she returned to her lodgings. There was a warm glow inside her which had nothing to do with the heat of the day. The more she thought about it, the more convinced she became that Hartley intended to propose to her and the memory of the warm, comforting way he had held her in his arms was very pleasant. He had kissed her too when they had said goodbye, very properly, on the cheek like a brother, but that was something he had never done before.

It was not of course that she was in love with him. Such a one as she could never fall in love with Hartley Shawcross! Oh, no. He had none of James' presence or nobility. He was much too plain and ordinary. Yet she counted the hours until she saw him again. Hartley never let her down. He was good and true despite his shyness. She did not miss the balls and the parties and the O'Briens when she was with him. In their simple way, she and Hartley had more fun together and it was good to know that someone cared. If he should propose again, she might just have him if Polly wouldn't. Of course, he did not respect her like he did Polly, but then she didn't respect him like she did James. As Polly said, one could do a lot worse than Hartley Shawcross. He would always be her dearest friend.

The trouble with life is that it cannot be all outings and lemonade. It has to go on, day after day in the workshops and the offices of the Madame Arlotts and Elmer James's with endless routine. Life changes but sometimes changes so imperceptibly that we do not notice and think everything remains the same.

Caitlin did write to Stewart's, without Hartley's knowledge, asking for a job. The staffing manager wrote back to say that, at present, they required no more young ladies. Any other shop than Stewart's did seem a comedown. As a result, she stayed disappointedly at Madame Arlott's. In the meantime, Hartley racked his brains for a solution. He did ask Frau Kleist, but she, regretfully, said no. He asked Ralph if his father's family could conceive of a situation for Caitlin. But they felt that she lacked the education for it. So, Caitlin stayed at her stitching, and the winter drew on once more.

≈

14th December 1852

My Dear Mother,

Thank you for your letter. I was sorry to hear that your health has not been good and trust that you are now feeling a deal better, please God. How I wish I could persuade you and Jeremiah to join me over here! It is true that the climate is more extreme, and just now, New York is exceedingly cold. But the spring and autumn are delightful, and the only fault with the summer is that it becomes a little too hot in July and August. It is never damp and inhospitable the whole year round as it is in England, however.

I am well settled in my new post as secretary to Mr Elmer James, Ralph's father, and I learn a great deal about business. There is good reason to believe that my advancement in this firm will be slow but steady. In a few more years, I reckon I will know enough to run any business, maybe even start my own if I can!

It is true, of course, that New York is a busy, bustling city, and very crowded. But it has life and vitality. The whole world is here. Folks are open and speak to you plainly. Everyone is launched on the sea of opportunity, and I guess it is every man for himself. But there is help and friendship along the way, as I believe my experiences have demonstrated.

My kind German family are doing pretty well now, although Herr Kleist still seems somewhat ill-adapted. But I think that is his nature. Ralph continues to be a faithful friend. Even young Tim, whom I still see from time to time, seems to prosper on the canal-boats and is growing up a deal better than I feared at one time.

I am sorry that Mr Dickens' articles on his American travels were so unfavourable. But really, Mother Dear, I do not think one can judge fully without being here for some time. Of course, I understand that Jeremiah is happy in his new country parish up on the Moors.

But, believe me, there is a great need of preachers and pastors in this land, too. I guessed from your last letter that you felt a little lonely since moving out of Bradford and leaving all your friends. I expect you have settled now into your new home and met new people. But I hope it is not too draughty and cold for you at this time of year. The proximity to the moors will hardly keep out the winter winds.

You have heard me speak many times of little Caitlin, my Irish Madonna. She has fallen on rather hard times since Mr Regan's unfortunate death as the family removed to Boston and were obliged to leave her behind. She does not enjoy her work as a seamstress, which I must say sounds pretty wretched. But I have plans for us both. If I can get another raise soon, I fancy we could live together modestly, so I intend to ask her to be my wife. Recently, she has given me some cause to believe this would not be entirely unacceptable to her.

There has never been anyone else for me since the first time I saw her, as you know, and every moment that I have been with her since convinces me more. When she is happy, she is like a breath of spring air. But she is too often sad and sorely needs a protector. I know I can fulfil this role and that I could make her smile again. If she will have me, we might marry in a year or two, and then you really must come out and see us for a visit, at least. I hear they are bringing steamships onto the crossings now and it is not as arduous, nor as drawn out as it has been hitherto. Naturally, I would send you and Jeremiah the fare. I hope he would feel able to countenance a Catholic as his sister-in-law, though I am well aware of his views on the matter.

I long to see you again, Mother, and wish that all these happy events could take place straightaway. Still, it does no good to be impatient.

I must trust in the fullness of time and God's goodness. The day will come. I am sure of it. You see the confidence that being in America instils! People do get on if they are prepared to work hard.

Rest assured that you are not forgotten, although so far away and that you are always in my thoughts,

Your loving and affectionate son,

Hartley

Chapter Five

Towards the end of the winter, Caitlin fell ill. It was not a serious complaint to begin with, merely a hard, dry cough that refused to go away. But she felt intolerably weary and slow in her work. Every day was dreary, and she felt she must break away. There must be something else she could do. Indeed, she knew there was, though she shrank from it. Anyway, she lacked any stamina at the moment to put any plan into action. Hartley was still her mainstay and her friend, but their relations had not advanced.

He'll never ask me to marry him," she thought dully. What a fool I was to think it! Why should he? What can I, a mere seamstress, offer him? I cannot even love him like I should. Perhaps he senses that and knows it is no good.

The day before her fever came on, she felt especially low. Standing in the street after the day's grind, it came into her mind with especial forcefulness that it might be better to throw herself under the hooves of the next pair of horses pulling a streetcar. Such accidents did happen. But when they came, they were clip-clopping along so slowly in the gathering gloom that she could not be sure of an easy death that way, only pain and dreadful injuries. She was surprised how logically she thought about it. Nothing of that sort had ever occurred to her before. A little shocked at herself, she stepped inside and sat down.

"Five cents," said the attendant who was collecting the fares. Her fingers in their mittens stumbled over the change. The car was noisy and crowded. She had been lucky to get a seat. Her head felt as if it was floating above them all in the strangest manner. When it was her turn to get off, she swayed as she rose to her feet.

"Watch yourself now, little lady," said the man next to her, steadying her arm. "'Tis easy to slip. Careful how you go." He was looking at her white face with some concern. She thanked him, and he touched his cap. Dimly, she recognized the fact that he, too, was Irish. Then, he was gone amongst the crowds. *No Irish need apply*, she thought bitterly as she struggled against the wind all the way up the street.

Her landlady was setting the table in the dining room as she left her wet umbrella in the hall. The room was bright and warm from the stove, but the dinner, whatever kind of stew it was, did not smell appetising. She thought of the unfriendly crush round the table.

"I shan't be down, Mrs Plunkett," she called out. "I don't feel well and shall have an early night." The lady of the house nodded briskly and removed one of the place-settings.

Her own room was cold and dark and made Caitlin regret her decision. She took off her wet cloak, her boots and her bonnet but found she couldn't stop shivering. Throwing a cover over the canary's cage to hush its trilling, she got into bed with all her clothes on and pulled the blanket up tight. Almost immediately, she fell asleep.

In the morning, she woke feeling thirsty. Her throat was sore and dry, and fifty little men were beating hammers inside her head. She called out, but no one heard her, and she felt too weak to move. When the maid came in to see to the room, she asked her to fetch Mrs Plunkett. Mrs Plunkett eventually came in a bustle of annoyance to see what was wrong.

She was persuaded to send the maid with a message to Madame Arlott explaining that Caitlin would not be in for a day or two. With some relief, she learnt no food was required by the patient, only a flagon of water, which was duly brought. Caitlin changed painfully into her nightclothes, wrapped two shawls about her trembling body and returned to bed.

It is never so wretched to live alone as it is when one is ill. Mrs Plunkett was not intentionally unkind, but she was not solicitous either. Every evening, she sent up an unpalatable mess of leftovers, which Caitlin would not have liked to eat even when well and left untouched. Whilst she was busy during the day with the laundry, she did poke her head in occasionally though Caitlin suspected this was only to see if her tenant had expired in the room, thereby leaving it available for another 'guest'.

Caitlin slept miserably on and off. Her chest now hurt her to breathe, and she was continually vacillating between shivering cold or sweating profusely. On the fourth day, she felt a little better and was informed by Mrs Plunkett that Mr Shawcross had called, but of course, she had sent him away. This was too much.

"But I wanted to see him!" she cried and turned her wet face to the pillow. Mrs Plunkett grumbled all the way downstairs about what hussies young girls had become these days and how they had no sense of the proprieties.

Even so, the next time Caitlin awoke, it was to see Hartley's face before her. He had obviously been there sometime and was watching her breathing with concern.

"Hartley!" she croaked and strove to get up. He put his arms about her firmly, and she clung onto him, relishing the clean, business-like smell of his suit.

"Have you had a doctor, Cait?" he asked anxiously.

She shook her head. "No, I don't think I could afford one."

He felt the pulse at her wrist banging away. "I shall bring one. Don't worry. I will pay for him."

She tried to thank him, but he was looking round the room, more than a little angrily, she thought. In fact, he was wondering if he should remove her to his own rooms which were at least warm and comfortable whilst this place was not. But of course, that whole operation would be fraught with impropriety.

The maid appeared with a curled-up specimen of sausage on a plate, luke-warm, hard, and reeking of spices. Caitlin shook her head.

"Take it away," Hartley told her with authority. "And ask your mistress to come up here directly."

"She's busy in the kitchen, sir," said the girl.

"I don't care. Tell her to come up now!"

Caitlin saw that he was angry. She had not seen him so before. Mrs Plunkett came, wiping her hands on her apron and grumbling under her breath. She had a good idea of what was coming and stood there defiantly.

"Why is there no fire in the grate?" Hartley demanded. "This room is freezing. There is ice inside the windowpane."

"Beggin' your pardon, sir, but Miss Murphy never asked for one."

"She is very ill, and anyone can see that she needs attention."

Mrs Plunkett remained obstinately silent.

"I am going to fetch a doctor," continued Hartley. "And when I return, I expect to see a good fire. She also needs clean bed linen and fresh water. This room is filthy, and the chamber pot needs emptying."

"We thought it best to leave her undisturbed."

"You were wrong." Even Hartley was surprised at his own sternness and strength in mentioning such matters, but he was determined that his Madonna should not be treated in this way.

"When I come back, I expect to see everything done."

"There is the question of the rent .... unpaid this week," Mrs Plunkett pointed out. She was not one to give in lightly. "It's meant to be in advance."

Hartley took out his wallet in disgust and handed over a wad of dollar bills.

"I trust that will suffice for the next few weeks," he said boldly." For such a miserable little room. Now begone and set these things in motion. If they are not carried out to my satisfaction, I shall make it known that you run a very disreputable boarding house."

Just how Hartley intended to do this he had not considered. But Mrs Plunkett was visibly shaken as she stumped crossly off and the maid, left hovering nervously behind, who had never heard anyone speak like that to Mrs Plunkett before, thought Hartley quite wonderful.

A doctor duly came and was ushered into a transformed sickroom. The grate had been swept and the fire lit. Lamps had been brought and the invalid was propped up on clean sheets and an extra pillow. Even the canary's cage had been cleaned and the bird fed.

The doctor sounded Caitlin's chest and pronounced a nasty infection which could well turn into double pneumonia. He prescribed plenty of bed rest for a while yet, goose-grease to rub on the chest and an evil-looking physic to break up the phlegm. Hartley paid for his visit and went to the drugstore. On his return, he found a chastened and embarrassed Caitlin who had endured many comments of Mrs Plunkett's about 'not runnin' a bleedin' hospital' and 'never in my entire life avin' 'ad any complaints before.'

"What time is it?" she asked weakly.

"About seven."

"In the evening?"

"Yes, of course! In the evening."

"Will you let Madame Arlott know I am not better? I cannot afford to lose my job, no matter how I hate it!"

"Don't worry about that. I'll see to it. You must take your medicine now."

She obeyed him, although it tasted horrible. "Hartley?"

"Yes?"

"I am so lonely. Will you sit with me a while?"

"Of course, dearest one!"

"I am sorry I have been caused you so much trouble."

He pressed her hot hand in his. "Nonsense, you have been no trouble."

"You were so angry."

"But not with you, Cait! Only you should have sent for me before."

"I thought it would pass," said Caitlin, "I suppose, and then I thought perhaps I would die, and that would be for the best. No one in the world would really miss me."

"I would miss you terribly," said Hartley, stroking a strand of hair off her forehead. "You know I would miss you, surely?"

"Yes," she said, "I think you would, a little."

"More than a little!"

Perhaps he did love her after all, then. If only he would tell her so!

"And if I wrote to Polly," he said, trying to cheer her more. "You know she would be here by the very next train."

The mention of Polly spoilt the effect for her. "Yes," she said dully. "Perhaps she would."

"I have no doubt about it. In fact, don't you think I should write? When you are recovered, you will still be weak for a time, you know, and not fit to go back to Madame's straightaway. A visit to Boston would do you good ... "

"No, Hartley!"

"Or if that were not possible, Polly's company down here for a while would help."

"No, you mustn't write. Promise!"

"Well, we must think of something to help you regain your strength. Oh, I almost forgot — I have brought you some soup. Could you manage to try a little?"

"Perhaps just a little."

"Frau Kleist sent it for you. I will warm it over the fire. She said it was very strengthening."

"That was good of her."

"Yes."

"I shall soon be strong again," said Caitlin. "You must not worry about me, Hartley. I know that I must go back to Madame Arlott's as soon as I am able. I can't thank you enough for all you've done."

He thought how wan her face was and how, in fact, more should be done. Perhaps he could speak to Elmer James about a raise. Perhaps he could take a second job, in the evenings, although then he should hardly see Caitlin at all. Once she was back to her normal health, he must settle the question between them once and for all. Somehow, he intended her to be his wife.

Yet the winter dragged on without anything being said or done. Caitlin recovered and returned to work for Madame, a little worn down but trying her best to remain cheerful. Elmer James left on a business trip before Hartley could pluck up the courage to speak to him and would be away for a month or two.

Then suddenly Hartley found himself caught up in the affairs of the Kleists again. For there was no mistaking any longer that Friedrich Kleist was deeply unhappy. To determine the cause was more difficult. Ever since they had changed premises the business had been thriving steadily and Rosa was much gratified by this. The children were well, the boys in school and growing steadily. There seemed to be nothing now which could stand in their way. Yet Friedrich was not happy.

He had borne the seeds of isolation within him to their new country — they were German but Jewish, Jews yet no longer Orthodox. When they had cast themselves adrift from their own country it had no longer wanted them. Yet who wanted them here? Rosa had compensated. It was she who chatted to the customers in her broken but quick English, she who made friends with the neighbours, and approved of everything new. Friedrich could not.

Rosa begged Hartley to take him out again in the vain hope he could be taken out of himself, and Hartley complied willingly. But it was difficult. The man had to be prised out of his workshop, even though he sat there in silence doing nothing but staring endlessly into space. Although he would accept a drink, he would say nothing unless spoken to, and sometimes not even then. Hartley could not find the means to reach him even when he tried to speak of music and art.

Rosa had given all the directions in the shop for some time now. She only needed Friedrich to sew but that, in the end, he seemed unable to do. Orders were late or improperly done. When she chided her husband, he merely put on his hat and coat and disappeared for hours on end on long, solitary walks, leaving her to wonder what on earth he could be doing. Poor Rosa! She could see her husband's disintegration before her eyes, but she had no remedy because there seemed to be no cause.

"What should I do?" she asked Hartley in a rare moment of desperation.

Hartley shook his head. "Try not to worry," he said kindly. "He is a melancholy man by nature. But this phase will surely pass. In the meantime, we must try and make life easy for him."

However, New York life was not easy, as Hartley well knew. He was at a loss how to help. So, Friedrich continued to walk the streets and wander down to the docks to watch the ships come in. On the way back, he would pass the doors of the synagogue and hear faint strains of well-remembered voices from within. They gave him an inconsolable ache in his heart, coming as they did from an earlier time, a different world where life was not as complicated. It made him stand before the door for a long time, thinking, remembering, sometimes trying to pray. Yet he could not bring himself to go into the synagogue. He was supposed to be a Christian now.

Rosa had no need of the old faith although they kept up many of its customs through habit and neither should he. How would the rabbi understand all the things he had done? Only Rosa's father could do that, but he might as well be dead and gone back in the old country. Even he could not take away the taint of failure, failure of the people, and the old stains of blood on the barricades and in the streets. That was Friedrich's burden.

He knew he was failing Rosa and the children too. Somehow, they must get an assistant, one who would understand this new-fangled sewing machine and new fashions better than he did. Yet they could not afford it until he earned more money. He must work, he must! Yet here was another gloomy day gone by with nothing done. Rosa would be angry and rightly so. If it wasn't for Rosa, he would have given up long since. Now Rosa, although he loved her dearly, seemed lost to him.

$$\approx$$

The snows were gone long ago, and the city was freeing itself from the iron grip of winter at last. Caitlin, like Friedrich, found little delight in the lengthening days and the promise of the tight buds on the trees in the squares of New York. What cause did she have to hope? Ever since her illness, she had been resigned but felt a permanent sense of weariness and growing despair. Every day, she felt the need to escape. Only where could she go, and what could she do? Her resolve was worn down by the drudgery of her life. She continued to see Hartley, but nothing new ever happened.

Chapter Six

One evening, when Caitlin arrived back at her lodgings, Mrs Plunkett informed her that a man was waiting to see her in the communal sitting room. Surprised, for Mrs Plunkett always referred to Hartley as '*that* Mr Shawcross', she entered with a curiosity unfelt since her days at the Regans. For an instant, she did not recognize the man who stood there in fine winter furs. His face was hard and tanned, dark and unsmiling, his body lithe and active-looking. Then he spoke her name, and she gasped.

"Owain!"

For a moment, they stared at one another, registering their changed appearances.

Owain spoke first. "My poor Caitlin," he said. "Everything fell apart then, despite your uncle's good intentions."

"Yes," she said with bent head, for then she had to tell him the whole story and it was not one she relished, though it poured out of her. "But what of you?" she asked at length.

Owain's face brightened. "I have bought my own land," he said proudly.

"That's wonderful!"

"And I intend going out there directly. It's in Kansas, see, where they grow first-class corn and crops of all kinds."

"You must have earned good money on the railroads."

"Not the railroads. For nearly two years now, I've lived rough up in the Adirondacks and hunted and trapped for skins and furs. I've been able to sell them for good money and save."

Caitlin murmured further astonishment and approbation. "You've done well, Owain."

He grasped both her hands impulsively in his own. "Will you come with me, Caitlin?"

"Come with you?" She couldn't believe she had heard him correctly.

"Yes! I have a deed of sale for the land. I have money for tools and horses and a wagon. The only thing I lack is a wife. Will you marry me, Caitlin? I have long thought of it. If I must go alone, I will, but how much better it would be to have a wife! It would make me strong and happy to have you by my side. Please say yes, Caitlin! You don't want to remain in New York all your life, do you?"

"Indeed not!" said Caitlin.

All the while Owain had been making his speech, an uncomfortable excitement had begun to possess her. Nevertheless, she still pulled away from him.

" I hardly know what to say, Owain! It has come so suddenly."

Owain did not appear to understand. He followed her across the room and faced her with eyes that were feverish in their intensity. "I know I am not offering you anything great, Caitlin. Life will be difficult at first with hard work. But many succeed, and it is a chance to make a new and happy life further out west."

"Yes, I understand, Owain. It is not that I would spurn such a life. Far from it. But I must think. Why, Owain, we scarcely know each other!"

He looked wounded. "Did we not spend six weeks together on the boat?"

Yes, of course, and I shall never forget them. But they were... well, not like real life at all! We cannot trust that. And I can see you are a different person already! Your fear has gone, and you are confident and strong ...."

"Does that bother you?"

"No, of course not. I am glad to see it. Only Owain, I am not sure...."

"I love you, Caitlin. I fell in love on the boat. I don't ask for love in return, only the chance to take care of you. We *do* know each other and can make something good of our lives."

Caitlin felt a sense of panic. Yet why? This was not in the least like Cornelius O'Brien's proposal. There was no doubt in her mind that Owain did love her. Wouldn't it be wonderful to have someone of her own at last? Not to mention escaping Madame and New York? She found she was tempted but not at all sure. Could she ever forget what Owain had done in the past?

Oh, but he had been good since he got here. He had tried so hard. Having her would surely keep him good. Why, it was almost her duty to marry him! Hadn't she confessed she would never be able to marry for love anyway, with James gone? What did it matter? She liked Owain well enough. In his new incarnation there was even something exciting about him. Had she not longed for something like this to happen? How would she end up if she stayed in New York? Dead surely, if she were to remain a poor drudge, and worse if she ever took the other option of risking herself on the streets as so many girls were driven to do.

Then what of Hartley? He wouldn't let her go on the streets and he would caution her against this too. She ought to find out more.

"This Kansas, Owain ..."

"Yes?"

"Is it far out in the country?"

"Oh yes. Far away from any ugly city! I have been told it is a beautiful land, full of green hills and pleasant streams and fertile soil. The climate is wonderful and everything that grows there ends up two or three times the size it would here. Most of the land is untilled, which is why they're real keen for folks to go. It ain't expensive like the farms in the Genesee Valley or up the Hudson where all the work's been done already. It's dirt cheap, and so it's a great chance."

"Green hills," said Caitlin thoughtfully. In her mind's eye, there floated a kinder picture of Ireland. "But will there be other people there, Owain?"

"Oh, sure. Settlers are going out all the time. That's one of the reasons I need you, Caitlin. I've forgotten how to talk to ordinary folks now that I've been alone so long. You're the one who'll make friends with the neighbours and look after the children and all."

It was an appealing picture, but she had heard about war like Indians. "And ... what about Indians?"

Owain laughed. "You don't need to worry about Indians! Not anymore. I came across some up north. They're not that bad when you get to know them. Anyway, most of them have been pushed out way further west."

Owain had not talked as much for two years or more. Now he could hardly be stopped as he went on to describe their new life there. Oh yes, he was a vastly different Owain!

"I'll ... I'll have to think."

"But you won't say no straight out?"

"No, no I won't. I will think very seriously, Owain, I promise you." She let him have her hand.

"I have no soft words," he said. "To woo you with. But I can take care of you, Caitlin, like no one else can."

"I shan't keep you waiting long — a matter of a day or two, that's all."

She called at Hartley's rooms the same evening, but he was out. She had not seen him for a week because he had pleaded problems at work.

Leaving a message that she must see him urgently; she returned home to her lodgings but could not sleep. Over and over again she reviewed her life in New York and found it wanting. This was surely the chance of a lifetime and another new start. It would be a decent life, honest and hard-working. She was not afraid of the land. She had grown up on it. What had happened since was obviously not for her, pleasant though some of it had been at the time.

The very next day, she gave notice to Madame Arlott. That made her feel more decisive, and she could not quell a rising excitement. She had made Owain promise to leave her alone for two days, but now she regretted this. Only the thought of Hartley poured a cold shower on her feelings and made her feel uncertain. Would he be driven to propose to her now? But if he did, could he offer her anything better? She stayed in all evening waiting for him, sitting in the communal room of her lodgings in a fever of impatience, but he did not come.

At last, just when she had given up hope and the clock in the room was striking half-past ten, she heard his step in the hall. She rose and went to the door. It was evidently raining outside for he was furling a wet umbrella and leaving it in the stand.

"Hartley! I am in here."

"Ah, you are still up? I was afraid you would have gone to bed."

"Wherever have you been?"

"I'm sorry, Caitlin. I have been looking for Friedrich."

"Herr Kleist?"

"Yes. He has gone missing. Since yesterday. No one can find him."

Caitlin saw in the lamplight that her visitor looked tired and anxious. That was unfortunate. Still, she couldn't help thinking how different he and Owain were. Owain was so dark and now suddenly so powerful in his enthusiasm whilst Hartley who was so fair seemed to be perpetually bothered about something or other. She shrugged her shoulders with pique.

To her mind, Hartley was too much taken up with this troublesome Kleist family.

"Well, surely he will turn up. Where have you looked for him?"

"In every bar and beer place I could think of."

"Is he a drunkard now as well?"

"As well as what?"

"Well, isn't he more than a little mad?"

"No, of course not ... nor drunk either. I had rather hoped he might take a drink or two, for he suffers so."

"Don't all men and women?" Caitlin was determined not to give a fraction of sympathy, such was her annoyance at being forced to hold back her own shattering news.

"They do not all feel it to the same degree. That is the conclusion I have reached lately through knowing him better. However, you did not ask me here to argue about Herr Kleist?" He smiled at her tenderly and not without humour. "What is it that gave your note so much urgency?"

Caitlin folded her arms with determination and turned away from him so he should not see her face. "Hartley ... I am going to leave New York."

"Are you going to join Polly in Boston?"

Polly! Why must he *always* bring up Polly when she wanted to discuss their mutual interests? She felt exasperated and it lent her tongue a sharpness she did not intend.

"No! I am not going to Boston."

"Then where?"

"I am going to Kansas."

"Kansas?" Hartley sat down and could not help but laugh. "*Kansas!* Have you the slightest idea how far away that is?"

Caitlin coloured. Now he was making her feel ignorant and stupid. "I wish it to be as far away from New York as possible!"

"But what on earth could take you there?"

"A proposal of marriage. A gentleman I know has bought some land out there and wants a wife to go and farm it with him."

Hartley was stunned. "What gentleman?"

"You don't know him. It is the stowaway I met on ship."

"The Welshman?"

"Yes." Was it her imagination or did Hartley flinch bodily at this?

"How on earth did he find you?"

"He went to Union Square and found the house burnt down. At the hotel they told him where I was living now. That hardly matters, does it?"

Hartley was trying to assimilate the shock. "Leaving aside the fact that a gentleman hardly stows away on an emigrant ship, I must point out you hardly know him!"

She had meant to ask his advice at this point but, seeing him already so negative, she began to defend herself instead. "Of course I know him! You can't spend six weeks aboard such a ship without getting to know someone well. He promised to come back for me if I was unhappy and he has kept his word ... as a gentleman would."

Hartley tried not to feel hurt at this. "Do you love him then?"

"I don't love any man, but I know that Owain will care for me and look after me. I ask no more." She tossed her head defiantly.

"Caitlin, I can understand your desire to escape —"

"It is more than a desire, Hartley. It is a necessity."

"But you really mustn't rush into marriage with any pioneer that happens to be passing because you must get away from Madame Arlott's!"

Caitlin stamped her foot. "He is not *any* pioneer!"

"I'm sorry, but surely you can see what I mean. What do you really know about him after all?"

A great deal, thought Caitlin sulkily. *A great deal more than I'd ever tell you!*

Hartley tried a different approach. "If only it were not Kansas, Caitlin. Anywhere else rather than there."

"Why? What is wrong with Kansas?"

"Nothing in itself. But it hasn't been admitted to the Union yet as the free state it should be. Before that happens, I fear there will be a deal of trouble."

"Pooh! American politics!" said Caitlin contemptuously. "What do I care for that? You can't believe all you read in the newspapers."

"Aren't you an American now?"

"No, I am Irish, and New York and New England do not want the Irish!"

Hartley shook his head. "They have little choice. You know full well there are Irish bankers and Irish businessmen now – politicians too."

"All men married to Irish wives because no one else will have them!"

"Then go to Boston and join Polly in her campaigning if that is how you feel! Only don't throw yourself away on a scurrilous coward like Owain!"

"How dare you?" Caitlin was stung to retort. "He has lived rough for two years in the Northern wilderness and scraped together enough money for his own land in Kansas. He has worked in mines and on railroads whilst you have sat at a desk and shuffled papers with your soft white hands and got precisely nowhere!" It was a terrible thing to say to him, and she knew it. But all her life, she had been hurt and cast out. Now it was her turn, and she was cruel in the rush of having a choice. Nevertheless, her heart misgave her when she saw the unhappy look on Hartley's face as he turned away.

"Have you already said yes?" he asked her quietly.

"Yes!" she lied. "And I have given notice to Madame Arlott."

"Then there is nothing more to be said. When will you go?"

"In a matter of weeks ... as soon as everything can be arranged. We wish to arrive before the end of the summer. How fresh and delightful it will be after New York!"

Hartley allowed himself a final word of caution as he picked up his hat and gloves.

"They used to call it 'The Great American Desert'," he said.

Caitlin lifted her chin an inch higher. He was only trying to frighten her. What did he know of it when he had never been out of New York?

"I am quite decided," she said.

"Then there is nothing else to say. I hope to see you again before you leave, and I wish you all the success and happiness in the world."

Caitlin bowed her head. Was that all? Were there to be no words of love? Would he not fight a little harder for her? No. Why should he when she had convinced him so well? She followed him disconsolately into the hall and answered automatically as he bade her goodnight. Then he was gone into the rain, and the night before, she could bring herself to stop him, forgetting his umbrella in his discomposure. It remained forlornly dripping in the stand. She waited for almost ten minutes, being sure that he would return for it.

But he did not.

Feeling unaccountably miserable, she extinguished the lamps and went upstairs with a candle. When she closed her own door, the noise it made sounded dreadfully final. Without any additional stimulus, she wept. All the things she had meant to say were left unsaid. If only it were possible to follow him and to tell him, who after all had been her dearest friend, that she was actually very unsure in her own mind what she should do, and not least because of him.

$\approx$

April 4th 1853

My Dearest Hartley,

I am so distressed that we parted the other night on such bad terms. I know that in the heat of our discussion I said things I did not mean and had been better left unsaid. Please try to forgive me, because I cannot leave New York knowing that you are deeply vexed with me. I do hope we can meet again soon.

Owain is very anxious that our affairs should be expedited as quickly as possible and there is much to do. We are to be married next Friday at the church of the Sacred Heart, off Madison Square at eleven. Do say you will come, then I will know you bear me no ill-will!

Your repentant friend,

Caitlin.

P.S. I do hope Herr Kleist has returned or been found safe and well?'

The reply cost Hartley dear to write, and Caitlin trembled as she read it, especially at the manner of its address.

≈

April 5th 1853

Dear Miss Murphy,

Do not chide yourself for our disagreement the other night. The whole affair came as such a shock to me that I fear I did not behave quite as a gentleman should. Of course, I forgive you and I hope that you will do the same of me. You know that I have been fond of you for so long and I wish you nothing but happiness and prosperity in your new life.

As to our meeting, I am not sure that is either possible or indeed appropriate and I am afraid I cannot attend your wedding. They took poor Friedrich Kleist's body out of the South Street docks yesterday morning, and he is to be laid to rest on Friday. I hope you will excuse me. My heart will be too full that day. I owe the Kleists so much for their kindness to me, and it would be unthinkable to desert them now in their hour of need.

I wish you God Speed, my dear,

Your faithful servant, Hartley Shawcross

≈

That Friday morning dawned as it must, bright but cold. Caitlin shivered in the thin wedding gown which Madame Arlott had lent her. There were no guests despite her finery. All along, she told herself that Hartley would relent and come after all. How could he stay away? But on her way into the church, she looked for his fair head in vain. Only Madame and one of the least unfriendly girls from the workshop were there as witnesses.

Madame Arlott had persisted in wearing her eternal black, and the girl was in working clothes, for they must return to their labours afterward. *At least I shall not be joining them*, thought Caitlin with a return of her spirits. Madame Arlott looks pleased. *She must be glad to have me off her hands at last with her obligation to Mrs Regan laid to rest. Well, I am more than glad. I am deliriously happy!*

Then the ring was slipped onto her finger, the priest intoned his final solemn words, and it was done so quickly she could hardly believe it. She had expected to feel more, not just happiness at avoiding Madame Arlott's. Still when they emerged into the sunlight again, she stopped shivering and smiled at Owain and felt proud of the way he looked. This was the beginning of their great adventure together, and she would never think about her disappointment with Hartley again. She and Owain were two of a kind, both runaways, both cast in the same mould with an intensity of feeling and desire. She would direct herself to loving this man as best she could. It would never be like it would have been with James, but she would endeavour to make Owain glad he had married her. For the first time in her life, she had someone to call her own.

Chapter Seven

Hartley awoke hollow-eyed. For too many nights, he had hardly slept. Ever since he realized he had lost Caitlin forever, nothing had felt the same. To make matters worse, he knew it was all down to his own stupidity and hesitation. As he shaved, he reflected that, in truth, his rooms were really not that bad. If only he had listened to Polly and Friedrich, (God rest his soul), Caitlin would doubtless have accepted him without demur had she loved him and had he asked her. That she had not loved him in the least, he still found difficulty in accepting it. Wasn't there a begging tone in her pitiful letter underneath all the brave certainties? His blade slipped, and he felt it sting his chin. Cursing, he washed off the soap and dabbed at the blood. He would never know now.

    It was two weeks since she had gone. He had been to work as usual with the exception of that fateful Friday when his grief at losing Caitlin, knowing it was her wedding day, and failing the Kleists had coalesced into one burning mass of regret.

    After his argument with Caitlin (better call it what it really was now) he had been unable to settle into the office the following morning and had gone down to the docks on some pretext or other. There, he had found news of a body being lifted out of the East River. It was as if he had known who it would be all along. The worst of his fears had come to fruition. He knew, even before he saw the body, that it was that of Friedrich Kleist's. The seamen who found him were relieved to settle the matter of identity so quickly, though for a moment, Hartley had hesitated.

Friedrich had been in the water for three days, and there was little recognisable of the shy and sensitive German tailor in that bloated face. But Hartley knew the shoes and the suit, the beard and the hair, and the hands of the German fob watch that still hung from his waistcoat pocket. By such little things are we known.

Someone had to go at once and tell Rosa and he realized it had to be him though he shrank from it. How loathsomely he had crawled along! With what laggardly coward's feet and unwillingness he had entered the door of the shop. But she knew in an instant from his face.

"Is it Friedrich?" she asked calmly. When he nodded, she put on her shawl and came with him, like the little Trojan she was, never saying a word. Where he stood and trembled, she was brave and forthright. She comforted the boys and explained as best as she could to Rachel — the very sight of whom tore at his heart. Friedrich was given a Jewish burial in the end, despite all the difficulties, because she knew that was what he would have wanted, and she did not shirk the rabbi in the end.

Afterwards he and Ralph determined to help Rosa all they could. Sensibly they sat down and discussed business. Of course, the tailoring side of the shop was over and done with. But, with a little help, Rosa thought she could maintain the quality second-hand clothes and the haberdashery and was unwilling to move from the premises where they were established, rightly so in the men's view. Then she had some wild idea of using the paper patterns Friedrich had made up — reproducing them and selling them to customers who were anxious to try out the new sewing machines for themselves. Ralph thought this was crazy, but Hartley could see the germ of a possibility in the idea. It might be a total failure but there was a chance that in time it could come good.

There was a risk investing in it, but Hartley had been weighing the matter carefully now for several days.

When he was ready, he left his rooms, but did not go to the office straight away. He felt he must call in to see Rosa and tell her what was on his mind. He had come to a decision with new firmness. He saw now that risks were continuous and necessary. It was no good waiting for success to come to one. He must proceed with the voyage he had embarked upon.

The shop was shut up, which surprised him, but at length, he made Rosa hear, and she admitted him, locking and closing the door behind him.

"You are not open, Rosa?"

She shook her head. He fancied that she might have been crying. Indeed, he rather hoped she had, for as yet, the calamity did not seem to have penetrated fully to her awareness, or, if it had, she kept it too well hidden.

She took him into the backroom where Rachel was playing, and the child immediately came up to Hartley with delight and climbed onto his lap when he sat down. Hartley fondled the head of dark curls with his hand. He wondered what was going on in her mind, and the thought gave him fresh pain. She showed him her doll and explained it was sad and very cross but would be better soon. Hartley glanced at Rosa.

"Come along," she said in German. "Run and play and leave Mr Shawcross alone. He has come to talk business with Mamma. Be a good girl and you shall have a new ribbon from the shop for your hair. You can go and choose one if you like."

The child ran off obediently.

"Well, Rosa," said Hartley gently. "I have been thinking a great deal about your idea of the patterns and I think it might just work if it is set up well. I would like to help you do that."

Rosa nodded, but there was no answering light in her eyes as there had been the other day.

"You are very kind," she said. "Both you and Herr Shames. So good to me."

Yet she appeared to be hardly listening. She had lost the bloom in her face and the shininess of her dark eyes that he used to like so much. She looked tired and he noticed for the first time that grey hairs were winging up from her temples amongst the once glossy black. Her arms were still plump and pleasantly rounded but she suddenly looked much older than her thirty- nine years.

She tried to concentrate. "Herr Shames....he did not think it such a good idea."

"Well, no, that's true, but I believe he's not looking far enough ahead into the future, Rosa. That's where we're going, isn't it?"

"I don't think I'm going anywhere anymore, Hartley."

It was the first time he had ever heard the smallest note of despair in her voice. He became doubly gentle.

"That's how it seems at the moment, Rosa. It's difficult for you, heaven knows. But there are the children — Friedrich's children and yours. They will help you, and so will I."

She seemed unable to speak.

"Shall we have another look at the patterns? Or shall I come back some other time ... a little later on, perhaps?"

"No," said Rosa staunchly. "I will not have you wasting your valuable time on my account. That would be ungrateful indeed. I will go and get them if you really think there is a chance." She got up stiffly from the chair, then faltered for a moment.

"Are you all right, Rosa?"

"Yes, yes, it is nothing." She went forward into the shop, and he could hear her talking distractedly to Rachel. Hartley looked around the neat little room with its rocking chair, piano, plants, and pictures. The rugs were old and faded, but what a wonderful job she had done so uncomplainingly over these last three years. He suddenly felt angry, angry at Friedrich, angry at the world, and angry with Caitlin. Rosa returned. She looked ashen-faced and sighed as she spread out the papers on the table between them.

Hartley rose to his feet. "Rosa, I think you are not well this morning. I will come back."

"No, don't go, please. It is not so very much. You see, I have another child growing inside me. It is Friedrich's last gift. It makes me very tired. But that will pass. All things pass."

Hartley was horror-struck. "Did Friedrich know?"

"What? Oh ja, Friedrich knew." She smoothed out the paper pieces. "See here ... this is for the shirts, the pants, the shacket. Friedrich was very good at the shackets," she hesitated. "Perhaps it is too difficult? Who could make them as Friedrich could?" She looked at him despairingly, and he saw large tears begin to roll down her fat cheeks.

It was dreadful for him to see her weep, this strong woman who had struck him with her pride and her fortitude from the first moment he had seen her. She bent her head with shame so that he could not see her face, but the tears continued to fall. He could see now that the grey streaks ran right through her hair. He was filled with an immense flood of pity and unbearable love. Not trusting himself, he turned away. She must have thought he meant to go after all, for she sobbed, "I am sorry! I am so sorry."

He turned again and put a hand on her bowed hair.

"Oh, Hartley," she cried. "What are we to do?"

He could not walk away. Taking her in his arms, he held her close, and she buried her head against his shoulder.

"You have nothing to excuse yourself for," he said, and his voice shook. "Nothing at all. No one can be brave all the time, Rosa. Not even you."

"Why did he do it?" she asked fruitlessly. "Why? I loved him so much. But I could not stop him. I could not make him happy. Why could I not stop him from destroying himself?"

"No one could stop him, Rosa. It was his nature. It was the way he was made."

She wept some more, and he waited until the paroxysms of her grief faded. Then he took her ravaged face in the palms of his hands.

"It is good for you to cry," he said. "And I am glad I was here to hold you. But listen, Rosa. This shop will go on, with some changes, of course, and I am going to set up and manage this pattern business for you. I know it will work. Maybe not the shackets but other clothes. Will you trust me? I can easily manage it as well as my work for Elmer James, and I will enjoy making it a success for you. Will you let me?"

She nodded, still overcome.

"You are going to be fine," he reassured her.

"I am sorry," she repeated with a sniff. "You shall not see me cry again nor be so foolish or weak."

At that moment, she had to be as unlovely as he had ever seen her, with swollen eyes and trembling lips, her whole body overwhelmed by the situation. It still came as no surprise to him when he said the words he had no intention of uttering earlier that morning:

"Rosa, I am going to take care of you. I would like to marry you."

She drew back in astonishment. "But you cannot! You are a young man with all his life before him, and I am old and ugly. I cannot let you do that!"

"You are not old and ugly," he said. "You are going to have a child. Old, ugly women don't have babies. Anyway, there is no such thing as ugliness in a woman like you!"

"Oh, yes, there is! I am not blind, Hartley, nor a fool!"

"Then you will not have me?"

"I am afraid I am tempted to have you ... that is it. It would not be right, Hartley!"

"I do not expect you to love me so soon after Friedrich."

"But Hartley, I do love you. You are like a grown son to me! You are such a worthy young man ... I know that."

"But I am not your son."

"No."

"Then marry me, Rosa. We need each other now."

"Ah, it is because you have lost your young and beautiful, headstrong Irish girl! But you must not grieve for her that much, Hartley! You must not throw yourself away on such as me. There will be others."

"I do not want others, Rosa. I want you."

She was exhausted and had to admit at last that she wanted him. She bent her head in shame, and he kissed it tenderly. He had never been more sincere in his life. Yet there was a great, dull ache in his heart.

Part Five

Towards Disaster

Chapter One

It was one year and one month later, and Caitlin's heart sang as she prepared supper in the cabin. It was simple enough fare: chicken in the pot and cornbread. But she had become an expert at cooking it, just as Owain was an expert at catching and killing their food. She smiled to herself as she put the pot on the stove. He was so tough and so hard-working. They had accomplished much already.

Wiping her hands on a cloth, she went outdoors to drink in the warm evening air. Her hands were roughened with hard work, but she didn't care. She was tired, for she had been working all day in the field alongside Owain and then had the livestock to see to, but it was the kind of tiredness that made you feel good about yourself and content with your life.

She looked out at their fields: three so far, two for corn and one for vegetables. The rest of their land grew wild with prairie grass, broken up by dirt mounds thrown up by gophers, but it was staked out to emphasize their new claim. Beyond it, the essentially flat earth rolled onwards. The sun had dipped in the west, leaving a vivid orange light in the sky behind. If she strained her ears, she could hear the waters of the nearby creek and a warm wind rustling through the few trees by its edge. One of their horses, Betsy, a dark bay mare, was cropping the grass nearby. Owain had ridden the other horse into town to the store. He had some goods to pick up and had been away for some time.

She was used to being alone. Sometimes, these days, she almost forgot how lonely she first felt out here. Leaving the door open, she went back inside to sit down in her chair. You could not feel too lonely when you knew there was a child growing inside you, even though it was still small. Something convinced her it was a boy, and that made her feel glad. In time, he would be able to help Owain.

She smiled as she thought of all that had happened since they left New York. She had been little more than a child herself then. For despite all the calamities that had already befallen her in her young life, despite the hardships of the voyage and all the tribulations of her three years in the city, she now knew she had been totally unprepared for the challenge of Kansas.

Of course, it had been exciting that first morning, with all her sudden inexplicable reluctance to leave New York. There was a great sense of adventure in both of them as they boarded the train. When the boxcars rattled along, she forgot her fears of the unknown in the novelty of being out in the countryside.

In due course, she discovered there were other cities in America besides New York, and some of them were much finer — Philadelphia, Baltimore, and Washington. So many places of civilisation and people hitherto undreamt of. After Washington, they steamed through the beautiful state of Virginia, full of glorious, verdant trees and pleasant, winding rivers with hazy, blue hills in the distance. The farmland here seemed very fertile, and they often saw black slaves toiling in the well-ordered fields. In her ignorance, Caitlin asked Owain if their lives could really be as bad as they were painted. For she had seen many fine houses and elegant carriages along the way, and the sight made her wistful. She could not imagine that these plantation owners could be so very cruel. They seemed such refined people.

Owain answered her stoutly that the most important thing in life was to be free. If he were a slave, he should not care for the best of conditions, knowing that he was not at liberty to leave nor to take any significant action without his master's consent. She supposed he was right — of course, he was, and yet she could not help thinking that the factory workers, the seamstresses, and the shopgirls of the North only endured a different form of slavery.

Owain was noticeably quiet. Not at all the frightened young boy she had met on the boat. In his silent Adirondack wilderness, he had become a strong man, but he had also absorbed much of its silence. She did not complain, for she knew they were still shy of each other, and that was surely normal for a newly married couple, though she wished he could be a little less serious and a little more talkative. Hartley would have been interested in the plantations and the people, she felt, and more willing to discuss the politics. "Look at this," he would have said. "Look at that. How different it all is from New York." Still, she mustn't think about Hartley. He was only her friend and not her husband.

It took them three days to reach Cincinnati and another two to St. Louis. She liked Cincinnati. It had broad and airy streets with clean red and white houses and attractive gardens, and it raised her spirits. St. Louis was different. Some of the wooden houses in the old French quarter were picturesque, with tumbledown galleries at the front, reached by ladders from the narrow streets. But the rest of the town mushroomed out into a mass of warehouses and wharves equally as nasty as any in New York. Their growth was due to the town's position on the great Mississippi River. It provided its very reason for being, and it was the reason they had come here — for this was the end of the railway line. From here, they must take a steamboat upriver.

The river water was muddy brown, the land around it wet and swampy, and there were many mosquitoes when night fell. She could not believe it was a healthy place and felt depressed and tired.

It was a full eight days since they had left New York, and now they were to spend another five on this monstrous contraption of a paddle steamer before they reached Kansas. In truth, she had not realized before how far away they were going, but now she did. The river was soon loathsome to her: the banks were low, flat, and monotonous, covered with the sparsest of stunted trees, interrupted only occasionally by the most wretched of settlements and steep bluffs. There were fewer emigrants aboard than she had expected, and all of them had a great deal more baggage and general paraphernalia than Owain and herself, even though she had insisted on bringing the canary in its cage, which she still hadn't brought herself to sell.

She grew anxious and voiced her worries aloud to her husband. Was this the sort of land whither they were bound, where everything lay listless and flattened? What if they could not buy tools, livestock or a wagon in Kansas?

Owain took her small hand and patted it rather absent-mindedly. He assured her there was no cause for alarm. Once they reached the great junction of the Kansas River with the Missouri and headed west, all would be changed. He had been told he could buy all he needed in Independence near that junction.

"Only think of that, Caitlin, there is a town called Independence in Missouri!" He patted the money belt he kept strapped around his waist, under his shirt, much as he had patted her hand. They were at the forefront of all the settlers that were bound to come and so they would be assured of the best land. Yet she wondered how he knew.

There was an Indian on the boat ... the first she had seen, and he fascinated her. Contrary to her expectations, he did not wear feathers or warpaint, merely an old, battered hat, a red shirt, and moccasins. He sat cross-legged on the deck, never moving, nor speaking, nor being spoken to. He was very tall, and his brown face stretched over high cheekbones with its nose hooked like an eagle's, remained impassive and proud. Supposing, thought Caitlin nervously, he cut their throats in the middle of the night with the gleaming knife strapped to his waist and made off with Owain's money bag?

She found it difficult to sleep. The motion of the train over rails had lulled her off even though the seats were uncomfortable, but the vibrations of the boat jarred upon her nerves. This Western steamship was different from any other vessel she had seen. It had no masts, rigging or tackle like the Yorkshire, only a couple of paddle-boxes and funnels. At every turn of the paddles, the funnels belched forth a great pall of smoke. She could not forget from the clank of the machinery that there was an immense furnace of a fire burning below their deck. The night was very dark, a good deal darker than she would have liked it to be. They lay on pallets on the hard deck, and the heat from their bodies attracted mosquitoes. Once, they passed another leviathan like theirs and saw the bright body of fire below blazing out over the water. Then it was gone with the swish of paddles churning muddy water, and they were alone in the darkness again.

The packet was not overly crowded, and there were certainly many empty cabins above. At least the food was regular, though monotonous, with three full meals a day of dried beef and pork, pickles and pumpkin, and as much hot cornbread and water as you could eat and drink. But the Missouri seemed much like the Mississippi to her, and the people on the boat grew no less unfriendly whilst the Indian never spoke. It was a vast relief to reach Independence at last. The town was a trading post, and the stores adequate.

It even had a hotel where they put up and where Owain ordered a fine meal of wheat bread and chicken fixings as opposed to cornbread and 'common doings'. They slept in a bed for the first time since leaving New York. Caitlin was still unaccustomed to the feeling of having Owain's body beside her and was nervous, but fell asleep immediately.

The next day, she felt better. It dawned brightly and fresher, and they were able to order most of the items they needed and purchase a fine, covered wagon, two sturdy horses, a cow, some hens, and a pig. There was no going back now. Over the next few days, they gradually organized all the tools and the household items in their place in the wagon and acquired wood (at great cost, for it was scarce here) for furniture. Caitlin fell in love with the horses, learnt how to milk a cow and not to mind the pig who was a pregnant sow.

Restored to high spirits, they set off along the Santa Fe Trail. Caitlin drove the wagon, uncertainly at first, but then with growing confidence and pride whilst Owain studied the rough map of the territory he got in Independence. It seemed they had reached another land after all, away from the river and the moist, stagnant pools surrounding it. This was a dry trail that led them through rolling land past pleasant creeks. All around them were green, waving grasses. It was like an ocean rippling in the wind. They knew that they had crossed the border and left the United States behind. Gone were the cities, the towns, the villages, the farms (for there was precious little evidence yet of other settlers). They had left all that they knew and much of it that was decent and comfortable.

Before them stretched infinity. The sky was vast, and the horizon almost circular. A bright prairie sun swam slowly across it. Underneath, the land stretched out and onwards, as far as the eye could see and further still.

Perhaps forever. They were filled with a sense of elation at the grandeur and brightness of it all and hugged each other without constraint for the first time. There were no forests, no blessed stumps to clear, as Owain said cheerfully, almost no cover at all except for a few elms and oaks, hickory and scrubby cottonwood which shaded the odd creek or watering hole. Instead, there were flowers of every shade that grew wild in the grass and the air was full of the hum of busy insects, though not the harmful whine of mosquitoes thankfully. There were many birds and once they saw a distant herd of grazing buffalo….no longer kings of the plain but still magnificent creatures. Everything was virgin and wild and, for the first time, Caitlin understood why Owain so desperately wanted his own land here.

She sat, for all the world, like a dirty gypsy woman, on the wagon with her cotton skirt covered in dust from the trail and a common bonnet tied round her head, a million miles away from New York and its fine parties and fussy ballgowns. The sun lay warm on the back of her neck, and she could swing her bare legs against the wooden board of the wagon. Beside her sat this small, dark, wiry man who was so strong and was hers alone, and behind her swayed the beginnings of their first home together with the canary chirping sweetly. She thought she had never been so happy.

Towards nightfall they stopped in the place Owain had marked out. It had no name but was situated way up a creek at the top of the Osage River. According to the map, the river was also called Marais des

Cygnes. The French had given it that name because it was a breeding ground for swans. They could hear the loud beat of their wings as they took off from the water. There were plenty of ducks too and geese and fat prairie turkeys. No shortage of food then.

The nearest settlement was Prairie City, and then Palmyra to the north. Not really cities of course, but mere collections of shacks, stores and saloons. Further south lay Osawatomie on the Pottawatomie Creek. All Indian names, which Caitlin found charming once she learnt the Indians were long gone into reservations, driven out like the buffalo. The largest settlement was Lawrence, way up to the north on the Kansas River. Around them for several miles, there was nothing.

Night dropped swiftly, and the dark brought a renewal of Caitlin's fears. In her naivety, she had imagined coming home to the site of a future log cabin surrounded by others. Instead, there was nothing but the empty land. Owain pitched a tent for the night, tethered the horses, and settled the livestock. Caitlin sat huddled round the fire and shivered, for it was colder now, and she felt uneasy and exposed. They roasted some bacon on the fire and ate it with cornbread. It tasted good out in the open, and she felt a little better. Then, the howl of a coyote nearby startled her and made her feel frightened again. Even the stars looked different and strange. Surely, there were more of them here than there had ever been in the city.

"What if it rains?" she asked timidly, gazing at the sky.

Owain, who was entirely in his element, laughed. "It's not going to rain!" he said. "The sky is as clear as anything. Anyway, what if it did? We have the tent. What a baby you are, Caitlin! I thought you were a country girl!"

But this was very different from Ireland. She looked crestfallen and ashamed of the fear she could not control. "I can't help it." Her voice trembled. "I'm so cold."

"It isn't cold, Caitlin!" Then he remembered she'd never spent a night in the open before. He smiled more kindly and pulled her down into his arms. This was the opportunity he had waited for, and it was time he took it.

"Come here," he said in her ear. "Listen to me. I know the land and I know the wild. Trust me, Caitlin, I know how to look after you."

And yes, she believed that he did and gladly let him hold her tight. She had believed she could never love him and would never love anyone but James. Here, underneath the night sky and the cold, unseeing moon, she found she felt differently. They had not begun their 'married life' as yet. In New York, she had not let him consummate their vows and there had been little chance since. Now, out here in this primitive place, she responded to his fumbling caresses with some ardour, and it was a relief to discover that she liked it well enough.

≈

A year on, she smiled to herself in her reverie in the rocking chair. What a baby she had been! But she wasn't like that now. Since then, they had both worked tirelessly. Owain had built the cabin, not out of logs for the trees on the creek were too precious to cut down, but out of prairie sods. It was very rough, and the walls were streaked with mud when it rained. Inside they had a stove, although it smoked the place out when the wind blew in the wrong direction. There were chairs and a table and a trestle bed. She had second hand crockery and utensils, blankets too for when it grew cold.

Owain had fenced off the land and laid his claim at the sutler's office as soon as he was able. The price was a little over a dollar per acre. They had sixty, but years and years in which to pay. They had ploughed and seeded the first three fields, and there were, after all, neighbours, a good few miles away, but within reach on horseback: Meg, a tough Welshwoman, oddly enough, with five children and her husband Billy, and to the South, the Pattersons, whom Owain didn't like much because they came from Missouri and had brought two slaves with them, though they were hardly monsters for all that.

That first polar winter was a shock. It had been really cold then, with biting winds which brought deep snow. Even in the fall, it turned nasty. One morning, Caitlin had been raking out the stove as usual when there was an angry hiss. To her horror, she realized she had disturbed a sleepy rattlesnake, which must have crawled inside the ashes for warmth. She had never seen one before, but there was no mistaking the danger. It uncoiled its markings, reared up its head, and darted out a forked tongue flickering towards her. She backed away and screamed. Luckily, Owain wasn't far away and came running. She had been paralysed with terror, the poker useless in her hand, but Owain had seized it from her and smashed the creature's head in. Even so, she kept on screaming until he took it away out of the cabin and came back to console her.

After this he tried to teach her to shoot. She managed the mechanics of it well enough but couldn't aim straight. She didn't know why. She could see Owain thought her stupid but there was nothing in the world she could do about it. That first winter had been long and hard with only the light of the sour-smelling tallow candles she made and a bit of buffalo-dung for the fire. So cold every morning when the stove had gone out and there was ice to break on the water troughs before the animals could be fed. So dark. The sow littered but squashed four of them though they still had plenty of salt pork to eat.

Now Caitlin's eyelids drooped, and her reverie dipped into dreams. But at the sound of a horse approaching, she awoke. Owain was back.

She rose to busy herself about the stove. When he came in, he looked agitated. She expected him to kiss her as usual, but he didn't. Instead, he threw himself down into his chair, muttering something unintelligible.

"Did you get the kerosene?"

"Yes."

"And the planks for the chicken house and the nails?" Owain was building a more secure shack for the fowl as they had lost one or two recently to foxes and prairie dogs.

"Yes, I got everything and there was a letter for you." He took it out of his pocket moodily, smoothed out the creases and handed it over.

Caitlin glanced at the writing briefly. "It's from Polly." She tucked it away happily into her apron. News! "I'll read it after we've eaten." A letter was something to be cherished and made even more precious through anticipation.

"I got a newspaper as well. I want you to read it to me."

"All right. After supper. Is anything wrong, Owain?"

"No, nothing."

"You seem cross."

"I am, but not with you."

"Didn't you get a good price for the chickens?" she asked.

"Fair enough."

"You were a long time. Was Billy there?"

"Yes. We were forced to stay. We couldn't get away."

"What do you mean?"

"The store was full of border men. All drunk. Laughing and celebratin'."

"Celebrating what?"

"The passing of the Kansas-Nebraska Bill. The president signed it today. They made us drink a toast to squatter sovereignty,"

"What's that?"

"A new law for Kansas."

"What does it mean?"

"It means that every damn Missouri ruffian can come here with their slaves if they want, and we can't do a damn thing about it. It means Kansas ain't ever going to be a free state in the Union."

"Oh! Eat up your chicken before it gets cold. Will that be so very bad?"

"Of course it will!" Owain sounded impatient. "Don't you see? How will our small farms compete if they come here with all that cheap labour? Anyway, it's completely wrong."

Caitlin chose her words carefully.

"Everybody knows it's wrong," she said, "but if they already have slaves, I guess the people who have them have the right to come and settle in Kansas like everybody else."

"You don't understand a thing," said Owain, contemptuously. Caitlin felt annoyed. *Maybe not,* she thought. *But it's me who can read the newspaper better than you.*

"There's plenty of room for everyone," she insisted. "In time, slavery will be abolished. Polly thinks so."

Owain shook his head. "There's going to be trouble," he told her. "These Missourians ... they ain't that keen to settle really. But they're going to come swarmin' in and fix elections. That ain't fair, is it? And they say they want to string up every abolitionist in the Territory."

"Isn't that just the whisky talking?"

"You haven't seen them, Cait." Owain broke his bread savagely. "They're wild, fighting men, bristling with guns and swords. They wear hemp in their lapels and goose feathers in their hats. That's to show they're 'sound on the goose' — means they all stand fast on the slavery business. And they forced Billy and me to drink on it."

Caitlin eyed Owain anxiously. She knew anything unfair still riled him hugely.

"You didn't say anything, did you, Owain?"

"What about?" He had become cagey now.

"You know. About slaves. About it not being right and all."

Owain chewed a mouthful of chicken and spat out a small bone in disgust.

"No, I didn't say anythin'. I couldn't, could I, with there being so many of them and Billy hangin' on my coat-sleeve like an idiot prayin' for me to be careful? I'd have liked to, though. I'd have liked to shove their bits of hemp right down their throats or up their arses. Didn't do no good anyway, saying nuthin'. They knew alright."

"That you weren't sound on the goose?"

"Yeah."

"Oh, Owain!" Hadn't he promised her he'd keep out of trouble? But that seemed a long time ago.

"Don't you go worryin' now!" He laid a reassuring hand on hers across the table. "I'm not goin' to let anyone force me to give up this piece of land."

"Is that what it'll come to?" Caitlin was alarmed.

"It might. But there's plenty of us round here, and there's going to be more. Lawrence is full of —"

"Abolitionists?" she interrupted.

"Northerners."

"Don't they think every Northerner is an abolitionist!"

"Well, they are, aren't they? Look at your friend Polly. Sounds like a real fine lady to me. She knows the right side to be on."

"Yes, but ..."

"But what?"

"Not all Northerners are like Polly."

Most of them, thought Caitlin, *couldn't really give a damn about the slaves.*

"Well, we do and don't you forget it. Sometimes, Cait, I wonder where your heart really is. What's Polly got to say anyway?"

Caitlin broke open the seal on the envelope in some confusion. *Of course, I believe slavery is wrong,* she thought, thinking of Uncle Tom's Cabin. *How could any decent person not? But I just want to be left alone in peace on this farm, with my new life working out. I've put everything else behind me. I've really tried, though it hasn't always been easy. I don't want any trouble. I don't want to lose everything again. Is that so wrong? What can ordinary people do anyway?*

She unfolded the letter and started reading it quietly to herself. Then she gave a cry of delight.

"I don't believe it!"

"What?"

"I just can't believe it." But she laughed all the same where a moment ago she had been sad. She read on, one hand clutching her bosom excitedly. "It's incredible. Ah, I see now. How perfect! Yes, it's perfect for Polly!"

"What in heaven's name you going on about?" asked Owain.

"She's going to be married. Polly's going to be married!"

"Can't see anything strange in that."

But Caitlin remembered two girls in New York, brushing each other's hair and being so confident they would never marry.

"It's strange for Polly. She always said she would never marry. But he's a minister. A Baptist minister ... oh dear!"

"What's wrong with that?"

"She's a Catholic like me. Only now she's going to give that up."

"Go to Chapel instead of church?"

"Yes."

"So. What's wrong with that?"

"Nothing, I suppose. I don't know." Caitlin realized she was shocked, though. It was Father Francis, of course. The old litanies which never faded even when you no longer really believed in them.

"She says his family were not best pleased. But they're coming round to it. How could anyone not love Polly? Her mamma is delighted because he is such a nice young man and not without money from his family, though she doubts they will spend it aright! Oh, listen Owain! John, that is his name, is heavily involved in the New England Emigrants' Aid Society. Polly says they are quite enthusiastic about coming to Kansas themselves as missionaries! Only there is still so much work to be done in Boston. They applaud our courage in being here. "What, (uneasily now) do you think they mean by that, Owain?"

"It's easier to talk about it in Boston." he shrugged.

"But wouldn't it be wonderful if they did come?"

"Nice for you," said Owain.

Caitlin looked at him and sighed. "She wants me to go to the wedding, though she understands it would be difficult. I can't, can I, Owain?" It was a statement of fact rather than a question though a wistful one.

"I'd like you to go if you wanted. Only it's a long way and we haven't the money. Anyway, it's not safe for a woman to travel on her own from here."

"I know. I didn't really think I could. But wouldn't it be lovely if they came out here? Perhaps they will one day." She went on shoring herself up with this remote responsibility and Owain had the grace to feel guilty.

"I'll take care of you, Cait. Don't you go frettin' now 'bout what I told you."

"No, I won't. Truly, Owain." She leant towards him and kissed him lightly over the table. "Sure, and I'm lucky to have such a good, strong man, all to myself."

"What else does Polly say?" Owain asked, cleaning his plate with bread. Most of Caitlin's meal lay untouched in her excitement.

"Let me see. Oh, lots about John! She says he is tall, dark, and handsome (of course!) and has a friendly, open manner, and is the kindest man in the world. She feels he is truly another half of her spiritually and that they are meant to do God's work together. But I mustn't think him 'a stuffed shirt' because of that because he isn't." Caitlin's mouth twisted a little wryly at this. "Oh!" She read on silently.

"Something else?"

"No, not really. Just about wedding arrangements and the like." Caitlin folded up the letter and left it lying on the table. She was safe to do so for Owain found reading a strain, especially where Polly's literate letters were concerned. Thanks to James and Edmund Burke, Caitlin found it much easier.

"Well, I suppose that's enough excitement for one night." She got up to clear the dishes. "Would you like me to read the newspaper now?" She glanced at *The Kansas Free State*. It was full of condemnation of the Kansas-Nebraska Bill.

"No, it'll keep," Owain yawned and got to his feet. "I'd better shore up that hole in the chicken house with the new planks, seeing as I got them. And if I catch that darned fox prowling round, I'll pepper him with shot!" So saying, he took his rifle from the wall and went outside, leaving the door open.

Whilst they had been eating, the moon had risen, so it was not completely dark. It was very quiet. The howl of a coyote, a sound Caitlin was accustomed to by now, broke the stillness of the night, but it was some way off.

Caitlin took up the letter again and moved the kerosene lamp, which was a great improvement on the candles, closer. The paragraph she had not read out concerned Hartley.

He has his fourth stepchild now, of course, Polly had written. *'Another boy they have named Friedrich. Rachel remains the only girl. But bless me, Rosa is pregnant again, this time with Hartley's own child, so there will soon be five of them. Hartley has become a family* man and seems happy with it from his letters, though I own I sometimes wonder why he took so much on at such an early age.

Because he wanted a mother figure, Caitlin thought sourly, with a small, green flame of jealousy curling in her heart. *He was sore at me leaving him. Although even when we were together, Rosa Kleist always had a hold over him. It was hardly a surprise to me when they married, despite the age difference.* She read on:

He has left his position at Elmer James'. The company was convicted recently of having dealings with a slaver, and they were heavily fined. Of course, Hartley and Ralph were mortally ashamed and knew nothing of it. Ralph felt bound to stay and support his father, but Hartley felt the time had come to move on, though they remain great friends. He is seeking another post but not very actively, as he is busy managing the store for Rosa. They have opened a second floor, taken on assistants, and bought sewing-machines. Already, they are gaining a good name for quality and reliability in New York. They are also selling paper patterns for people to make their own clothes with, which seems a bit strange as they are in the business of making clothes themselves. But I am sure you wish them well, as I do, and will be interested to hear this news.

Caitlin put away the letter. *He will do well,* she thought, *in time. He has the patience and the perseverance for it — like an animal beavering away quietly, almost unobserved. I hope he thinks of me sometimes and treats his seamstresses better than Madame Arlott did. If I had stayed, I might have worked for him, but he would only have employed me out of pity. It would never have worked.*

She followed Owain out into the night but went to the stable — makeshift lean-to against the crude barn and pig shack. Inside, there was a sweet smell of hay. Betsy and Trooper, Owain's horse, raised their heads enquiringly and came nuzzling for the carrots she had brought. Trooper took his greedily, but Betsy snuffled gently over her outstretched hand and took hers daintily like a lady.

"I love you, Betsy," Caitlin murmured, laying her face against the mare's warm neck. "You're such a good girl." *I am happy,* she thought. *Far happier than I ever was in New York. Please, God, let it stay this way forever.*

Chapter Two

A week later, Owain rode over to Billy's place on some errand. At least that was what he called it. Caitlin suspected it was all on account of Billy's having told Owain there were new rifles to be had in Lawrence — Sharp's rifles shipped in from well-wishers in Boston, the very latest design that had the capacity to fire repeatedly.

"What would you be wanting with those?" asked Caitlin. "There are other things to spend our hard-earned money on!"

Owain said they must be ready to defend themselves if worst came to worst. She was left behind, (though she would have liked to see Meg and even go to Lawrence herself) as somebody had to get in the new crop of potatoes.

She harnessed Betsy to the wagon to help her. It was a beautiful day, dry and hot, with a warm wind soughing over the plain. The air was full of the scent of flowers and the noise of cicadas. She was used to picking potatoes — though they weren't potatoes like they'd had in Ireland — used to working, used to being on her own and not in the least afraid. It was a little past noon when she started to unload them in the yard whilst Betsy stood, untethered but obedient and patient as always.

They came with a thunder of hooves over the horizon. Too many to be Owain and Billy, and too soon. The dust they raised made a cloud that travelled with them, but, as they drew nearer, Caitlin saw they were six in number. She shaded her eyes with curiosity. Who were they? No one she had ever seen. She felt a prickle of fear, but there was nowhere to hide. Anyway, this was her land. She had the right to be here.

Nearer they came as she stood and watched them. Then, with harsh whoops and cries, mimicking Indians to terrify her, they rode into the yard and drew rein dramatically in a flurry of dust, spume and whinnies. Betsy was startled and backed off and Caitlin went to hold her head and stroke her. The action of calming the horse gave her confidence, though the men had moved round her and the wagon in a circle, fidgeting their horses by pulling savagely on their reins, which she didn't like at all.

"Who are you? And what do you want?" she demanded crossly. "What do you mean by riding in like this and scaring my horse?"

One man spoke for all. Like the others, he had a rough, brown face, dirty and unshaven, with long, uncombed hair covering his neck and shoulders. His boots were caked in dried mud and drawn over coarse, soiled trousers. He wore a bright red shirt with an eagle braided on the breast. Over it swung a rifle, and a sword dangled at his side. In his belt were two revolvers and Bowie knives stuck out of both boot tops. On his head was an old, slouched hat with a cockade on the side and a single, white goose feather sprouting from the top. They must be the border ruffians of whom Owain had spoken.

"Where's your husband, ma'am?" The words were polite enough, but the way they were spoken was not, and he did not remove his hat.

"He's not here."

The man swore vilely and spat tobacco juice into the dust at her feet. Betsy snorted and moved her feet restlessly.

"Quiet, Betsy!"

At a curt nod from their leader, two of the men dismounted. "Well, is that a fact, little lady? You won't be minding now if we just check that out?"

Of course, she minded! She minded like hell but deemed it best to shake her head as if puzzled.

The two men who got down went into the cabin, and she could hear the careless overturning of furniture and the deliberate crashing of plates. Grimly, she gritted her teeth whilst the leader of the men sat back in his saddle and lit a cigar, grinning at her. The search moved on to the barn and each shack in turn. It didn't take long. Indeed, there was no place much to hide. Caitlin heard an agonized squawk, and one of the men returned with a chicken hanging from his belt, the blood from its freshly slit neck dripping onto his boots. How dare they, she thought, quivering with anger. How dare they!

"Well, ma'am, seems he ain't here."

"I told you he wasn't. What do you want with him anyway? We don't know you."

"Well, we sure do know him, ma'am. Oh yes, we sure do!" All of them laughed. "Had a little drink with him last week." The spokesman leaned forward and spat on the ground again. "What we ain't too sure about is just how he's a-goin' to vote in the elections this fall. Didn't seem clear enough about that, to us."

"Well, I don't know, I'm sure."

"Reely. Is that a fact? But you looks like a fine young gel with some sense in her, for all you're a damned Yankee ..."

The other men began to laugh again and cluck and make chicken noises.

"Reckon you'd better start talking some sense into that man of yours. Because if you don't ..." he broke off and drew a finger expressively across his neck. "Just like that ole' squawking chicken there."

The man with the chicken took it from his belt and threw it at her feet, "Get my meanin', honey chile?"

They all guffawed and began to circle their horses round her and the wagon until she felt dizzy.

"I get your meaning," said Caitlin. She was beginning to panic. How much more of this was there going to be? Would they do anything else to her? *But they're just threats,* she thought. *That's all. I mustn't let them see I'm afraid.*

"Now get out and leave us alone!" she said with an attempt at spirit.

"Sure. Wouldn't want to overstay our welcome, would we, boys? Not on an abolitionist farm!" The word '***abolitionist***' was spat out with venom.

"We're not abolitionists. We're just immigrants trying to make a decent living."

"Well, I sure am relieved to hear that! Now don't you be forgetting it. Otherwise, your man ain't gonna be goin' nowhere, no more." He nodded to the others and turned his horse around.

Caitlin let the relief flood over her too soon. For instead of riding away, they only drew back to spur their horses into a gallop around the dirty yard. As each of them passed Caitlin, they drew a revolver out from their belt and fired it up into the air, with a wild shriek. Once she realized they were firing into the air, it didn't frighten her too badly, but Betsy didn't like it. She whinnied in terror and her eyes began to roll.

"It's all right, Betsy, it's all right," Caitlin told her desperately, hanging on to her bridle.

The leader reined in his horse again. "Jest another thing," he said, his eyes narrowing cruelly. "Mebbe it'd be better if you weren't around to vote in the fall at all. Reckon it'd be better to move on while you still can. Otherwise, next time, it'll be the cabin and the fields."

He pulled a rough torch of bound straw from the pommel of his saddle and lit the end of it with his cigar, waiting till it caught properly. Then he tossed it nonchalantly into the back of the wagon behind her. The others whooped in glee. Then they turned for the last time and were off as swiftly as they had come.

The wood of the wagon was as dry as tinder. It caught straightaway. Betsy heard the crackle and smelt the smoke behind her. She neighed wildly and began to struggle in her traces so Caitlin could hardly hold her.

"I'll get you out," she panted. "Don't fret! Oh, stand still, there's a good girl."

The flames were fanned by the wind off the prairies and roared up. Betsy began to plunge wildly. as Caitlin's fingers stumbled over the buckles of the harness. Jesus, Mary and Joseph, there were so many of them! She should have got a knife but there was no time. Instead, she dashed around the other side when she had got one side free, hanging onto Betsy's head all the while, trying to keep her down. Betsy shook saliva all over from her mouth, then reared upwards, jerking the reins out of Caitlin's desperate hands. She just managed to catch them again as the mare's hooves reached the ground. The flames leapt higher, but she was on the last fastening now.

"Nearly done, my darling," she cried. "Nearly free! Oh, don't fret, don't fret!" But the leather was stiff, and Betsy, knowing quite well she was nearly free, kept on pulling it through her fingers. With a tremendous straining forward of her hindquarters, the mare broke the last strap and suddenly bounded forwards, carrying Caitlin, still clinging onto the reins, with her. She fell but didn't let go and was dragged a few yards. Then the mare stopped, bucked, and kicked out at the encumbrance, just as Caitlin was struggling to her feet, bruised but not too badly hurt — until one iron hoof caught her right in the stomach. She let go now in the agony of the pain, and Betsy bolted.

Caitlin lay on the ground, winded and gasping, with the wagon still burning behind her. God, it hurt! She wanted to be sick. Gradually, the waves of pain ebbed away and were less sharp. Then she raised herself like an old woman. *I'm all right,* she thought. *She hasn't killed me. It's over now, thank God, it's over. I'm not going to cry, I won't! It's only a wagonload of potatoes and a runaway horse that'll soon come back. It could have been worse. It could have been the cabin. It could have been the corn. Oh, dear God, the corn!*

She suddenly realized that the wagon was burning so intensely that it was sending a great shower of sparks high up into the air. And the wind was taking them, not towards the cabin, but down to the first field, only a hundred yards away. If the corn caught, the whole lot would go! She had to do something. She must get water.

In a frenzy, she ran to the stable for a couple of pails, then down to the creek to fill them. They were almost too heavy to lift, but she ran back, though her arms felt as if they were being wrenched out of their sockets, and she lost a good deal of water with it all slopping over the sides.

She flung it on the wagon where it made a pitiable sizzling noise and barely any difference at all. More, she must get more! Back to the creek. Back to the wagon. Hurry, hurry! Why did she have to be so slow? After the third trip, she realized it was better to take the buckets to the cornfield itself and throw them over any sparks which had landed and seemed to be in danger of taking hold. She got a broom to beat them out as well, and that seemed more successful.

At last, the flaming wagon died down, more from lack of fuel rather than from her strenuous efforts. It was subsiding into a charred, twisted mass. The floating sparks came wafting along less frequently. The water did better now. She'd done it though she stood guard for a long time with the broom.

At last, she felt able to leave, having lost count of the trips down to the creek and back. She was exhausted. Her face was smeared with ash and dirt. Her clothes were torn, and her feet hurt so badly she could hardly walk. But she was proud of herself. She had saved the corn. Wearily, she staggered through the cabin door which had been almost torn off its hinges by the border men.

A sorry sight met her eyes. The chairs were overturned, the table-legs broken in two, and crockery lay smashed all over the floor. Worst of all, the empty birdcage lay on its side with its door hanging open. The canary was gone. Her last link to Hartley had flown. Flown free just as she had once said it should.

Subsiding onto the floor, she put her hands over her streaked face and sobbed. After a while, she dried her face on her skirts and pushed back her tangled hair. *I did save the corn*, she said to herself. *Owain will be pleased at that. Damn and blast those men!* Now she knew why Owain wanted those rifles! If she'd had one in her hands, she would have found her aim and shot at them alright!

She ought to look for Betsy but felt too tired. Her whole body ached. It didn't really hurt where she had been kicked now, it was just a bit sore, but she had a funny feeling inside, a kind of dragging, draining sensation. She closed her eyes. Yes, she ought to sit quietly and rest. She would leave this mess and go and lie down on the bed for a while.

When she opened her eyes again, she realized she must have slept for some time, for it was growing dark. But she was still alone so it couldn't be that late. Could it? Supposing Owain had met the men on the road? No, she mustn't think of that. She had an awful, gnawing ache low down in her back and she realized now that was what had woken her.

She rose with some difficulty from the bed. The dragging feeling was still there, in fact, it was worse, and she felt sticky and wet, as if she had been sweating a lot around the stomach and legs. She found a candle as she couldn't find the lamp and it was probably smashed anyway. Going over to the stove, she pushed the candle into the dying embers.

When the candle flickered into life, she almost dropped it again, overwhelmed by a nasty cramp in her stomach which doubled her up. It went away but when she straightened up and held out the candle and looked down at her skirt, she saw a great, red stain there and cried out. Stumbling to the door, she threw it open and staggered outside.

"Owain!" she shouted. "Owain!" Her voice sounded thin and reedy and full of panic. A flock of geese took off, startled, from the creek and she heard the slow flap of their wings. Nothing else. There was no answer.

Only the dusk softening the great plain, the stains in the sky a pale and ironic imitation of the blood that was flowing from her. Betsy was cropping the grass and gave a shy whinny from somewhere near at hand, for all the world as if to say she was sorry.

Caitlin staggered back into the cabin and fell onto the bed. The pain came again worse than before and there was more blood. There could be no doubt she was losing their unborn child.

When Owain got back two hours later, it was all over. He came thundering up the track with Billy. The sight of the burnt-out wagon frightened him. Bursting into the cabin, he ignored the scene of destruction as if that was only to be expected and flung himself down at her bedside.

"Caitlin! Are you alright? What have they done to you? I'll kill them! I'll kill them if they've hurt one hair of your head!"

Caitlin sobbed out her story. She was all right, just sore, shaken and sick, but she knew she had lost the baby. Owain's face was drained of colour.

"I'll kill them!" he repeated bitterly. "I swear it."

Caitlin put her hand out to his cheek. They hadn't really meant to harm her, she said, merely to frighten them. The business with Betsy had been mis fortune, and of course, she'd had to struggle with the fire, too. But they hadn't known she was pregnant. He mustn't, for the love of God, do anything rash. There was nothing he could do anyway.

All the while she was talking, his face grew twisted. When she had finished, he got to his feet, picked up the new rifle he had brought back with him, and plunged out of the cabin.

"Go after him, Billy!" begged Caitlin. "Don't let him ride off! Make him stay!" Billy disappeared at her bidding.

Even Owain knew he had no hope of finding the border men now. He had not gone back to Trooper. His intention was different. As Caitlin strained to get out of bed, she heard a shot. Horrified, she dragged herself to the open door. Billy stood alone in the yard. He had found an oil-lamp, lit it, and carried it with him. She followed the direction of his gaze. Owain had gone to the paddock. She saw him return now, his rifle still smoking, and she saw what he had done. He had shot Betsy through the head.

She screamed at him. "How could you? It wasn't her fault. She was frightened. How could you?"

He never said a word but, returning to Trooper, led him off to the stable. Caitlin fell against the doorpost. Billy came to her then and helped her back to bed. She was hysterical.

"Hush now!" said Billy kindly. "Don't take on so about an old horse. And don't blame Owain too much. He had to do something. We've been holed up in our place all afternoon and evening, exchanging gunfire with those pesky raiders. At last, they gave up and rode off, and we came straight out here. Owain was beside himself with worry that you'd come to some harm as you did. Rest now. You shouldn't get up yet. I'll send Meg over to see you tomorrow. She'll know what to do. I reckon it's best to leave you two on your own now."

He pulled on his hat as Owain came back into the cabin. "We'll come over tomorrow," he said, shaking his head. "It's a bad business." Then he left.

Owain stacked his rifle silently in the corner. He came over to the bed and held out his arms, but Caitlin shuddered and turned her face to the wall.

"You shot her."

"She deserved it."

"She did not, and you know it! You shot her because the border men weren't there, and she was. You lost your temper!"

"Well, it's done now."

She said nothing.

"I'm sorry. But we can't have a horse round here that frightens that easily."

"What do you mean 'that easily'? She is — was — a darned sight calmer than Trooper."

"Well," he said again hopelessly. "it's done now. Didn't know you'd get so upset over it!"

"She was my horse. How am I going to get into town now?"

"I'll mend the wagon. I been looking at it. The wheels are all right. It's just the body. Then you can drive Trooper."

"What if I want to ride?"

"You'll drive from now on. It'll be safer, and I'll come with you."

Caitlin began to cry, and Owain put his arm around her shoulders but she shrank away and shrugged him off. "You did well about the corn," he said. "I'm proud of you. How could you think I'd let any man or beast get away with hurting you?"

"You shouldn't have done it! I never wanted you to do that."

"Sometimes it's right to do the wrong thing, ain't it?"

"I don't know," she replied in misery.

"We're not going to be driven out of here, right?"

"No."

"Then we got to fight back."

"You think those men'll come back?"

"Not now. But maybe some time."

Caitlin knew she wouldn't grieve one bit if all the border ruffians were shot but she grieved for Betsy and could not forgive Owain for what he had done. Something more than the baby had died inside of her. And the beautiful dainty yellow canary had flown away, never to be seen again.

≈

The men didn't return all summer long. It was a good summer despite many crashing thunderstorms and a good crop of corn, vegetables, and fruit. Nevertheless, for all the exhortations of Northern and Southern states alike, few new settlers came, even though they were paid to do so. Nearly as many trickled out as in. The territory had its first census, and turned up only 8,500 inhabitants, including women, children, and slaves. Of the American born males of voting age, more than sixty-two per cent came from slave states. The South had a clear majority and duly elected its own candidate as the Territory's delegate to Congress. Many votes were cast illegally by border men crossing the Missouri for the elections. There was no need for them to have done so but they were determined it should go no other way. Owain and Billy muttered about it like all the other free-soilers but there was nothing they could do, given the encouragement already meted out to any new white settler.

Caitlin felt relieved for it seemed the troubles might settle down now. The ruffians had not returned and there was time to fill the cracks in the cabin before the return of the cold winds found them out, to lay in timber, make more candles and salt pork ready for winter. Kansas had a governor now sent from the States, and Caitlin hoped he would be able to keep the peace.

In February, there came general elections for a state legislature. This time there was no doubt they had been fixed. Well over three times the known and expected vote was cast. Once again, the Southerners won. This time the free-soilers fought back by forming their own party and their own convention. Owain attended their first meeting at Big Springs but came back disappointed. One of the leaders, Jim Lane, had advocated a free-soil state for Kansas because "everyone knew they didn't want no niggers in it at all".

"So that's it, is it?" asked Caitlin. "You've done with politics now? Realized what they're all like?"

"They're not all like that," Owain protested. He was dispirited though. Nobody had spoken the real truth, he reckoned. They lacked a leader of real worth.

"You've done with them, then?" Caitlin persisted.

"I guess so."

He kept his word all next summer, too, despite the fact that raiding and intimidation had broken out again on both sides. But Caitlin and Owain were blessedly left alone.

Chapter Three

It was a cold winter night in New York when Hartley's son was born. Outside, a freezing rain was falling, whirling down in a wet maelstrom under the streetlamps. Inside, Hartley's mind was hardly less turbulent.

One week ago, he had renounced Queen Victoria with great solemnity and his right hand held high and became a citizen of the United States. He had also learnt in a letter from Jeremiah that his mother had passed away. If only she could have waited a little while for his news! If only it had been possible for her to visit them, for now, he had the money to send her the fare. He felt sure that, if he could have gotten her away in time from that draughty Yorkshire parsonage, all would have been well. As it was, Jeremiah blamed him for breaking her heart in leaving and never going back.

Hartley paced up the room in some agitation. The shop, transformed since Friedrich Kleist's day, was locked up for the night. The little Kleists were all banished upstairs in the care of the woman he had engaged to look after them, though Rachel, a dark little rosebud, kept on escaping and coming to peer down through the bannisters at him hopefully. She was still his favourite, and she knew it, but he did not want her around tonight. In another room above, Rosa sweated in labour with the midwife in attendance. Hartley had arranged everything with forethought and with great care. Yet he felt sick with worry.

It seemed so gross of him to have inflicted this upon Rosa so soon after the last little one. He had not meant to. After all, though Rosa was a devoted wife and he loved her, he did not find her that attractive. He had married her to look after her, Rachel and the boys. Yet her bed was warm and inviting, and his sexual appetite had grown. It horrified him that he should succumb so regularly. Still, he had regenerated Rosa, although he suspected she still loved Friedrich at heart, as he did Caitlin. Since their marriage, she had blossomed. Together, they made a good team.

At Hartley's suggestion, they had kept on the tailoring side of the shop by employing other tailors. The sewing-machines had come in. They had stretched themselves to buy the premises next door and now had a much larger workshop. The name of Kleist still stood on the sign and people were getting to know it. Under Rosa's direction, the merchandise in the shop was growing. She knew how to make goods look attractive and he knew how to manage. The paper pattern business had not as yet taken off, but Hartley was determined to stay with it and Rosa agreed. They were ideal business partners.

And that, thought Hartley, is how it should have stayed. Only he had married her, and now they seemed to be creating an unwanted dynasty. Unwanted was perhaps unfair. They both took delight in the children. Rosa was as devoted as ever to the family. She fussed over them endlessly and took control of them all, Hartley included, and she delighted in it. There was nothing she would not do for them, and she had been proud to bear Hartley's own child, prouder than Hartley had been to bestow it. Now, the moment had come when it must enter the world, and Hartley felt afraid. What have I done, he thought, in terror, what have I done?

When a knock came at the door, he seized upon it eagerly and welcomed Ralph inside. His friend, his warm, male, sensible friend!

"No news yet?" Ralph asked him cheerfully.

"Not yet."

"Well, never mind! These matters take time. See, I brought a bottle of whisky. Thought you might need it! Let's sit by the fire and talk. It's damnably cold out."

They settled themselves comfortably. Hartley wanted to change the subject, not to have to think about what was going on in such hot, cloistered secrecy upstairs. So, he began,

"I haven't seen the paper today. Is there any more news from Kansas?"

"Governor Reeder's letting the election stand, despite everything. Talk is, he'll soon be replaced for that. Though God knows what anyone else can do."

"No more trouble then?"

"No. But it's bound to come, of course. Settlers are still getting shot every other week in some dispute or other."

Hartley looked into the fire.

"You're worried about Caitlin?" Ralph asked.

"Yes."

"Polly said she was all right in her last letter, even though she'd lost a baby. Doing well. I guess it won't affect those that keep their heads down."

"No, I suppose not."

Ralph refilled their glasses. "You got to let her go, Hartley. I know how you felt about her, but she's not your concern anymore. Hell, you got enough responsibilities here!" Ralph had not really approved of his marriage to Rosa.

"Yes, I know," said Hartley, a little wearily. "I just think about her once in a while, that's all and I wish she wasn't in Kansas."

Ralph deemed it wise to change the subject. "My father wants to know if you'll come back. He wants to make you a manager. Knows he's lost a good man."

Hartley smiled but shook his head. "No, I don't think so, Ralph. Like you say, I've got a lot going on here. It may not be that impressive now, but it's going to be."

"You don't hold that darned slaver business against him, do you?"

"No, it isn't that. I don't hold that against him any more than you do."

"Sometimes I do." Ralph grew moody. "If war came now, I'd feel bound to go, you know? To make some reparation. Would you go with me, Hartley?"

Hartley shook his head. "Let's pray to God it doesn't come to that."

"But it might." Ralph's eyes were shining now with excitement.

Hartley saw that he wanted the chance to prove himself. "But you don't believe in war, Ralph, any more than I do! You're a moderate man, not a firebrand."

"Maybe. But to do something for the Union! Wouldn't that be a fine thing? You must feel that now you're an American too!"

Hartley considered this with a frown. "I don't know. I thought it'd make me feel different but I'm not sure that it does. I keep on telling myself I'm an American, but underneath, I know I'm still Hartley Shawcross." *And I let my mother die without seeing me, thousands of miles away*, he thought. *Because I believed that it was easy to get rich in America. Now I know better.*

From upstairs, there came the cry of a newborn infant, the unmistakable protest of angry bewilderment at being dragged into the world without its consent. Hartley jumped up from his chair and Ralph got up too, with a grin.

"Not so," he said. "Hartley Shawcross, you may have been an emigrant, but you just fathered a native American child! Congratulations! There ain't no turning back now!"

Hartley took a gulp of whisky, his heart hammering away. What Ralph said was true. His son wasn't going to be a Yorkshire lad. He was half Jew, half Gentile, solidly European, if not entirely English, and yet American! He raised his glass once more with Ralph.

"God save America," he said quietly.

Sometime later, the midwife came downstairs, nodding and smiling. At her invitation, Hartley bounded up the stairs two at a time, Ralph following a respectful distance behind.

Rosa lay quietly, tired but serene, against white pillows. Her hair was now entirely grey. She looked at least fifty, though she was barely forty, and Hartley's eyes prickled with tears. She let him kiss her on the cheek, then motioned him to the cradle at the foot of the bed.

"It's a boy," she said proudly.

Timidly Hartley approached. The new child lay loosely wrapped with tiny fists, exploring the air. He had a crown of damp, dark hair. But his face was that of a Shawcross. A great lump rose in Hartley's throat.

"You can touch him," laughed Rosa. "He won't break!"

Very carefully, Hartley picked him up. The little eyes fixed onto his own. It was odd, but he looked like a baby version of old Jeremiah — Jeremiah as he had been before he became sanctimonious, found God, and lost people, the once beloved companion of his boyhood years. This then was his son. Hartley kissed the damp brow and swore silently to himself that he would make the business flourish for this boy. It should be his as much as it was Johann and Reuben's and Friedrich's. He felt filled with new purpose.

On the way downstairs, they were waylaid by a sleepy but sulky Rachel, escaped from her charge yet again. She stretched her hands up towards Hartley pleadingly and he picked her up, smiling, swinging her into his arms.

"You've got a new little brother," he told her. But, as far as Rachel was concerned, little brothers were two a penny. She pouted.

"Hartley still love me?" she asked, striving to conceal her anxiety, and failing.

Hartley kissed her tenderly. "Of course. Hartley always love Rachel. Always! No matter how many little brothers. Rachel is Hartley's little girl!"

The nurse came wearily out of the children's room with apologies, yawning and rubbing her eyes, and Hartley handed Rachel back to her.

"It's alright," he said.

The men returned to the fire and the whisky bottle.

"No," said Hartley to his friend. "No, Ralph. I do not think I could ever go to war with you. Not now. I have mouths to feed, and bodies to clothe, and minds to educate. These are more important than any war. I could never go and leave Rosa alone with all of this."

≈

In Boston, Polly was setting out with her new husband to another lecture on the evils of slavery. The speaker was a man recently returned from Kansas, where free soilers had set up their own legislature in defiance of the fraudulent elections, which the Governor had let stand. Obviously, trouble was on the way, and the free soilers urgently needed cash, food, and clothing for new settlers and for arms to defend themselves. An appeal was to be launched and the wealthy Bostonians exhorted to give freely for the cause. Polly was concerned to know something about conditions in Kansas and how she could help her friend best, though they would have given what they could for the cause anyway.

Polly was happy with John who strode beside her. As she had told Caitlin, he suited her very well. They lived in a small but comfortable row house in the South End which was undergoing much rebuilding. It was not yet the fashionable area it was briefly to become, but it was near John's newly built chapel and his ministry to the poor. The area was overcrowded with immigrants who lived twenty to a cellar and were frequently flooded out as if that were not bad enough. Polly's strivings for service had been amply fulfilled.

They had taken the ageing Mrs Regan, who had never entirely recovered from the fire in New York, with them. She suffered pangs at leaving Aunt Sophie's more established Beacon Hill residence but now seemed reconciled to the change and found a new role in housekeeping for her busy daughter and son-in-law, although she still found it impossible to understand them.

It was a cold but crisp winter evening, and the squirrels were scurrying about foraging under the trees as they crossed the gas-lit Common and made for the lecture rooms near the grand, golden-domed City Hall. There, they would meet friends as friendship here was based on like mindedness: abolitionists, writers, journalists, women's rights' workers, and other ministers with their wives. The culture and elegance of the hilltop city reached out to envelop them in its civilized safety.

≈

Over one and a quarter thousand miles away in Kansas, Caitlin and Owain were preparing to flee their home. It was a bitter night. Yet only a few miles away, a veritable army of Missourians were camped on the Wakarusa. It was ironical. That spring and summer several new settlers from the North had moved into the area. Free-soil families now outnumbered the pro-slavers. There had been no further raids and Caitlin had begun to feel secure. That feeling was much needed for things had not been the same between Caitlin and Owain since the dreadful day of the border ruffians' visit.

Although the corn grew high and the squash swelled large and colourful, that first intoxicating joy at their land had vanished. For a long while, Caitlin looked up fearfully at the sound of approaching hooves. Most of all, it took a great deal of time for her to forgive Owain for shooting Betsy. She didn't want him to touch her, and they hardly spoke when they worked alongside in the fields. Owain was miserable and angry, though he tried to put her indifference down to grief over the loss of the baby. This winter was as long and drawn out and cold as the last, and eventually, they became intimate again. By the spring, Caitlin was pregnant once more. They were busy with ploughing, sowing, and planning ahead.

So, it surprised her one evening to hear Owain speak of doubts over whether they had taken the right step in coming here after all. He was tired; she knew that, for he had been working every daylight hour to turn more land and put in more seed than last year, but she had not realized that he had become so despondent.

It was all very well, he said, this small-scale farming. But there seemed little profit to be had. It wasn't like raising sheep or cattle. They planted, and they grew, and they harvested, but for what? Why, merely to buy more seed to put in next year. There was never much left over. By now, he had hoped to be building a timber-framed house for her, to have more furniture, clothes, and a new horse. But the land which he had thought so kind swallowed up everything. To expand, he realized he needed extra hands to work more fields but there was no possibility of paying for labour at present.

Caitlin felt worried. When she looked up, his face was still young in the lamplight, but it looked weary and disappointed and wretchedly unsure of itself. She put down her sewing and knelt at his feet, searching out his hands with her own. Had they not everything they really needed, she asked? They had plenty to eat. They worked hard but they were out in the open all day long and life was a hundred, no, a thousand times better than it had been in New York. Timber was expensive here because it was scarce. But one day they would have a fine house. Till then, the old prairie cabin suited them well enough. She did not mention its shortcomings. Nor did she point out that there was no labour to be had unless you owned slaves, for each settler was stubbornly bent on tilling his own plot. Instead, she spoke cheerfully of how she would raise him an army of sons.

He smiled at this and fondled her hair but then grew absent again and mentioned the new laws that the pro-slavery legislature had introduced: you could be jailed for expressing doubts about slavery and harbouring a fugitive slave had been made a hanging offence. That wasn't right. How could a country get along that way?

Caitlin told him firmly that didn't concern them. They had nothing to do with slaves, no more than they did with the Indians. No one cared about them, did they? No one talked of fighting for their rights, though they had been pushed out of their own lands and forced to live in reservations No, not even in Boston! There was nothing they could do about it anyway. One day, it would all be sorted out and put right, no doubt.

And hadn't he found the free-soilers' meetings as senseless as any? Hadn't he promised her, above all, not to get involved? He agreed that he had, a little ruefully. It was only that he wanted to do better by her.

She cried at that and said it was nonsense and they were friends again.

That had been in the spring. Summer followed hot and wet with thunderstorms that made them quake in the cabin, fearful of the jagged blue lightning that forked to earth. Nevertheless, the powerful rain nourished the corn. The land was peaceful again, and there was an influx of new and welcome settlers of the right kind.

The blight came unexpectedly when Caitlin miscarried again without warning. This time, there seemed no reason. There was no Betsy to blame, no fire, no border ruffians — nothing but misfortune. She felt a failure. Naturally, she had continued to fetch and carry, to scythe and to gather in the harvest as well as going on with her housework, but every woman round here did that whether pregnant or not. The fear stole over her it was something to do with her alone, something that had happened to her inside, last time. She cried bitterly and knew that Owain was terribly disappointed too.

This time, she was ill with a fever for some days afterward. It seemed to drain all the strength out of her and, when she recovered, she felt small and inadequate, and the land seemed much bigger. Owain would not talk about it, and she grew lonely again.

There was an Indian summer in the fall, almost as hot as the real thing, and it made her more listless. The sky lay on the land so full of light that it seemed to set the golds, reds and bronzes of autumn to flame. Indeed, there were many prairie fires that burned day and night and they had to be vigilant over their corn. Acrid smoke wafted in the air amidst the crackling of grass.

Then rain came with a chilly spell, followed by late warmth once more, though not as fierce. By November, the year was winding down toward winter again. Their harvest had been good and Owain had a little money to spare after all. Should he buy another horse? he asked Caitlin. She shook her head, not wanting a replacement for Betsy. Trooper did them well enough, she said. Better buy another couple of pigs to keep up the stock. Then it began — a small spark at first, but enough to set the tinder.

At nearby Hickory Point, two squatters fell into a fight over a piece of land. There had been bad blood between them for a while. One was a free-soiler, and one a pro-slaver. The land was valuable being one of the few sites of hardwood growing around. Fists and skeins of rope came out on both sides, then pistols. The free-soil man was killed, but the local sheriff made no move to arrest the culprit. There was nothing new in that, for it had happened often enough before. Everyone knew the Sheriff had pro-slavery sympathies and was hostile to the free-soilers.

But the dead man had a friend — one Jacob Branson by name — who happened to head the local free-soiler society and was dedicated to the cause. Realizing his danger, the killer had fled, leaving his wife and children with friends in the neighbourhood. Branson took his chance and rode against those friends, threatening them with their lives if they did not give the family up, though settling in the end for burning their homes to the ground. The injured parties complained to the sheriff, giving him a Godsent reason for arresting Branson, which he promptly did. However, the posse was ambushed, and Branson freed. Now the Sheriff had his excuse to march against Lawrence, where free-soilers were suspected of sheltering Branson.

The Sheriff's posse camped on the Wakarusa, and its numbers swelled alarmingly, with upwards of fifteen hundred border ruffians thirsting for revenge. The army, for such it was, was camped less than five miles from Owain and Caitlin's homestead, and Owain thought they should leave and get into Lawrence for safety.

Caitlin was uncertain. Lawrence was the target, after all. Wouldn't they be better off staying put? Owain thought not. It seemed unlikely that a Sheriff of the county — no matter how unfairly elected — would really dare to attack Lawrence for all his bluster, but he might decide that any local free-soil farmer would do to provide an example if the townsfolk failed to give Branson up. Even if their lives were spared, their homestead might be burnt down. At least in Lawrence, they would be surrounded by supportive, like-minded people. The townsmen regularly drilled, like militia. Even if Lawrence were attacked, they would stand a better chance there. Out here, they could be picked off at any time with no-one the wiser.

There was little to pack. Owain harnessed Trooper to the rebuilt wagon, and they tied the cow behind. She would slow them down, but they couldn't afford to lose her, and she couldn't be left. The pigs and the chickens were turned out into the paddock with plenty of food, and the shed doors left open for some shelter from the cold winds. Perhaps they would never see them again, but the livestock would have to take their chances whilst their owners took theirs. It couldn't be helped.

Caitlin drove the wagon and Owain rode behind, his shotgun at the ready. The greatest danger was in meeting some marauders along the road. They had waited till dark to leave, which meant it was bitterly cold, but they wrapped themselves up as best they could. As they left, the moon swung up over the rolling sea of land, and Owain cursed it. Caitlin looked back once and saw in its ghostly light how small and pathetic their place looked — just an untidy cluster of shacks with a mud cabin surrounded by a few acres of tilled land, a mere blip in the vast ocean of wild, frost-covered grass.

Her heart thumped uncomfortably in her throat as she flicked the reins gently over Trooper's smooth flanks. They couldn't progress beyond a walk, or the cow would protest noisily. In the distance, they could see the glow of campfires. They kept well away from them, though it meant taking a circuitous route. To be discovered could mean detainment or even death. There could be no other reason for being on the road tonight other than fleeing to Lawrence.

The next ten miles seemed endless. At first, they met no one. Then, another wagon rolled out of the night shadows to join them. Caitlin caught her breath, and Owain clicked back his gun-hammer, but the driver of the wagon signalled to them in a conspiratorial silence and fell in quietly behind. Owain knew him. Then they were joined by Billy and Meg with all their children bedded down under blankets in the back. Another two miles and another wagon appeared and then another. They had safety in numbers now.

By the time they reached Lawrence, a silvered dawn was breaking, and there were six of them, all bound for refuge. Some of them had brought pots and pans, some livestock, some furniture while others had little apart from themselves. But they were all armed, all caught up in the inexorable march of history, though none of them saw it like that at the time.

It was the first of December 1855, and that very morning, the new governor, a man called Shannon, had travelled to Kansas City and sent an urgent telegram to the President of the United States, requesting authority to summon federal troops to assist in 'executing the laws and preserving the peace and good order of the Territory.'

Lawrence was in a state of chaos. There was nowhere to stay, for all rooms were full, and the settlers had to camp out in their wagons despite the cold. Still, there was plenty of food to be had if you could pay for it, and campfires were lit on the streets. The residents were free with their welcome, for all were grist to the mill. The garrison of townspeople drilled daily and toiled ceaselessly, building defences. Their numbers were roughly a thousand. Only they wouldn't make much difference for even a child could see the town's position was indefensible.

It stood on an open prairie sloping to a belt of timber that marked the course of the river. To the west, it was commanded by a bluff which rose steeply enough from the town but then sloped gently down as if in invitation to the open country. One portion of the crest of the bluff was within five hundred yards, well within artillery range, and, in addition, there was a deep ravine suitable for covering the approach of troops at night. In short, Lawrence had not the ghost of a chance of holding out despite the bravado of its citizens. The only factor they had on their side were those Sharp's rifles from Boston ranged against more antiquated weapons, and luckily, both sides knew it. Only this held the border ruffians in check. There was no attack that Sunday nor on Monday either.

On Tuesday, Governor Shannon received his answer from the President. He was promised federal troops as soon as proper orders could be made out. This put the Governor into a cheerful frame of mind, but, as he was dressing, an express arrived from the Sheriff to warn him that his men were getting restless at inaction and that, if Branson were not handed over soon, there would be bloodshed. At the same time, two men from Lawrence itself sought him out, sent by their committee to appeal for the Governor's protection. They insisted they were not responsible for Branson's rescue and claimed the real culprits were not even citizens of Lawrence.

"Only they are now!" the Governor said, rummaging through a pile of newspapers on the table. He picked out a September issue and made the free soilers read their declaration of defiance against the legislature.

In answer, the free-soilers pointed out all their provocations and encounters with the border men and, indeed, the Sheriff himself. They told the Governor that the Sheriff had called all men of Lawrence traitors and threatened to wipe out the town, even at the expense of the Union and the ensuing civil war. Governor Shannon was shocked. The situation was a time bomb. He realized he could not wait for federal troops any longer but must visit the Wakarusa camp himself to plead restraint.

Great fires burned in Lawrence all that night and the next. The men were engaged in building earthworks for defence. In parties of fifty, they took turns plying spades to complete three great earthen forts and entrenchments connecting them. Owain laboured hard amongst them. He no longer felt tired or dispirited. A kind of charge ran through him at this challenge to everything he had worked for.

Meanwhile, candles burnt all night in the rooms of the Free State Hotel, where Caitlin was taught by the other women of the town to make cartridges from powder, lead and rifle caps. She became quite an expert but found herself wondering fearfully if they were all going to die. This was not what she had come West for.

Still the morale of the town was high, encouraged by these feverish preparations. Even a howitzer had been smuggled in right through the Southerners' lines. Perhaps they would not have to use the Sharp's rifles after all. If they did, they told themselves they could scarcely be better prepared. Some of them ached to fight and fight at once. They had been listening to a newcomer from the east. Owain and Caitlin had seen him arrive in a wagon bristling with bayonets stuck on warlike poles. He was tall and fierce looking, with a long beard like an Old Testament prophet, and he spoke like one of those prophets, too, in a strangely powerful voice which made everyone stop and listen. He had come with four fine sons, and his name was John Brown.

Owain and Caitlin listened, too. The message was simple enough. Slavery was an evil abomination in the sight of the Lord, and he, John Brown, had been sent to halt its insidious spread. Not by a president, nor a governor nor a colonel. Nor even by one of these brave, sorely used fugitive slaves who stood at his side. But by a higher authority. By God Himself. That God who was now calling each and every one of them to join him!

"Which side would they be on? Would it be God's? Or was it to be the Devil who rode with those whisky-swilling, gun-toting Southerners? There was only one way to stop them, and that was to match guns with guns and bayonets with bayonets. There was no choice but to fight — if not today, tomorrow, or next year. Let it be now! Let those that had no stomach for the fight depart but let them remember the Devil went with them, and if any man doubted that, let him look on the scarred back of this poor Negro beside him. Let him look long and not forget it; then let him go and see the body of Thomas Barber, one of their own townspeople, who had tried to ride out of Lawrence yesterday to visit his relatives and ensure they were safe and had been brought back murdered for his pains, riddled with Southern shots ..."

Caitlin tugged at Owain's arm. "Let's go, Owain. I don't want to see these things."

But Owain's eyes were shining in the torchlights. "How can you say that? I want to listen to him."

The black back with its knotted scars like worm tracks under the skin was shown, and the crowd murmured angrily.

"Come on, Owain. Let's go. I'm so very tired, I must lie down."

Reluctantly, Owain came, and they made their way back to their wagon. Dark tatters of cloud streamed across a great, white moon. Night had come, but the streets were still feverish with activity and wild talk.

"That man is the one to lead us," said Owain. "The one we've been waiting for so long! He speaks the truth. There is no way out. There never is. In the end, we must fight."

"Didn't you see his eyes?" asked Caitlin wonderingly.

"What about them?"

"They were on fire like a madman." She noticed then that Owain's eyes were burning, too.

"That's his zeal. If we had more like him, we would not be in this wretched situation, holed up like rabbits!"

"Perhaps." Caitlin lay down in the wagon and wrapped herself in a blanket. "I wish," she said in a small voice. "That we were back home!" Owain came to himself and put his arms around her.

"Of course you do, my sweet!" he said. "You are a woman. You cannot understand such things. I see that now."

Caitlin felt an immeasurable gulf open up between them. "You think I'm a coward!" she accused him angrily.

"No, no." Owain smiled distractedly and stroked her hair. "I know you are not. How can I forget that you once saved me when others would have turned their back? You are my own sweet woman, that is all! I do not expect you to know about these things!"

"Don't you, Owain?"

"Why no! Don't worry. I feel now that all will come right."

"I don't."

"Never mind - you will see in time."

Caitlin saw only too well. She saw that in a matter of moments in this strange, wild night under the stars, under siege in Lawrence, she had lost Owain and lost him to a hard, wild, and powerful man who would never give in. Yes, it was for just cause, but a violent one. Wearily, she closed her eyes.

"I must sleep," she said. "I'm so tired, making those endless cartridges all day and all night. And with all of the waiting. Perhaps tomorrow it will be over."

"I think it must be," agreed Owain. "They will attack, and we shall be ready for them! Would you mind if I left you alone for a while to see what the other men are saying?" Owain got up and seized his rifle.

"No, I only want to sleep."

"I shall be back soon," he promised as he kissed her. But knew he wouldn't.

He was far too excited, and she felt afraid.

Chapter Four

"My dear," said Hartley, "I had not expected to see you in the shop so soon!"

Rosa breezed across the floor towards him, confident and happy, her dark eyes beaming. "Oh, but I am well," she assured him. "I have never felt better.

You have no need to worry. And you know, the girls work much better when I am here."

"But the children, my dear!"

"The nurse is with them. She is good. If you would permit it, I should like to keep her on..."

"Of course."

"It is good to be back in harness again! Ah, I see one of our best customers is in. I must have a word. Excuse me, my dear."

Hartley bowed stiffly to her and retreated. There was no doubt that the store functioned better with Rosa around. She was right. His role was different. He must do the accounts and he must think, always be thinking, how to make the business better. He had no need of another position now. Their own business was growing daily, and they needed him to nurture it.

Seeking their private rooms, he returned to the vexed question of how to distribute and advertise those blessed paper patterns, how to persuade people they wanted, nay, needed them. Rosa, in the confidence of her blossoming store, had almost forgotten them. Hartley had not. He owed it to Friedrich because they were based on his designs. Like a dog with a bone, he worried away at the idea which seemed so unlikely and yet still intrigued him.

Sometimes he had the feeling that Rosa hardly needed him at all these days. So, he was anxious to prove his worth. He would never have expressed it to himself in these terms, but deep down inside, he felt the need to justify his existence as more than a husband who had simply replaced Friedrich Kleist. He wanted to make the business truly his own, not something merely gained by chance.

Although intending to work, his attention was distracted by the daily papers. Automatically, he turned to the pages which chronicled the daily doings in Kansas. It seemed that civil war there was inevitable. He thumbed the news anxiously.

However, the news was good. The 'Athens of Free State Kansas'. In other words, the town of Lawrence was still under siege but had not been attacked yet. The governor was attempting to mediate with the pro-slavery camp, and, against all odds, the free-soil leaders in Lawrence had kept their own men from fighting their would-be attackers despite the intervention of a now notorious man named John Brown.

≈

Governor Shannon had managed to persuade the pro-slavers and their sheriff that a surrendering of arms on the part of Lawrence would make up for the lack of recapturing Branson. He then put forward this face-saving solution to a committee from Lawrence. Only he found the free-soilers far from amenable.

He was beginning to feel impossibly beleaguered for there was no doubt the outcome of this affair rested squarely and horribly on his shoulders. Yet he seemed thwarted at every turn. Next morning, he had to accept the citizens of Lawrence could not be held responsible for Branson's actions. So, he promised to disband the sheriff's posse, providing the free-soilers signed a pledge to aid the execution of any legal process against all criminals.

At last, they agreed. With some relief, and under the influence of a considerable amount of liquor to calm his shattered nerves, he spoke to the townspeople about the peace treaty. Hardly had he finished when John Brown turned up and climbed onto a soapbox to denounce his 'damned concessions'.

"These laws we denounce and spit upon and shall never obey!" Brown cried.

There was an uproar. Nevertheless, the leaders of Lawrence succeeded in convincing the crowd there had been no concessions. John Brown and his boys left in disgust whilst Governor Shannon took along leaders from Lawrence to meet the pro-slavers and ratify the agreement. He wasn't popular there either for the pro-slavers were equally indignant that the Sharp's rifles hadn't been surrendered. Everyone blamed the governor for playing them false. Tempers ran high in the Wakarusa camp, and it looked as if there might be an attack after all that very night.

Then the weather changed with the suddenness of a whirlwind as so often in Kansas. A wild gale blew up with the darkness and drove a snowy sleet before it. Added to that, the whisky supply gave out and so the Sheriff's posse struggled homeward. In Lawrence, the Free State Hotel was jammed with a victorious celebration. But Owain had insisted on leaving when John Brown left, so Caitlin missed that. Instead, they were battling back to their smallholding.

≈

It was a cold homecoming. Most of the pigs were still rooting around and glad to see them, but all of the fowl were gone, picked off by hungry marauders or coyote. The late squash, ungathered in the panic, had frozen in the field. It took an age to get the stove going and infuse any warmth at all into the cabin. The next morning, it was even colder, and they were on their way to a very white Christmas with a foot of snow outside the cabin. War was frozen now, along with everything else. Mere survival had taken over.

On Christmas Eve, it was seventeen below zero - on Christmas morning, thirty below. The water froze in the tumblers on Caitlin's breakfast table and the bread had to be held to the fire to thaw between the cutting of each slice. They were in the throes of the bitterest winter they had ever known.

It was four days after Christmas and still bitterly cold. Waking up in the morning was the worst time for the bed had grown cold, and their bodies stiffened. Fresh snow had blown through the cracks in the cabin door in the night again. The stove had to be rekindled if they were to survive and that meant getting up. The cow needed to be milked in the shed outside.

Caitlin thought longingly of the warm drawing-rooms of the well-to-do in New York. She had slept in her clothes, for it was too cold to do otherwise. On rising, she piled on extra layers, two thick shawls, and a scarf wrapped around her head and pulled on her boots. Outside, the freezing morning air cut into her like a knife.

At least the cowshed, stacked round with bales of hay, felt warmer. The cow looked at her mournfully then went on chewing as she got out the pails. There was a slight stirring behind the bales. Probably mice. Caitlin didn't mind mice. Compared to coyotes and snakes, they were pretty harmless.

"Come on, beautiful," she said sleepily to the cow. "Don't give me any trouble this morning. Just nice, warm milk."

As she squatted ungainly over the stool, she heard a baby cry and stopped in disbelief, her sore, red fingers poised over the cow's first udder, ready to squeeze. There was more rustling behind the straw, and the baby's cry swelled into a hungry wail.

"Jesus, Mary, and Joseph!" Caitlin exclaimed. "Come out at once, whoever you are!"

Slowly, from behind the bales, a man's head emerged and stared at her in fright. Caitlin gasped. It was a black head, blacker than she had ever seen, with tight, fuzzy hair, a broad, flattened nose, and big thick lips. His teeth were very white, and his enormous eyes rolled in terror. Dropping the bucket in her fright, Caitlin grabbed the rifle that always stood ready in a corner of the shed and backed away, pointing its long, thin barrel at the intruder.

"Come out with your hands up!" she cried. "I'm not afraid to shoot!"

The smell of fear was strong in the shed. Slowly, they came out. The black man and a black woman, diminutive and thin, with a dirty bandanna wrapped round her head and a tiny black baby clutched in her arms.

"Jesus!" said Caitlin again, more calmly. "Whatever are you doing here?"

It was the man who spoke. "Please Missy, don't shoot! We don't mean you no harm! We're just a-sheltering here from the cold. We's a-sorry. We'll go now, straightaway if you wants."

Caitlin took a deep breath and lowered the gun. "You're runaways!" she declared.

"Yes, Missy. But we don't mean you no harm. No trouble, no ways. We jest shared with the cow 'cos of the cold. We go now, Missy, right away!"

"I'm not a missy."

"No, ma'am. I's sorry. I didna mean to be disrespectful."

Caitlin stared at the woman who was looking hungrily at the cow. The tiny child was held close to her exposed black breast to stop its wailing but both breasts were shrunken and flat.

"Where will you go? There isn't another cabin for miles." Caitlin stated.

"I don't know, ma'am. But we sure as hell git out of your way, don't you worry!"

Caitlin let out a sigh. "There's nowhere else for you to go!" she said. "There's too much snow on the ground since last night, even if there were. Don't be foolish! Jesus, you would have to come here, though!"

"Yes, Missy - I mean ma'am. It very stupid of us. We real stupid, see."

"Stay here, I'll fetch my husband. It's all right, he won't hurt you. He'll know what to do. Don't move. Do you understand? We won't turn you in. We can at least give you a meal and some milk for the baby."

White teeth flashed in a smile. "Missy very good white lady! We understand. We not make any trouble."

Caitlin turned and went back to the cabin. Owain had gone back to sleep, but she roused him. Together, they fetched the pitiable family inside and Caitlin put some soup on the stove to warm.

"Where are you from?" asked Owain.

"We from Kentucky, mas'r," the man answered

"You don't need to call me that! It's a mighty long way!"

"Yessir. We run on Chrissmas day, sir, when everybody's a-busy rejoicin' and dancin'."

"But how did you get across the Missouri?"

"It frozen, sir. Frozen real hard. We ran and ran and then we walked and walked."

Caitlin gasped and looked at their feet. The man's boots were out at the toe, and the woman's feet were bound up in what appeared to be rolls of cloth.

"Was your master a bad man?" she asked.

"No, ma'am. He not bad. Mas'r a good mas'r."

"Then why did you run away?" asked Owain.

"Mas'r need money real bad. He gonna sell me down south. I ain't no common field nigger. I's a good house-boy. So, he get plenty money for me." This was said with a touch of pride. "But Kitty here not much good. She have to stay behind and then she dun gone and have this chile' on Christmas Eve. I didna want to leave them!"

Caitlin ladled out a bowl of soup and pressed it into the black woman's hands. She was so young, scarcely more than a girl. Pretty too, despite the fact that her hair was cropped shorter than any boy's under the bandanna. A lively, cheeky face. Yet her quick movements had a kind of grace and elegance even though she was so thin and frightened.

They had said they had not been ill-treated. No worm scars here, no beatings nor starvation. They said their master was good. So how could he separate them forcibly when she had just borne their first child? Caitlin thought about 'Uncle Tom's Cabin'. It was true then. It was all real. It did happen.

She looked at Owain. "What can we do? We've got to help them, but I don't know what we can do."

Owain read the sympathy in her eyes and smiled more warmly than he had for some time.

"I do. I know," he said, then addressed the negro again. "Look, what is your name?"

"Washington, mas'r. I mean, sir."

"Washington?"

"That's the name mas'r gave me. I ain't got no other."

"Well, look now, Washington, where do you want to go?"

The reply was unhesitating. "Up north."

"Up north," the girl echoed him dreamily, speaking for the first time. "Where all folks are free!"

Caitlin's eyes filled with tears as she looked at Owain. He seemed undaunted.

"That's a long way, Washington."

"I knows, sir. And we don't know the way. But others say that in Kansas there's white folks who come from up north and they help. Is it true, mas'r? That's why we run here."

"Yes," said Owain firmly. "It's true. I know of a good man who lives not far from here who will help you. He knows how to get slaves up north. I will take you to him. Only we'd better wait until dark."

Washington nodded his curly black head. He was beaming now. "Yessir! We do anythin' you says!"

Caitlin was looking at Owain in disbelief. "But we don't know anyone!"

"Yes, we do. John Brown! He'll get them safely away for sure."

"But we don't know where he is!"

"I do. I heard it in the stores. He's staying at Osawattomie with one of his sons."

Caitlin felt the cold gnaw into her stomach. She shivered. "It'll be dangerous, Owain. And such a long way at night over the snow!"

"I've got sled-rails on the wagon."

"I didn't mean that. I meant if you should get caught."

"What else can we do?"

Caitlin looked at the family huddled round the stove in the lamplight, hardly daring to believe their luck. "Nothing," she said flatly.

"Even if we get caught and hang for it?"

Caitlin swallowed hard. "Even then."

"That's my woman! That's settled then. We'll lie low till dark and then I'll take you to this man — the very best man you could find to send you north."

The faces of the negroes were ample reward. Caitlin smiled at Owain, suddenly contrite.

"You are a fine man, really" she said humbly. "I always knew it." Then she spoke to the family.

"You'll need to rest," she said. "Because you'll have to travel all night. You can have our bed. I'll go get some milk from the cow for the baby."

The black girl gazed at her in wonder, still holding onto the infant.

"It's all right," said Caitlin. "I'll feed the babby for you. I - don't have any of my own, but I know how to do it. I've looked after ..." her voice faltered. "Some."

Kitty smiled and handed the baby over. Caitlin took the light bundle, asleep now, its tiny hands curled into tight fists against its cheeks.

"When you wake up, I'll cook you a proper meal. We haven't got any fowl. They were all picked off recently. But there's plenty of pork, isn't there, Owain?"

Owain nodded cheerfully. "I'll kill a pig, then you can have it fresh and cooked hot."

He went out into the cold morning, letting a freezing blast of air into the cabin. Caitlin grimaced. She hated the killing of the pigs: the squeals, the mess, the violence, and the blood on Owain's hands. But it had to be done. They must survive.

Later, while Kitty and Washington slept without fear, rolled up together, Caitlin rocked the baby in her chair. Its tiny black fingers explored the air, its mouth continually seeking and sucking everything, even the tentatively offered white finger when the bottle of milk was done, its little face screwed up all the while. It was no different, she thought, no different than a white baby. Why did they have to do these things to each other?

Then Owain came in with a hacked-up carcass and she had to leave the baby and get busy to prepare their meal. She hated the cleaning and stripping of fresh meat. Nevertheless, it would give them all the strength which was needed for the trial ahead.

When night fell, the frost came down harder than ever. Owain went to get the sled ready. Caitlin opened the box in the corner of the cabin, which they had brought from New York, and rooted about until she found something that rustled softly in paper. She unwrapped it and gave it to Kitty. It was a shawl that Polly had sent from Boston for the babies she had never had, and it was crocheted in snowy white wool. Kitty's eyes grew round as she touched it. Caitlin folded it around the small, black body of the baby.

"I can't take this, missy! I ain't never had nuthin so fine. It too good for us."

"No, Kitty, you must. It's so cold and the baby needs more protection. Anyway, I want you to have it."

Owain brought the sled to the door in the dark. The wind was bringing more light snow with it, drifting off the plains. It sparkled in the lamplight. Washington was quiet now, tense at the thought of their journey through the open land and what failure might mean. Kitty was more eloquent as she cuddled her baby close to her in its fine, new white shawl. When she turned to Caitlin to say goodbye, her face was polished with a serene smile,

"I ain't never gonna see you again," she said simply. "But I goin' to pray for you every night. I pray you have lots of little chillun of your own."

"I don't know that I can, Kitty. I lost two already you, see, and another hasn't come."

"I knows it," said the girl. "Leastways, I felt it. I seen it before. But you will one day. Kitty knows it."

Caitlin put her arms around the girl impulsively and hugged her thin shoulders. She couldn't speak.

"Don't cry, missy! I know you will one day. I'm gonna pray so darned hard for that good, white lady in Kansas."

"But Kitty - I'm not good!"

"Yes, you are, missy. 'Course you are. You don't know it but you are."

Caitlin shook her head dumbly. Her heart was very full.

"Lots of folks think they's good," Kitty said. "But they ain't. It's folks don't think so that are." She climbed up into the wagon, and Caitlin shut the tailgate behind her.

"Goodbye, Kitty," she said, still choked. "I won't forget you either, and I hope, oh, I do hope the North will be what you expect it to be!"

"Get down now," said Owain, curtly. "Under the blankets. And don't show your heads for love nor money." He nodded to Caitlin.

"Don't go worrying now. I'll be a while 'cos I'll make certain to give every homestead a wide berth."

"I know."

Then they were off — a grey shape melting into the whiteness and the dark, with Trooper stumbling to find a foothold on the icy track. Kitty disobeyed instructions so that Caitlin saw her black face, surmounted by its dirty bandanna, pop up briefly to give one last grateful wave.

She went into the cabin and sat down by the glow of the stove, feeling suddenly tired and weeping without knowing why or for whom. She felt as if a great test had come and passed away and yet, in its passing, had left so much more to come.

Chapter Five

It was dawn when Owain returned and she found she had slept in the chair and not worried too much after all, though she had managed to keep the fire going.

"Well?" she asked him anxiously. "Did you all get there?"

"Yes."

"And John Brown?"

"Was wonderful. He was so pleased to see them."

"They will make it then?"

"I'm sure of it. With him to guide them. He knows who to pass them on to next on the Underground Railroad."

"Thank heaven! I'll get you some broth. You must be cold and tired."

Owain sat in his chair and whistled through his teeth.

"Not a bit of it," he said proudly. "I feel good. You know, in Brown, we have a great leader, we really do."

Caitlin looked at his face and saw he was happier than he had been for a long time. For once, she thought she understood why.

≈

Spring that year made many false promises but at last there came a thaw and the air grew mild. Flocks of birds arrived on the creek as a staging-post on their way north and the air was full of their cries of courtship. It was time to turn the earth again and plant seed. Caitlin lay in bed late for she had found with a frisson of excitement that she was pregnant again and this time she was determined that nothing should go wrong. She was half inclined to believe that Kitty's prayers had already been answered.

It was a premature hope. Within a couple of months, she had miscarried. She was ill again, and Owain rode into Lawrence for a doctor. He listened to Owain's story and came to shake his head over her. The third time, did they say? Well, she was not meant to carry children then. Indeed, he had only to look at her narrow hips. Nature could be wise. They should give up the attempt. Repeated episodes like this would weaken her constitution. This time, she would recover with care, but he could not vouch for her safety again.

At first, she felt nothing but the fact that all energy had drained from her. Later on, sitting wrapped up in a blanket outside the cabin, watching Owain doggedly work the fields alone, she felt a failure. She dozed but always awoke to the same scene: Owain toiling, the newly turned soil, prairie grass beginning to grow tall and green again, waving in the wind below a vast bowl of sky. When she was a little stronger, she walked slowly and stiffly, like an old woman, down to the creek. Once, she thought she saw a quick flash of canary yellow in the trees but then it was gone She sat for a while by the flowing water under the hickory and cottonwood trees and watched the wild turkey strutting and preening their feathers, blowing their chests out to ridiculous proportions to attract their mates. 'Look at us!" they seemed to say, "We don't toil and labour like you do. This land was made for us. It doesn't matter if you put a ball of lead in one of us now and then for there will always be more of us. But not of you. You should go home.'

At least, that was what she felt they were saying. For what was the point in being here, in working so hard, if they could not renew themselves and pass on the land to their offspring? She thought of all the women she had seen out here, of Meg with her strong, healthy brood. She even thought of Frau Kleist in New York City, who was so much older yet still fecund and able to go on giving Hartley children just as she had done her first husband. Only she, it seemed, could not. It wasn't fair when she wanted it so.

Owain, never talkative, grew positively taciturn. They did not discuss the problem though he repeated what the doctor had said to make sure she understood. He said he knew it to be true and he would not put her through this anguish again. He would make sure of it. She believed him but how were they to get through the cold winter nights without any comfort? It had taken her a good while to return to Owain's arms after Betsy but in the end she had. It was difficult to believe that part of their lives was gone forever.

Owain did not express grief, but she was sure he felt it keenly. His interest in the land waned further. He still worked it but without the old enthusiasm and often grew moody and resentful. Sometimes he talked longingly of Wales. *It's my fault,* she thought bitterly. *I have failed him.*

Gradually her strength returned — not evenly but flowing back one day and ebbing the next. She resumed her tasks regardless: feeding the livestock, milking the cow, collecting the eggs from the chickens they had been hard put to replace, washing their clothes in the creek, and spreading them out to dry, raking the fire in the stove, cooking their food, sweeping the cabin, mending clothes, making candles and butter, working in the fields. She had to prove herself worthy of at least this. Owain didn't seem to notice. Once the busy time of planting was over, he hung up his farm tools and was continually saddling Trooper up for a ride. At first Caitlin didn't mind. He was restless and needed the exercise, she supposed. Then he was away for longer and longer stretches at a time and she suspected he was visiting John Brown and his sons in Osawattomie.

With the thaws of spring, the dormant troubles of Kansas began to raise their heads again like snakes in the grass. Every day there came a new rumour that a large force was preparing to march on Lawrence. The border men took to patrolling the river and went so far as to board steamers bound for the town. They made one notable haul of Sharp's rifles to the value of four thousand dollars. That sent a shiver down all free-soilers' backs, though they told themselves the Missourians were so stupid they wouldn't know how to use them.

≈

The Sheriff of Douglas County was active again, continually searching houses in Lawrence on some pretext for transgressors of the law, which gave rise to several skirmishes. He was eventually shot and wounded for his pains, but not killed. The shocked citizens disclaimed responsibility and said a Southerner had done it. There were many isolated fights and killings up and down the land, and it was no longer safe to travel abroad alone.

Early in May, the Court of the Federal judiciary declared that any acts against the elected Territorial powers amounted to treason against the U.S. Government. The free-soilers reaffirmed their resistance, though many of their leaders were prudent enough to escape for a while and fled back East.

"They're lily-livered!" said Owain when Caitlin read out this story to him from the newspaper. "Not like John Brown."

"What else can they do?" asked Caitlin. "No point in staying to get arrested and killed, as they surely will if they carry on causing trouble."

Owain eyed her coldly. "That's all you ever think about," he accused her. "Staying out of trouble! Have you forgotten Washington and Kitty?"

Caitlin felt hurt.

"Of course not. I'd do the same thing again tomorrow. You know I would. But this constant fighting is wrong. It's not going to change anything!"

"It's the only way to change things, see," Owain replied. "The Southerners started it, but we have to fight back and fight better. If everyone was like you, the slaves'd still be slaves in a hundred years. I don't expect you to understand. You're only a woman."

He did not add, "and not a very good one at that." But she wondered if he thought it. He seemed to have grown harder towards her: impatient, dismissive, and scornful of her views where he might once at least have listened.

With spring coming late after a severe winter, much damage had been done to trees and plants. Heavy rains had delayed the ploughing and sowing of seed. Yet now it was all done. The harvest might be late, but it would come again. It was a time for repairing and rebuilding and the mating of livestock, except Owain wasn't interested in that anymore. The only time she saw him animated was when he returned from being with the Browns. She dared not ask him what they did, though she suspected he was taking his revenge for the day the border ruffians had ridden onto their farm.

One day, he turned up leading a horse. He explained it was for her. He needed Trooper all the time now, for 'business', and he didn't like to leave her alone without the means of getting away if she had to.

It was a fine chestnut quarter-horse, big and strong enough to do farmwork and of a reasonable enough temperament for a woman to ride. Caitlin was a little doubtful. Betsy had been small in comparison, just a Mustang really.

"But where did you get him?" (For she knew he hadn't the money.)

"Never mind that. What do you think of him? Will you be able to manage him?"

Her hands stroked the firm chestnut nose and noted his large, kind eyes and the affectionate nuzzling of his mouth.

"I think so. He seems gentle enough. Have you ridden him?"

"Of course. He's responsive. A bit lazy perhaps. But I thought he'd do for you. We'll have to paint his blaze out and his white fetlocks though."

"You stole him, didn't you? From a Missouri farm!"

"So? I thought you'd be pleased."

"I suppose I am, really. But what if you'd been caught?"

Owain laughed. "The men who ride with Old Brown don't get caught. We've got God on our side!"

Caitlin sighed. It was useless to argue with him.

"Take him in and give him a good feed. Then he'll want to stay."

She led him into Betsy's old stall and tied him up. He gave her no trouble but looked at her so intelligently and expectantly she had to laugh.

"It's hardly right, I know," she said, falling into her old way of talking quite naturally to horses. "But what can I do? Owain shouldn't have stolen you away, and perhaps someone is grieving over you now. To look at you, I should have thought that likely, only remembering what the border ruffians were like, maybe not. But I can't take you back now or turn you loose. I'll look after you well, don't worry. I wonder what your name is. You'll have to have a new one now."

In the end she called him Paddy after her father because he reminded her of an Irish horse. He was big to sit on after Betsy, and she felt a little frightened the first time because she hadn't ridden for so long, but he proved to be a gentle giant, and she was glad of him.

Three days after Paddy's arrival, Owain came riding into the yard in an excited state.

"Lawrence has been sacked!" he yelled, galloping round and scattering the chickens all over, squawking in terror. "Lawrence has been sacked!"

Caitlin almost dropped the pail she was carrying. "When?"

"Yesterday morning."

"What happened?"

"Hundreds of border men smashed all the windows, shelled the hotel, burnt the houses, and drove the townspeople out."

"Was anyone killed?"

"No, only one, and that was a Southerner. He was struck by a wall and serve him right!"

Owain threw himself off Trooper and landed at her feet. "It's war now," he said. "This'll be the start of it."

She could see he was glad. Beside himself with excitement, in fact.

"At least no one was injured. Nobody killed. No real harm was done."

Owain yelled at her. "Can't you see it's a crime?"

She picked up her pail coldly and went back into the shed. "I'm glad we weren't there, that's all," she threw over her shoulder,

"I wish I had been!" He insisted on following her in his feverishness. "You'd have only got yourself killed ... for nothing." Caitlin put the pail down and picked up a pitchfork. She was in the middle of cleaning out the stables.

Owain took a good hard look at her for the first time for months. She was still a beautiful woman though she had lost the first edge of her prettiness. Her face — so pale after the miscarriages — was beginning to brown again in the Kansas sun. She remained slim and her shoulders and the curves of skin down to her breasts were still finer and more desirable than any woman's he had ever seen. Her hair grew long and free in dark curls and her blue eyes still flashed but her dress was poor and ragged, and she wore a scarf wrapped round her head like some negro field worker.

For a moment, he wanted to throw her down in the hay, straddle her, and subdue the rebellious mouth that didn't approve of him. She was not the same woman he had met on the boat nor in New York. She was tougher and more resilient and that was all to the good. But she was stubborn and seemed angry with him all of the time, just as he was with her.

"I may have to leave you for a day or two," he said curtly. "But you'll be alright, won't you? The spring work is all done. You've got a horse of your own now, and you know how to use a gun."

She interrupted him. You're going to join John Brown, aren't you?" To join his band of maniacs ..."

He felt like hitting her now. "Don't say that! You're not fit to call him that."

"There are those who say madness runs in his family."

"They would! It's just an excuse for their own cowardice and damned inaction, that's all." His black eyes burnt with fury. "Nothing you can say will stop me. There's work to be done. But it's only for a day or two."

Her eyes wandered past him into the yard where the late afternoon sun was making the dust motes golden.

"Trooper needs seeing to," she said. "He's all of a lather. You shouldn't ride him so hard."

"He's alright. You see to him if it worries you. I've got other things to do."

She walked the horse round the yard to cool him off, then took him back to the stables. Owain retired to the cabin and began cleaning his rifles.

Chapter Six

24th May 1865

It was a black night, black enough for an avenging angel. Down at Dutch Henry's Crossing on Pottawamie Creek, a man called James Doyle heard a knock at the door. He hadn't heard the alarm of either of his two bulldogs because five minutes earlier, Owain had slit their throats.

There were eight men waiting at the door and they were all bristling with pistols and broadswords. They asked where one Alan Wilkinson — a member of the Territorial Legislature — lived, and Doyle gave them directions in good faith. Then, the men pressed him back into the room.

Their leader was a tall man with a long beard and the face of a hard, proud eagle. He demanded a surrender in the name of 'the Army of the North'. Doyle was unarmed, as were his three sons: William aged 22 years, Drury 20, and John only 16. The father was asked to step outside and questioned as to his beliefs on the slavery issue. Then the sons were ordered out, too. William and Drury went, but their mother shed tears and asked that John might be spared because of his age. Three pistol shots cracked out through the dark. In the morning, James, William, and Drury Doyle were found dead, their skulls split like melons, their sides pierced, and their fingers cut off.

Wilkinson was up late when John Brown and his men called at midnight. His wife was sick with the measles. The same routine was followed, though this time there was no sound. His wife thought he had been taken prisoner but, in the morning, he was found a hundred yards away, with his skull split and his side pierced.

The last call of the night was to the home of one James Harris. It wasn't Harris but a guest of his called William Sherman who was asked for. Harris was spared, providing he promised to leave the territory.

But Bill Sherman had his skull hacked and his sides pierced, and his hands severed. The next day, James Harris was seen leaving for Missouri in a dazed condition, his wagon piled high with household goods and his wife weeping.

The very same morning, Owain returned to Caitlin. She was still in bed when he arrived for it was not yet light. The sound of Trooper's hooves and his nervous whinny woke her. She rose wearily and, wrapping herself in a shawl, sat on the edge of the bed in the grey dawn. When Owain came in, the first thing she noticed was a sword dangling at his side.

"It's cold," he said, approaching the stove.

It was then that she saw the dried blood on his clothes. "Owain! What have you done?"

"I've been on a raid."

"A raid? What do you mean? What kind of raid?"

"One to set an example to every man in this county. We killed five pro-slavers. That's all. I could have wished it had been more. But the message is clear enough."

Caitlin recoiled physically from him. "That's all! How could you?"

"John Brown said it was God's will." He took off his bloodstained shirt and stuffed it into the rekindled fire, holding it there with the point of his sword until it caught and began to burn. Caitlin sank trembling into the chair at the table and put her head in her hands.

"Listen to me, Owain. Rustling horses is one thing. But murdering in cold blood is quite another!"

"They had it coming to them. It wasn't murder. It was an act of war."

"That's what John Brown says, is it? No, it wasn't. It was murder! And you did not shrink from it! I know you killed once in anger, and I understood that, afterwards, you were ashamed and meant to do only good. But this…. this is different! This was planned."

"I do not repent, Caitlin, and it is right you should know that."

"Who were they?"

"I told you; they were pro-slavers. They were on the list."

"John Brown's list?"

"Yes"

"The man is a fanatic. Not godly at all."

Owain's eyes narrowed. "Don't speak of him like that. And I will be careful. I will lie low for a few days."

"We need things from the store."

"Then you must go and say I am sick and have been home in bed all night."

"I can't say that."

"Then I shall have to kill you too."

She gasped. "You cannot mean that!"

"A wife should not betray her husband."

Their eyes met, and Caitlin saw no warmth. "Please don't go with Brown again, Owain. I beg you!"

Owain shook his head. "You don't understand. But now I must wash and sleep. Have the rifle ready for me in case anyone comes. Go outside and watch the track."

When he was asleep, Caitlin stood and watched him for a while. In sleep, the hard lines on his face were softened. The intensity of his eyes was veiled. A mop of dark hair flopped over his brow. He looked like the young man she had met on the boat again. The one who had taken his tarring and feathering bravely because he knew in his heart, he deserved more for the dreadful deed he had done.

She went outside. He had redeemed himself for that first crime in her eyes by taking good care of her and Maeve on the boat. Then he had worked hard and stayed out of trouble, earning his dream of buying a farm and he had loved her once. To say what he just had was dreadful. What had happened to him, six years on? She strove to pinpoint the moment of change and it all came back to shooting Betsy. She had never really forgiven him for that. But she had at least understood why. Then there had been John Brown.

Would it have made a difference if they had children running around now? Surely it would! Yet the influence of this man Brown ran so strongly in him that perhaps it would not. He did care, she knew, for what he believed in. He had risked his own life to help Kitty and Washington. He thought he was doing right now. He had reconciled himself to it. But she could not.

She realized there would always be some cause somewhere for Owain and some justification. He was also a killer. And her husband. At her request, he had built the crude terrace of wooden planks outside the cabin, where she liked to sit, to stop so much mud being trailed inside when it rained. She cooked his meals and did his washing and shared his bed. She sat on in the rocking chair with the rifle across her knees and thought uneasily how she no longer wanted to do any of these things. She did not want him to touch her again.

Nobody came, thanks be to God. It was a beautiful day. The air was fresh and sweet with the scent of flowers. The birds were singing, almost as sweetly as canaries, and the prairie grasses waved in the wind. It was very much like the first day they had arrived from Independence. Yet how different.

In the evening, she cooked him a meal when he woke at last, fed the animals, lit the lamps, and sat down quietly to do some mending. They said nothing to each other. When he went back to bed, she slept in the chair. The next day, she drove Paddy into Prairie City for provisions. In the store, she bought a copy of the Kansas Free State newspaper. It said nothing about the killings, but all over town folks were muttering about it in low voices. She fancied once or twice she attracted some hostile glances, and that frightened her. In the post office, she saw Billy.

"What happened, Billy?" she asked him. "Will there be trouble?"

"You mean after the massacre? I reckon so." Massacre! That was a word of some weight. "The general opinion round here is that the Comanches did it."

Caitlin stared at him. "That's ridiculous. They stick to the High Plains. They don't come here."

It was true. Since the day they had arrived, the only Indians she had seen were poor, ragged fellows who came into Lawrence or the trading posts singly or in twos and threes. She was no longer afraid of them. Nobody was.

"Sure, it is. But their reputation for butchery in the past makes it kinda convenient to lay this at their door. It sure goes against the grain to think any of ours could have carried out such atrocities."

Butchery, massacre, and atrocities It had been truly brutal then.

Billy paused to heave a wad of tobacco from one side of his mouth to the other before continuing. "We know the truth in our hearts though. It was John Brown and his men alright. Folks is just too shocked to admit it."

"Have there been any reprisals?"

"They say John Brown Junior's been arrested. Turned over to the dragoons who took him away in chains, though he swears he weren't there. Actually, I'm inclined to believe him, for he's the weakest of the sons, you know, a bit soft in the head."

Caitlin longed to tell him about Owain but knew she could not, must not.

"Do you think there'll be raids on our farms?"

"Could be. Don't get frightened, Cait. You got Owain to protect you. Why ain't he here today, by the way?"

"He ...he stayed to guard the farm."

"There you are, you see. You won't come to no harm. I reckon the pro-slavers will know who's to blame..." With these far from encouraging words, Billy tipped his hat to her. "Troublesome times," he said. "Sometimes I just wonder where it's all a-gonna end. Reckon we must just stick together and keep our heads down."

Caitlin thanked him for his news and passed on. Before returning home, she went back into the store and bought a Southern newspaper. Back at the wagon, she took off Paddy's nosebag and climbed on to the box to read it.

The headlines made her hands shake. It was described as the Pottawattomie Massacre. Women and children terrorized in the middle of the night. Free-soilers' dirty doings showing them up for what they were! Five good men, two scarcely more than boys, murdered and their bodies mutilated. No gory detail was spared. By the time Caitlin finished reading she felt sick.

She drove back to the homestead without seeing anything to left or right, unharnessed Paddy, stabled him and put the provisions away hurriedly. Then she entered the cabin with dragging feet and a reluctant heart.

Owain sat at the table, engaged in the everlasting task of cleaning his rifles. "Any news?"

"Plenty." She laid the paper down in front of him.

He glanced at its title. "What you buy that for? It's a Southerner's newspaper, full of lies."

"Not this time, Owain! It tells the truth. Doesn't it?"

He looked sullen. "I asked if there was any news."

"Oh yes," she said. "John Brown Junior's been arrested and taken away in chains."

He was startled. "But he wasn't there! Truly he wasn't!"

"You should know, Owain."

He got up and, picking up a saddlebag from the floor, began to pack it.

"Where are you going?"

"To John Brown's hide-out."

"You mustn't."

"But he may need me if he's planning to get his son back."

"And after that?"

"There's a lot to be done. Who knows? This is only the start."

"You'll be away for some time then?"

"Maybe. But you'll manage till the fall."

"That's not what concerns me, Owain."

"No?"

"No. But if you go now ..." she struggled to find the right words. "there'll be no hope for you. Don't you understand, Owain? It'll be the end of you."

"I'm not afraid!" He continued to pack his bags. "And I don't regret what I've done. I'll see it through. Brown has great plans. I shouldn't tell you, but I will. We're gonna raise an army so that folk will have to listen. We're gonna get the blacks to join us. It's a revolution, and it's coming soon. One day, you'll be proud of me, Caitlin!"

"I don't think so," said Caitlin in a low voice. "Not if you carry on doing it this way by killing and maiming innocent folk." But she saw it was already too late for him, and she would have to play her last card. Doggedly, she followed him out to the stables where he saddled Trooper and got him ready to ride.

"If you leave me now for this, I don't ever want you back. I mean it, Owain! Not ever."

He swung himself up into the saddle and adjusted his packs and rifles. "I reckon I won't be back for some time. Time enough for you to change your mind. Billy'll help if you got problems and I left some money from the fund in the cabin. You see, I ain't heartless. But I got to go."

"I mean it, Owain!" She was desperate now. "I shan't have you back, for I'll not share my bed with a murderer no more."

He led Trooper out and swung his hard, lean body into the saddle. "All right, Cait. I hear you, and I understand you don't understand. Guess there's no more to be said."

She couldn't believe he wouldn't get down from his horse, even now, but he didn't. His dark eyes rested on her a moment longer, angry, disappointed, and resentful. Then he turned the horse abruptly and kicked him away. He rode out of her life in a cloud of dust without a backward glance.

After he had gone, she did not cry. She walked round the farm, looking at everything, assessing what was to be done and if she could do it, building her anger up into a crescendo so she would not feel the pain. It wasn't so bad. She had a good horse and a wagon, a cow and a heifer calf, several chickens, and three pigs. But who would kill the chosen pig in the fall?

Best not think of that. Owain could be back by then, with his tail between his legs, admitting she was right.

There were three full fields of good, strong corn. She would have to harvest them herself when the time came and pray the weather held. There were potatoes and beans and squash. Plenty to sell if she could but harvest them. She could shoot, after a fashion, and ride. She could look after the animals, and she would do that better than any man. Billy's dog had had puppies this spring. She would ask him for two of them to guard the place now she was on her own. She would show them all!

Deep inside, a still, small voice of reason told her she should go back East, joining the wagonloads of folk bound for the steamers every day. But she could not give up so easily. She would be perfectly safe. Neither a pro-slaver nor a free-soiler would be bad enough to slay a woman in cold blood, surely? She had already known the worst, and that was because of Owain.

It would be lonely, but she tried to put that to the back of her mind. Hadn't she been lonely in New York? Her only other option would be to write to Polly, telling her what had happened and throwing herself back onto charity. She could imagine the reaction — how Polly would instantly write and tell her to go and live with them. Doubtless, she would be trotted out at various abolitionist meetings as an example of what the pro-slavers had done to poor white women in Kansas. No, she couldn't do that. In her mind's eye, she could already see Polly's wistful letter to Hartley Shawcross: *'Our poor Caitlin is back from Kansas and has had a terrible time. Owain had to go and become a freedom fighter. Our hearts are with his bravery. Poor Caitlin. Of course, we knew from the start she should not have married him.'* Well, it wasn't quite like that, and she would not have them thinking it was.

Something inside her still wanted to succeed on her own if need be. Then perhaps she could sell the farm as a growing concern one day and go back with money in her pocket. She went to bed tired but not completely downcast.

Harvest-time was hard. It was back-breaking enough for two and for one doubly so. Every day she was up at dawn to scythe and gather and bind the sheaves. Then she loaded the wagon with the dry stooks and took it to the barn. There was always more to be done, and she knew she was too slow. Every night when she fell into bed, aching in every muscle, she worried if the weather would hold. Then disaster came from quite a different direction.

She had just started the second field when it happened. She saw a cloud approaching, which advanced more quickly than any thunderstorm. It puzzled her. Then, the sky grew dark and noisy with the beat of thousands of insect wings. Locusts! She ran to get a broom. She had heard of them but had never seen them before and vainly thought she might beat them off.

Wildly, she flayed about her, but the air was full of them, and she screamed as they flew into her face, her mouth, her eyes. Horrible, yellow, sticky bodies everywhere! It was useless. Within seconds, the thrumming of wings ceased, as if by common consent, as they settled on the fields and their jaws took over. She ran about hopelessly, flaying corn and insects alike with the broom. It was all over in half an hour. They rose again as one and made off in the air to the next farm.

Every blade, every ear of corn was gone. Only bare stalks waved forlornly in the wind. Two-thirds of her crop had been eaten. She fell down exhausted in the field and cried her eyes out, beating the ground in impotent rage. Nothing had prepared her for this catastrophe. It had never happened before. It wasn't fair they should come this year. Now, there would be only enough grain to feed the livestock and herself over the winter and nothing to sell. It could not have been a worse start.

Still, she had the money from the fund left her by Owain, though she had once sworn never to touch it, knowing it came from John Brown. Now she would have to, blood money or no. Otherwise she could not buy new seed in the spring. Only spring was a very long way off.

The fall came, and the land burnt under the sun, and still Owain did not return. Hadn't she told him not to? She wasn't sure whether she was glad of it or not. All summer long, the troubles had raged. There had been several retaliatory raids against Osawattomie by the Missourians. Houses had been burnt, and another son of John Brown's

— Frederick, also a mental deficient — had been killed. Palmyra was plundered.

Meanwhile, Brown's army fought back by attacking the Missouri camp and killing half the men savagely. Federal dragoons rode in to disband the two sides but failed to arrest Brown. Then, the action moved south to two new forts the Southerners had built on the Missouri. These were attacked by free-soilers under Jim Lane. There were rumours of another march against Lawrence, but it didn't happen. 'Jayhawking' was the order of the day — sporadic burning, pillaging and killing.

In the late fall, the news fell off. It was said in town that John Brown had gone back East, and Jim Lane had retired with his army to Nebraska. Still Owain did not return.

November 4th was election day in the States, and in Kansas, it was the first day that snow fell. The Democrats won, though the new Republican party did pretty well. The new president was James Buchanan, a weak man who was to prove unable to control subsequent events. It meant little to Caitlin, though she still read the newspapers, expecting every day to hear some dreadful news of Owain's doings.

That winter was not as hard as the last, though hard enough for Caitlin. It was only the care of the animals that kept her going, for she grew mournful in her solitary confinement. Sometimes, she dreamed of New York ballrooms with ladies in pretty gowns that fluttered like butterfly wings and wished she had married Cornelius O'Brien. She had given up writing to Polly, though she missed the letters in return.

When the thaws came, she paid a visit to Billy and Meg.

"I must have a hand," she said, "for the ploughing and sowing. I can't do it all on my own. I can pay him. Could you find somebody for me?"

Billy promised he would try.

Chapter Seven

A week later, Billy turned up at Caitlin's cabin with a young Indian in his wagon.

"Oh no," said Caitlin quickly, taking one look at his high-boned, insolent face, his long black plaits, and the eagle feather in his hat. "That isn't what I meant. I don't want his kind."

Billy took her firmly inside the cabin by the elbow, leaving the Indian waiting outside. "Let me explain to you, Caitlin," he said. "Let me tell you about him first."

"He's not Comanche, is he?"

"No. Kickapoo."

"What's his name?"

"George."

She laughed. "You're trying to fool me, Billy!"

"No, I'm not, I swear. Everyone round here calls him 'Injun George'. He's a half-breed."

"A what?"

"His mother was a white woman. Some say that she was kidnapped, others that she ran off with an Indian thirty years ago. Don't suppose it matters much either way now. Anyway, this boy was born as a result, and she named him George. I expect the Kickapoos have another name for him. When he was about ten or eleven, she took off her paint and her feathers and beads and came back to Lawrence with him. God knows why. P'raps her man'd gotten himself another squaw. Maybe he'd died or maybe she thought George oughta get some kind of education. Nobody'll ever know now as she fell ill and died soon after and nobody spoke to her when she was living. Jest plain ignored the poor woman.

"Well, since then young George has had to fend for himself. I guess we all thought he'd go back to the Kickapoo, but he didn't, though Lord knows, he's kinda Indian through and through. Never came to much good. But he's survived. Must be nigh on thirty years now. Every spring and summer he turns up to get work on the farms. Then when the harvest is over, he takes his pay and goes off and drinks himself silly. No one sees him all winter long. I guess he goes up on the plains and lives rough. Then, every spring, he turns up again like a bad penny looking for work.

"Now, I know this ain't much of a recommendation, but Injun George ain't a baddun. A bit lazy, but he'll work all right if you ain't too soft on him. He fancies the idea of working for a white woman for a change."

"I bet he does!" said Caitlin suspiciously.

"Well, I think that might be somethin' to do with his mother. Anyway, I reckon he would be pretty loyal to you. And there ain't no white men, Caitlin, for love nor money. They've either got their own hands full like me, or they're off fighting like Owain," Billy paused.

"He's good with horses," he added as an afterthought.

"He'll not ride Paddy!" Even so Caitlin considered a frown puckering her brow. "How much would I have to pay him?"

"Eight dollars a month."

"That isn't much!"

"He won't expect more, provided he gets his food thrown in reg'lar."

"Where will he sleep?"

"Oh, he'll be happy to bed down with the horses or the cows."

"But will I be safe with him, Billy?"

"I wouldn't have brought him if I thought any different, Cait. Providin' you show him who's boss."

"It's a bit like having a slave," said Caitlin pensively. "Paying him only eight dollars and treating him like dirt."

"Oh no it ain't! If Injun George ain't happy, he'll take off and go somewhere else, make no mistake about it! You don't want to go feelin' sorry for him."

Caitlin sighed with misgivings. "All right, Billy. I'll take him on. I guess I have to."

He stayed with her for the next three years, on and off. That first year, he didn't say much. His work was pretty fair, and it certainly made a difference to her. She gave him his meals outside on the stoop and he ate them greedily and appreciatively with his hands though she had provided him with his own knife and fork. He never came inside the cabin. Though she would have denied it strenuously, she still felt a little frightened of him.

Then one day a terrific thunderstorm blew up whilst he was eating his supper outside. The wind whipped dust-devils across the yard and the blue lightning forked electricity down from the sky. Tremendous torrents of rain came crashing down. Caitlin dithered. Then she kicked open the door of the cabin and motioned him curtly inside. He scurried in like an animal at bay, his old Indian blanket sheltering his precious hat, one hand firmly held onto his plate of food. He squatted down on the floor with his back to the door. With another jerk of her head, she indicated the table and chairs. His eyes looked at her foxily, but he obeyed. She sat on one side of the table and he on the other, in Owain's place, and they both ate in silence. After that they always ate together though his table manners did not improve.

The harvest was successful that year. No locusts, no struggling alone. The race against the elements had evened up again. The heat blistered the land, but they would get it in before it shrivelled.

One day, when they were both scything together, Injun George looked up to the cloudless sky and sighed.

"What is it, George?" she demanded, irritated at his sighing.

"Storm coming. We stop now. We get Paddy back to stables and animals in."

She glanced up angrily. Another excuse for a break! Billy had told her to be hard on him and so she was. Did he still think her soft then because she was a woman?

"Don't talk rubbish!" she said. "The sky's perfectly clear. There's been no sign of rain for weeks."

"But storm on its way now, white lady."

She paused and straightened her aching back, pushing one hand across her sweating brow.

"How do you know?"

"Thunderbird tell George by way he fly. Thunderbird a messenger from Thunder God. He know."

Caitlin squinted up into the brilliant sky, following the line of George's finger. High above, a black speck soared and glided.

"It's an eagle, George, that's all. Birds aren't messengers from God."

"George, go get animals in now?"

"No, damn you! Get on with your work," and she slashed away with the scythe again.

Ten minutes later, the sky had grown very dark, and the lightning was starting to flicker. Paddy, always nervous of storms, was whinnying sharply and shifting about in the traces of the wagon. George looked at her expectantly.

"Go on then!" she muttered through clenched teeth.

He downed his tool and moved over to the horse. As the rains came crashing down and the thunder rolled, Caitlin ran to herd up the squealing pigs and drive them into the shed. The dogs ran about barking wildly, creating chaos. By the time they got back to the cabin, they were both soaked to the skin. Caitlin began to dry her hair crossly. Injun George sat cross-legged and smiled, his plaits dripping unheeded onto the floor.

"White lady listen to Injun George next time," he said triumphantly.

Caitlin grimaced. He had been good with Paddy. She knew she couldn't have got him unharnessed so fast and held him when he was frightened nor got him into the stable and tied up so quickly, calming him down all the while. The knowledge infuriated her.

After the harvest, she paid him off for the long pause of winter. He took the dollar bills without counting them, thrust them into his pocket and made off with ne'er a thanks nor farewell, hugging himself in the dirty blanket, walking with a spring in his step down the track. She had meant to ask him to kill the pig but now it was too late.

He won't come back, she thought with a pang. *Why should he? I've been so bloody to him. All because I'm angry inside. He's off to get drunk and to wash the memory of that crotchety, embittered white lady out of his system and I don't blame him at all.*

Next spring, when the thaws came, Caitlin opened her door one morning and almost fell over him, sitting patiently, cross-legged on the doorstep. After so long alone, it came as a shock.

"Darn you, George!" she cried. "What are you doing here?"

"White lady not want Injun George this year?"

"Oh yes, yes I do! I'm sorry. You just scared the wits out of me!"

It had been difficult this winter. Each winter was hard, but this one had been different in the quality of its hardness. Last year, she had buoyed herself up with the hope that Owain would come back one snowy night. This winter, she knew he would not. She began to drink a lot of whisky. Some nights, huddled in front of the stove, as close as she could get to keep warm, wrapped up in blankets like Injun George, she could hardly remember what year it was nor how long Owain had been gone. She gave up wearing skirts — instead, she found a pair of baggy corduroy trousers which had belonged to Owain and tied them at the waist with rope so they fit. She wore them with a shirt and a battered felt hat when she went outside. What did it matter? There was no one to see. Skirts were too cumbersome and blew about too much in the wind, and there was always wind here. Night after night, she heard it moaning about the cabin. She didn't kill the pig but sold it instead to buy meat. It was her one weakness. Apart from that, she was acting like a man. She wore men's clothes, she drank, and she swore all the time. She even spat. No one should say she was soft. She had given up crying, though deep inside, she felt a kind of despair at her life passing all the while. It was a long winter.

So, it was with a great sense of relief that she found Injun George on her stoop in the spring. She had missed him. Strangely enough they were on much better terms straightaway, having got the first year out of the way.

"White man coming back soon?" Injun George asked within the first few days of his return.

"Oh yes. He'll be back real soon now."

"White lady say that last ploughing time. And last harvest. But he not come."

That annoyed her but she didn't condescend to answer. They were sitting together at the table, eating supper after a hard day's work turning the sod. Caitlin was very hungry with the work she had done and laid down her knife and fork to pick up and gnaw the bones in the same way that her Indian hand did. After a while, she asked,

"What do you do in the winter, George? Where do you go to? You're like the flies that disappear, and no one knows where."

"Flies much damned sense!"

Caitlin laughed. "Well, where do you go?"

"I go to the High Plains."

"To the Kickapoo?" Her curiosity was fired.

"Not Kickapoo." George's face glowered. "Kickapoo call George 'Paleface Boy'. George not a boy no more! George thirty summers. Should be Indian brave and big man. But to Kickapoo, George always 'Paleface Boy'."

Caitlin glanced at him. His indignation was proud and genuine. She felt sorry for him. He belonged nowhere, and he knew it. That was awful. Yet he remained uncrushed.

"So, you spend the winter alone on the High Plains?"

"Yes, white lady."

"What do you do when the snow comes?"

"George kill buffalo long before then. Take it to his dug-out under the earth. Dug out very good and dry. George have buffalo and furs and fire."

And firewater no doubt, thought Caitlin amused.

"Dug-out good place for winter. George eats and sleep."

"Don't you ever feel lonely, George?"

He didn't answer. Perhaps he didn't understand what the word meant. She tried again.

"The High Plains are dry and deserted, aren't they?"

"Drier than here. But buffalo still there and gopher and prairie dog. High Plains not so bad. No white man."

"Ah yes," said Caitlin. She sucked her fingers clean. "That sounds good. No white man."

George looked at her knowingly.

"White lady want to see High Plains?"

"Too far."

"Not on horse."

"Perhaps."

"White lady come to George dug out in winter? We sleep and make babies, yes?"

She was shocked back into rectitude. "Certainly not!"

George was chastened.

"Anyway," said Caitlin, slopping whisky into his glass as well as hers, so he should know she did not hold it against him. "This white lady don't make babies ... she can't."

George thought about this.

"This why white man leave," he decided.

"No, it is not why white man leave!" Caitlin pushed away the table and rose to her feet crossly to clear the plates.

Then he really surprised her. "Injun George sorry," he said. She could see in his face he still thought he was right and perhaps he was in a way. But he had said sorry.

She shrugged. "It's all right," she said.

Another year gone. Another dreadful winter survived somehow. Another ploughing and another harvest to come.

"Why white lady not go back East?" said Injun George.

"You haven't seen the city, George. You don't know what it's like."

"White lady should go back."

"Why?"

"When Injun George go town, he hear talk."

"What sort of talk?" Caitlin felt alarmed.

"I ignorant injun. Not understand!"

"Don't play games with me, George! You understand very well. What do they say?"

"They say white man gone with John Brown to fight for the slaves. Some of them want to burn down this farm, but then they laugh and say no point, only a crazy injun-loving woman live there that wear trousers and be drunk and half-wild."

"Well, I don't care what they think or say." Caitlin stuck out her chin. "They won't come burn the farm. That's the important thing."

"It not good for white lady."

Why should he worry? But he went on to tell her.

"One day white lady fall ill, and nobody come. White lady will die alone."

So that was it. He was thinking of his mother. Caitlin shook her head.

"That won't happen to me, George. I'm still young and strong."

"Everyone think they young, even when they grow old. Everyone strong till they die."

His words cast a terrible chill over her.

Chapter Eight

Harper's Ferry, Virginia, 6th October 1859

It was a miserable night. A cold grey cloud drizzled rain from mountainous crags above the small peninsula, which jutted out into the meeting place of the Potomac and Shenandoah rivers.

John Brown's army was marching on the federal arsenal situated at Harper's Ferry. It was still a small army: four free blacks, one escaped slave, and sixteen whites, including Owain Griffith. Their numbers seemed of little consequence to them. There had been no reconnaissance of Harper's Ferry, no effort to alert Virginian slaves, no emergency plans for escape in case of disaster. That too, was of little concern for Brown was convinced that, once they were in control of the arsenal, slaves from the whole of Virginia and beyond would flock to the cause. Theirs was the tinder to set the flame. God was on their side, and so they could not fail.

Owain's heart was drumming with anticipation. For the last three years, John Brown had shuttled between Kansas and Boston, leading marauding parties in the West and raising money from supporters in the East. He had devised grand plans. Men had come but also gone. Owain had remained loyal all of this time. He had always been there when needed, fought savagely and then lain low in the quiet times, foraging for himself and living rough like he used to, which was what he liked best. He had become one of Brown's most trusted leaders and earned a reputation for being a fiery little Welshman with a strong heart, never to be crossed if you knew what was good for you.

Now, at last, after all the waiting, worrying, and chastening times, they were marching to their goal.

Had he ever thought of Caitlin during those long, cold winter times alone when there was nothing to be done and no killing to be had?

All the time. Sometimes, he even dreamed about her on the farm at the Osage River. He had no doubt she was coping, that she had grown strong. He did not worry about her, but he felt bitter when he remembered how she had sent him away.

He had no intention of returning until he had proved himself a hero in her eyes as well as the world's. She should welcome him back with open arms then, with never a question as to how he had carried out his deeds. Everything would be justified, and it would be as it had been that first night when they had reached the Kansas Plains. Then God would see fit to give them children. He saw that now quite clearly.

As he marched, the butt of his rifle bit into his side underneath a long grey shawl. Though hidden, it was primed and ready just as every nerve in his body was taut and every muscle stiffened. Yet it was all so easy. Crossing the covered bridge over the Potomac that led directly into Harper's Ferry, they posted guards and sent sentries to the other bridge into the town. The remaining handful of men marched down the dark main street unchallenged. Past the blacksmith's, the apothecary, the general store, the saloon, and the armourer's home. All slept on unawares.

The watchman at the arsenal was taken completely by surprise when John Brown's voice rang out with authority.

"I come here from Kansas, and this is a slave state. I am going to free all the negroes in this state, for I have possession of the United

States Armoury, and if the citizens interfere with me, I will burn the town and have blood."

It had begun. This was what he had come to America for — nay, had been sent for, been chosen from the start, and spared and directed to this end. Why was it that women never understood these things? For, in his mind, Elen, his mother, had begun to run along closely with Caitlin.

They captured the Hall's Rifle Works nearby without any trouble. Then, a small party of men were sent to seize hostages from the town. They returned with a prize indeed — Colonel Lewis Washington, a prosperous slave owner and a great-grandnephew of the first American president, amongst them. That was a wonderful moment. With him, they brought his sword — said to have been presented to his great-granduncle by Frederick the Great — and John Brown seized it and strapped it round his own waist. He declared that when all the slaves had come and been armed from the arsenal, he would lead the campaign for liberation onwards with this sword.

Meanwhile, the night was dark and long. The guards stopped an eastbound train at the bridge and warned the engineer to back away. No supporters came tumbling out of the cars. Only nervous passengers stared with pale and frightened faces out of the windows. A railroad baggage man loomed up quickly out of the dark and was shot by one of Brown's men in an excess of nervousness. He was a free black, as it happened. An unfortunate accident, but no one was to blame. The train was allowed on its way. Very shortly, telegraph wires began humming all over the East with news of a Negro insurrection, fire, rapine, and pillage at Harper's Ferry.

With the dawn came the townspeople's wrath, expressed in blistering gunfire. More significantly, during the day, the militia arrived, and the raiders were pinned down.

After four hours, they suffered their first casualty, and it was one of the blacks. Faced with a siege, Brown withdrew most of his men and the hostages they had taken to the fire engine house next to the armoury, and they barricaded themselves in. Soon, after one in the afternoon, he sent out two men to negotiate under a truce flag, but they were shot down without mercy. One of them was John Brown's son, Watson, who struggled back to the engine-house in agony.

The battle went on. One of the raiding parties tried to run and was savagely shot to death. Then, his body was used for target practice. The last men were driven out of Hall's Rifle Works and butchered. John Brown tried to parley and offered to release the hostages if he and his remaining fourteen men were let go. The townspeople didn't care much for this. By the time night fell and the gunfire temporarily ceased, no deal had been made.

Owain's fingers were stiff and aching with the constant loading and re-loading of rifles, and his shoulder hurt from the repeated discharge of his weapon. He didn't know how many men he had killed, but he knew it wasn't enough. By now, Brown's other son, Oliver, had been wounded too and lay beside Watson, both of them dying in excruciating pain. Oliver begged his father to kill him to put his misery to an end. The reply was curt, "If you must die, die like a man!"

Sometime later, all went quiet, and John Brown called out to Oliver. There was no reply.

"I guess he died," he said without emotion.

For the first time, Owain's blood ran cold in his veins. It looked mighty bad. They had never been holed up like this before. They were used to the lightning strike, the swift meting out of punishment and revenge, and the rapid, exhilarating getaway. For the first time, he realized he was bound to die unless Brown could be persuaded to surrender without reservation in the morning. Owain knew that he would never do that.

Was it possible that John Brown himself should die, too? He still looked determined, unrepentant, and unafraid. Owain realized it did not matter to him. He knew his death would have meaning. Perhaps martyrdom would have even more meaning than his life.

But what of the nameless ones? What of those that history would soon forget? Owain struggled with his feelings. Long ago, when he had committed his first crime — such a small one as it seemed now — he had been afraid of death and had run. He had atoned for that. But since then? His blood seemed to stagnate now. It was the darkest hour, and he drowsed over the barrel of his gun without meaning to, then jerked suddenly awake.

"Caitlin!" he said, though he didn't know why. Panic flooded through him. He had been so certain, but now everything was dissolving, and he had to fight to hold onto any meaning. He sank onto his knees but could not pray, could not even frame thoughts, never mind find the answers.

I have done wrong, he acknowledged to himself. *I have done shocking things, but I did them for the right reasons. Oh God, what will happen to me?*

Caitlin....the name returned unbidden. She would never be proud of him now. Nor would Elen. Bitter tears crowded into his eyes like hot salt. He had sworn to look after Caitlin. Now, he would never see her again.

Then he took a hold upon himself lest someone should see him, maybe even Old Brown himself. It would not do. These were only shadows and nightmares. The only matter of significance left was to die well, to be brave and not to cry out. He steeled himself, and his heart hardened as he did so. *Nothing I did,* he thought, cannot be redeemed by this. *It's only the night which troubles me, and dawn will soon come. Maybe we'll even get out of here ...*

But the view outside their fort in the morning was daunting. Row upon row of hostile, armed men stood there, including a company of Marines, newly arrived from Washington. They were obviously preparing to storm the engine-house, for they were armed with muskets, fixed bayonets, and sledgehammers. The power of the whole Union was on their side. Their commander was Lt. Colonel Robert E. Lee, and being a fair man, he sent a lieutenant forward under a white flag to demand surrender and promise protection for the renegades.

John Brown met him at the door. He stood tall and upright with his long beard flowing proudly and his eyes burnt like coal. The counter-proposals he made were clearly impossible. In a moment, the lieutenant had jumped aside and waved his hat as a signal for the Marines to charge.

Owain bent his eye steadily to his sights as they came on in waves. He fired and fired again, but they had a battering-ram to the door, which suddenly disintegrated, and then they were in the room itself. His sweating fingers whirled the rifle round to face them and fire again. Except he heard no sound other than a distant explosion and felt a great thud in his chest. The black curtain came down as he hit the floor.

For an instant, it parted, and he had a hazy impression of John Brown being bludgeoned to the ground with a blunt sword. He was then seized and dragged off. Owain groaned. There were a tremendous number of men above him, swaying, moving, shouting, but everything was soaked in a red mist.

"Caitlin!" he said again, without knowing why, though he knew now he was weeping. Then he felt a great outpouring within him, sweeping away all the pain but also his life with it. He found it difficult to remember who he was. All identity was lost in the surging of what seemed to be black paint coming out of his eyes. It was so hot and heavy. Then, the folds of the curtain enclosed him forever.

It was Billy who brought the news a few days later, riding over to the farm on Osage Creek on a flaming October day. Injun George had already left for the winter, and Caitlin was alone, resting in her chair on the stoop, shading her eyes against the sun, struggling to recognize her neighbour approaching down the long track.

She had not seen Billy for some time, but the dogs remembered him and ran excitedly to bark and yap around his legs when he dismounted. Caitlin took off her battered hat shyly and fanned her flushed face with it. She was wearing an old shirt and Owain's corduroy trousers as usual, and her hair was tied back from her face.

Billy," she greeted him without rising, wondering at the awkward look he gave her.

"Caitlin." He came unwillingly onto the stoop. "I guess you haven't seen the newspapers then."

"No. What is it?"

He laid one paper carefully on her lap and stood back a little, embarrassed, not relishing his task. She glanced at the headlines.

Harper's Ferry. Where was that? Virginia — a long way from here. Then she caught the name of John Brown and read on with a sinking feeling in her heart. He had been arrested, indeed already tried, and sentenced to hang with his followers. But only four of them had survived the raid. The dead were listed and the name of Owain Griffith was amongst them. He had at least escaped the hanging he had feared so much.

"I'm very sorry, Mrs Griffith," Billy said.

She didn't know what to feel. "It was bound to come, Billy." "Yeah, I reckon so. Meggie told me to say if there was anything we could do ..."

Caitlin shook her head. "That was kind of her. But no, there's nothing to do."

"I suppose not. Reckon they'll have buried him there. Perhaps you'll get a letter."

"Perhaps. Though I doubt they'd know where he came from."

"You'll be going back East now?"

"I don't know. Do you think I should?"

"I thought there'd be relatives there ... yours or his."

"No, there's no one."

"I see. I'm real sorry."

"I guess I'll have to stay on, at least for a while. It won't be that different for me after all."

"No, I suppose not."

Only somehow, it was. After Billy had gone, she walked slowly down to the creek. It had always been her thinking place. She watched the waterfowl dipping and bobbing in the evening sun. Billy was right. There ought to be something to do, but there was nothing. She wished Injun George was still here. She still clutched the newspaper in her hands: '*Harper's Ferry: conclusion of the trial - fear of Southern whites - Republicans' vehement denial of support*'. All the outrage, anger and fear of a nation.

Abruptly, she tore the paper into shreds and scattered the pieces on the waters, where they floated quietly away. Nothing was left then...nothing at all.

≈

1st November 1859 (Written to Fedwr Gog in North Wales)

Dear Elen Griffith,

I do not know if this will reach you, nor even if you are still alive. You do not know who I am and will be shocked to receive this letter from a stranger after such a long time. I am sorry, but I believed I should write, though I wish I had done so before now. I married your son, Owain, six years ago and came with him to Kansas Territory to farm.

I know what made your son run away from Wales. The reason was not as bad as you might have believed, though the action was. We met on the boat on the way over when he was scarcely a man. I saved him from being sent back as a stowaway because I felt sorry for him, and I too, was alone. Owain was sorry for what he had done and worked hard to earn enough money for his own land out here. Many is the time I asked him if I could write you on his behalf, for I thought he had done well, and you would be glad to know it. But he would never allow it. I think it was because he had big dreams he wanted to fulfil first, to prove his worth to you and everyone back home.

Times out here have been very hard. I failed to give Owain any living children, and we were both sad about that. Also, it was difficult to make the farm pay. But there were other matters, too, which will be hard for you to understand. I shall try to explain.

This land has been torn apart by troubles and fighting over the slavery question and the different ways of life in the North and South. Owain fell in with a man who was fanatically committed to the anti-slavery cause and was prepared to shed blood for it. He joined this man's private army. I thought he was wrong to go away with him and still do, even though I agree slavery is wrong. Nevertheless, Owain died bravely in what he felt to be a just cause, attempting a rebellion. His deeds along the way are best passed over. But I had not seen him for three years.

I do not believe your son and my husband was totally bad though, I do think he was corrupted by the times and this particular man. His aims were good, but his passion spoilt them by carrying him into the darkest anger. I would like you to know that he was always a good husband to me until the day he left. Also, he once risked his life to save two runaway slaves and their child, and that was probably the best thing he ever did. He was not afraid of hardship and had become very strong.

Now I must forget him as if he had never been, for my own sake, but I know that you will not. I believe he is buried in Virginia in Harper's Ferry, although I suppose that name will mean little to you. I wish now that I had disobeyed Owain and written to you before, that you had known something from me other than this grief. I wish for many things that never came to pass. But I remain, sincerely yours, Owain's widow and your daughter-in-law,

Caitlin Griffith

Caitlin had written to Padraig years before from the Regans but never received any reply. She had written to the hotel in Liverpool where they had stayed, but it seemed Padraig and Bridget had never left a forwarding address, despite Padraig's sentimental protestations. She hoped this letter to Elen would fare better across the waves to North Wales.

Chapter Nine

Injun George returned in the spring, and Caitlin told him what had happened.

"Now, white lady go back East," he said promptly, as she knew he would.

"I don't know about that, George. I haven't made my mind up. I guess I just don't see how I can. Anyway, there's the ploughing to be done and the cow is going to calve again."

He shrugged at her stubborn adherence to work but shouldered his own labour again, willingly enough. It was an unusually hot, dry spring with no rain above a sprinkling, and the winter had been dry too. The hods of earth were rock hard, and Paddy had to struggle valiantly under the plough.

The omens were not good.

"Land no good to plant seeds this year," George announced baldly.

Caitlin was horrified. "But we must! If we don't plant, we'll have no crops!" That would mean no money and no food. The fund Owain had left ran out long ago.

"No crops, no way this year," George told her firmly.

She was badly frightened. Surely, it must rain soon. It was yet but spring. Even George could be wrong, though usually he was not, as she had found to her cost many times.

"Keep your money this year," he urged her. "No buy seed. You need money."

"No, George, we must plant!"

He shook his head over her sorrowfully as a hopeless case.

"Jesus, we only need a few storms! You're always after prophesying doom, you good-for-nothing half breed!" She was angry with him against her better judgement as always, but he knew it was because she was frightened. Only he was as stubborn as she was.

"Not this year," he repeated with intransigence, though he did as she asked and planted the seed.

There was a pedlar passing through Palmyra when she went to buy the seed and, against all her common sense, she was allured into buying some merchandise from him. Silly things she had no use for: a new comb, some soap, pretty ribbons, a mirror and even a bale of cotton cloth in sprigged green for a new dress. She who never went anywhere and never saw anyone and had worn trousers for two years! But she was sick of never buying anything but seed.

It was a mistake though, especially the mirror. When she got home, she took a good long hard look at herself and was horrified. Her complexion of pale porcelain, so admired in the drawing-rooms of New York, was utterly changed. It was brown and tough-looking and dry. Her eyes — always large and blue — looked positively enormous, but they wore a harassed expression and round them were the beginnings of lines. A permanent angry frown was beginning to etch itself on her forehead. *This cannot be me,* she thought incredulously! *Me, who men have always run after, whether I wanted them to or not. I am but three years short of thirty and already I look nearer forty.* The sun and the rains, the endless toil, and the worry (and maybe the firewater) were exacting their toll. She had nothing to show for it, no husband, no children, no timber-framed homestead, and not even a fertile farm now it seemed, nestling in the prairie sun. It was a severe shock. I will make up the dress, she thought, and I shall wear it when I go into Lawrence.

The drought continued and split open the soil so that the newly planted seeds shrivelled and died. Injun George showed them to her with a look on his face which spoke volumes.

"I can get more," she said defiantly. So, she could - just - but after that, she would have nothing.

He shook his head sorrowfully. "Don't do that, white lady."

"I must. Oh, don't shake your head at me like that! We won't plant them straightaway. We'll wait for the rain to come. It must come soon."

But the vast sky remained obstinately cloudless day after day. This time she went to Lawrence for the seed, as if the supplies might be better there. It was a substantial town now, thriving and flourishing, and one in which the free-soilers were at last gaining the upper hand in the Territory so the townsfolk were no longer afraid. The talk was not of farming but of railroads. The drive west continued, and the tracks being laid were coming nearer — not merely to link Kansas with the East, but in an urgent desire to cross the desert and reach California where gold had been found. Even virgin land might yet be sold to a railroad company.

It was in one of the general stores that she first met Andrew Tyrrell. He was not a local but a Yankee from the East, a big and prosperously dressed man with flaming red hair. The very same Andrew Tyrrell that had come over on the Yorkshire in first class, had she but known it, and he had done well in the new world. He propped up the counter with a whisky in one hand and a cigar in the other, oozing confidence and wealth and speculating keenly on the value of land owned by each incoming customer and whether it would be worth his while to buy.

He was not from the railroad company but, being a shrewd racketeer, intended to buy up land cheap to resell to the railroads for a large profit.

Caitlin thought him contemptible. A man clearly without an ounce of moral fibre or courage in him and yet one who had obviously achieved much success.

She had come into town shabbily and eccentrically dressed as usual, despite her good intentions, for the sprigged cloth was still not made up, and she received haughty looks from the Lawrence women because of it. Injun George sat and waited in the wagon for her outside — another affront to delicate white, abolitionist sensibilities — whilst she bludgeoned her way uncaring down the street and up the sidewalk into the store, an odd little figure in her man's clothing and battered hat.

Yet despite all this, Andrew Tyrrell noticed her. She realized it as soon as she walked in, for he did not attempt to conceal it. His eyes alighted on her face and rested there a long time, though he never spoke a word to her and smirked at her appearance as did the rest of the shop. Even so, he saw her fine face under the ridiculous felt hat, and his eyes undressed her from her old clothes in an instant. She saw that at once. It was still there, then, that old power of hers, only half understood, to attract a man. Despite everything, it was still there.

In her heart she did not want to attract such a man, but he was attracted to her, and she felt excited after her long years alone. He was not entirely unpersonable. Big and bluff with small, rather mean eyes and that auburn stubble. He had a kind of energy, a wickedness about him that was somehow appealing in her desperation. In no way handsome, nor worthy, and certainly not kind. Dangerous, in fact.

She bought the seed whilst appearing to ignore him yet listening all the while to what he said. He was bargaining with a little ferret-like man for a piece of land. He was staying in the Free State Hotel. He would be there several days if the fellow wanted to change his mind

She left in the knowledge that his eyes followed her out and ordered Injun George to drive her home. That night she sat up long and late considering her predicament. This last winter had been the hardest of all, knowing that Owain would never be back now. It had almost broken her. She did not relish the idea of another. All her life, she had been tossed about like a reed in the wind with no folks of her own. Even when Owain had come back for her in New York and brought her out here, the decision had hardly been her own. Was it not time to act and take matters into her own hands? She knew she could.

She also knew Injun George was right. There would be no rain. She could not delay planting the seed forever. The drought would continue and ruin it like the first batch. Then she would have nothing, only the dread spectre of famine to face, without money, and without any protector. Hunger and poverty. Had she come so far across the seas, propelled by these, only to encounter them again and sink back into suffering? Heaven forbid! Injun George was right — no-one would help her, and she would die alone. She must sell now while she could and go back East.

Andrew Tyrrell might be her last chance.

Would he want the land? She had no idea how valuable it was. Probably not much. It was far from certain the railroad would take such a route; indeed, it seemed unlikely. She must link it with the offer of herself, detestable though the thought was. The money from the sale would only last a short while whereas Andrew Tyrrell could be a meal-ticket for life.

Her next two days were spent making up the cotton bale from the pedlar into the semblance of some sort of gown, using her old skills as a seamstress. It was not a very good gown, for she had never been a very good seamstress, but it would suffice. She cut the bodice deliberately low. Unsullied by childbirth, her breasts were still tight and firm, her waist trim, her stomach flat. The pattern of the cloth was very pretty. When she had finished it, she tried it on and thought it quite fetching. Its green shade suited her well. She had no fashionable bonnet to match but would do up her hair with the ribbons she had bought, and it would look better for it. The effect was perhaps a little young for her but would not be noticed. Hardly the widow's weeds she ought to be wearing, and she wondered briefly if a black veil would be more intriguing.

As she undressed for bed, her courage almost deserted her. She thought of Father Francis. Jesus, what was she doing? How could she even contemplate this? But then Father Francis didn't have to face starvation in Kansas. Doubtless, he would advise her to throw herself on Polly's charity — That she could not do. She tried to console herself with the idea that all would turn out for the best. Yet she knew Tyrrell was a beast. She was much wiser now than she had been when she met Owain. Dear God, what would Hartley say if he knew? Oh, but it was useless to think of that! She had to survive, and it was the only way she could think of. It was impossible to ride Paddy in all her new finery of course so she had to call reluctantly upon Injun George's services as a driver. He stood taken aback when he saw her emerge from the mud cabin in her new dress.

"What's the matter?" she demanded angrily.

"What white lady doing now?"

"That's no business of yours, George!" She settled herself demurely in the back of the wagon whilst he continued to stare. "You ignorant Indian boy, right? I pay you to work for me, and you do what I say. You drive me into Lawrence."

He got into the driving-seat, muttering and mumbling to himself all the while.

A devil inside her drove her on. "How do I look, George?"

"White lady look very fine."

"Thank you."

"But white lady up to no good."

"Injun George should keep his thoughts to himself," she said, tartly. "Shut up and drive!"

He turned round on the box and looked at her hard and long.

By the time they reached Lawrence, she had screwed up her resolve once more and swept into the Free State Hotel with a satisfying rustle of long, forgotten petticoats and green cotton skirts.

"I must speak with Andrew Tyrrell right away," she demanded at the front desk.

"Mr Tyrrell?" asked the hotelkeeper stiffly, looking down his long nose at her bonnetless hair. "Do you have an appointment? Mr Tyrrell usually has appointments."

"No, I don't believe I have. But he'll see me. It's about a property deal."

"A card, perhaps?"

"No card."

The eyebrows were raised several inches above the long nose. "A name then?"

"No name he would know. Only he met me in the store here a few days ago."

She must rely on his curiosity, if not his memory. The long nose disappeared, and she swept through into the public lounge to sit and wait. A moment of panic filled her. It was here where she had made cartridges under siege four years ago. So much for that. She had tried a good man and it had ended in disaster. Now it was time to take on a bad one and perhaps she would fare better.

She became aware of his presence and lifted her eyes to the doorway. Tyrell stood there, blocking it very effectively with his big, red body, a shadow fallen across the sun. For a minute he looked at her and she at him, then he advanced into the room, and she rose, coyly extending her hand.

"I don't believe I've had the pleasure of your acquaintance," he said, altogether cunning and charming at once, though she could tell he recognized her well enough.

"No," she agreed firmly. "I don't believe you have. My name is Caitlin Griffith. But I've heard of you, Mr Tyrrell."

He liked that of course though his eyes narrowed as he pressed the hand she proffered, pinching the hard band of her thin wedding-ring against her skin. She had better explain that quickly though, in her new canniness, she knew it would do her no disservice.

"Oh, and what have you heard of me?"

"That you're interested in buying land in these parts."

"Depends on the land, ma'am. What land would you be offering?"

"Sixty acres on the Osage Creek. Only a little of it is ploughed and seeded, but I don't imagine you're interested in that. There's a cabin too, some livestock and tools."

"The Osage Creek." He pretended to consider and smiled. "I don't think so, ma'am. As you rightly surmise, I'm not interested in farming."

"Neither am I, anymore. My husband was killed in the troubles, and I don't have the heart to carry on." She placed a hand over her bosom so that he should see it heave with suppressed emotion. He was not slow to notice though he was unimpressed by the emotion.

"I'd like to help you out, ma'am, but really, Osage Creek, that's too far down south for the major railroad, you know. I don't think so."

"One day there'll be branch lines, won't there? Linking up the whole of this Territory to the main line. Settlers are still coming here."

"Maybe. But you're talking ten, twenty years ..."

"I can give you ..." she hesitated. "a very good price." She looked at him and smiled invitingly.

"You sure it's yours to sell?"

"The stake is."

He laughed and shook his head. "You got enterprise, ma'am, I'll say that for you. But the answer's still no."

"It is mine. No one else has a claim to it. I can show you the papers. Why don't you come out and see it — no obligation, of course, but if you're staying in these parts a while longer ..." Her voice trailed off, but she moved closer to him and engaged his eyes with a knowing look. He was, she realized, much larger when she stood so close to him. The desperation of her mission made her feel faint. She plunged on.

"If you have the time, that is. Of course, it's not much of a place to an important man like yourself, but it's very pleasant ... won't you come? You won't regret it."

"Maybe I will. I'm not promising, mind."

She smiled again, looking up at him. "I understand, Mr Tyrell. Perfectly. I'm sure it'd be worth your while."

"We'll see."

"I won't take up any more of your precious time, but I'll look forward to your visit. Good day."

"Good-day, ma'am."

She swept out neatly without a backward glance though she felt his eyes follow her. Her heart was hammering away, and she had to lean against the wall outside for support to recover herself. She felt the taste of cheapness in her mouth but swallowed it. Had she done enough, said enough? Now she could only wait and see.

Injun George was sitting stoically in the wagon. "Where now?" he asked.

"Home, of course."

"You mean that's all?"

"For the moment. No, wait! Take me to the store. I want to buy some more cloth. I must have more than one dress."

He shrugged his shoulders in resignation at her madness.

≈

Tyrrell paid his visit three days later, when she had almost given up on him. In the meantime, she had made up another dress, this one in plain black to suit her widowed status, but again she had cut the bosom low. It suited her even better in its simplicity. She walked him round the farmstead but could see straightaway he wasn't really interested. He must have looked at maps in the meantime and seen it was worthless. Yet he had still come. She must continue to work on him then.

"It ain't prime land for my purposes," he said bluntly.

"Maybe not. But it's close to the creek at a good crossing-point. Surely that counts for something?"

He merely shrugged.

She took him back to the cabin, which was neatly swept, where a good pot of chicken was bubbling on the stove.

"You'll do me the honour of taking some supper with me, Mr Tyrrell?"

"That's mighty kind of you."

She made him sit down and served him with the food. He ate well and obviously enjoyed it as he was a man with a hearty appetite. She produced a bottle of whisky and made sure she kept his glass filled though she herself drank little. He lit a cigar and pushed his chair back, contemplating her shrewdly.

"You've farmed this place alone for how long?"

"Three years."

"With nobody around but that Indian hand?"

"That's right. He comes to help out in the spring and summer."

Tyrrel took another puff from the fat cigar, and his small, hard eyes almost softened for a moment.

"You got guts, lady!" he said. "You know that?" His admiration was genuine. "Most of the women I know'd faint at the prospect."

She met his gaze levelly. "It ain't a lot of use fainting, Mr Tyrrell, is it? Nor complaining. Not when you're up against it."

He acknowledged this with a nod of his head. "Worst part of it is, I'd expect an old hag to hang on here somehow, but not a good-lookin' woman like you."

She looked at him coolly. "I'll not disguise the fact I sometimes feel the need for a man around, Mr Tyrrell. That's why I want out." She saw a gleam in his eye.

"And what plans do you have, just supposing, just supposing now, I might buy?"

She leant over to him across the table and refilled his glass with a smile. The tone of their conversation was becoming more intimate, and she sensed the seeds of victory. She must choose her words with care now, though she had begun to sweat.

"Oh, I don't know. I'll go anywhere. Back East for preference. But I'd like to travel a bit. Where are you going, Mr Tyrrell?"

"Virginia. Though I move around a great deal. But that's where my home is." "Virginia!" she said with unfeigned delight. "Oh, I've always wanted to go to Virginia. Perhaps we could travel back together. That'd be real pleasant."

His eyes had narrowed again. He was wondering if he was reading her right. She still leant towards him smiling and the creamy valley between her breasts had opened up for him. Of course, she was a common little gold-digger but a darned attractive one. He made his move.

"I like to sample goods before I buy."

She rose quickly to her feet and went to fetch another bottle of whisky — her very last — to cover her revulsion. Her hands trembled on the cork as she thought quickly. Well, it had to come. Why not? The first time was bound to be the worst, but she might as well get it over with. Only no! She must think as hard as him if she were to win him. If he had her now, he would go away sated and maybe never return.

By the time she returned to the table she had regained her composure and was smiling again. She refilled his glass, set the bottle down, and then deliberately seated herself upon his knee. Laughing with a forced gaiety, she let her hand caress his hair. He was sweating now, his head thrown back, his cheeks flushed red, his lips parted, his big, ugly hands seeking her breasts.

"Well now, Mr Tyrrell," she said coquettishly. "I can see you're an excellent businessman!"

His hands had found her breasts, undoing the laces of her tight black bodice and she hoped fervently he would not detect the hammering of her heart underneath them. It was essential he should believe her strong now.

"But I'm not bad at business either and I don't think the goods can be yours until you put your money on the table."

She thought he might be angry, but he laughed loud and long at that. She caught his mirth-shaken head in her bosom and kissed it, hating herself all the while. He returned her embrace with fervour. Dear God, he was strong — so large and hard! He could take her now no trouble if he wanted to and she knew that he did, but she was cunning and raised her head suddenly.

"What's the matter?" His words were slurred with whisky and passion.

"Just listening."

"Listening! What in hell's name for?"

"Injun George."

He stared at her uneasily, and she smiled. "He's out there?"

"Yes." She had no idea whether he was or not. "He's very devoted, you see, very loyal. He's a Comanche. They're very possessive of their women. Not that I'm his woman, of course though he'd like me to be. I won't tell you what he'd do to you if he knew what you were doing but it wouldn't be pleasant. They're awful good at... mutilations."

She rose to her feet and walked away from him carefully, rearranging her dress. Like most bullies, he looked terrified at the idea of a challenge.

"Of course," she went on brightly, "I wouldn't dream of taking George to Virginia. I'd turn him off. But that rather depends on me getting there first, don't it?"

He wiped his wet mouth nervously with the back of his hand. "What do you want?"

"I want you to buy this land. Then I want you to take me to Virginia with you. After that, we'll see. Only you won't find me ungrateful. Who knows? We could be two of a kind."

He roared with laughter again at that and she felt relieved for he had been looking peevish at being outmanoeuvred before. "Darn it, you're right, Mrs Griffith! All right! I'll buy this hellhole and take you with me for as long as I want. You'll like it. I promise you that! I got a fine house in West Virginia. I'll dress you up in silks and get rid of those widow's weeds. You'll sure make me the envy of any man with you on my arm dressed proper. We'll have darned good times!"

"Yes, we will!" Caitlin threw back her head with spirit. "Darned good times! You'll get your goods, Mr Tyrrell, don't worry! I ain't no shrinking violet but I know how to act real fine too. It's a good deal." She had done it, she had him, and she was ashamed of how triumphant she felt. It wasn't until later when alone and she could cast off her act that the guilt and her true feelings returned.

It didn't take long to dispose of the livestock, the tools and the wagon, nor the unplanted seed and the little furniture she had. The prairie cabin would just fall into decay, yet another small monument to failure. The dogs went back to Billy, but she kept Paddy with some half-brained idea of taking him to Virginia with her, unable to bear the parting.

Her half-breed Indian hand was still hanging around, although she had told him repeatedly, she was selling the land and he would have to go. On the last day, before Tyrrell came for her, she wandered into the stables and found him there, stroking the horse's head, silent, impassive but disapproving.

"What are you still doing here?" she asked him angrily. "Jesus, haven't I told you over and over again to just go?"

He looked at her reproachfully and her heart smote her. "Injun George say good-bye to Paddy." The horse blew and snuffled its agreement.

"All right, all right," she said irritably and sat down heavily on a bale of straw, her head in her hands. A wave of depression engulfed her.

Injun George stood and watched her. "White lady don't have to do this," he said quietly.

Caitlin exhaled her breath wearily. "But I do, George. Yes, I do. You were right, you see. I knew all along you were. That's why I've been so mad at you. There's been no rain and there'll be no harvest this year. I should have gone back East long ago. I can't starve."

"White folks always worried 'bout starving. No need. High plains good. Still buffalo."

"I can't kill buffalo, George. I can't even kill a pig." He fell silent. "What do you know about it anyway?" she went on miserably. "Mr Tyrrell will take me back East and feed me and dress me up real fine. Isn't that enough?"

"That white man bad," said George simply. "White lady better than that. White lady need not do this. She know that."

Caitlin broke down and wept without reserve, for the first time for years. Why did he have to torment her so? As she sobbed, she felt the touch of his hand against her arm, shy yet firm, and looked up.

"George understand," he said. "Perhaps it not so bad. White lady not want to die alone like George's mother."

Caitlin sniffed and wiped away her tears with her hands. "I mustn't cry anymore, George. It'll make my face swell and my eyes go red and he won't like that."

"White lady always beautiful," said George.

Caitlin smiled half-heartedly. "I've been bad to you George, you know? Bad and cruel and unkind. I'm sorry."

He shook his head and his big plaits swung slowly from side to side. "White lady always good to George. She not mean what she say. She cook real good meal and look after George and pay him well and give him firewater."

Her tears flowed again. "I'm glad you think so, anyway." She looked at him for a moment and came to an impulsive decision. "George, I want you to take Paddy."

He was astonished.

"I want you to have Paddy as your horse. Wouldn't you find it useful to have a horse to take you to the high plains and back?"

He nodded so hard she thought his head would fall off; his bronze face was wreathed with smiles now. "White lady sure? George never had horse of his own!"

"I'm sure. Mind you feed him properly now and look after him well or I'll come back and skin you alive!"

"And look," she went on, feeling in the pockets of her skirt, "here's some money. I haven't paid you this year for your work, not enough anyway." She pressed it into his hands, pleadingly.

"No, white lady," said George, holding it out. "Work no good this year - no money."

"But it wasn't your fault the seeds didn't grow. Keep it. You'll need it for firewater come the fall."

"A few dollars." He took them but gave back the rest. "White lady need the rest. She must leave white man soon as she can."

Caitlin was chastened. They heard the sound of a buggy's wheels outside and she drew her black veil hastily over her face, for she had decided to travel in her mourning dress.

"Thank you for staying with me, George," she said. "All that time." She reached up and kissed him lightly on the cheek, to his amazement and her own. "I hope you have many years of Paddy." She stroked the horse's forelock for the last time, then turned away.

They went out into the bright hard light of the yard where Tyrrell's buggy was waiting. He greeted her heartily enough despite casting a doubtful eye at the Indian.

"Get on up then if you're ready! Those your bags? You ain't got much."

Less than I came with, thought Caitlin sadly. She climbed up. The bags were put in hastily and in a second they were driving away.

Too soon for Caitlin. Yet she dare not look back for fear of too much emotion at the last sight of the little farm on the Osage Creek. If she had, she would have seen Injun George standing proudly with Paddy, his very own horse beside him, one hand raised in farewell, following with his far-sighted eyes the mark of their carriage-wheels in the dust. She may even have noticed a tiny bird perch on his shoulder in a flurry of yellow feathers.

Part Six

Armageddon

Chapter One

New York, 19th April 1861

They swung down Broadway in one vast blue tide, strong limbs rising and falling to the rhythm of a march. The points of a thousand bayonets bobbed in the air, the wind uncurled red linings from officers' cloaks and the sunlight glinted off the polished steel of sabre and sword and gun-barrel; the elite 7th New York militia were on their way to defend Washington from attack.

In every doorway, out of every window, and from every rooftop crowded a mass of figures, and a cheer rose from every throat. The Stars and Stripes fluttered from every flagpole and the sidewalk was a crush of eager bodies. Each lamppost had its own swarm of little boys, waving caps and neckerchiefs in excitement. The noise was deafening.

Hartley and Ralph watched them go by.

"What a sight!" sighed Ralph, with eyes alight.

"It'll be you soon enough."

"I cannot wait!"

At last, the throng started to disperse, most following in the soldiers' footsteps, eager to wish them well to the very last. Hartley and Ralph disentangled themselves with some difficulty and walked back into Union Square. It was almost deserted now but, on the morrow, it would be crammed again for another war rally.

"*He's* coming tomorrow," said Ralph with awed respect. *He* was Major Robert Anderson, the commander who had held out in Fort

Sumter under Confederate siege for three months. "Look! There's the fort's flag."

From the statue of George Washington hung a forlorn sample of the Stars and Stripes banner. It was ragged at the edges and pocked with shell-holes. You could still see the marks of nails on its left-hand border where the federal troops had raised it again and hammered it to a spar, after a Rebel shell had shattered the pole.

The two friends sat on the grass nearby and gazed at it. Hartley sighed and Ralph glanced at him sidelong.

"I do believe you're having second thoughts," he said. "Are you, Hartley? I would so like us to go together."

Hartley smiled and shook his head. "I don't think so," he said.

"Did you speak to Rosa?"

"Yes. She told me she'd understand if I felt I had to go. I didn't think she would after Friedrich's involvement in the German revolution. But she said that she did."

"Well then?"

Hartley remained silent, but Ralph would not let him alone.

"I know you think Lincoln's right. Ever since he spoke at Cooper's Union."

"Of course I do. But he's still hoping to avoid war, and I hope so, too."

It was Ralph's turn to shake his head. "Not a chance! A good thing, too. It's him who's calling for volunteers now."

"There's no shortage apparently. Tell me, what did Miss Fitzsimmons say?"

For at long last Ralph had been persuaded to marry and Miss Fitzsimmons was his fiancée, a girl of class, kindness, great wealth, and good looks. She would make a fitting wife for Ralph in every way.

Ralph lay back on the grass and laughed carelessly, pushing a wavy lock of hair from his forehead. "Sophy? She told me she darned well wouldn't marry me if I didn't go!"

"That's very stout of her."

"Wonderful, isn't it?"

She would kiss the sword when he left no doubt. It was only typical of the times. So much had happened in a year. Far too much. It had been coming for a long time. War talk, and nothing but war talk was the order of the day. Anyone who believed war was something to be avoided was branded a coward — except for Mr Lincoln. In the speech Ralph was referring to, he had won the hearts and minds of many by convincing them that the new Republican party were moderates to be trusted, despite his deep moral convictions, and that they were indeed *'no more radical than the Founding Fathers'*. Ralph was correct. Hartley had been impressed.

That speech had been way back in February of last year when Lincoln was campaigning for the Republican nomination for president and the first time his name had become widely known. In May, he was declared the Republican candidate, and several slave states threatened to leave the Union if he was elected because of his anti-slavery beliefs. He was elected as president in November, and on the 20th of December, South Carolina seceded, closely followed by Mississippi, Florida, Alabama, Georgia, Louisiana, and Texas, further incensed by Lincoln's call for military coercion.

All of these states had taken the Union forts and arsenals in their territories, and only Fort Sumter, on an island off the coast of Carolina, along with Fort Pickens at Pensacola Bay had the tenacity to resist. The seven Rebel states had already formed their own constitution for a 'Confederate States of America' and elected their own president, one Jefferson Davis, in Alabama. Now there was talk of other Southern states joining them, a new flag known as the 'Stars and Bars' because of its broader stripes had been adopted and, much worse, they had authorized a domestic loan of fifteen million dollars and called up 100,000 volunteers for an army.

Only a few days ago, Fort Sumter had been bombarded and Major Anderson had to surrender as he ran out of provisions and ammunition. Lincoln had been forced to act to declare the secession amounted to an insurrection and announce he would use the Federal Army to put it down. Hence the call for volunteers to swell the ranks. Now Virginia, the closest Southern state to Washington, had voted to secede and Arkansas, Tennessee and North Carolina were sure to follow. The Confederate capital would be moved to Richmond, Virginia and already the battlelines were being drawn. Old classes of West Point were being split apart between the two camps.

"You see, Hartley," Ralph went on earnestly "the more there are of us at the beginning, the quicker it'll be over. Of course, the South doesn't stand a chance. But they know they've gotta strike quick to make any impact at all, and Washington, being just across the Potomac, is in real danger. Just imagine, having those scallywags in the Capitol itself before we've even finished building it! Then again, the whole thing'll probably be over by Christmas. Imagine how you'd feel at missing it!"

He did not add that it was somehow ignominious not to volunteer but Hartley knew he thought it. He sighed again and wondered what had become of his good friend's common sense over the past year.

"I know, Ralph, that everything you say is true. But it's not easy to contemplate leaving Rosa on her own with the business to run and six children to look after. I swore I'd look after her."

"Is it six now? I'd almost lost count! Guess you'll be glad when she's too old for it at last!"

Hartley was in too serious a mood to be amused.

"How old is Johann?" asked Ralph. He was the eldest.

"Nineteen."

"And you said he's bright and proving to be a dab hand in the business."

"Yes, he is. But we hope he'll study some more. Rosa wants him to become a lawyer. Reuben's only seventeen and altogether a different type. He's a dreamer. He only wants to play the piano and write poetry."

"That's not much of a life for a boy!"

"Maybe not. But I don't criticize him. He reminds me too much of Friedrich. Rachel's ten now and going to be a lovely girl. Young Friedrich is six and a bundle of energy as you know. Jeremiah and my other little one are too young to even understand why I should go, if I did. It's impossible, Ralph, no matter how honourable, for me to take off on some crazy adventure with you!"

He could see that Ralph still did not really understand.

"You're too much married!" was what he said, and "It's not crazy! How can you say that now you're an American too? Doesn't the Union mean anything to you?"

"Yes," Hartley replied. "Of course, it does. But I don't think it does to Rosa."

They sat on in silence for a while, with the feeling of a new constraint between them. Then Ralph said,

"I met Tim at the recruiting office. Remember him?"

"Of course I do. I expect he was enlisting?"

"Sure thing. He wanted to go into the artillery. He asked me what you were doing for the war effort, so I told him about the uniforms. He laughed and said that was typical of Mister Shawcross to be so canny!"

Hartley's face flushed red.

"That's not why I'm staying!"

"Did I say it was?"

"Not exactly, but you weren't far off it."

Ralph saw he'd wounded his friend and jumped to his feet, proffering his hand.

"I'm sorry," he said, beaming in his usual open manner. "I didn't mean what you thought I did! Honestly, Hartley! It's just that I'd hoped you'd be with me, and I can't get rid of the feeling of disappointment you're not going to be. Forgive me, old pal! Only think some more about it!"

"No use," said Hartley. "I take your apology but not your offer. I wish you well, Ralph, but I'm not going unless I'm conscripted, and that's final."

On his way home, Hartley felt depressed. He couldn't rid himself of the suspicion that his friend thought him a coward and a money spinner to boot. *Perhaps I am,* he mused. Perhaps my concern for the family is merely an excuse to cover cowardice. He caught sight of himself in a shop window and grimaced. Why, he was becoming positively middle-aged! His fair hair was still unfaded by age, but his frame had thickened. The cut of his frockcoat and pants, the affluence of his waistcoat and silk cravat, the set of his top hat, and the addition of a cane marked him out as a man who was succeeding and prospering. Add to that a wife of sterling worth, six healthy children, and a growing, thriving business and you had Hartley Shawcross at thirty-four, a former steerage emigrant now very much on his way up. That was exactly what he had wanted when he had been impelled to come to America all those years ago. And yet, why must there always be an 'and yet'? He was no longer as sure, as certain of life as he had been. Perhaps it was this damn war that had done it, made him question his beliefs and his reasons for being here. For now that he had enough money to live moderately well, he had the luxury of asking himself how one should live.

He still missed Caitlin. It was like a secret sore that would never heal and left a taste of disappointment about his life. He had not been idle since she had gone. Apart from marrying Rosa and launching himself into the creation of new progeny, he had worked hard to transform the business. Two years ago, they had moved premises again. They now had a much larger shop for the 'odds and ends' as he thought of them, the haberdashery side, run by Rosa, which was doing well. They also had two very good-sized workshops in the older part of town, which were full of sewing machines to turn out reasonably priced, good-quality clothes. It was almost a factory. The second-hand clothes side had been dropped along the way as they moved up in the social echelons. A third building housed the paper patterns workshop, which was beginning to make some impact, though it continued to struggle.

The family itself still lived above Rosa's shop, albeit in a more spacious and better-furnished apartment. All of the children old enough went to school, dressed well, and had respectable friends.

Now, this war was threatening to disrupt everything. Normal business was suspended. Within the last few days, he had been offered and accepted a large contract to make Army uniforms and to make them as quickly as possible. Everything was to be given over to that. Tim was right, of course. He would make money out of it. The idea was distasteful, that he should send men off to war in his uniforms and yet not go himself, but what else could he do?

It was not as if he didn't have any problems - there were plenty. Each day, they lost more of their tailors in the mad rush to enlist. Only yesterday Rosa had asked him what was to be done about this. He had told her they must advertise for women, the best they could find, and only those who knew how, or could quickly learn, to handle the new machines.

"Why should they come to us?" Rosa had asked.

"Because we'll pay them more and make sure the conditions are good."

He would get them; he was sure of that. What was more, his managers could run the place well enough under instruction now, even if he was not there. So, he could leave the business for a while and enlist. Only what would happen to them all if he never came back? No, it was unthinkable, despite his misgivings and the shame of being called a coward.

He let himself into the apartment and climbed the stairs after glancing into the shop. Rosa was not there. She would be preparing tea upstairs. He greeted the younger children in the living-room but then went straight on into Rosa's kitchen. He wanted to tell her that, despite Ralph's entreaties, he would not be going for he knew she had fretted over it, despite her fine words.

There she was, banging away with the tea kettle at the stove, her back emanating what he took to be mere disapproval but then found was little short of hysteria. Johann and Reuben were in the room, sitting together at the wooden table. The younger boy looked distressed for some reason whilst his brother appeared angry and defiant. Hartley went up to Rosa and caught her by the waist, smiling. Rosa could no longer be called plump even by the kindest of persons. She was plainly fat as her fine figure had broadened and welded itself together. Still, she was dear enough to him and normally calm and steadfast. So, it shocked him greatly when she let out a positive shriek as soon as she saw him.

"Reuben!" she shrilled. "Out of here. Now!"

"But my dear! Whatever has Reuben done?"

The boy picked up his books hastily and departed.

"It's not Reuben, it's Johann!"

Rosa wiped her hands on her apron and stood facing them both, arms akimbo, breathing heavily.

"Then what has Johann done?"

Rosa looked at her son angrily. "Tell him!" she commanded harshly. "Go on, tell your stepfather, who's never been anything but good to you and had such great hopes for your future, what it is you have gone and done, like the fool you are!"

Johann looked sulky.

"I haven't done anything wrong, sir," he insisted.

Rosa wailed. "Mein Gott! Nothing wrong, he says! Nothing wrong! He's only gone and broke his poor mother's heart, that's all! Only gone and put himself down for a soldier, that's what. Gone and enlisted himself to fight in the war!"

Hartley felt a cold, cold stone drop suddenly into the bottom of his heart. It weighed him down in a moment and he felt suddenly old; wise but useless.

"Is this true, Johann?" he asked quietly. "Have you really enlisted?"

"Yes sir. This morning." Hartley saw that he was very proud of it. Rosa grabbed Hartley's arm and gripped it hard.

"You must go down there," she said. "To the recruiting office. Tell them it was all a mistake. He is only a boy. Tell them to let him out of it. They will listen to you!"

"I'm not a boy, Mother!" Johann shouted furiously. "For God's sake, I'm nineteen!"

Hartley laid a hand warningly on Rosa's arm. He knew what he said now was vital. With a great effort, he tried to make light of it.

"No," he agreed. "Johann is not a boy any longer. He is a man, man enough to consider his own future. Is that tea you're making, Rosa? I'm thirsty. Let's sit down and have some tea and talk about this calmly."

Rosa turned away to the stove with a sob as Hartley drew out a chair and sat down. He saw that Johann had his lips together in a stubborn line and smiled frankly at the boy.

"Now, Johann," he said. "We all know your mother would like you to be a lawyer."

"I don't want to be, sir. Lawyers are nothing but a set of rogues!"

"Mr Lincoln was a lawyer," Rosa interposed with a sniff. "Now he's President of the United States!"

"They don't make Jew boys president, Momma!" This was said with a great deal of scorn.

His mother turned on him savagely. "You're not a Jew boy!" she retorted. "Not anymore. You're a Christian and an American! You're a clever boy, good at book learning. You're not going to get killed for nothing, not if I have anything to do with it!"

Johann opened his mouth to argue, but Hartley held his hand up for peace. "Rosa, my dear, I think it might be best if you left us alone for a while," he said tactfully.

Rosa plonked the teapot on the table with another injured sniff. "You better make him change his mind!" she said. "Or I'll never forgive you!" She flounced out of the room, wringing her hands, and throwing her apron up to her wet eyes.

Johann raised his dark eyes to the ceiling. His face was lean and arrogant, good-looking like his father's, and he had recently grown a tiny moustache.

"Of course," he said insolently, "I know you're on her side. She always gets her own way: nagging morning, noon, and night. Do this! Do that! Help me, Hartley! Finish your schoolwork, boys, eat your meals, look after your sisters, go to Church every Sunday like a good Christian so folks'll know you're not really a Jewish boy! I'm tired of all that, and she won't stop me doing what I want! Neither will you. You're not my real father! You can't forbid me to go. If you do, I'll run away!"

For the first time since he had married Rosa, Hartley's hands itched to crack his eldest stepson smartly across the face. He who had never struck any of his children! He controlled the impulse and pressed then firmly together.

"You never said that to me before, Johann," he said sadly. "Not once in all the years I've cared for you. It hurts, you know. And I've never, ever heard you speak about your mother like that and never want to again, no matter how old you are. Do you understand? Have you forgotten all the things she's done for you? How she struggled to get you boys out of Germany and over here to a better life? The effort to get on here broke your poor father in two but it didn't break her. She'd have done anything for you and still will."

"I've heard the story before," Johann said. But his words were more defiant than the tone in which they were spoken, and he had the grace to look ashamed.

Hartley sighed. "She did these things because she loves you. Do you want some tea?"

"No, thank you."

"Well, I do." Hartley poured it out wearily into Rosa's precious china cups, brought all the way from Germany. "Do you want to know what I've been doing today? No, I expect not but I'll tell you anyway. I've been watching the parade of the 7th New York militia. I suspect you were there somewhere in the crowd too. Stirring, wasn't it? Glorious! Even I, Johann, felt stirred. Then I spent the next hour listening to my friend implying I was a coward for not going and actually wondered if I should, after all. It's very easy to be swept along in the excitement of it all. But I decided I had far stronger claims upon me, upon my life, for that's what we're talking about, Johanna. I have to continue to take care of your mother and the family. I'll go if they make me but not before. Even if Ralph does think me a coward."

Johann shuffled his feet uncomfortably under the table. "You're not a coward, sir!" he said, more amenably. "I never expected *you* to go. Of course, you have to look after Mother, and the others and the workshops, but you don't have to look after me. I'm old enough to look after myself and I don't have such responsibilities."

"No, but you're going to cause a lot of heartache at home. I wonder if you realize how much? Think awhile, Johann. We're not soldiers, you and me! We've had no training, no experience, not just in military matters, but of anything physical. Have you really thought what it's going to be like? Can you kill, not just one man, but many? Do you really want to risk your own life? You say you don't want to be a lawyer, well that's fine! I'm not going to make you be one. But I had thought of late you'd make a darned fine businessman and I'm willing to keep you in the firm as long as you like and give you more responsibility."

Johann squirmed again. "Afterwards, maybe," he muttered. "But not now. I've got to do this first."

"There may not be an afterwards, Johann. And for what? What is the Union to you?"

"But what about the slaves, sir? Anyway, it's done now! Oh, please don't make me go back to the office and say I can't go after all! I'd be a laughingstock. I couldn't bear it!"

Hartley looked at him shrewdly. "Are many of your friends going?"

"Just about all of them, sir!"

"I thought so!" Hartley sighed. "They may not be doing the right thing either, Johann. Haven't we brought you up to decide what is right for yourself?"

"But I have, sir! It is right. I know it! Mr Lincoln thinks so, and I know you have a deal of respect for him!"

Hartley felt as if he was beginning to be tied up in knots and getting nowhere. "Did your friends say you'd be a coward if you didn't go?" he asked sternly.

Johann flushed.

"Did they?"

"Yes ... they said it'd be just like a Jew boy to go sneaking off and making a fortune out of war uniforms instead."

Hartley dropped his head into his hands and groaned. "These are your friends, are they? I wish you'd told me all this before, Johann."

"Yes sir. But that's not why I'm going. I really want to. I'm sorry to cause you and Momma pain, I really am, but it's something I must do. Anyway, we're going to get trained really well. It'll be all right; I know it will," he grinned and looked more boyish than ever. "We're going to whop those bluffing Southerners pretty darned quick!"

Hartley could see it was no use though he had another stab at it. "I know you don't think you're young," he began ineffectually. "But the fact is you are. I was twenty-two when I emigrated, and I thought I was a real fine fellow and that the streets here'd be paved with gold. I'm not saying I regretted it but ..."

"Yes, sir?"

"Well, things turn out a little differently, that's all, to what you expect. It's much harder than you first believe. Do you understand what I'm saying, Johann? Everything is so much more complicated, especially where other people are concerned, as they must be."

"Yes, sir, I understand."

Hartley could see by the impatience on his face that he did not. "There's nothing else I can say, is there?" he asked sadly. "To stop you going. Nothing at all."

"No, sir."

"Which regiment is it?"

"The 12th New York." Only the twelfth! The seventh had marched that afternoon.

"Then I wish you luck, my boy. Come, let's have a proper drink to toast you!" He got up to find the whisky bottle.

Johann's face was radiant with triumph. "What will you say to Momma?"

God knows, thought Hartley miserably, but what he said was, "I'll try and make her see there's nothing we can do."

Hartley lay in the dark with Rosa beside him. She still would not speak to him though he knew she was not asleep nor would be for a very long time. Every now and then a great sob would shake her large body.

It had been a wretched evening. For the first time since their marriage, apart from when she had been engaged in delivering babies, Rosa had felt unable to serve dinner and had retired to her room in distress. Hartley had made shift to do it himself, but Rachel had pushed him aside, saying, "I'll do it, Papa."

He sat useless in his masculinity, waiting until she had finished before mouthing the usual prayers. Normally, he was not aware of the mixed nature of his family, but tonight, it bothered him, and he felt the words of the prayers were inept. The food turned dry and tasteless in his mouth. No-one but Johann was happy. Reuben, in particular, was more subdued than usual.

I must talk to him, thought Hartley in a panic. *Later, after Johann has gone. Who knows what he might be thinking and feeling now? He never shows anyone his poems.*

Rachel was important but grave in her assumed role. She was very fond of her eldest brother, who came second only after Hartley himself in her affections. They all seemed to know what was going on. Jeremiah created an unfortunate tantrum over some article of food he would not eat, and Hartley ordered him irritably from the room when Rosa would have cajoled. Now, they were all in bed and it was Rosa herself who must be cajoled. Hartley put out a hand, but she shrugged it away.

"Rosa," he said earnestly. "I must speak with you! I swear I did my best. We talked for a long time. But it's no good. He has to find out for himself. We can't tell him what to do anymore."

"But he'll die. I know he will!"

"Possibly. But maybe he'll be one of the lucky ones. Not everyone will die. Perhaps he'll just be wounded and sent home early on."

"Easy for you to speak of it when he is Friedrich's child!"

Hartley threw aside the bedclothes and rose angrily. "That's harsh, Rosa and unfair." He paced moodily to the window.

Rosa sat up in bed with a tear-stained face. "I did not mean it. It is only because I am afraid! And I know that you are, too. Come back to bed, please, Hartley!"

Hartley had thrown aside the curtains and was looking into the street. There was a woman below, a streetwalker, obviously. He started as he saw her. Just for a moment, he had thought ... there was something in the profile, the turn of the head that reminded him of Caitlin. But no ... that could not be! He leant faintly against the window frame.

The woman drew away, lifting her skirts way above the ankle as she walked, swirling them provocatively from side to side. No, it was not Caitlin, but the incident had given him a shock, and he shivered. What would happen to her in wartime out in Kansas? What might already have happened?

He went back and sat on the end of the bed gloomily and sighed. He wished he were a thousand miles away.

"I know you are concerned for Johann," Rosa repeated. "It is the older men who should fight wars, not the young ones. Hartley, you must go with him!"

"What?"

"You must go with him. Get them to let you into the same regiment. Then perhaps you can protect him."

"Rosa! There are times when you are the most unreasonable of women. Do you imagine for a moment that I could protect him? We're talking about war, not a picnic!"

"You might be able to. Please, Hartley! Do it for me! If I could go, I would, God knows! It's not as if you haven't thought about it. I know you have."

"And what would you do without both of us?"

"I shall manage. You know I could. Please do it, Hartley! I'll never ask anything else again."

Hartley laughed hollowly. "That's what you really want? To get us both killed?"

Rosa sounded tearful again. "That's not it. You are cruel to say that!" Hartley sighed.

"Very well, Rosa. I'll do as you ask. It's very likely for the best. I'll enlist tomorrow morning."

In a strange way, he felt almost relieved. Yet how ignominious to have the decision made for him in this way. There was no pride in it now. Damn Johann and all young hotheads!

Chapter Two

Leesburg, Northern Virginia, April 1861

Spring came gloriously that year, ushered in by long golden days of dappled warmth and shade. The roadsides were awash in the wild colour of flowering dogwoods, sumacs, and redbuds. Caitlin's brief memories of the beauties of Virginia were not false.

They had arrived last summer, alighting from the eastbound train at the hillside town of Harper's Ferry, of all places. Caitlin had not expected that, and it came as a shock. Whilst Tyrrell went to see about their onward travel arrangements, she stepped out of the station and gazed down the long main street with a weak feeling in her legs. It was all very ordinary, and hard to believe what had happened here.

Tyrrell was soon back. He told her there was no chance of further travel until the next morning. They would have to put up at the local hotel. She followed him meekly, as if in a trance, still in her black dress and widow's veil. The woman at the hotel desk looked at her suspiciously when Tyrrell booked one room.

"Her father died recently," he said curtly, interpreting the look correctly. The woman proffered her condolences.

In their room, Caitlin sat down before the wooden dressing-table and looked at her face in the mirror. It was very white. Somehow, her imagination had never got her beyond this point. She knew it had to come, but it should not be here, of all places!

The room was cramped, and, in consequence, Tyrrell seemed much larger. His broad body took up too much space and he had to stoop to get through the doorway. His red beard looked uncomfortably fierce, and his hands were much too large, the backs of them covered with freckles and thick auburn hairs. Caitlin felt frightened at the sight of them. She had scarcely said a word on the journey, and he had done nothing to put her at ease.

"You'll not wear that dress again," he said. "It's ridiculous to shroud yourself in widow's weeds and it makes folks curious. Take it off and put on your green one."

"Very well. I didn't want to get it dirty travelling. That's all." However, she shrank from the idea of undressing before him. That should be in the dark. It should all be in the dark.

"I'd like to take a walk first. I want to see the arsenal where the rebellion was."

"I'll take you there if you get changed."

"No, thank you. I would prefer to go alone." He wasn't pleased at her defiance.

"I'll only be a little while. That's where my husband was killed, you see. When I come back, I'll do as you ask."

"Damn right, you will! I've kept my side of the bargain and it's time you kept yours, Mrs Griffith." That was all - no sympathy, no understanding. Well, she had been a fool to expect any.

She left swiftly before he could change his mind. In the street, she had to ask the way and drew more odd looks. Why was everyone so inquisitive here? Perhaps it was just that her nerves were stretched taut.

The group of buildings that composed the arsenal stood by the riverside. They were still shell marked. Otherwise, there was no sign of what had occurred. It was over and done with — a mere few days out of many, already receding into the past. In a short while,

Confederate troops would arrive to take it over, strip it of all its munitions, and blow up the bridge that spanned the river, but no one knew that then.

Caitlin stood and stared at the firehouse. It was so small and insignificant. No one had written to tell her what had actually happened. She had to make it all up. She dared not ask about graves, but he must be buried somewhere near, lying in Virginian soil.

Behind her black veil, the tears flowed. She had told him never to come back, and he had taken her at his word. He had been so determined, so wrong, and yet so convinced he was right. There was nothing else she could have done, given what he had done at Pottawattomie.

"I'm sorry, Owain," she mumbled in a choked voice. "I'm so sorry. But I wrote to Elen for you as best I could."

She could not go back directly and walked up and down in a state of distraction. Crazy thoughts came, thoughts of running away, of trying to make out alone like she had always intended. Only she didn't know how.

Gradually, she became calmer, and her natural spirit reasserted itself. She mustn't think of Owain. She must survive. She would get drunk after dinner. Tyrrell drank heavily, and she would, too, to blur the edges of her sensibility. Men were neither all good nor all bad. This one at least wanted her, and she would use him. If it was wrong, then she couldn't help it.

All she wanted was to eat and drink and sleep in comfort without having to break her back and her health working. She wanted to wear pretty dresses again and to have money and a comfortable home, as she had done at the Regans. She would not have pushed Thaddeus Regan aside now. At last, she was prepared to accept the workings of men's minds. No one should ride into her domain ever again to shoot, burn and kill. She would at least have someone to protect her. Setting her face against the wind so that the black veil fluttered against her drying cheeks, she bent her head and trod with determination back to the hotel.

That first night was the worst. Anaesthetized though she was, it was not enough. Tyrrell was rough and not tender as Owain had been. Also, he wanted her to do things she had never dreamed of. But it was no good shirking her chosen task. So, she gritted her teeth and did them anyway.

In Leesburg, where Tyrrell had his house, she felt a little better. It was a pleasant town, shaded by trees, too good for the likes of Tyrrell, who spent every night drinking and gambling. But Caitlin thought the house was wonderful. It was timber-framed with a classical portico and proper furniture inside. She had a fine carriage all to herself and two black servants (free blacks, though Tyrrell's treatment of them was hardly any better than if they had been slaves). The wardrobe in their bedroom was full of fine clothes. She did not ask who had worn them before nor what had happened to her. Tyrrell was pleased with her unfeigned delight, and their affairs proceeded on a lighter footing. He was often too inebriated to bother her in bed.

Only Caitlin discovered a different kind of loneliness here. In the day, she was mistress of the house and could arrange matters as she pleased, though the servants were too afraid of Tyrrell to become her friends. When she went shopping in her finery, the respectable ladies of the town, no kinder than the ladies of Lawrence, looked the other way and crossed the street to avoid her. The shopkeepers were cool and restrained and served her last. Consequently, she had even fewer friends than in Kansas, for one could not count the bawdy, rough men whom Tyrrell brought home.

Worst of all was the behaviour of her keeper himself. It was true that he was generous, for it pleased him that she should have the best of everything and be admired by his friends. He was not often downright unkind as long as she appeared gay, but if she showed she was feeling morose, or if he had lost out on a lucrative deal, then he would lose his temper, curse, swear, and sometimes even strike her.

He had a lively sense of humour, though she found it difficult to laugh at the things which made him laugh. He was so far from understanding her that she felt as if she were living with an unconcerned stranger whom she knew secretly held her in contempt. Sometimes, he went away to Washington or Richmond on business, and then she could relax and feel safe. He was excited and exultant at the prospect of the coming war. Being Yankee, Caitlin thought they might have to move further north. But Tyrrell saw no necessity for that. If Virginia became a battlefield, as he hoped it would, he reckoned he could gain commercially from the bargains able to be struck with both sides. He might even become a spy, and the idea of that made him guffaw loudly and long.

Over and over again, he assured her they would be in no danger as civilians and would stand to make a pile of bucks. Slapping his thighs, he would pull her down onto his knees and begin to fondle her in a merry mood. She supposed it was affection of a kind, and she could not afford to reject his advances.

Sometimes, usually, when he was gone, the full force of what she had done came home to strike her, and she wished she might die, wishing that troops from either side would come marching into

Leesburg and blow the town and everyone in it to pieces. On such days, the whisky bottle was her only comfort. Yet each time she woke, she felt conscious of the fact that she was sinking further downwards.

≈

Camp Anderson Washington, July 14th 1861

My Dear Rosa,

The indications are very strong that we shall move in a few days, perhaps tomorrow. Our movements may be of several days' duration and of considerable conflict and danger. If it should be necessary to fall on the battlefield for America, then I am at last ready, and indeed, I pray that it is I who falls and not my dear stepson.

We have no misgivings that what we fight for is not right. Johann acquits himself admirably and I am proud of him, and sure you would be too. Ralph has been elevated to the position of Captain and is straining at the leash. Though not as daring and enthusiastic, I confess it means a great deal to me now to be at his side when I sit down and consider what we are fighting for and how Mr Lincoln depends on us.

This is the only sustenance I can give you should we not return. Johann has never wavered. It is rather he who comforts me. Believe me, I shall do everything in my power to protect him. He has the strictest instructions not to leave my side. But if I fall, as I may, I know he would have to fight on alone.

If I should not return, I know I do not have to entreat you to bear before you, at all times, the sustenance of our dear children. I pray that I may have done enough to make this easier for you. It wounds me to the quick when I imagine them fatherless again despite all my care and good intentions. Yet I know that none of them could wish for a better or stronger mother. Take especial care of Reuben. I know he is much troubled by thoughts of the war.

I can hardly describe to you my feelings on this calm summer night where at least two thousand men are sleeping round me, perhaps enjoying their last sleep. Many such letters are being written tonight. Johann sleeps in the confidence of youth, but I fear I shall not.

I am very conscious that we did not part on the best of terms as we should. I do not blame you for it, but it grieves me sorely. Believe me, Rosa, that my love for you continues as before. I am mindful of happier memories which comfort me still. I can see you now as you were the first time I saw you in Liverpool, before we ever got to The Yorkshire, leading a tearful Friedrich onto the wagon which had come to take us to the dock. You were so proud and strong and striking; it has stayed with me always. I have never told you this before. Did you realize we were quartered in the same dreadful boarding-house, without knowing it? It seems that our paths were meant to cross from the beginning. I did not realize it at first, but, when poor Friedrich had gone, I own I had always respected you so much it was bound to turn to love.

Forgive my many faults. I know I have sometimes been thoughtless or foolish and that I let you down in the matter of Johann. If I should die on this battlefield, his will be the last name on my lips. It is very strange, but I feel tonight as if the soul of Friedrich is here too, watching over us both. He is here in all his former glory; he knows our trial is near, and he approves of what we do, most heartily. Is that not strange?

If it is possible, perhaps my soul shall flit around the earth unseen, too. In that case, rest assured, I will always be around to guide you in the gladdest days and darkest nights. Perhaps this is all nonsense, but even so, do not mourn for me over much, I beg of you.

As for the children, tell them how I died and why and that I did it with love still in my heart for them. Only Jeremiah may remember me from my own, and that not for long. I shall become a dim figure in his childhood. Yet in him and the other little one, something of me will go on just as something of Friedrich goes on in Johann and Reuben. Perhaps, after all, this is what life is about. I feel sorry for Ralph and Tim here with us who do not know parenthood as yet and perhaps never will.

Rosa, I repeat again that I have unlimited confidence in your maternal care. I feel that God will bless you for your struggles. As I read over this letter, I am aware it seems full of gloom. Naturally, I hope that my death will not come to pass and that we will be reunited before long, but I do not retract a word, for it is necessary to face our prospects with realism.

May God keep us all,
Your Loving Husband, Hartley.'

General Irwin McDowell, the commanding officer of the Unionist Army in Northern Virginia, was not a likeable man. Although he forgoed the habitual comforts of alcohol and tobacco and even tea and coffee, he was an eater of massive proportions, a glutton in fact. He had won his promotion for gallant services in the Mexican War, but his attitude towards his subordinates was appalling. He could remember neither faces nor names and appeared incapable of the simple function of listening, treating everyone with brusque indifference.

For all that, one had to feel sorry for him in the July of 1861, for he was in a desperate dilemma, and he knew it. For some time, he had come under relentless pressure to attack the enemy with an army which was entirely unready, his officers being either inactive veterans or inexperienced youths. His enlisted men were short on weapons, ammunition, equipment, and even uniforms. Although they had been drilling for weeks, their training was far from adequate. He had no reliable maps of the difficult terrain of Virginia and lacked enough cavalry to provide the details to draw up new ones. What he needed above all to remedy these matters was time, but time had run out.

His superior, General Winfield Scott, was an ageing man in ill health, and likewise reluctant to advance. He would have given more time gladly had he been allowed, preferring a slower, less bloody campaign to throttle the Confederacy by blockading its ports and controlling the Mississippi River. Only the decision did not rest with them but with Lincoln, and the president was under relentless pressure to attack by a fretful Northern press and public, incensed by the knowledge that a Rebel army was virtually knocking on the door of the nation's capital.

McDowell did complain to Scott that his troops were green, but Scott only replied that, although that was true, so were those on the other side. They were all green together.

McDowell's plan looked sound enough on paper. The federal army would divide into three columns to improve its pace and mobility. These would advance westward on roughly parallel lines, seizing the Confederate outposts at Fairfax Court House, sixteen miles from Washington, and at Centreville, five miles beyond. Here, two of the columns would push forward and make an attack on the likely centre of the Confederate line at Bull Run. The third column would skirt the enemy's flank and strike southward, cutting the rail link to Richmond and threatening the Rebels' rear. The Confederates would then be forced to retreat some fifteen miles to the next defensible line along the Rappahannock River, a more respectable distance from Washington.

The success of this plan involved using large numbers of men to intimidate the Confederates. It also depended on other Union forces harassing a second Confederate Army out to the west in the Shenandoah Valley to prevent them from joining the men at Bull Run. McDowell was assured this could be done, and the necessary preparations were made. A whole reserve division was added to the Unionist Army so that the force stood at 35,000 men, the largest ever assembled on North American soil. At two p.m. on July 16th, it staggered off uncertainly toward the enemy.

Meanwhile at Manassas Junction, twenty-five miles ahead of the Yankees, McDowell's old West Point classmate of '38 and his rival, General P.G.T. Beauregard, was anxiously waiting. He had spent the last month suffering similar delays and shortages and his plans had changed many times, shifting back and forth uncomfortably between attack and defence. At last, the order came from Richmond to take the defensive. President Davis and General Robert E. Lee knew the army was not strong enough to initiate an attack. Feverishly, they fed in extra regiments and Beauregard put them into a long battleline at Bull Run, south of Centreville.

The five-foot-high banks of the stream made a formidable barrier, and there was only one bridge that could support the weight of an army wagon's traffic. But there were several fording places so Beauregard had to spread his army thin to defend them all. Nevertheless, he felt certain that the Unionists would try to cross at Mitchell's Ford or the adjacent Blackburn's Ford half a mile downstream, and that was where he concentrated half his forces and planned to stand fast at Bull Run.

The long line of Yankee soldiers dragged their feet, sang, and bragged, choked on dust, and sweltered in their thick woollen uniforms under the heat and humidity of the Virginian sun. Sometimes they broke ranks casually to stop for water, to urinate, or to wash the caked grime from their faces, even to forage for chickens in direct defiance of their officers. Hartley was disturbed to see this and forbade Johann to do the same.

They were held up for hours at the most trivial of creeks, marshalled into single file to cross a narrow log bridge, until one man decided to wade and discovered it was only knee deep. When night fell, they kept on marching. It was ten o'clock before they reached their objective and were allowed to bivouac. In all they had covered little more than six miles though it felt like sixty.

Early next day they resumed the march and the first of them arrived at Fairfax Court House in the middle of the morning. The Confederate outpost had long gone, amply warned of their clumsy approach. McDowell was disappointed, especially when he learnt from the scouts that Centreville had also been abandoned.

He issued his orders for the next day. Brigadier General Tyler was to pass through Centreville with his men at first light. Then he was to march towards Bull Run and simulate a noisy assault, although not actually bring on an engagement, merely giving the impression of massive numbers coming forward to distract attention from the outflanking maneouvre of the third column.

At seven a.m., General Tyler duly moved out. With him were the 12th New York militia under the command of Colonel Richardson amongst other brigades. They were to be the vanguard. McDowell then rode off to establish what any reliable map of the area could have told him: that the terrain was far too difficult for any third column to cross Bull Run at the chosen point so their plan to outflank the enemy could never have been put into operation.

Hartley and the other men knew nothing of this. All they knew, with a mixture of apprehension and excitement, was that the time had come at last to fight. Hearts beat fast as they approached the little village of Centreville. It was deserted as Beauregard had pulled his troops out during the night. The more rightful occupants also appeared to have fled, leaving only chickens to run around squawking, scattered by the men's boots.

Richardson was a seasoned and combative West Pointer. 'Fighting Dick', they called him. He took his men on and through the place with no respite. He also rode out with Tyler two miles or so, to a rise that overlooked Bull Run at Blackburn's Ford. Although open fields ran down to the stream, the banks themselves were thickly wooded and covered with dense underbrush. They spotted an enemy battery some distance behind the ford and a few pickets here and there but little else. Tyler could see the town of Manassas where Confederate troops were stationed with its crucial railroad, just three miles off in the distance and the sight of it filled him with excitement. Surely the Rebels would fall back under an attack as they had done before? Then the glory of the day would be his!

Directly contravening orders, he sent Richardson back to call up all of his men before the ford, ready for a probe, and in the meantime ordered two twenty-pounders to open fire on the Confederate battery spotted beyond the trees. Two companies of Massachusetts men were sent forward as skirmishers to draw the fire of the Rebels along the creek and force them to reveal their positions. These men soon discovered that a few houses and stands of trees on their side of the Run concealed enemy marksmen and an hour of skirmishing followed as the Confederates staged a fighting withdrawal back across Bull Run. The closer the Yankees got to the stream, the hotter the resistance became. Several men were killed in heavy crossfire from hidden positions up and down the bank.

Eventually the Massachusetts men were ordered to withdraw and doubts now rose about the wisdom of continuing the engagement. An adjutant of Macdowell's, rode up and advised Tyler to call a halt. He had done enough. They had uncovered the enemy's position and strength and done that well.

But Tyler had the scent of combat in his nostrils now and he had a full brigade on hand under Richardson. He had no intention of withdrawing. Instead, he positioned the 2nd and 3rd Michigan and the Ist Massachusetts to the right of the guns, facing Mitchell's Ford whilst he had the 12th New York militia moved to the left above Blackburn's Ford. They were lamentably exposed on the hilltop and uncomfortably within range of some of the Confederate marksmen. Already the bullets were beginning to whistle round. When the fire began coming out of the woods, it at last suggested to Tyler that they were getting in too deep. Fretfully and belatedly, he decided it was time to call off the attack.

At that precise instant, Richardson gave the order for the 12th New York to charge, believing Tyler to still be covering him.

The New Yorkers were left out alone on a limb. Before them was ranged the full gunpower of over half of Beauregard's entire army ...

≈

Blackburn's Ford, Bull Run

Hartley was gripping his rifle so hard that the flesh of his fingers hurt. Underneath his blue uniform, the sweat was pouring. They were out in the open fields now in the harsh bright light with bullets whistling by. He glanced at Johann's face beside him. It was tense and white and frightened.

"Stay close," he muttered. "Stay close to me!" His legs felt as if weighted with lead. Ralph was in front of them, his sword drawn, leading them on. Ahead of them was thick pine underbrush. If they could reach that, they would get some cover. Ralph ordered them on faster and they broke into a run.

Suddenly the air was full of an almighty boom. The trees and brush erupted with flame. The earth and the sky itself seemed to be on fire.

"Drop!" yelled Hartley in a panic. "Drop down, Johann, drop!" But he had already dropped without a sound.

Hartley dropped too, fired, and rolled onto his back to re-load his rifle. It was an old U.S. Model 1842 musket and he had never been happy with it. Now, with the sky exploding above, it seemed an impossible task. He stabbed wildly with the ramrod at powder and ball to get them down the barrel.

Johann was lying very still. Why wasn't he re-loading? Hartley twisted his body sideways to look. It was then he realized the boy had fallen backwards and not forwards. Rolling back onto his front, Hartley discharged his weapon again without knowing what he aimed at. Then he writhed forward on the ground to his stepson's side.

Johann's limbs were spread-eagled wide over the ground. His neck lolled as Hartley tried to raise it and his blue cap fell off. His dark eyes were open and staring but saw nothing. There was an enormous hole in his neck where the shell had passed right through, and it poured out warm, sticky red blood.

Hartley let his head fall back in horror. Kneeling over him, he picked up the boy's rifle. It hadn't even been fired. There hadn't been time. Something made him look up, God knows what. Through his nightmare, he dimly saw a grey monster running out of the brush, launching towards them with a rifle aimed to fire.

With a howl of rage, Hartley raised Johann's musket and fired at point blank range. The figure fell with a look of surprise. As his hat came off, Hartley saw that he was only a boy too, and not a monster at all. He had fallen beside Johann — someone else's son.

The brush still belched fire. Hartley lay down flat on the ground and shook. He no longer attempted to re-load. He put his hands over his ears. All around him men were falling with wild screams as the murderous volleys carried on and tongues of flame spurted from the bushes.

He did not know how long he lay there but it seemed an eternity. Then he heard his name called out. It was Ralph come up from behind, his brown hair flopping into his eyes, his sword drawn, and his mouth twisted into a shriek.

"Come on, Hartley! What the devil are you doing? We're falling back! Come on!"

Hopelessly, Hartley tried to lift Johann's shattered body, but Ralph tore him away.

"Don't be a fool! You must leave him! Come on!"

Dragged on by his friend, sensing that Ralph had risked his own life to come and get him, Hartley began to run. The field was a sickening mass of confusion now. All the corpses had stained the grass red. Men with gaping, grimy holes in them lay dying in terrible agony. Ralph urged him on. Even when they were back in the relative safety of the rest of Richardson's forces, most men kept on running wildly in any direction. Horses plunged and whinnied in terror. Gun carriages were trapped in ruts. Soldiers sat dazed and wounded on the ground. It was total bedlam.

They saw 'Fighting Dick', his sabre flashing in the sunlight, wheeling his horse, and standing up desperately in the stirrups, striving to rally the fleeing New Yorkers and send the whole brigade in again for a charge. It was useless so he had to withdraw himself and try to collect his battered men together.

The Battle of Blackburn's Ford was over.

≈

The tired Rebels were returning to the south bank although the artillery of both sides would rumble on for another hour or so. McDowell had arrived to berate Tyler for his breach of orders and the humiliating performance of the men. They marched back to Centreville to lick their wounds and for McDowell to reconsider his plans. For two days they sat around dazed in camps and slowly recovered.

Hartley thought he would never recover. They were told that the Battle at Blackburn's Ford was just the forerunner, as indeed it was, and that they must all return to fight again. Hartley did not care. His most earnest wish now was to die. Why had he lain immobile when he might have died fighting beside Johann's body? His shame ran deep.

"He never even got to fire a shot," he told Ralph bitterly. "He did nothing, nothing at all. It was all so unnecessary!" Over and over again he cried, "What do I tell Rosa?"

Whilst they sat in the camps, screwing up their courage to attack again, a throng of civilians arrived from Washington. They had followed the army in buggies or on horseback to witness the grandest spectacle of their time: the thrashing of the Rebels. There were several hundred of them including senators, congressmen, photographers, reporters, artists and even elegantly dressed ladies with picnic-baskets.

"How dare they?" asked Hartley bitterly. "What do they know? They think all they have to do is mouth a few inane prayers to their white American God and all will be accomplished within a few hours!"

Ralph was worried about his friend. This was not the same upstanding, reverent man who had left New York with him. Of course he was in shock. Ralph was shaken and disillusioned too but they had made him an officer and it was his duty to inspire resolve.

"There were bound to be early sacrifices, Hartley," he said, quietly but firmly. "Bound to be. And there were blunders and terrible humiliation. The troops were untried. We were not ready. It's terribly hard Rosa's boy should be one of the first to go. I know that you wish it had been you. But you've got to stiffen up now. The country needs us. We must fight again, and then you can avenge Johann's death."

Hartley stared at him. "Avenge his death?" he repeated, with a hollow laugh. "What good is that to Rosa? I already had my vengeance, and I wasn't proud of it."

"It was him or you, Hartley!" For Ralph had already heard about the young Confederate Hartley had killed, heard it over and over again till it was driving him mad. It was clear that his friend's nerve had gone, and had to be restored, brutally if need be. "You're acting like I'd expect the boy's own father to act!" he accused him, sharply. "I mean Friedrich Kleist of course. That's no help to anyone. You've got to be a man now, Hartley!"

Hartley looked at his friend of so many years' standing. He knew in that moment, although they would always love each other, there would no longer be the same understanding and trust between them.

"You need not worry!" he said, sarcastically. "I'll fight for you, Ralph. I'll fight like a demon if needs be. I have nothing left to lose and I know I need to prove I can do better."

Ralph clapped him on the back and left to write a letter full of valour to Miss Fitzsimmons. The distortion of the truth was necessary for, hell, a man had to keep his spirits up somehow. He had other letters to write too, as the commanding officer of his unit, letters to the relatives of those men who would not be returning, including Rosa.

As he sat alone at his desk in his tent, he heard the whistles of trains in the distance, blowing from the junction at Manassas. He tried to shrug them off. Doubtless they were bringing in small numbers of disorganized troops for the Confederates from Richmond, seeing as the rail link had not after all been broken. Of course it was disturbing that the whistles could be heard every few hours, but the rumours might not be true. They had it that those trains bore brigades of the Second Confederate Army from the Shenandoah Valley.

Back in his tent, Hartley was surprised to receive another visitor: Tim O'Reilly. No longer young Tim O'Reilly from Ireland and a great scamp to boot, but a fully-fledged Union Artilleryman of twenty-five years old. His face was still freckled and youthful looking however, and he had the same cocky grin though he was solemn enough now.

"Evenin', Mister Shawcross."

"Why, Tim! How glad I am you are safe!"

"'Course I'm safe. The artillery's a darned sight better off than you infantrymen. Thought you'd have the sense to see that, Mister Shawcross, beggin' your pardon!"

Hartley sighed. Tim sat down beside him and wound his fingers awkwardly around each other for a while.

"Heard you saw the elephant today?" he said finally.

"Saw what?"

"The elephant, Mister Shawcross. Jesus, don't you ever listen to what's going on around you? The men here's all talking about 'seeing the elephant'. Like when you goes to a circus for the first time and sees one. You'd heard there were such beasts and what they were like and how big they were, but it's not until the first time you see it with your own eyes that you actually believe it and realize. Same thing with war."

"I see," said Hartley. "Yes, Tim, it's a good phrase. I saw the elephant alright, and I didn't like it one bit. I didn't conduct myself very well either."

"Not the only one, Mister Shawcross, not the only one by a long chalk!"

Hartley smiled at him, weakly. He guessed Tim was being gentle and respectful for a reason.

"I heard about your boy," Tim said the next moment, confirming it. "The Kleists' boy that was. Horrible luck that."

"Yes, Tim. It was." He tried hard to sound stout. It would not do to cry in front of Tim. "I hardly know what to tell Rosa, yet I must write and send it with Ralph's letter."

"Jesus! I'd rather face several of those darned Southern brigades have to do that, Mister Shawcross!" Tim spat tobacco-juice vigorously from the side of his mouth and Hartley winced. "Funny, but all I can see is that quiet, half-scared little boy on The Yorkshire, hiding behind his mother's skirts. Jest can't believe he's grown up and dead already. Don't seem right at all!"

Hartley's eyes brimmed over as he nodded, but Tim pretended not to notice.

"Guess it's not what we came to Americky for, is it, Mister Shawcross?"

"No, it certainly isn't." Hartley wiped his eyes with the back of his hand. "Why on earth did you volunteer, Tim?"

"Oh, I don't know, this and that." Tim spat again. "I was getting bored with canal boats, I guess. You know me, Mister Shawcross, have to be where the action is. At least I went into the artillery and not the bleedin' infantry! Could have knocked me over with a feather when I heard you'd done that."

"I couldn't let the boy go alone."

"S'pose not."

"Well, now we've paid a thousand times over for the money we'll make on those uniforms."

"You didn't oughta think that way, Mister Shawcross," said Tim severely. "If folks are stupid enough to go to war, somebody's gotta provide 'em with the clothes to do it. Good luck to you, I say!"

"I suppose you're right."

"Shouldn't make 'em so bleedin' hot, though!"

"It's army regulations. I expect we'll be glad of it in the winter." Yet Hartley smiled at him. For all his irreverence, Tim was making him feel a little better than Ralph had done. They sat together for a while in companionable silence. Then Tim said,

"Gave me good advice 'bout those railroad shares, all those years ago, Mister Shawcross. I been putting all my hard-earned money into those, and they been doin' real well."

"I'm glad of it, Tim."

"Yeah, well I reckon I'd best be getting back now."

"I'm very touched you came Tim. God bless you!"

"Yeah, well next time you go into battle, Mister Shawcross, you just remember you got Tim O'Reilly covering your backside and then you'll feel better."

"I know it, Tim. Thank you."

Only they didn't go into battle again. Not to begin with, anyway, not the 12th New York at Bull Run. It was a punishment for Tyler and his ignominious performance. They spent the whole day shifting about from one side to the other, never getting near any real action when the battle recommenced.

To start with, all seemed to go well for the Unionists But McDowell's early triumph was premature. What was more, he spent so much time riding back and forth, rallying his men, that he lost track of the battle as a whole and failed to bring up his strong reserves. Like a miser, he doggedly continued to field one brigade at a time, dribbling away hundreds of lives needlessly, without anything to show for it. Now and then a Unionist unit would gain the summit of Henry House Hill where the most savage fighting took place, only to be thrown back with heavy losses.

Backwards and forwards it went, whilst men on both sides collapsed with heat and exhaustion and thirst and from breathing the dust filled air. Some even died from sunstroke rather than bullets or shells. Orders could not be heard over the general din. The confusion was increased by the unfortunate fact that some Unionist regiments still wore grey, and some Confederates were still in blue. Orders to hold fire were given until too late because of it. Soldiers became disorientated and fired their weapons into the air. Many were unable to fire at all, having neglected, in the heat of the moment, to put a percussion cap on the nipple at the rifle's breach and they died because of it. Others forgot to remove the ramrods from the barrels and sent them sailing over the field like flights of arrows. A number of them dropped paralysed as Hartley had done, or ran.

But most fought bravely if without skill. Jackson stood fast with his troops for the Confederate side and earned his nickname of 'Stonewall'. Blenker's Brigade held its ground for the Unionists and opened fire on the Confederate cavalry.

The tide turned during the afternoon. By 4.30pm, the great Unionist retreat had begun, orderly at first but soon degenerating into a fleeing rout. The Confederates were too exhausted to follow up their advantage. The Federals were supposed to stand and form a defensive line at Centreville, but half of the army streamed back in a chaotic tide towards the Potomac, performing no better than the hapless New Yorkers had done.

"A shambles!" said Ralph, bitterly. "Nothing but a bloody shamble!"

Bloody was right. There were three thousand dead or missing on the Unionists' side and two thousand on the Confederates'. To add to the misery, a drenching rain began during the night, turning the roads into quagmires. Disorderly men struggled along with crazed, half-mad looks in their eyes. There were cavalry horses without riders and wrecked baggage-wagons or pieces of artillery without horses dragged along by hand.

There would be many more 'bloody shambles' to come. Many more blunders, incompetent generals, stupid actions, and inactions, and many more casualties. The war would not be 'over by Christmas'. In the safety of the North, public and press alike, beginning to realize this, berated Mr Lincoln, and the Government, for acting too hastily, quite forgetting their earlier point of view. The romantic visions were gone, shattered by Bull Run and its authentic reports of a rout. They had all finally seen the elephant.

≈

Northern Virginia, August 1862

Miss Caroline Cholmondeley (who had long ago abandoned the 'Honourable' prefix to her title) never showed that she was tired though inside of her there lurked a deep and growing exhaustion. For over a year, she had followed the Unionist Army from Bull Run to Ball's

Bluff, to Mill Springs, to Shiloh, and all through the wearisome Peninsular Campaigns. Her presence was self-imposed though financed of late by the Women's Central Relief Association for the War. Her task was to help organize the field hospitals and make sure the nursing was as good as humanly possible. It was not easy for the nurses were not trained and generally came from the lowest ranks of women. Once the Army moved on, it left whole wardfuls of 'lucky' men: men who were blinded or paralysed or who had lost limbs, men who were wounded, sometimes not badly, yet who were still in danger of dying from the biggest killer of all which was infection.

No one knew why so many wounds went 'bad'. Miss Cholmondeley held decidedly eccentric views on the subject. She was convinced it was due to dirt but not the dirt the soldiers came in with, as the surgeons believed. No. She said it was due to dirt on the floors, dirt on the trestle beds (if they were lucky enough to get them), dirt on the sheets, dirt on the bandages, and, worst of all, dirt on the clothes and hands and instruments of the surgeons and nurses themselves. She had even come to believe recently (anticipating her contemporaries here by some years) that dirt, albeit invisible, lurked in some mysterious fashion in the very air. There was little she could do about that, but she waged war on the other culprits with soap and water, turpentine, and chloride of lime as her only allies.

Miss Cholmondeley was not popular for this. Every ward she entered had to be scrubbed down repeatedly. Wounds had to be washed and turpentine or even the demon alcohol applied. All bandages had to be clean and changed frequently. The more sluttish of the nurses learnt to fear the very sound of her tread on the boards and called her an interfering old busybody. Most of the surgeons were of like mind but some of them respected her and valued her help. They began to see that the amputations in particular did better in those wards she passed through. And the men loved her. Although they did not understand the war she waged, they knew she would listen when they poured out the horrors which invaded their minds during the night. They believed her a saint and perhaps she was, though she would have been the first to refute that suggestion.

They told her so many things, and she had learnt so much over this past year, above all, not to judge them. Always, there were worries and fears over loved ones and little ones left behind. That was only natural and proper and that she could cope with. But there were many other things, too, things she would rather not have heard. Always the question if they could still be a man had they been wounded below the waist. Tales of great bravery but also cowardice and horrible deaths: the memories of friends, fathers, sons, brothers, and yes, even lovers, blasted into pieces whilst they stood next to them — the ones they could not get out of their minds.

Miss Cholmondeley had not known about this kind of lover before, but she knew now. The guilty admissions shocked her at first, but she had come to realize that the loss of such a lover was no less painful, no less hard. She never told anyone what she had heard.

Now, a year later, she was back at Bull Run, in preparation for the second battle in that cursed place. It was night and she was passing the door of the hospital's main office when she heard voices coming from within. One was contemptuous and condemnatory, and she recognized it as one of her senior nurses, a woman she secretly despised. The other voice was timid and uncertain yet pleading.

She paused, hesitating, then pushed open the door of the room and went inside. There were two women inside. The older nurse, a corpulent, heavy-breathing woman with a distinct moustache and a permanently flushed face, was seated squarely at the desk and a stranger was standing before her. The stranger was a young woman dressed fashionably, even opulently, and in over-bright colours. Her bonnet sported a purple plume. However, Miss Cholmondeley noted she looked *clean*. Her face, underneath the outrageous bonnet, was a fine one though her startlingly blue eyes looked strained and unhappy. It was strange but she thought she had seen that face somewhere before though this seemed unlikely.

"Well," Miss Cholmondeley addressed the nurse briskly, "What is going on here?"

"Just another woman volunteering for the hospital," her colleague replied. "You told us we should be more careful about who we had, so I've turned her down. She has no experience and is not suitable in her station."

Miss Cholmondeley bristled. What did the woman mean by not suitable? The volunteer had clean hands and clean fingernails — a rarity indeed. Oh yes, she could guess why the nurse had turned her down, but she had no right to condemn her. She said as much. Now it was the nurse's turn to bristle, but she said nothing. She dared not. Instead, her looks said it for her. Can't you see, they said, that this woman is a trollop and a whore, a kept woman if ever I saw one?

"I shall take over the interview myself," said Miss Cholmondeley coolly. "Kindly leave us!"

The old nurse heaved herself up onto her feet, swearing under her breath, but left the room. If Miss Cholmondeley wished to recruit tarts and prostitutes that was her affair.

"Now," said Caroline Cholmondeley, kindlier now the older nurse was gone. "Sit down, my dear."

Caitlin sat at the opposite side of the desk, and Miss Cholmondeley cleared her throat.

"Do you have any experience?" she asked.

"Not really, that is no."

"Can you tell me a little about yourself then, my dear?"

Caitlin thought. Not of the past two years but before. "I lived and worked on a farm in Kansas for some years — a good part of it alone. My husband was killed, you see. I'm stronger than I look. I can do most things. Cope with minor accidents, certainly."

"I'm afraid you'll see more than minor accidents here." Miss Cholmondeley sighed. "Very much more."

"Oh yes, I realize that. I'm not sure I can cope but I want to try!"

Miss Cholmondeley brightened up at this. She thought it an honest attitude which boded well. "You'll learn very quickly, I'm sure. I have no fear of that. Take no notice of that old harridan who calls herself a nurse. She understands little, I'm afraid. I am more than willing to take you on. Don't be afraid. None of us know if we can cope but we do somehow." She paused: "You must forgive me, but I hardly think you obtained such clothes to wear in Kansas. If you do come, I will expect you to dress more plainly."

Caitlin dropped her eyes, feeling ashamed before this upright woman and nodded. "Of course. It was foolish of me to wear this to come here but I can dress as plainly as you like. Why, in Kansas, I even wore trousers!"

"Dear me!" said Miss Cholmondeley. "I hardly think that will be necessary." But she looked up and smiled as she said it. The girl had spirit and she appreciated that. "You can start as soon as you like. Another offensive is planned, as you probably know, and we shall need all the hands we can get."

Chapter Three

"You want to do what?" Andrew Tyrrell, deep in his cups, roared with laughter: coarse, obscene laughter and his red beard jerked up and down convulsively. "You're not a nurse, my dear, you're a whore!"

Caitlin set her chin against him. "No, I'm not! At least, I wasn't till I met you."

Tyrrell's eyes narrowed meanly. "You were always a whore!" he said, contemptuously. "I saw it in your face as soon as I saw you. Some women are born like that!"

Caitlin dropped her head, hating him.

"It's because you're a whore," he went on, belching into his drink. "That you got this crazy notion. Want to see all the soldiers, do we, those brave young lads in blue and paw their wounded, young bodies if we can?" She looked as if she might be going to cry but didn't. God, she was a disappointment to him! Always so meek and mild despite the promise of their first meetings. He did not realize that was down to him.

"Lots of women are volunteering," Caitlin said lamely. "It seems the decent thing to do. Especially when you're making so much out of the war. It's a way of giving something back." She did not add that she was desperate to get away from him, desperate to feel she had some worth left in her, something honourable that even she could do after all.

"S'prised they'll have a strumpet like you!" he said. "Though come to think of it most nurses are strumpets, anyway. Do they pay you for it?"

"No, I shall be a volunteer, not a regular nurse."

Tyrrell snorted. "Don't know when you've got it made, do you? All right then, go if you want to. I reckon you'll soon be back! It won't be as glorious as you think. You'll be back wingeing in a couple of hours!"

Only she wasn't. It was, truth to tell, harder than she had thought. When the first wave of casualties came in, she felt appalled at all the raw suffering. She stood reeling, wanting to be somewhere else: anywhere, even in Tyrrell's bed, to be away from the crying and groaning, the dirt and the smells and the blood. She felt frightened and inadequate but if she could steel herself to stand it and do this one small act of mercy, then perhaps God would forgive her the rest. Besides, she knew Miss Cholmondeley was watching her and wanted to prove her worth to somebody, to that particular woman above all.

Miss Cholmondeley, for her part, saw that she learned quickly and was an apt pupil, conscientious, gentle, and tireless. Above all, she was clean.

After a few days, she called her into the office for a discussion. Caitlin went reluctantly, fearing a dismissal or at least a stern lecture over some tasks not well done. She grew more nervous when Miss Cholmondeley sat for a time, not saying anything but dissecting her face and demeanour.

"What is it, Miss Cholmondeley? Have I done something wrong?"

"No, no," Miss Cholmondeley recovered herself. She had been wondering about the angry bruise under the girl's left eyelid. It had been there several days now, and it wasn't the first one she had spotted. "Far from it, my dear. I am very pleased with your work."

"Thank you." Caitlin felt relieved. What then had Miss Cholmondeley to say to her?

"Can you tell me a little more about your life?"

Caitlin stared.

"It isn't idle curiosity, I assure you. It makes no difference to me. I will not be as shocked as you think."

A woman who listened to tales of death and horror every night was not going to be upset by such obvious stories a kept woman could tell her, after all. "Only I have the feeling it may help you to talk about it. You see, I don't think you're the kind of woman who ought to be dressed in the clothes you were when you first came here."

Caitlin blushed. "I'd rather not say," she muttered.

Miss Cholmondeley sighed. "What was that? You must speak louder. I fear I am becoming a little deaf." It was true. She had noticed it of late. Sometimes she thought it was due to the dreary boom of guns in the distance. Except she had heard Caitlin's ashamed murmur well enough.

Caitlin lifted her chin then. "Of course I am a kept woman," she blurted out. "It's obvious. I know that. He buys me gaudy things. He wants me to wear them, and I do. I sold my farm to him in Kansas and came to Virginia with him because I didn't know what else to do, and I didn't want to starve and die alone. Will you send me away because of it?"

"Send you away?" said Miss Cholmondeley in amazement. "What must you think of me? On the contrary! I want you to stay as long as you are able. But tell me," And her eye returned to the bruise. "Is he not a good man at heart?"

"No," said Caitlin, miserably. "He is detestable."

"Do you have children?"

"No, I cannot bear children. I always miscarry and so I have none."

"Then there is nothing to stop you from leaving this man?"

"Nothing," said Caitlin, wretchedly, " and yet everything."

"Do you love him?"

"Indeed no! It isn't that. It is because I have no one else."

"My poor child!" Caroline Cholmondeley could not resist the challenge. She saw her duty clear before her. Besides, she liked this girl, liked her spirit, her fine face, her quick mind and especially her clean fingernails. She was determined to save her from herself. "Well," she said. "You must not feel like that any longer and you must certainly not allow yourself to be struck and bruised anymore! You are my best nurse, Mrs Griffith. I do not say it lightly and I cannot afford to lose you!"

"I don't understand."

"Soon it will be time to move on. The Army will have gone, and we will have done what we can here. But I am afraid there will always be more to do elsewhere, until this terrible war is finished. The men need you, Mrs Griffith, God needs you, I need you! I want you to come with me!"

Caitlin was astounded. She swallowed hard. Of the three claiming to need of her, she found Miss Cholmondeley far and away the most powerful.

"It would mean leaving him," she said.

"But of course. Would that not be a great relief?"

It would. Caitlin saw it with a great rush of feeling. Only dare she do it? "I have no money," she said.

"I can arrange for you to lose your volunteer status and to be paid. Of course, it will not be much but ..."

But it would be hers, gained honourably. Caitlin hesitated. She feared she was not up to it, after all. But oh, what a blessed relief it would be! If only she had the courage. Miss Cholmondeley saw the conflicting emotions pass across her face.

"You do have the strength," she said simply. "I know you have." Then she rose to her feet, signifying the interview was at an end. "Whether or not, I shall be glad to have you as long as I can." She wisely left the room to leave Caitlin alone with her own thoughts. She felt rather tired. Had she made any impression on the face that had come to her underneath a nodding purple plume? She rather thought that she had but it remained to be seen.

≈

Caitlin went back to the timber-framed house in Leesburg that evening and packed her bags. She would take nothing that wasn't hers, she decided - only the simple items she had arrived with. For a moment, surveying the fine silks in the wardrobe and looking round the opulent room with its expensive furnishings, her determination wavered. The future lay ahead cold and uncertain.

Yet it was her last chance. She saw that clearly. It would never come again. Left to her own devices she might never find the courage. Rather she would go on drinking and shutting away her conscience, sinking downwards in a slow but sure spiral with a man she hated who was bent on dragging her down. Better by far to accept Miss Cholmondeley's challenge.

Now there was the leaving itself to be got over. Tyrrell was downstairs in the parlour. Quietly, she took her bag down the stairs and left it in the hall. The black manservant saw her do it and his eyes widened.

"Missis leaving?"

"Yes, Olly."

"Mister Tyrrell, he know?"

"Not yet."

The black face became anxious. "You not tell him, missis. You go quick now. He not in good mood."

"No, I can't do that. It's right he should know."

Olly shook his thick head of curls as he watched her go into the parlour.

"Jest hope you come out agin," he muttered to himself and scuttled off to the kitchen in fear.

The curtains were drawn inside the parlour; heavy, plush folds of red velvet that lent an atmosphere of oppression to the room. It was crammed with expensive furniture, figurines, and tasteless trinkets. The many candelabra were all lit, and the air was stifling and close. Tyrrell slouched in an armchair, his waistcoat unbuttoned, his collar undone. Beside him, on a small table, stood an empty decanter and glass.

Despite his attitude, he was neither happy nor relaxed. Someone had got the better of him that day and he could never abide that. Even now he was planning how to take his revenge. His small eyes bulged when he saw his mistress, still in her drab working clothes.

"Why are you dressed like that?" he demanded. "Why haven't you changed for dinner? I have people coming."

"I am going back to the hospital," said Caitlin.

"Now? You can't! I told you, there are people coming. I want to make a good impression. And I told you before, I won't have you working nights there."

"Miss Cholmondeley has asked me to go."

"Miss Cholmondeley, Miss Cholmondeley!" He chewed on the words in a grumbling manner and spat them out as if they were the butt end of a cigar.

"Seems to me you take too much notice of that woman and her darned hospital of late!"

Caitlin hesitated, then plunged on. "I'm about to take more notice of her."

"What do you mean?"

She took a deep breath and prayed for courage. "Miss Cholmondeley has asked me to travel with her to the next field hospital, and the next. I have agreed. It is something I can do. I shall earn my keep again. I intend to go - and not to come back."

He stared at her with a mounting colour in his cheeks. Then he gave a hollow laugh.

"Well, aren't we the little Saint Theresa then? You Irish whore! After all I've done for you!"

"You don't want me," protested Caitlin, her heart beating fast. "You think you do but you don't! I've kept my side of the bargain we made for two years and it's more than enough. You can always find somebody else."

He rose from his chair abruptly and crossed the room towards her. She shrank back.

"My women don't leave me!" he said. "I throw them out!"

She tilted her chin upwards. "Very well. If you must."

The sharp slap of his hand stung her cheek. She put up her hand and turned her head away. "You've done that once too often. You don't know how to treat a woman."

He swore. "Didn't you have enough, then? Enough to eat and drink and a roof over your head with servants and plenty of fine clothes? What more do you want? You knew I wouldn't marry you!"

"No, thank God!" said Caitlin with a shudder. "Nothing is enough to make up for living with you! You shut me out and made me feel low and cheap as I believed I was. You dragged me down all the time to your own dirty level! There's not an ounce of common humanity in you, and no love — no love for anything but money."

He grabbed her by the throat and shook her. "You'll stay with me, by God or be damned!"

But she had begun it now. Launched herself on the road out. She would not slip back. "No!" she cried. "Leave me alone! I'm going!"

She felt his big hands squeezing around her neck and felt panic. He could knock the breath out of her so quickly. She read the idea in his face. What a fool she had been to ignore Olly's advice! She gagged. Then he hurled her away with contempt and she fell on the floor with a sob.

"You're right," he said peevishly. "What do I care?" He returned to his chair and, finding the decanter empty, swept it off the table with his arm. It crashed and broke into a thousand pieces on the carpet. He rang for Olly to clear it up and bring him another one.

Caitlin panted for breath. Her throat hurt. But the ordeal was over. He was not going to kill her. She struggled to her feet and turned to go. He should have no word of farewell now.

"Wait!" The command was harshly spoken, and she drew up, fearful.

"Have you got any money? I know you can't manage without money. You need your whisky!"

She shook her head scornfully. "I've taken nothing that isn't mine."

He reached inside his waistcoat pocket and took out some dollar bills. They were rather dirty. Slowly, he began to peel them off with his thumb, counting.

"No," she said. "I thank you, but no! I shan't need it where I am going."

He looked amazed.

"You're a hard woman to please," he said, in a placatory tone. "But you got guts after all. I'll say that for you. You don't have to go ..." He became pleading and cajoling now. "I'll treat you better, I swear."

She knew that he wouldn't for all he meant to. It would last a week, no more. Still, this reversal of his was harder to take than his blustering and ill temper.

"No," she said. "I'm sorry. It's too late."

Olly stood in the doorway, nervous and shaking, summoned from the kitchen by the bell. She knew Tyrrell would beat him when she was gone to vent his anger on someone but there was nothing she could do to stop that. Tyrrell didn't see him yet. His head had dropped deep onto his chest and his hidden face was morose. She almost began to feel sorry for him but knew he remained a monster underneath his self-pity. Quietly, she walked out of the room without saying another word.

In the hall, she picked up her bag and put on her travelling cloak. The front door opened to her touch, and she passed through. It closed firmly behind her with a sharp noise. In the street, she drank deeply of the warm night air with an immense sense of relief.

The buggy to take her back to the hospital was waiting at the end of the road. It had been easier than she had thought. She should have done it months ago. Now, at last, she was free again. The future lay ahead: uncharted, uncertain, but hers alone.

Chapter Four

Antietam Creek, September 17th 1862

Caroline was tired, deathly tired. Caitlin could see it in her face. She was tired too, but not in the same way, for she knew now that Caroline Cholmondeley, underneath all her bravado and brisk sales in full flow, was desperately ill. The enormity of this wretched battle was the last thing she needed. For the first time, that evening, Caitlin had seen her falter, looking at the rows and rows of wounded men as still they came in, wave upon wave.

The hospital could not cope.

When Caitlin darted into the office for fresh supplies of bandages, she found Miss Cholmondeley, that odd, pucker-faced, brave figure, sitting with her head in her hands doing — remarkably for her — nothing.

"Caroline," she said, alarmed. "What is it? Are you unwell?" Miss Cholmondeley hardly raised her head at all.

"There are too many of them," she mumbled in a daze. "We do what we can, but there are always more. And more again. There are too many of them." Caitlin slipped quickly onto her knees beside her. She had changed much these last few weeks away from Tyrrell. She was tough and courageous; she had absorbed all that Caroline had taught her, and she had seen enough blood and suffering to last a lifetime. But she had not lost the newly learnt art of caring for someone other than herself.

"Caroline," she said again, tenderly, a hand round the older woman's shoulders. "Let me make you some coffee."

"Tea," said Miss Cholmondeley faintly. "My herbal tea."

Caitlin smiled and went to do her bidding at the big stove which overheated the room. They had neither of them had anything to eat all day — there hadn't been time. Her back and neck ached intolerably with bending over. Now she had stopped for a moment she felt quite faint. How much worse then must Miss Cholmondeley feel?

"You must rest, Caroline," she said. "Why don't you sleep for a while? You've been working all day."

"So have you."

"But I am younger and in better health, I think."

"How can I rest when I must see to the men and make sure everything is clean?"

That was impossible, thought Caitlin sadly, with the wounded pouring in an overwhelming tide of broken, bleeding bodies. If only she could accept that and not drive herself so hard! At least she accepted the tea gratefully.

"You'll take it too." It was an order rather than a question. Caitlin thought privately she would have preferred a good slug of whisky to get her through the night to come but gulped the tea down.

"I have been a failure, Caitlin."

"Oh no! You mustn't say that! You're just tired, Caroline, exhausted. No one can go on forever. You must sleep and then you'll feel better. I'll go back to the ward and see things are done as you wish, at least, as best I can."

With much soothing of protestations, she managed to get Miss Cholmondeley laid out on the floor — there was nowhere else to put her — with a blanket rolled up under her head and another to cover her up. Within seconds she was asleep.

Caitlin braced herself for the return to the ward. Even so, the fresh sight took her aback and made her reel again. The very stench of the place was enough to make one's stomach turn. The smell of blood itself was in the air, warm and sickly. Only it wasn't just that. It was the awful sight of them: in wretched row upon row, laid out, left bleeding, moaning, grimy, unrecognisable, shattered men. And still the orderlies brought them in on stretchers. Nothing could be worth this, surely? Nothing. It made her want to go out and scream at the soldiers to stop.

Swiftly she passed down the lines with her bandages and tourniquets. Soon they would run out and then what would they do? As she passed, men cried out for water, but she ignored them. That was someone else's job. She was supposed to stop serious bleeding if she could. Nine times out of ten she couldn't but she went on trying. There was no hope of cleansing wounds at the moment. No wonder poor Miss Cholmondeley had collapsed in horror.

*We **are** failures,* thought Caitlin in desperation. *Most of these men will die. Yet how can we be anything else, faced with all of this? It's never been quite so bad before.* She was right. This single day at Antietam turned out to be the bloodiest of the entire war.

She passed down the lines. Miss Cholmondeley had always told her not to become involved with individuals, whilst being involved herself all of the time. Here there was no need for the warning. All personalities were submerged underneath the great mass of human suffering. There were only the dead and the not yet dead.

Caitlin began to feel disorientated. She was aware she had started her rounds again in the wrong place and missed some men out.

It couldn't be helped. Nothing could. Best not think about it: move on to the next one and the next. Jesus, this one was bad! He had a great hole in his side. He was surely dying. It was a wonder they had bothered bringing him in at all. She tried to signal to the nurse carrying the precious stocks of opium to come over, but she couldn't attract her attention. She was too busy. Anyway, it was almost too late already.

She felt sickened but moved on automatically to the next one. A shoulder wound. Jesus, Mary, and Joseph, if only they wouldn't groan so! She knew they couldn't help it and felt guilty at the thought but knew she would fall asleep eventually, though not tonight by the looks of it with that sound echoing in her ears.

The next one had a leg wound. She moved away the blood-soaked blanket. It was gaping below the knee and slowly oozing. She had seen worse. How much blood had he lost? She glanced at his ashen face and was struck as if by a thunderbolt.

Hartley!

Her own blood seemed to drain away from her too. Hartley Shawcross! Surely it couldn't be? She must be mistaken. But it was. All the experiences of her life seemed to meld together in that one moment, all the people she had ever known and loved: James, Owain, Polly, and Hartley — Hartley!

He wasn't aware of her. She could see that. His face looked ashen, grey, and clammy. He had lost a good deal of blood. Otherwise, he looked the same though immeasurably older. Lined and harder, as they all were, even the youngest of them. She checked him over again. No chest wound, nothing on the arms. She looked at the slowly oozing right leg again and decided to apply a tourniquet. Not too tight though. She might not be able to come back for a while.

He ought to recover, she thought. He ought to, given time and all the things they no longer had like clean bandages and water and pure air and no infection. For Caroline was, without doubt, correct in her obsessions. She ought to move on now, straightaway, but she couldn't. That would be shabby of her. Instead, she bent her head close to his.

"Hartley," she said urgently in his ear. "Hartley, it's me, Caitlin! You're going to be all right. Can you speak to me?"

His eyes flicked open, once, twice, watery blue grey as she remembered them, but the effort was too much, and he could not recognize her.

"Never mind," she said. "I'll be back. Don't you worry now, Hartley, I'll look after you. Don't give up on me! You're going to make it."

He groaned slightly as he tried to move. She had nothing to give him, like all the others, and passed on with an effort, feeling confused. Until now they had all been someone else's people. This time the face stayed with her and did not blur into the mass.

It had been a Confederate victory of sorts but at terrible cost: 13,700 of their casualties compared with 12,350 on the Unionists' side. The problem for Lee was that this number comprised a third of his entire army whilst for McClellan (who had long since replaced McDowell, though with no more success) it was only a sixth. Lee was forced to retreat, and so Mr Lincoln was able to cleverly proclaim it a Unionist victory after all. He did more than that: on September 22nd, he announced that, as a war measure, based on his powers as Commander-in-Chief of the victorious army, the slaves in all areas presently occupied by Rebels should be forever free, as from the first of January 1863.

It was a grand declaration though it had little practical effect for the slaves as yet. But it uplifted Unionist hearts and made them feel that in the end they were going to win. It also put paid to the prospect of the British coming in to help the Confederates.

But such international matters were of little importance in the hospitals left behind at Antietam. The situation was a little easier now, mainly because so many had died and been removed over several nights for burial in mass graves. There was no time for sentiment. And they had fresh supplies at last. It was now that the real work had to be done on the survivors.

Caitlin reached Hartley on her morning round of dressings. "Good morning, Hartley," she said. "How are you, today?"

He tried to smile and signalled he was fine, but she could see that he wasn't. He knew her now.

"I'm dead," he had said wryly when he first recognized her. "I'm dead and gone to heaven, haven't I, with you here?"

"I don't think so," she had laughed. "You have a strange idea of heaven! Anyway, I'd be dead too then, wouldn't I, and I know I'm not?"

"But whatever are you doing here? I thought you were in Kansas."

"I was but now I'm here." She didn't tell him anything else for the moment. It wasn't necessary.

She undid the bandages with a sense of unease. His wound had been festering for four days now. This morning it was worse. She mopped up the green pus. That was only to be expected. But the redness and swelling above the wound had spread further in the night. It had reached the knee. The skin was bulging and tense and hot to her touch. The wound itself smelt vile. Her spirits sank. Hartley was sitting up with an effort to see, but she swiftly covered the wound again and made him lie down.

"Is it getting better?" he asked her, anxiously.

"Yes, it's getting better. But I shall ask the surgeon to look at it today. He may want to ... clean it up a little." She couldn't tell him, she really couldn't, though she knew perfectly well what the surgeon would say. "How are you feeling, Hartley?"

"I don't know. A little strange. Very cold. It's so cold in here." He shivered. She lay a hand on his forehead. It was burning and he looked exhausted and grey again, worse than yesterday. She would ask the surgeon to see him as a matter of urgency.

"You can tell me, you know," said Hartley bluntly, seeing the anxiety in her face. "I'm ready to die. They've all gone, you see — Johann, Ralph and even Tim. It's only right I should join them. Only I could wish it were quicker and less demeaning. I can't stop shivering but it's not because I'm afraid."

"Nonsense!" said Caitlin fiercely. "You're not going to die, Hartley Shawcross, so don't let me hear you talking like that! What about Rosa and all those children? I'm going to get you another blanket."

She sought the haven of the stores before he could see there were tears in her eyes. It was expressly against the rules of course. Freshly laundered blankets and sheets were like gold. They were only to be given out when strictly necessary. But Caitlin no longer gave a damn for the general good. It was Hartley's condition that wrung her. However, she had been observed.

"What are you doing, Caitlin?"

It was Caroline, of course, with eyes like a hawk, standing blocking the doorway.

"I'm getting an extra blanket for a man with a gangrenous leg. He's feverish."

"Is it Private Shawcross?"

"Yes."

"It won't do him any good, my dear. You must ask the surgeon to see him."

"I know. I will but he's cold. Shouldn't he have some comfort if he's going to lose his leg?" She folded the blanket over her arm and held it, fiercely protective, to her body.

"Of course. But you mustn't become involved, Caitlin."

"I can't help it. I know him."

Caroline sighed and put her arm out for support against the door. "I'm sorry, my dear. But you must try not to let that make a difference."

"I can't. I won't have him die alone with no comfort from anyone who really cares."

"We all care, Caitlin." Miss Cholmondeley was severe. "We care for them all. We don't want anyone to die or suffer. It's merely the way things are."

Caitlin dropped her eyes, ashamed. It was true, of course. But the feeling inside her now was stronger than reason. Naturally she didn't want any of them to suffer and die. But she especially didn't want Hartley to. She would not put the blanket back. She looked up, intending to argue, but Caroline had gone. She could hear her footsteps retreating down the corridor and knew she intended to look the other way. Triumphantly, Caitlin hurried out, clutching her prize. She went and covered Hartley up.

"Is that better?" she asked. He was asleep and didn't hear her.

When the surgeon eventually arrived, he was brusque and to the point. He did not speak to Hartley at all, only to Caitlin. That was not to say Major Douglas, as he was called, was a bad man. He was a good surgeon and one who approved of Miss Cholmondeley and her work. He would even scrub his hands between cases. But it was a darned sight easier for him to talk to Caitlin who understood. It was the sixth leg like this he had seen that morning.

"It'll have to come off," he said sharply. "Well above the knee. Tell him, would you, and get him ready? Give him some whisky. Hopefully, it'll be in about an hour. I'll try and do him first because his general condition isn't too good."

Then, he was gone as quickly as he had arrived.

"What did he say?" asked Hartley, alarmed.

"Wait a moment. I have to burn these." Caitlin removed the filthy dressings. When she came back, she had a clean strip to cover the wound lightly and a bottle of whisky. They had crude anaesthetics now — to pull the teeth of rich people in Boston — but not enough for thousands of wounded soldiers. She covered the monstrosity the wound had become and poured him out a large tumbler.

"What are you giving me this for?" Hartley asked, astonished.

Caitlin knelt on the floor beside him, the bottle in her hand. She couldn't shirk it anymore. "He's going to amputate, Hartley. Cut your leg off. Drink it, please."

"Oh," he said. Just that. Nothing more, for a while. She allowed the news time to sink in. With relief, she saw he was going to be brave, and her heart went out to him. He drained the glass, and she took it back, only to refill it.

"Expect it's for the best," he said, squinting down at his leg. "To get rid of it, I mean. It's just a mess, isn't it?"

She nodded. "If he doesn't do it, you'll get blood-poisoning and die. It's much, much better to be rid of it. Drink that up, please and I'll give you some more."

Hartley protested. "But I haven't had anything to eat yet. They wouldn't give me my breakfast. I'm not used to drinking spirits in the morning. I'll be raving drunk!"

She looked at him awkwardly, unable to say anything which would make it easier.

"I suppose that's the idea, isn't it?"

"Yes. I'm sorry."

Hartley looked rather white and emptied the glass, holding it out now for more. She noticed that his hand shook slightly.

"Will I be able to walk?" He said it as casually as he could, striving hard to give the impression that it wasn't really of much consequence to him.

"Yes, you'll be able to walk. With crutches. You've still got the other one. You're lucky. It's only a leg." She didn't mean to sound hard, but he had to be bundled through this catastrophe somehow, as quickly as possible. Yet he was still Hartley and still her dearest friend after all the long, intervening years. She softened and caught his hand. "You'll be fine. Really, you will. Once it's over. Don't be afraid!"

"I'm not!" He grimaced. "What am I saying, dear God? Of course I am!" He raised his eyes to the ceiling, and they were moist.

She took the glass from him and refilled it hurriedly though he was still struggling through the last generous measure. How many was that? Three or four? Not enough, but she mustn't give him too much or else he might vomit. They did sometimes and died choking on it. It was a risk.

"It's not that I'm afraid of being lame, at least I don't think it is. But I'm afraid I shan't be brave."

"Nobody's brave in these circumstances, Hartley. It doesn't matter."

"But what if I scream and shout so much, they can't do it?" He was sweating now. Caitlin hesitated. She didn't want to tell him, but he had to know.

"It won't be like that. They'll tie you down. And this surgeon, he's not good with words, but he's good at his craft. He'll do it quickly, as quickly as he can. And…and you'll pass out. Most of them do."

Where had she learnt all this? Hartley realized she had seen it done many times before. He put a hand up in wonder to her face and stroked her dark, curly hair and she let him. His Madonna! That she should know such things! He felt rather awed. The whisky was beginning to make him feel as if he was floating.

"Will you be there?" he asked.

She hesitated. She had been going to ask another nurse to take her place under the circumstances. "Do you want me to be?"

"I don't know. I don't think so."

She rose to her feet gratefully. Her knees were aching intolerably from the hard wooden floor. She knew it was frail when she thought of the pain he must go through, but she couldn't help it.

"Do you want any more whisky?"

"No. I don't know. Yes, perhaps."

She poured out one last measure and gave it to him. God, she hoped it wasn't too much. At least she'd managed to stop them giving him any breakfast.

"I expect," said Hartley, beginning to hiccup quietly. "it's like going into battle. I was the most dreadful coward at first but then I got used to it. You do. When the time comes, you just have to go, and it all happens. Then it's over. Right?"

"That's right, Hartley," Caitlin agreed. "That's just how it'll be. You just go and it happens. It'll soon be over. Try not to worry. See if you can sleep now."

$$\approx$$

Afterwards, he woke up in the night tormented by the most sickening pain and writhed about.

"Caitlin!" He tried to cry out, but his voice was hoarse and cracked with all the shouting done earlier for it had taken him a long time to pass out. Only an agonized whisper came out. She was there, sitting at her desk at the end of the ward, waiting for just such an event. The other amputees had been restless too. She had other staff to help her, but she wouldn't let anyone else go to Hartley.

"Hartley! I'm here. What is it, dearest? Is it the pain?" She bent over him with concern, the light of the oil-lamp glowing on her sensitive face.

He moaned. "They haven't done it, Caitlin!"

"What do you mean?"

"They haven't taken my leg off! It's still there! I can feel it right down to the toes. And it's hurting so! Why didn't they take it off? Will they do it tomorrow?" His hand grabbed desperately at hers.

She squeezed it and put the lamp down so that she could enfold it in both her own. "Listen to me, Hartley. Calm yourself. It's all right. Your leg **has** been amputated. It's gone. It's the stump that's hurting."

"No, no," he cried. "It's my leg! The knee and the wound and the foot. I can feel the foot. It's like being in hell!"

She had heard them say so before. It was very strange but there was truth in it. It wasn't merely the product of a fevered, confused brain. It pained them far more than the real site of the trauma. She didn't know why but it happened.

"You must believe me!" said Hartley in tears.

"Hush now, I do! I know, Hartley. It happens. Other men have told me the same. Lie still. Try not to writhe so. I'll go and get you some opium."

When she returned, he had vomited on the floor and was sweating profusely.

"I'm sorry!" he groaned, ashamed.

She smiled.

"It's all right, Hartley. I'll clean it up. Don't you worry. It happens all the time. It doesn't matter."

He still groaned. She gave him the opium and went to fetch cleaning materials, wondering why it was always the trivial which worried the most decent men more than anything else. He was a decent man, she realized and winced at the memory of calling him a stuffed shirt. She thought of the first time she had met him in Union Square, his tentative visits to the Regans' house, the gift of the canary in its cage, the way he had looked after her when she was ill in New York when he had been her only friend. Oh, why had she not waited for him, however long it had taken? Why had she been so foolish as to marry the impetuous Owain and take up with a rogue like Tyrrell? Now he belonged to someone else who had appreciated his worthiness all along and would never be hers. The thought was bitter for she realized now that she did love him and had always done so without knowing it.

When she returned, his breathing was a little easier. The blessed, magical opium was beginning to work. She sat with him for a while until he drifted off into sleep, mopped his brow and cooled his hands.

"Don't you ever sleep?" he asked her drowsily when he awoke, before falling away again.

"Not tonight," she said.

"Will we ever get out of this mess?" he asked longingly, and she had the impression he was not just speaking about the war.

"One day," she said.

She had not been present during his operation. Caroline had taken her place, had offered to do it in the briskest manner as if it were the most normal thing in the world and doing her the favour, not Caitlin, though she was terribly tired. *If only I could be like Caroline,* thought Caitlin, returning sadly to her post at the desk. She feels for everyone with no thought of her own selfish satisfaction. *I am different. I must have someone. If I cannot have Hartley, I must at least make sure he survives this: I shall nurse him and make sure he doesn't die. He will recover through my efforts no matter what.*

However, the next day he was delirious and did not know her. The stump was clean enough, thank God. She dressed it herself (clean hands, clean bandages, clean fingernails). No one else should touch it. It was the old infection, not a new one, coursing through his blood, heightened by the trauma and shock of surgery. Had they been too late in what they had done for him?

"Never fired a shot!" he said to her angrily, struggling to sit up. "Did you know that? He never even had a chance to fire his gun!"

Who was he talking about? Ralph, Tim, Johann? She did not ask.

For days, he went on like this, sometimes lucid, sometimes rambling. He began to cough, too. Perhaps he had pneumonia. Many of the men had. She prayed for the first time in years. *Dear God, if you just let Hartley live, I'll do anything. I'll never do anything bad again! I'll really try to be like Caroline!"*

Then, one morning, he woke, weak but without a fever at last. The stump was still clean, and he asked for food. He hadn't given up on her after all. He was going to live.

Chapter Five

The day came when Hartley was ready for discharge. His stump had healed well, and he was gaining strength all the time. They had given him two wooden crutches and taught him to walk again after a fashion, ungainly and lopsided though it was. Caitlin watched him struggle to master it courageously. What more could they do? His war was over, and he ought to be thankful for it. A wagon waited outside to convey him and several others to the railway station for a train back to Washington and then New York. They were the lucky ones. They were going home.

Miss Cholmondeley was thinking about moving on, too, after the army, which was about to make a push southward toward Richmond before winter came on. Caitlin knew she would not see Hartley again. He was going back to Rosa and all those children who needed him, and Rosa would, if she had any sense at all, welcome him back with open arms. He still had his business to run. That would be good for him. Slowly the horrors would fade as he resumed normal life. He would never forget it, but he would survive. She was truly glad. Why, then, did she feel so wretched inside as she went about her work in the wards? Why did she bang bedpans and slop water jugs and speak crossly to the orderlies under her command?

Their leave-taking was dismal. There was no privacy, of course, and no time to say anything worth saying. Just polite farewells and profuse thanks from Hartley, shrugged off by herself with a careless laugh.

"Take care of yourself," she said, and he nodded. Then she watched him go, awkwardly and messily, with crutches thudding on the floor, leaning to one side heavily, moving the sound leg with a great effort, throwing the crutches forward again.

Caroline said something strange whilst they drank their tea in the afternoon.

"Are you coming south with me then?" she asked.

"But of course. Why shouldn't I?"

"Nothing. Only I thought you looked very fatigued of late and possibly needed a break."

Caitlin repeated her mentor's own words. "There will be no break until it's over."

But Caroline was right, of course, as always. It was true that she was sick of it. Nursing Hartley so intensely had taken something out of her. Easing the suffering of those who were dying or patching up the war wounded to send them home was one matter. Patching up the rest to send them back into battle was another. There seemed to be no end to it, and now she needed one. She was not like Caroline. She could not go on and on until she dropped.

It was with a great sense of depression inside that she let herself be driven back to her lodgings in the town that evening. She was not looking forward to the long evening ahead. On the other hand, she needed to be alone with her thoughts and declined Caroline's company. It was already getting cold. She went directly into the public room to warm herself by the fires for a moment.

She saw him immediately. He was sitting by the fire with his fair head bowed, his crutches leaning against the mantelpiece. He was sitting, waiting for her but gazing into the fire with a faraway expression in his eyes.

"Hartley! What are you doing here? Didn't the train leave today?" (Perhaps that was all it amounted to.)

"Yes, the train left."

"Then why aren't you on it? Whatever is the matter?" She could see that there was a deal of pain in his eyes.

"I can't go back. Not like this."

She sat down opposite him quietly, wondering, and warmed her hands at the fire.

"What about Rosa and the children?"

"I don't know. I must write to her first. Tell her I've been kept here for a while yet. It's been so long. It seems like another life, almost belonging to someone else. I am a different man."

She saw that, although they had cut off the gangrene and patched up his leg, the wounds of war were still there, eating into his heart. They had not been able to heal those.

A noisy crowd poured into the room, heading for the bar, filling the whole place with an untimely invasion, laughing and talking too loudly.

"Come up to my rooms," she said. "We can't talk here."

It was a struggle for him to manage the staircase, which was too narrow for her to help him. In the end, he made it, though it exhausted him. She had two rooms, one to sleep and wash in and a small sitting room where a fire was laid but not kindled in the hearth. It was a shabby place after the house in Leesburg, but she found it a comfortable enough haven. He sank onto the old sofa whilst she bent down to light the fire.

"Why can't you go back, Hartley?" she asked gently. "It's not just because of your leg, surely? Is it because the boy, Johann, is dead?"

"It's because of all of them," he said wretchedly. "There were four of us that set off. Johann was killed at Bull Run before he fired a shot. Tim always said he would be all right because he was artillery. He could hide behind the big guns. Only he wasn't all right in the end. They got him on the Peninsula in the Seven Days' Battle. I saw Ralph die at Antietam just before I was shot. He was standing right next to me. He was engaged to be married. They've all gone except me, and I deserved to survive least of all. I'm the only one going back."

She looked up at him. His fair head was bowed in his hands. "What do you mean by 'deserved it least', Hartley? That's nonsense. It could as easily have been you. It just wasn't, that's all. It's the fortunes of war. You mustn't feel guilty over it."

He continued to talk as if he hadn't heard her. On and on, as he had never talked to anyone before, in the growing flame of the little fire, for, although the darkness was gathering, she had neglected to light any candles or lamps. It would be easier for him like this. It was all about the war. Johann again. He was talking about Johann. How could Rosa ever forgive him? Even though she had written to say she had. Those were just words in a letter. She couldn't really mean it.

"I'm sure that's not true," said Caitlin. "She'll be so glad to have you back." She could see he didn't care about that. Saw, too, that although he felt badly for having failed Rosa, he did not really love her anymore and never had. It had only been pity and a sense of respect which had made him marry her.

"I can't go back," he repeated. "I haven't been back for two years. The children will have forgotten me, and even if they haven't, they won't expect a cripple."

"But Hartley, you must have had leave!"

He had but had not taken it in New York, she discovered. Even then, he had felt unable to face them. He had stayed in Washington.

He carried on. About Tim O'Reilly, who had left him his railroad shares in a letter found in his possessions because, he said, he had no one else to leave them to, and he reckoned Mister Shawcross, who had been his only true friend, would know best what to do with them.

"More blood money," said Hartley bitterly. "Like the uniforms."

She didn't understand what he meant, but she let him go on about his cowardice and fear. About all the men he had killed. Sometimes, he imagined that if they made a line of them, those grey uniforms would stretch all the way back from here to the Potomac. At night, he dreamt about them: a line, head to toe, of other men's sons whom he, Hartley Shawcross, had filled with lead. He had once believed in God but now he did not.

He could not look at a line of trees without feeling afraid that they would rattle with gunfire. Any loud noise, anything at all, made him start out of his skin and reach for a rifle that was no longer there. He could not go back and take up his old life in New York, where the workshop was full of the din of sewing machines, and women would look at him strangely and think him a cripple who had gone mad. He could not continue to make money out of Army uniforms.

On and on, he went into the night until at last, he could no longer talk and just sat there, with his hands covering his face. Caitlin felt relieved at the silence. Everything was out now, poured into one vast stream of misery that she felt she would never be able to wash out of the room. It was more difficult to deal with than blood. She was aware that it should have been Rosa who had heard it all and not her but was glad it had not been.

Stiffly, she rose to her feet (all this time, she had stayed kneeling by the fire) and lit the candles at last. They made the room brighter, more comfortable in an instant, enveloping it in a warm glow. Her love for him lit up with them.

"Would you like me to bring you something to eat?" she asked. "I can fetch a tray from downstairs if you like."

"No," he said, "no, nothing to eat."

She passed into her bedroom and lit a candle there too. Drew the curtains, folded back the bedlinen, undressed slowly, got into her chemise, and brushed her long, dark hair. When she went back into the sitting-room he had not moved and still sat with his head bent. No, he did not need food, but he needed the comfort of her love.

"Hartley," she said softly, breaking into his reverie of despair. "It's late. It's time to sleep."

He looked up then and saw her in her flowing chemise. For a few moments he appeared mesmerised, seeing her like that in the luminescent glow. Then he recovered himself and reached for his crutches.

"Yes, it must be late. Forgive me. I must book a room here, somewhere."

She stepped over to his side and took the crutches out of his hands before he could struggle to rise.

"No, Hartley. That isn't what I meant. I'm not asking you to leave." She sat down beside him and held out her hands, waiting for his. They hung in the air, soft, white, and lonely, offering all of herself to him.

Finally, he took them but looked awkward and doubtful. "I can't!" he said, faintly.

"Why not?" She feared he would say something about Rosa, his children, his self-respect, even his concern for her.

"I've only got one leg."

"Oh, Hartley!" She leant over and kissed him on the lips, her eyes shining with unshed tears. "Didn't I tell you before? Tis only a leg! Not the rest of you. It's not the end of the world. I love you, Hartley and I thought you loved me."

"I do." His voice was choked. "But don't you mind? I thought all that would be over, that women would not ..."

"Then you were wrong!" She stood up, seeing she had to make it easier for him. She handed over the crutches and extended her other hand. "Come."

She took an age seeing to the fire whilst he slowly undressed in the other room and got into bed. All the time her heart was thudding with expectation, but she knew he needed the time to cope alone, to get himself decently covered so that he would look just like other men. It didn't matter to her. She had seen it many times, but it mattered to him.

When she went back into the bedroom, she saw that she had been right. Lying down in bed, with the sheet thrown across his naked chest, he looked as if he felt more comfortable with himself. Even his face was more like the old Hartley, younger and shining in the candlelight.

She slipped in beside him and turned to face him with a hand held out to feel his face.

"Cait," he said, with wonder in his voice. "My beautiful Caitlin. My Madonna!"

"Don't call me that," she said, surprised. "I'm anything but that! Whatever made you think of it?"

"I'm sorry." He smiled. "It's just the first time I saw you I thought of that."

"In Union Square? In heaven's name, why?" "No, not there. On the quayside in Liverpool. With a baby in your arms. I thought it was yours, you see. I didn't know it was your sister. And you looked so alone, as if you'd been deserted."

The words pierced her, and she began to sob.

"What have I said?" Hartley was shaken to the core. His arms went round her, and she pulled him closer desperately, still sobbing. All the pent-up grief and emotion of the long, lonely years and the exhaustion and strain of the last few weeks filled her crying. "I'm sorry!" he said. "Dearest Cait, I'm so sorry. I'll never call you that again, I promise!"

"Don't leave me, Hartley," she begged. "Please don't leave me now! Please always love me."

He said that he would never leave her, would always love her, had always loved her from that first moment, had wanted her so much in New York yet never dared to ask for fear of being turned down. He knew only too well that he had lost her because of his darned foolishness then. Well, he had learnt his lesson now and would never lose her again. His arms were strong and warm. They kissed each other, and she ran her hands through his soft fair hair and let him play with hers.

Finally, he blew out the candle and made love to her without hesitation for all that he had to twist and turn his body so awkwardly. She was surprised at the depth of his passion and stirred by it. Despite her other men, Caitlin had not felt such happiness before, whilst Hartley felt a vast tide of relief flow through him with his climax. What he had feared most was removed. He had lost his leg, but he wasn't impotent. Caitlin had been correct and, seeing straight through him had known he needed to be shown that he was still a man

The next day, Caitlin went to Miss Cholmondeley and asked to be released from all further duties in the hospital. She would not, after all, be travelling south with her.

Caroline eyed her up shrewdly. "So, he didn't go home then?"

"Who?" asked Caitlin, guiltily.

"Private Shawcross. I have eyes."

"No, he didn't," said Caitlin. "We patch up arms and legs and sides and faces but not hearts and minds. He needs me to do that."

Caroline was checking over a list of requisitions. She frowned. "His wife should do that, my dear."

Caitlin flushed. "She can't. She's much older than him and doesn't love him."

"You don't know that." Miss Cholmondeley laid down her pen and looked at Caitlin severely. "You know it is wrong to steal another woman's husband, Caitlin!"

"I'm not stealing him. I'm just borrowing him for a while. He doesn't want to go back." She knew she was probably lying and would have liked to add that he was hers first anyway but didn't dare. Caroline made her feel too mean and small. "Why is it so wrong?"

she demanded. "After all he's been through. He needs me. I didn't ask him to stay. He did it of his own free will."

Miss Cholmondeley shuffled her papers. "I can make no comment on that," she said. "I know the men have been through a great deal. But I wonder if you are helping him as much as you believe, that is all. Also, I hope to see you back in, shall we say six weeks' time?"

Caitlin continued to think that would never happen for the next month. It was the happiest time she had ever known in her life — that he had known too, she was sure of it. She saw his smile return, not the twisted, wry one he had worn in hospital to cover his pain and fear, but the old, pleasant smile that lit up his agreeable face and his kind eyes. He even laughed at her antics for she had grown very carefree of a sudden. Well, perhaps it was recklessness.

All the same, Caroline's words stayed with her like a thorn in her side, continually twisting and growing bigger. She felt bad about deserting her and she knew what she was doing was wrong. Not as wrong as the time she had spent with Tyrrell. But she felt she had been forced into that through the threat of starvation. This was a different decision, and she had made Hartley comply.

She told him all about her life, one night when he had been dismayed to discover she could drink as much whisky as he could. She told him to force disillusionment and as a catharsis for herself, just as he had told her about the war.

First, she spoke of her father and Bridget rejecting her, of James shooting himself, and how Mrs Regan had sold Maeve to Mr Hooper in Rochester. She even told him about Thaddeus Regan, followed by the story of her life with Owain, how hopeful it had once been, yet how disastrously it had turned out.

"You were right," she admitted sadly. "I didn't really know him. Not the dark side even though he had confessed it. However, he wasn't all bad. Perhaps if I could have carried his children, it might have been different. But once John Brown got his hooks into him, there was no hope."

So, she told him then about Pottawattomie Creek and Harper's Ferry. About the long, cold, lonely winters when she'd taken to drinking and wearing trousers, waiting desperately for Injun George to return, and finally, about Andrew Tyrrell.

"I knew it," said Hartley. "I felt it all along, that you were in some terrible danger."

"Because of what was happening in Kansas?"

"Not just that. One night in New York — it was the night I'd failed to persuade Johann against joining up — I looked out of the window and saw a woman on the street. She was a little like you and, for a moment, I really thought it was you. It gave me great pain."

"She was a streetwalker," said Caitlin, intuitively.

"Yes, and I felt at that very instant you were in the same kind of danger."

She had thought he would be more shocked. He always had been shocked at the slightest impropriety. Now she saw he understood about larger events and did not judge them, for he had grown in stature of mind. She could suddenly see him as an old man, a rather crusty but kind old gentleman in New York, particular to a fault about the small matters such as how people were dressed and whether he could buy the right newspaper, and if children and grandchildren were behaving correctly and yet, underneath all of that, harbouring a great lake of understanding and love. It would be easy to carry on loving him then.

Except he wasn't going back to any of that because she had made him promise.

"So, you see," she said, pouring some more whisky defiantly into her glass, "I have done far worse deeds than you, Hartley Shawcross. I am not your Madonna and never was."

Contrary to her expectations, he refused to be disillusioned and merely smiled at her and squeezed her hand. No, no, he said, that wasn't true. Just think of her courage in leaving Tyrrell, and what good work she had done since! Then he told her how he'd bought a booklet listing the wealthiest citizens when he'd first arrived in New York as a raw emigrant and how he'd imagined, no *seen*, his own name there already. What a fine fellow he'd thought he was! No wonder Caitlin had thrown him up for Owain, he said. Somehow the things he'd thought important once didn't matter a damn now. Not a single flutter of ambition or desire did they raise in his soul. His greatest regret was that his mother had died far away without ever seeing how well he had done. But if the whole factory and shop went up in flames tomorrow, he shouldn't care, as long as Rosa got the insurance.

Caitlin looked at him in distress. "But Hartley," she said, uncomfortably. "You were doing so well. You could again. There was nothing wrong in that. Don't you think that when this depression has passed, you will feel differently?"

For she could see that money was soon going to be a problem as always. He no longer had his Army pay and she did not have her wages from nursing. Their resources were dwindling fast living in a hotel which was expensive. Caitlin could see she would have to get employment. Perhaps she could rejoin Caroline near Richmond and take Hartley with her? But that would never do. Caroline might not take her back under those circumstances and she could never force Hartley back so near the fighting. Yet there must be somewhere they could go and something they could do to live a normal life together.

At the beginning of the second month, Caitlin could see a certain sadness returning to invade Hartley's face. She did her best to distract him, but his dejection soon returned. In her heart she knew why. Their charmed time together was unreal and should be drawing to a close. She tried to push that knowledge to the back of her mind, but it was no good. The sadness grew.

One morning in bed, she found him particularly quiet and reflective, one hand on the stump which was still tender and gave him a great deal of discomfort. She pulled his hand away and wrapped it round herself instead.

"Don't you know?" she asked sleepily but affectionately, "that you are the most marvellous lover that ever was? Hasn't Rosa ever told you that?"

No, he smiled wryly, he couldn't recall that she ever had. There was a short silence. Rosa, he explained after a moment, rather submitted herself to all that as a duty, in the same way she did to childbirth. Though he supposed he could hardly blame her when the two matters were so highly connected in her case. He became more thoughtful and then began to speak of Rachel, his stepdaughter. She was a grand girl, he said warmly. She would be a real beauty and had a good mind with it. His most earnest wish was that Rachel would never have such a hard life as her mother; never have to work her fingers to the bone and worry and grow old before her time like Rosa had. The man she married would have to be a great deal more than decent to satisfy him, though of course, he must be that as well. For he had reached the conclusion that in many ways women's lives were harder than men's.

"Except we don't have to fight," said Caitlin.

"Not on a battlefield perhaps. But everywhere else."

That reminded him of something else. Had she seen in the paper yesterday they were talking about bringing in conscription soon? Of course nothing was more likely, and it occurred to him that Reuben would now be eligible. That was a terrible thought. Reuben would not go off like Johann had. He was a different boy altogether. He would also know exactly what might happen. He would hate it — not just the battles, but everything: the coarseness, the filth, brutality, and stupidity of it all. Reuben, he said, was highly sensitive like his father. Little Friedrich and Jeremiah would be too young to be called up, thank God, even if the war went on for several years yet, and he sometimes thought it might. His youngest was another girl.

Caitlin rose from the bed and put on her robe. It was not a hasty movement, but she could think of nothing to say and felt inadequate. She went to make the coffee so he should not see her face.

He followed her into the sitting room after a short while being much quicker at dressing now. To her embarrassment, he stumped right up to her, on his crutches.

"Have I," he inquired, touching her gently on the shoulder, "upset you by talking about my children?"

"No, of course not," she said, brightly. "Only I must go and get some coffee from the stores. That's the last of it, I'm afraid."

"You needn't go this very minute," he said.

Yes, yes, she must, she insisted. It was in such short supply these days and, even though it was such a high price because of the war, it would soon be sold out if she did not go early. She would fetch him his morning paper too. In a fever, she grabbed her bonnet, tying the strings hastily and, snatching up her cape, almost flew out of the room and down the stairs.

In the street, she could brush away her tears unseen. It was no good. Her heart felt dull and heavy as lead. No matter how much she loved him, it was not going to work. It also came to her in the store, watching the man weigh out the grains of coffee with scrupulous care that Hartley would never leave of his own accord, not after that promise which she had wrung from him so unfairly. He was far too honourable. It would have to be her who cut the cord that bound them.

On the way back she dragged her feet. It was so hard. Too hard for Caitlin Murphy. She realized she had forgotten his paper and went back for it. He must not be without that. After all, he had little else to do out here but read it every day from cover to cover. Was that not a sign of discontent itself? Bitter tears stung her eyes once more. But it was no good. She had to do it. If she didn't, she would just watch him grow a little sadder and guiltier each day, worrying over the children and what he could and could not do. They would end up with so much they could not speak about that there would be nothing at all left in the end.

She entered more calmly and went up to him, putting the paper and the bag of coffee down on the table between them. Then she cupped his chin in her hands and kissed him on the lips. "I love you!" she said. "I love you very much, Hartley Shawcross and I shall always love you." He hugged her and looked happy.

She sat down, took off her bonnet and laid it on the table, playing a little with the strings. Then she sighed and spoke at last. "But Hartley, it's time for you to go back to New York." He looked at her astonished. "You could be back in time for Christmas if you went now."

"But what about you? I can't leave you here alone, Cait!"

"I shall be fine," she said quietly. "I shall go and rejoin Caroline."

"But that will be terrible for you!"

"No. It won't be so bad. And God knows she needs me."

"I could come with you."

"No, Hartley, you can't. You would hate it. I wouldn't put you through that."

"But I could find work somewhere. I do mean to, you know."

"With one leg? Hartley, the only job you can do is the one you already have in New York. It's probably going to rack and ruin without you. I don't believe Rosa is managing as well as she'd have you believe in her letters. You have so much to do there."

"It's because I spoke about the children," said Hartley miserably. "isn't it? I knew I shouldn't have!"

Caitlin put her hand on his shoulder. "Hartley, how could you help but speak of them?"

"No," he said. "I couldn't help it. But I can't help wanting you either."

She hugged him.

"Do you really want me to go?" he asked doubtfully.

"Yes, I do. Not because I don't love you but because I do." She looked at his face hopelessly. "I can see you're not really happy here and I know what you're thinking, even when you don't say it. And I can't be happy if you're not." The more she said, the more she saw it to be true and the better about it she felt. "You must go back,

Hartley, for all our sakes. You couldn't have done it two months ago, but now I know you can."

"But I promised never to leave you," he said sadly.

"I release you from that promise. You made it too easily! It wasn't fair. We wanted to turn the pages back, but we can't. It's my fault just as much as yours."

"You're so brave," said Hartley, wonderingly. "Braver than me. I'll never break my other promise. I'll always love you. I always have."

She smiled.

He put on his Army uniform to go home. Might as well play the part of the wounded soldier coming home from the war, he said wryly.

"Well, why not?" countered Caitlin. Anyway, he looked very good in it, and she told him so.

"Especially with one leg," he grinned. At last, he could joke about it.

"Yes," she agreed, laughing with him. It definitely added authenticity.

They were making rather a gay thing of the leave-taking after all, and she was glad of it, for she had forbade tears.

"If you cry," she had said, "I shall too and I shan't be able to stop. So, you mustn't."

"Only you ought to have medals," she said a while later. "You deserve them."

"Medals!" he said, scornfully. "I don't want medals."

"I've often thought," Caitlin went on, "that we ought to give out medals to the best patients in the wards."

"Oh, would I qualify then?" He was smiling again. "I rather thought I hadn't."

"Well," she pretended to consider. "Certainly not all the times you were sick on my clean floor! But all in all, you weren't too bad. Shall I polish your crutches, Private Shawcross?"

"I think that might prove disastrous."

"Probably! Let me do up your buttons again then. They're all crooked."

Halfway through, he caught her to him and kissed her desperately.

"Hold still, now!" she said with mock severity. "We'll never get to the station if you keep on doing that!"

She felt proud of him on the platform. He did look fine, it was true, and handsome now. His fair hair shone in the pale winter sunlight, his face was solemn, but could soon break into a smile. His figure, after eighteen months of army life, was taut and trim with no paunchiness about it. He looked young and strong again and he was using the crutches more skilfully. Only she knew he still couldn't get that far without becoming too fatigued.

No one, she was glad to see, on the station platform, pitied him. The porters saluted him with respect. Women turned their heads and cast admiring glances at him, despite the missing leg. He would be all right, she thought with relief, when he got back to New York. He would be a success. Nearly eight weeks ago, he had come out of hospital a broken man. She had put him back together again and her heart swelled with pride.

The train was ready to go now, and she felt panic as well as pride. He held her for the last time, very tightly as if he would never let her go and kissed her in full view of the crowd. That Hartley Shawcross should ever do that!

"Thank God," she said, in a strangled voice, "you're not going the other way to Fredericksburg."

"I'll never leave you in my heart!" he said. "One day, we will be together again, I promise!"

"I don't think so, Hartley. It's better not to make promises anymore." Her voice was very low.

"If you don't tell me you believe that I shan't let you go," he whispered fiercely in her ear.

"Very well." She smiled as she stroked his cheek. "I believe you, dearest." Only she didn't.

"Time to get aboard now, sir," said the guard passing by. "Want any help?"

"No, I can manage." He did need help of course, and fortunately the man insisted.

Caitlin shook her head at him severely. "Aren't you the eejit then?"

He was in the carriage above her now, too high to reach and her panic mounted. She tried to impress his every feature upon her mind's eye before it was too late. Then the whistle blew.

"Hartley!" she cried. "You won't do anything foolish, will you? Tell me you won't!" The carriages were beginning to move, and she started to walk along with them. "Please!"

"I won't," he said.

"And you won't tell Rosa about us, will you?"

"No, I won't tell her." He was sliding away but she walked faster then broke into a trot. "I'll write to you!" he shouted.

"But you won't know where I am! Don't, anyway. I'd rather you didn't."

The carriages were beginning to pick up momentum. The porter came up and made her move back.

"Dangerous to do that, ma'am," he said. "Keep back now."

So then she could only stand and wave her handkerchief in farewell, as he did, until the train was almost out of sight, and they couldn't see each other anymore.

Chapter Six

Fredericksburg, December 1862

The battle had been over for three weeks when Caitlin arrived. On the hills above the town, fresh snow had covered the gashed ground, but the wards were still overflowing. Caroline welcomed her back with open arms.

"I knew you'd come!" she cried, hugging her joyously. Her haggard face was flooded with radiance like the touch of the sun. "I knew you would. Oh, Caitlin, I am so glad!"

At this, Caitlin bent her head on the older woman's shoulder and broke down into floods of tears. It was too much to bear such protestations of joy.

"Oh, Caroline!" she wailed. "A love like this will never come again, never! I'm so unhappy!"

Miss Cholmondeley comforted her as best she could until the tears began to subside.

"Just tell me one thing, my child, and then we'll speak of it no more. Did he leave you or did you send him away?"

"I sent him away."

"My brave girl!"

"But now I wish I hadn't!"

"Of course you do! But Caitlin, love will come again. There is always tomorrow. You are still young."

"No, never the same. Not like that."

"Then you must thank God for the happiness you had for a short while. And you did help him, Caitlin! You were right. There now, let's sit down."

Caitlin sank miserably into the chair by the desk in yet another cramped little office. They were all the same. She began to feel as if she had never been away. Only Caroline was not the same. Now that the delight had worn off her face, it looked very thin and pinched. There was a great gap between the collar of her dress and her neck. *Dear God,* thought Caitlin, feeling shocked as she looked at her properly. *What a deal of weight she's lost!* Miss Cholmondeley produced a bottle of whisky and two tumblers from a locked drawer in the desk.

"Come, let us have, what did you used to call it, a 'slug' of whisky to get us through the night!"

Caitlin's eyebrows shot up and she gasped. "Caroline!"

"What is it, my dear?"

"No herbal tea?"

"I threw it away."

"You can't have!"

Miss Cholmondeley was extremely amused. "Well, no, not really. But I must admit that, over the last week or two, I have discovered exactly why the surgeons tell us to give this stuff to the amputees. It does dull the pain somewhat."

"Pain?" Caitlin was alarmed. "Are you in pain, Caroline?"

"Did I say pain?" Miss Cholmondeley poured the whisky into the tumblers. "Not so much. Not actual pain. I didn't mean to use that word. It's more of an ache, really. Nothing much, you understand. But it keeps on nagging away, especially at night which is a nuisance."

"Whereabouts do you feel it?"

"Oh, somewhere here in the stomach." Caroline ran a hand vaguely over her abdomen. Caitlin realized, now she came to look at it, that her stomach was far too large for a woman of her size who was fast losing weight. It looked swollen and it had not been like that two months ago. Caroline saw her questing eyes. "The surgeon says I have a lump," she said.

"You consulted him?"

"Certainly not! But the man wouldn't let me alone until he'd poked and prodded around with his great, dirty hands. 'You have a lump, woman', he says in his loudest voice, as if he wants to announce it to the hospital at large, which of course he does. 'I am quite aware, Major Douglas,' I say, 'that I have a lump. I have been aware that I have had a lump for some considerable time, thank you.' Well, he looked a bit taken aback by that ..."

Despite the sadness in her heart, Caitlin smiled. She could see that Caroline had positively enjoyed discomfiting the surgeon. "What is more," Caroline continued, 'there ain't nuthin' I can do about it,' he said. 'It's gone too far.' 'Well, I could have told you that,' I said. 'You're wasting valuable time on me, Major Douglas.'"

An extremely young nurse popped her head round the door. "Excuse me, ma'am. Casualties coming in from a raid on a scouting party. Two of them are hurt bad."

"I'll be there directly." Miss Cholmondeley rose from the desk with some difficulty and rummaged in the cupboard behind her for clean bandages, her narrative immediately forgotten. Caitlin went to help her.

"But, Caroline," she said with concern. "If you have a lump that has grown so large, then surely you should go home?"

"Nonsense, my dear. What good would that do? Major Douglas agrees with you, of course. He wants to get rid of me, no doubt. 'It'll get you in the end', he says to me, 'you mark my words!' 'Thank you so much, Major,' I say, 'for your invaluable advice!'" Caroline chuckled. "It was naughty of me, I know. And, of course, he is right and was only trying to help, poor man. It will get me, and the end is coming nearer all the time. Sometimes at night, I think I can feel it on its way, silent but sure."

"Oh, Caroline!"

She turned to Caitlin and smiled, putting out a hand to lift her crestfallen chin. "Don't look so sad, my child! I have no fear of death. I shall welcome it. But I'm not going to sit down and wait for it to come whilst there is work to be done. The good Lord will take me when he's ready and not before. And hopefully not before this place is cleaned up! Come with me and you'll see what I mean." She steered her along the corridor to the ward. Caitlin had already temporarily forgotten about Hartley.

"We should have had this place shipshape by now," said Miss Cholmondeley, a little despondently. "It does vex me so that it isn't. Antietam was much worse to begin with. But I think the staff there were better in the end. I can't seem to get through to these people. Perhaps I'm just getting tired and not making myself clear. Now you've come, it will be better. You are such a comfort to me, dear. I've missed you more than I can say."

"And where," asked Caitlin, to deflect this eulogy. "Are the army going next?"

"I really don't know. General Burnside doesn't seem to be a great improvement on McClellan. There's a tremendous amount of shillyshallying going on by the sound of it. First we hear North, then we hear South."

It made no difference. North or South, there would remain plenty of work to be done. Caitlin took in the familiar long lines of wounded, battered men. Thank God Hartley was out of all this! She felt sobered as she watched the strangely emaciated yet swollen figure of her friend passing down the lines, dispensing comfort everywhere. What a shabby reward for all her work God was giving her, Caitlin thought bitterly! She swore silently that she would stay with her now until the end came.

≈

January was drawing to a close when Caitlin realized she was pregnant. At first, she could not believe it, but all the usual signs were there. It was extraordinary because she had spent two years with Tyrrell, and nothing had happened. Granted, he had often been away or drunk or she had managed to avoid him somehow, but she had come to believe that conception was no longer possible for her. Yet now, after only a little more than six weeks with Hartley, she found she was wrong. Foolishly, she felt a warm glow of elation inside.

The next moment she was cast down again. It couldn't succeed. The doctor in Kansas had said she'd never get beyond the first four months. Soon it would be over, like all the others. That would be for the best of course. It wouldn't make a difference to her life or leave her with an extra burden, but she would feel disappointed. Oh, well. She wouldn't tell anyone about it until she had to.

However, the very next morning, Caroline, her eagle eye undimmed by illness, caught her quietly vomiting into a basin in a dark corner.

"What is it?" she cried. "Caitlin, are you ill?"

Caitlin emerged sheepishly, wiping her mouth, a cloth hastily drawn over the basin.

"No, no, Caroline, it's nothing," she said cheerfully. "I'm not ill. I was merely overcome by ...by some spasm. It's gone now."

Caroline looked at her long and hard.

"No, you're not ill," she said eventually. "You're not ill at all. You're well, in fact you're positively blooming! You're with child, aren't you?"

Caitlin fidgeted nervously from one foot to the other.

"Well, aren't you?"

"Yes. I'm sorry."

"Come into my office for a moment."

Caitlin followed her with a sigh. But Caroline, she noted, was not in the least annoyed. She was looking for her quill and paper. "I shall write a note releasing you," she said. "Of course, I must do that. It's unthinkable that you should be lifting hulking great weights of men up and down all day! We shall say, I think, that Private Griffith was unfortunately shot down at Fredericksburg, and you need compassionate leave. No one will know any different."

"But I don't need you to release me, Caroline," Caitlin protested. "I can do the work. It'll make no difference at all. The pregnancy will fail anyway."

"Make no difference?" said Caroline, astonished. "Whatever do you mean?"

"You've forgotten," said Caitlin softly. She did forget, increasingly of late. "But I believe I mentioned it when I first came to you. I can't carry children, Caroline. I always lose them, early on. I suppose the work here might bring it on a little quicker but it's inevitable anyway, I'm afraid."

"Oh dear!" said Caroline, her pen arrested in the air. "I do hope not." She looked genuinely distressed.

"Hope doesn't enter into it anymore: I've learnt that. When it happens, I'll go and lie up in the hotel for a few days. If you could get me something from the hospital at that time, I'd be grateful. I shan't want anyone else to know, of course."

"But my dear child ...!" Caroline wrung her hands fretfully. "It could be dangerous for you!"

"Perhaps. The doctor in Kansas seemed to think so. But that was a long time ago, Caroline. I was weaker then. I'll get well again. Don't you worry!"

"I do hope so, Caitlin. It seems so very hard." Miss Cholmondeley screwed the paper into a ball. Her eyes were wet. She was thinking that, if Caitlin should by any misfortune precede her into the great unknown, she couldn't be sure, for the very first time in her life, that she could forgive her Maker for it.

≈

Gettysburg, June 30th 1863

Caitlin straightened up, one hand in the aching small of her back. Already the casualties were coming in, though the news was 'good', whatever that might mean. She bent down again to check that the bleeding from the soldier's arm had been stemmed. Yes, it had. He had a gash on his chest too, but that was only superficial. She cleaned it up and strapped a clean pad over it. He watched her do it cheerfully, fully conscious. He hadn't lost much blood. One of the luckier ones. Could have been treated on the lines really. Only she hoped he would fare better here. It was a dreadful irony when the lesser wounded ended up with blood-poisoning or pneumonia.

The man cleared his throat. "My wife is in your condition," he said.

Caitlin smiled. "That's nice."

"Wouldn't have thought they'd let the likes of you work here, though."

"Well, Miss Cholmondeley, who runs this ward, is rather a law unto herself."

"Ain't complainin'." He winked. Then he said, needing reassurance, "Been lucky haven't I, nurse?"

"Yes," said Caitlin. "you've been very lucky."

"Times this morning thought I wouldn't be. Thought I'd never see that baby born. I wouldn't mind so much only it's my first. I will get to see it now, won't I, nurse?"

"Don't worry, sergeant," she said, glancing down at the stripes on the blue sleeve she'd cut off. "We'll soon have you home."

Passing along the line, in her blessedly loose dress, she looked up and saw Caroline leaning against the opposite wall. Like her, she had put her hands into her back. For six months they had both struggled on through some of the worst battles of the war. They both had swollen abdomens now. But inside Caitlin's bump, a new life was stirring and kicking, hardier and more determined to survive than her others it seemed. For against all the odds she had not lost it whilst Caroline's tumour only bore the seeds of destruction.

For weeks now, Caitlin had watched her anxiously, expecting at any moment to see the legs that dragged her along fail. The time was overdue when she should have taken to her bed.

Now, even as she looked, her legs buckled underneath her, and she saw Caroline slip down onto the floor. At once she threaded her way through the lines of groaning men. Caroline did not groan though her pain must have been approaching a similar intensity for she was panting hard.

"Come on, Caroline. You're going back to the office." She helped her there and into a chair. It was a titan struggle. Caroline's face was grey. Surely this is it, at last, thought Caitlin desperately. She can't go on like this day after day, racked by these sudden spasms of pain and breathless if she moves at more than a snail's pace. It's not humanly possible.

"Shall I give you some more opium?" she asked.

Caroline shook her head. "No. It only makes me want to sleep. It'll pass."

"Whisky then?"

She nodded her approval, and Caitlin poured it out.

After she had drunk it, she said faintly, "You know, my dear, I have the strangest feeling from what they are saying. I feel this will be the decisive battle, the last of the great ones. The tide will turn with it. The end shall be in sight."

"Perhaps it will." Caitlin was less sure. They had said that before. The Federals were reported to be winning now but it was still early in the day.

"One thing's certain anyway," and Caroline attempted a smile. "It's our last battle, isn't it, Cait, you and I?"

"Yes," said Caitlin quietly. "It is. It's time for us both to rest now."

Caroline nodded and drifted off into a semi-conscious state, halfway between sleeping and waking. The door opened and one of the surgeons strode in in Army uniform. It was Major Douglas who had examined Caroline previously.

"Oh," he said shortly. "I see." That was all.

"I know it's a very bad time," said Caitlin, firmly, "with the men just starting to come in. But I really think I ought to take her back to our lodgings."

He nodded. "Undoubtedly. I'll commandeer the first buggy I can get for you."

"Would you authorize some medical supplies for her, too?"

"Of course."

"Thank you."

"Thank you, Nurse Griffith. I don't need to tell you how to make her comfortable, I'm sure. She's in your hands. Stay with her. It would hardly be right for her to be alone after all the suffering she's eased. And afterwards, I suspect I won't be seeing you here again either, will I? You should rest in your condition."

"Yes," agreed Caitlin. "It's time for me to go too. I'm very sorry. But I can't really manage very well, not during a major battle."

"No need to be sorry," he said gruffly. "I'm amazed you've stuck with it as long as you have. And I thought *she'd* be dead months ago. Should have been, you know. She's willed herself to stay alive."

He hesitated and Caitlin saw he wanted to say more.

"I'm sorry to see both of you go. Tell her that, would you?" He nodded his head in the direction of Miss Cholmondeley. "When she's clearer. Tell her I'll miss having her on my wards. I shan't have anyone to argue with anymore."

Caitlin smiled. What was more, she noticed as he went out, bluff and grumpy to the last, that his hands were scrupulously clean. She must remember to tell Caroline that. It would please her so much.

For the next three days, Caitlin nursed Miss Cholmondeley in the rooms they shared together. All the while, cannon boomed and roared up on the heights above the town. Caroline was too far gone to hear it. Her pain was severe, but Caitlin quickly stepped up the opium and she slept a great deal. In her conscious moments, she asked Caitlin to read to her from the Bible. Occasionally, she began talking unexpectedly though she sometimes drifted off again in the middle of what she was trying to say, leaving the words hanging in the air.

"I used to have money once, you know," she said in one of these periods. "Rather a lot of it. I came from what in England they call a good family. But it's all gone now, my share of it anyway. I gave it away, being mindful of the camel that couldn't pass through the eye of the needle."

Caitlin murmured something of praise. Caroline took no notice.

"Only I wish I'd kept some of it now. Not for me but for you, my dear. Oh, whatever will you do?" she asked fretfully, "When the child is born? With no one in the world to help you. All alone?"

Caitlin reassured her. She would manage, she said. Caroline must not worry about it.

Then again, sometime later, quite forgetting her earlier remark, "You must go home, Caitlin. When I am gone, you must go home to your family in the North. Battle-torn Virginia is no place to bring up a child. Go home to your family. I cannot believe they would turn you away. They will accept the child."

Caitlin said that she would. Her family would take good care of her and the child. She was sure they would. She felt it was an entirely justifiable lie.

Then, finally, Caroline asked if she could feel the baby move. Caitlin guided her hands to the likely places and prayed that Hartley's child would not take too long to comply lest the dying woman might fall unconscious again. Thankfully, it was co-operative, and Caroline smiled.

"I am going out," she said contentedly. "But another life is on the way in. I feel it will be an important one and significant somehow. That means a great deal to me. You see, Caitlin, the Lord is not stupid and is good after all. You don't think so, but He is."

"I knew it," she claimed, after a short silence. "From the very first moment you told me. I knew it would not die. It is the good which comes from your life." Then she closed her eyes again.

Those were the last words she ever spoke. After that, she remained in a coma, the harsh tide of her breathing rising up and down like the waves on the shore. The next day it began to falter. It would stop for a while, then start again and so on. When she died at last, it was so quietly and so peacefully, that Caitlin, dozing in her chair, was not aware of it until she woke a short time later. She started to her feet guiltily, but Caroline's deathmask was perfectly composed. There was almost a smile on her lips. No pain and no suffering anymore.

Carefully, Caitlin closed her eyes and folded her hands across her chest. Then she took some soap and water and gently washed her face and hands and combed her hair. Caroline, of all people, would wish to be clean and presentable to meet her Maker. *Though God knows,* thought Caitlin with conscious irony, *if he doesn't welcome this woman with open arms, He won't welcome anybody, Catholic or no Catholic.*

It was still daytime, yet the guns had stopped some time ago which was odd. In the streets of the nearby town, there was a great rumpus. The Yankees had won! For the first time, the Yankees had clearly and categorically won. The Yankees were coming! The townspeople were terrified. What was more, the telegraph was alive with news. Vicksburg had surrendered to Grant! It seemed that nothing could stop them now. The tide really had turned.

Caitlin knew nothing of this as yet. When she found out, she would wonder with awe how Caroline had somehow known in advance and reflected on how fitting that was.

For now, she reflected on other things, sitting quietly in her chair, watching respectfully over Caroline's body. She felt strangely calm and contemplative and not alone at all.

The baby continued to kick within her. It was growing stronger every day. She hadn't had a single problem with this pregnancy — not one — and was proud of it, though somewhat amazed. It had not, after all, it seemed, been her fault she couldn't give Owain children.

It must have been some mismatch between them, some ill reaction. She wondered at that and wondered too at Caroline's prophecy for the future of this child. Of course, it was just the fancy of a dying woman and yet Caroline, dear good Caroline, had been so wise. Might it not be true?

However, she couldn't sit here forever and contemplate the world. She had Caroline's burial to arrange. She also had to pack her own bags and make travel arrangements. She had decided some hours ago what she must do. Go home, Caroline had said. But she had no home. Still, she must go North now. There was no other alternative. She had been too proud to do it for herself, but the child must be cared for. A week later, she boarded the train to New York.

Part Seven

The Homecoming

Chapter One

July 1863

In New York she stopped overnight in the seediest of hotels, that being the only one she could afford. In the morning, she changed trains. She had forgotten how crowded and noisy New York was, and how hot it became in July; though she had once arrived on such a day, a greenhorn with wondering eyes in a green velvet dress. She wasn't a greenhorn now — she was an American.

I have paid you my dues, she thought. *I have battled through these streets; I have sweated in your workshops. I have been a pioneer and driven a covered wagon out West and scythed your corn and lost it all. I made ammunition for the Free State Party in Lawrence under siege. I have fought your campaigns and tended your war-wounded in Virginia. I have done all of that. Now I am coming home and carrying a new American inside of me. I once wore fine clothes and bonnets with silly plumes and carried a parasol. Now that is all done with. I am coming home to you as I set out, with less in fact, in a simple homespun dress of grey cotton, and I must ask you to do something for me.*

It was sweltering in the wagon car although it was still only morning. She took off her stiff grey bonnet and patterned brown shawl and ran a hand through her moist, dark curls as the sweat poured down the back of her neck. New York in summer was a burdensome place to be carrying a seven-month-old baby.

As the train set off and rattled further north, the air grew fresher, and she began to revive. They crossed the Hudson River on shining metal tracks, and passed lakes, shimmering blue under the sun. Leafy green trees, unscorched by the fires of war, reappeared. After some hours, the line of the old Catskill Mountains came into view. We will still be here, they seemed to say, when you are gone, and all this has passed away.

They steamed past somnolent little towns each with its own white church, and fertile farms where the pumpkins were beginning to swell in the fields. Sleepy Hollow country, all glowing golden in the midday sun. Here were towering chestnut trees and a gentle spell in the valleys. The whistle of the engine saluted each hamlet and town.

In Albany, they forked west, leaving the Hudson behind, following the line of the Genesee River and the slowly decaying Erie Canal. *I am going home,* she thought once more, the palms of her hands resting on her distended abdomen, *although I have never been there before.*

It was evening when she alighted from the train in Rochester. The journey, once thought to be so long and arduous, had paled into insignificance compared with her past travels. But she was stiff from sitting so long and glad to stretch her legs again. The sun seemed more golden than ever. *I am here,* she thought. *This is going to be my home and I shall see Maeve again though I will scarcely recognize her.*

She had to ask the stationmaster the way. Rochester was a bustling place where flour mills ground their machinery every day by the side of the tumbling Genesee Falls. The river mouth opened into Lake Ontario with British North America on the other shore. The place that all slaves dreamed about and where the Underground Railroad terminated. The place where, in the fall, flame leaves covered the graves of free blacks and liberal activists alike in its cemetery.

The stationmaster directed her to East Avenue, a broad road flanked by stately beech trees with mansions built in the classical style. This was surely the wealthiest portion of the town. Her hopes were confirmed. Mr Hooper was still alive, and he lived right here. The stationmaster even knew him. She guessed everyone in Rochester knew him.

She found the gateway and entered. There was a long sweeping drive and a beautiful garden, the most beautiful garden she had ever seen, full of flowering shrubs and graceful, many-toned trees, leading up to a vast white house with creeper on the walls and a columned doorway. It was grander than the sketch in Mrs Regan's drawing-room and it was here that her nerve failed her. What could she, Caitlin Murphy, possibly have to do with anyone who lived in such a house? Doubts rose thick and fast.

Supposing he was sick? He must be in his sixties at least by now. Supposing he was angry at her ridiculous presumption? Supposing he threw her out? How could she have imagined for a moment that she would ever be received in such a place?

She stiffened her resolve, for the sake of her unborn child who must have a home. She walked on down the driveway and up the intimidating steps of white marble. She rang the bell, a slight, dark figure in a poor grey dress swollen by pregnancy, carrying only a shawl and a bonnet with bedraggled strings and one small carpetbag.

A maidservant answered. Her sharp eyes narrowed in suspicion as she absorbed the caller's appearance and shape.

"We don't receive beggars here," she said, pertly. "Nor gipsies." She looked at Caitlin's long, dark curls and travel-stained face.

Caitlin wished for the earth to open up and swallow her. But surely at any moment she would hear the trip of young feet on the grand sweeping mahogany staircase she glimpsed through the door, and hear a girl's inquisitive, lively voice.

"I'm neither of those," she said, awkwardly, though of course that was exactly what she was. She began to panic. "I've come to see - Miss Hooper."

The maid looked startled. "Wait a moment," she said. "I'll fetch the housekeeper. "And she closed the door.

Caitlin waited. She was just about to ring the bell again when the door reopened. A big, black woman, well-dressed, bustling and very authoritative, stood on the threshold. *I's a free black,* her manner declared. *I ain't no Eliza, Thomasina nor Sophy. I ain't your Mammy. I's a Mrs and proud of it. I works for Mr Hooper but he ain't my mas'r. I's not a slave.* She looked at Caitlin crossly.

"What you doing here, woman, asking questions 'bout that poor chile?" she demanded.

Caitlin shrank inside. "I just wanted to see her, that's all. I looked after her for a while in New York before she came here. I only wanted to see her again and know how she was growing up."

The housekeeper's face underwent a strange spasm and she sniffed. "Then you come a mite too late," she said grimly. "Miss Maeve, she ain't here no more. She done gone an' took pneumonia two years ago and died. Mrs Hooper died the following fall. They said that was an attack of the colic, but it wasn't. It was a broken heart. And Mr Hooper, he ain't never been the same since, Lord bless him!"

Caitlin reeled against the columns of the doorway. In all her suppositions, she had never once considered this. She could not believe that death would dare to sweep down that driveway and knock at the door of such a grand house. Death was for the streets of New York and a thousand other cities and the grim battlefields of war, not here! She burst into tears.

"You come a long way to see this chile?" asked the black woman, kindlier now, seeing her distress.

Caitlin nodded.

"I guess you better come inside then." The housekeeper took her carpetbag and plonked it down in the hall, then returned to help her inside to a chair.

"Come on, now. I can see you ain't in no condition to stand."

She supposed the woman must have been some kind of nursemaid in New York. Caitlin sank into the chair and covered her face with her hands. In her imposed darkness, waves of misery engulfed her.

The housekeeper touched her arm. "Follow me," she said, and taking her up again, led her into an immense drawing-room off the hall. "Look!" she commanded. "You ain't got no reason to cry. That's Miss Maeve when she was four or five." She indicated a painting which hung over the hearth. "That's her puppy dog, Brutus on her lap. Brutus is an old dog now, but he's a great comfort to Mr Hooper."

Caitlin wiped her eyes and looked at the study in oils. A little girl with black curls and blue eyes looked back at her happily. She was plump in the face and shoulders and was dressed in a gossamer creation of white, sprigged cotton. A young black puppy sat on her lap. She was everything she had imagined her to be.

"And this," said the housekeeper, picking up a silver-framed daguerreotype from a polished table nearby. "This was taken shortly before she got ill. In her first real party gown."

Caitlin took hold of the frame in wonder. There she was, older now and slender, with the beginnings of sophistication, a rose at the bosom of her lovely dress.

"Yes," sighed the black woman, dabbing at her own eyes. "Miss Maeve, she had a short life. She wasn't quite thirteen when the Good Lord took her. But she sure had a happy one. Lor' knows, no chile was ever treated better. She had puppy dogs and kittens and ponies and fine clothes, and respectable chillun for friends. She had everythin' she wanted and the most devoted and lovin' of parents. Not that she was spoilt for all that. I took care to see to that." The housekeeper's face softened. "But I never had to scold that much. My Miss Maeve, she was a good chile. She had sunshine pouring out of her every day. These pictures always stay in here though Mr Hooper, he couldn't bear to look at them for a long time."

Caitlin thought of Bridget Murphy and of Mrs Regan. They had been right. So, she mustn't give up now. Like them, she too had a child to consider. She took a deep breath.

"I would so much like to see Mr Hooper."

The housekeeper's eyes narrowed. "I's not sure about that."

"Oh, please! I must."

"You better pull yourself together then. Mr Hooper, he too good a man to be upset by the likes of you and me!"

He was in the back garden. Another garden. The black woman led her out the back door down a terrace, flowering in profusion, past a splashing fountain and across a wooded lawn. He was sitting under the trees in a white bathchair. An aging man with snowy white hair and portly frame. Caitlin felt scared though his face was kind. He was trying to read a newspaper, but it was obvious that, for all his horn-rimmed spectacles and the aid of a magnifying glass he held close to the page, he couldn't see the print very well. He folded the paper away hastily when he saw them, but the housekeeper scolded him all the same.

"There you go, strainin' your old eyes again!" she accused him. Her tone was hectoring but Mr Hooper seemed to take it in his stride. "This woman come asking to see you at the door. Her name's Griffith. She came asking 'bout Miss Maeve. Seems she looked after her in New York. But I tole her what happened." And she retreated across the lawn, dabbing her eyes with a large red handkerchief and then pretending to swot away the flies with it.

Chapter Two

Mr Hooper sat in his cane chair next to a wrought iron table on which he had laid his paper. On the other side of the table was another chair, also in wrought iron. He indicated it to Caitlin, and she sat down nervously. They looked at each other in the ensuing silence. The sunlight shone through the leaves of an overhead tree and dappled them with chequered shadows. Everything was green and golden. The sound of the fountain splashing in the distance and the birds singing were the only disturbance beside the light breeze turning the leaves of the tree.

"I'm sorry you've had a wasted journey, Mrs Griffith," he said politely. His voice was rather gruff. He took a watch on a chain from his waistcoat pocket and examined it, resetting the hands before putting it back. She liked his face. It was broad and not at all shrivelled despite his age, though she saw now that he must be approaching seventy, at least. He had a wide mouth, a freckled skin and eyes that must have been merry once. "You looked after my Maeve in Mrs Regan's house?" he asked gently.

"Yes."

"I am sorry you had to come so far to find out."

Further than you think, thought Caitlin.

"We never kept in touch, I'm afraid. Once, when Maeve was growing up and becoming curious about her origins, we tried."

So, he had not concealed the truth. She was glad of it.

"But the Regans house had burned down apparently, and they had moved to Boston. We did manage to contact Polly Regan who told us her mother had been widowed but she never mentioned a nursemaid, Mrs Griffith..."

The time had come to confess. "I wasn't a nursemaid," said Caitlin. "Before my marriage, my name was Murphy. I was Maeve's half-sister."

She was unprepared for the strength of his reaction. He leant forward in his bathchair and adjusted his spectacles with a little cry.

"Caitlin?" he asked immediately. "You are Caitlin? Come closer, my dear. I want to see. My eyes are not good."

She moved her chair timidly, feeling embarrassed. "I don't know that we looked alike," she said apologetically. "We had different mothers."

"But there is something!" he continued with excitement. "Now I can see it. Not the eyes. Hers were not as blue as yours. But there is something in the face and the hair. Yes, the hair is the same. I wonder, would you mind indulging an old man? Would you let down your hair and bring it forward round your face like a young girl's?"

She did so shyly.

"Yes," he said at last, after a long inspection. "You are indeed her. You are Caitlin Murphy." He took off his spectacles in his emotion and she saw that his eyes were wet.

"I am very sorry," she said. "To upset you. Your housekeeper asked me not to."

He chuckled. "Oh, don't listen to her! She wraps me in wool. It's completely unnecessary."

She realized then he was intensely excited, as well as being moved. "What a humdinger of a day!" he exclaimed. "You see, you were the reason we wrote to Mrs Regan! Maeve wanted to know about my dear, her origins. I told her how she'd been brought to New York from Ireland in steerage with only an older sister to fend for her. 'What are you filling her head with that stuff for,' Mrs Hooper used to say? She didn't like it. But Maeve did. It was her favourite story because she could remember none of it. She wanted it told to her over and over again. What had it been like, she wanted to know? Had the ship been through a great storm? How old was her sister? What was she like? Was she pretty? What was she doing now?" Mr Hooper sighed sadly. "Of course, I didn't really know. So, I'm afraid I made it all up. But Maeve didn't mind. She knew I made it up. We made up stories together. About Caitlin and how brave she was. How you had probably married a fine man in New York, but we were sure that one day you would come to see us."

Mr Hooper folded and unfolded his spectacles in agitation. "Then we learnt what had happened to the Regans a considerable time after the event, I regret to say. Four wasted years. I asked Polly what had become of you. She said you had married but moved to Kansas, that she had received some letters from you but then they had stopped coming and she never understood the reason why. She had no idea where you were now, but she was afraid you might have been killed in the troubles out there, for she could not believe you would have stopped writing to her otherwise."

Caitlin's cheeks burnt with shame.

"I didn't tell Maeve that," Mr Hooper went on. "I couldn't. We went on making up stories instead. 'One day,' she said, 'Caitlin will come and find us.' Of course, I no longer believed that, but I told her I did. My dear child, why did you not come?"

"I never imagined," said Caitlin, her voice unsteady. "That it was like that. I never thought you would want me to. In fact, I believed the reverse."

It was Mr Hooper's turn to look ashamed. "I shouldn't tell you this," he said, "but truth will out in the end. When we decided to adopt Maeve, I wanted to take you too, but Mrs Regan told us you were wayward, and would bring us nothing but trouble. I thought that sounded like a great deal of nonsense. Only it made Mrs Hooper nervous. 'Just the child,' she said. 'We can bring up a child our own way but not change a grown young woman.' So, we just took the child. I fear we did you a great wrong, but Mrs Regan insisted that what you needed was a husband as quickly as possible and she could find you one in New York. She was a very strong woman, though not too proud to ask for money."

Caitlin thought bitterly about the unrelenting bosom in the Union Square house.

"Still," said Mr Hooper, even more sadly, "what's done is done. She's dead now, you know. We should not speak ill of the dead. No doubt she meant it for the best."

Then he slapped his hand on his thick thigh and appeared to cheer up. "But now you're here. You came at last!"

"Too late," said Caitlin in a small voice. "Through my own stupid pride. I'm very sorry, Mr Hooper."

"It's never too late, my dear. Is your husband here with you in Rochester?"

Caitlin lifted her head. "No," she said. "He was killed."

"Of course," he said. "The War. For a moment, I had almost forgotten about the wretched war. I am so sorry. Do you have other children?"

"No. This is the first I have managed to carry for so long. That is why I came to you, Mr Hooper. As you can see, I need a refuge. I am not afraid to work. However, I cannot work in my condition at present. Still, I do not intend to throw myself upon your charity like a pauper." She lifted her chin a little higher with determination.

"I shall be able to work again," she said, "once the child is born. I came to ask you for shelter, Mr Hooper, but also for employment. Not for pay, but in return for my keep and that of the child's."

Mr Hooper was bemused. "Employment? But, my dear, what could I possibly give you to do?"

"I can do many things. I can cook and clean and sew, and I am a very good nurse."

"But I have a housekeeper and a cook and maids. I even have a nurse and though I'd dearly love to be rid of her I cannot put her out on the streets! There is nothing I need. And am I to put my Maeve's half-sister to work like a common servant? It's unthinkable! Surely you can allow me to take care of you for Maeve's sake, for the mistakes made in the past. It would give me great satisfaction."

"No," said Caitlin with difficulty. "I cannot. You are most kind, but it's all happened before. I have always been a burden, and I cannot bear to be one again. I must earn my keep."

Mr Hooper was clearly flummoxed. It seemed preposterous. What was he to do with her? Then his eye alighted on the newspaper on the table, and he leant forward eagerly.

"Can you read? Yes, you must be able to read! Polly Regan told me you wrote her letters."

"Yes, I can read quite well. An uncle in Ireland taught me."

"Then read this to me. No, not there. Here!" He pointed with a stubby finger. "This is what I want to hear."

It was the transcript of Mr Lincoln's speech on his visit to Gettysburg.

"*Four score and seven years ago,*" Caitlin began, "*our fathers brought forth on this continent a new nation, conceived in Liberty, dedicated to the proposition that all men are created equal.*

Now, we are engaged in a great civil war, testing whether that nation or any nation so conceived and so dedicated can long endure. We are met on a great battlefield of that war. We have come to dedicate a portion of that field, as a final resting-place for those who here gave their lives that that nation might live. It is altogether fitting and proper that we should do this.

But in a larger sense, we cannot dedicate - we cannot consecrate - we cannot hallow this ground. The brave men - living and dead - who struggled here have consecrated it, far above our poor power to add or detract. The world will little note, nor long remember what we say here, but it can never forget what they did here. It is for us, the living, rather, to be dedicated here to the unfinished work which they who fought here have thus so nobly far advanced. It is rather for us to be here dedicated to the great task remaining before us - that from these honoured dead we take increased devotion to that cause for which they gave the last full measure of devotion - that we here highly resolve that these dead shall not have died in vain - that this nation, under God, shall have a new birth of freedom - and that government of the people, by the people, for the people shall not perish from the earth."

There was a long silence. Caitlin had read it well, with expression. Whilst she had done so she had thought of young Johann Kleist, little Tim O'Reilly, whom she had never met but heard much of, dear, cheerful Ralph James, Hartley and all the men she had ever nursed. She felt moved, and at the end of it, she thought of Washington, the runaway slave, not his famous namesake, and his wife, Kitty. Despite all the wrongdoing, the awful mistakes, the cruelties on both sides, this is what it had been about even if the North had fought for different reasons in the end.

"Yes," said Mr Hooper after a long time, "that is exactly what he should have said. He is a great man, and after the war, he will heal the nation, thank God. It will all come right." He sat back in his chair and smiled at her warmly.

"Well, my dear, you read extremely well, not quite well! You have your employment."

"But it isn't enough," protested Caitlin.

"It is more than enough. I daresay I shall need you to fetch my rug as well when the fall comes. I am sure I shall be querulous and trying when I require you to listen to me and to talk back. Don't you understand? I am asking you for companionship. I am a rich man, but I cannot buy it, and it is something I now value above all else. It is no mean thing to a lonely old man who only has memories left, cannot get about much anymore, cannot see too clearly, and cannot remember as well as he used to. Will you accept my employment, Miss Murphy, and my protection? It would give me a great deal of pleasure if you would."

She bent her head in humble gratitude. "Yes, Mr Hooper. Thank you."

≈

On August the twenty-eighth, her son was born a fine, strong, healthy boy. She named him Hartley. After the birth, Mr Hooper seemed to take on a new lease of life. He left his bathchair for hours at a time and stumped about house and garden with a stick, poking into everything, making plans, enquiring about the child's welfare every day and generally antagonising Millie, the housekeeper, in her renewed role as nanny.

"I feel," he said. "Like the grandfather I thought I would never be!"

Caitlin, lying in bed, warm and comfortable, with her baby son in her arms, smiled at him. By now, she knew him well and knew what was on his mind, though he was afraid to ask it.

"Would you like him to be?" she asked.

His face lit up.

So, the child became Hartley Shawcross Hooper.

≈

In April 1865, they celebrated Lee's surrender at Appomattox. Hartley Junior was almost two years old by then and growing fast — a sunny, happy little boy with fair hair and blue eyes, more like his father than his mother, but chattering away.

Long ago, Caitlin had woken up one morning and realized she was happy. She led a quiet life and did not socialize, though Mr Hooper had planned she should. The happiness had stolen up on her unawares. She was content enough and tranquil with the child and the old man's companionship and loved them both. At last, she had her own family.

He needs me, she thought, as a daughter as well as a friend, and he appreciates me. He never pours scorn on what I say, never minds how I look or what I do. And I am his eyes, for it was evident that he was rapidly going blind. She found, after all, that the greatest pleasure came from doing things for him and not what he was doing for her and her son. It was no longer necessary to be loved, though she was. She had found that loving was better. Just as she loved her son whom she knew was bound to leave her one day and yet always be part of her.

There were other matters she put right, too. She wrote to Polly and begged her forgiveness with an explanation of how she couldn't bear to continue to write after what had happened to Owain in Kansas. Polly wrote back immediately with great joy and invited her to stay in Boston. She went but did not stay too long lest Mr Hooper and little Hartley should grieve too much without her.

Polly had grown into a fine woman, as loving and good as ever, with a large family and the support of her John. After confiding in her friend and much pleading from Polly, Caitlin allowed her to write to Hartley Shawcross and tell him where she was and that she was safe and happy, though she made her promise not to tell him about his son.

That April of 1865 was marred by one tragic event, shocking and incredible. Abraham Lincoln was assassinated at Ford's theatre. Caitlin read the account of it to Mr Hooper from the newspaper.

"Don't go on," he said. "I cannot bear it. Reconstitution will never take place now. I fear for the South. The nation will bleed again and bleed repeatedly."

It was the only time she saw him sad, except when she related her experiences in Kansas and during the Civil War, for she told him everything eventually. She even told him about Hartley Shawcross one day after seeing a small piece in the newspaper about 'the amazing rise of the paper pattern industry.' It reported that The Friedrich Kleist Paper Pattern Company, based in New York, was about to open a mail-order branch and carried an interview with its owner and company director, Mr Hartley Shawcross, a Civil War veteran and supplier of uniforms to the Federal Army, a railroad king, respected industrialist, and philanthropist. Mr Hooper did not judge, but she made him swear never to tell anyone Hartley Shawcross was her son's father.

"Not if that is your wish," he said. "But don't you think Hartley — both of the Hartleys — should know?"

She shook her head, for she had told the boy his father had died gloriously in the War.

"But truth will out, my dear, in the end. It always does. Especially considering the way you have named him."

She cut out the newspaper article and kept it with a glow of pride and satisfaction in her heart. He was a great success. She hoped he was happy, too.

Chapter Three

October 1885

Twenty years passed, though now, looking back, it didn't seem like it. Where had they gone? Twenty falls, twenty winters when the snow fell deep in Rochester, twenty springs and summers. Caitlin sometimes found it hard to remember she had lived anywhere else or led any different life.

Young Hartley had grown into a fine young man of whom she was intensely proud. More handsome than his father, she thought critically, though very like him. Not as diffident. Nevertheless, he had Hartley's vein of seriousness and worthiness in him along with her spirit. His education was complete, and he had taken over the running of Mr Hooper's flour mills, though he had other ambitions, including political ones. He would soon marry a girl in Rochester, and Caitlin was fond of her and felt her son had chosen well regarding character.

Nevertheless, the idea struck a certain panic inside her. Mr Hooper was now a very old man fast approaching ninety, totally blind and almost confined to his bath chair, requiring a significant amount of care. His mind remained alert, and she still read the papers to him every day. But one day, he would die. And what will I do then, thought Caitlin? He will leave a great hole in my life.

Of course, I shall still see young Hartley, possibly even live with the married couple, as they have told me repeatedly, but how different it would be! She had to acknowledge that the best years of her life were over. She was fifty-one, and her black hair was shot through with silver.

Her figure had thickened slightly, without her meaning it to. There had been suitors over the years despite her desire to lead a quiet life, but she had turned them all down. Now, presumably, there would be no more. When she thought of Hartley's father, it was with an increasing pain and an awareness of having let life pass her by.

It was as if the events of her first thirty years had been too intense, too concentrated, too soon. Thereafter, she had sat back in relief and coasted along with the tide. Now, it was too late to do anything about it, and she was beginning to feel incomplete and unfulfilled despite the joy of her son and the care of Mr Hooper. She knew she was lucky to have no financial worries now. Mr Hooper had treated her like a daughter and ensured that would continue after him, in his generosity.

How different things might have been had she swallowed her pride to come to him earlier! But she should not complain. Everything had turned out for the best. Only she felt restive and uncertain. *I am going to be lonely*, she thought, *and it is no one's fault but my own. Why could I not have accepted any of those nice, well-meaning gentlemen? I have compromised myself before - why not once more? Why did my life stand still when I came here?* Yet she did not regret that. It had been the right decision.

In October, the trees in Mr Hooper's garden wept flame-coloured leaves once more onto the grass. The frosts had come early and sharp that year, and it was a brilliant fall. Soon, there would be deep, crisp snow. Caitlin felt depressed and was angry at herself for being so. She was writing a dispirited letter to Polly in the library when Mr Hooper's visitor was shown in. She raised her head as she heard the sound of low voices and the study door closing on them across the hall.

His lawyer, no doubt, come to draw up young Hartley's marriage settlement.

In a little while, she was summoned to their presence by the faithful Millie. She had not heard his visitor leave, but Mr Hooper was alone.

"Sit down, Caitlin," he said kindly. "Someone most unexpected has been to see me."

She sat down curiously. "I thought I heard someone," she said. "What did he want?"

"He wanted," said Mr Hooper gravely, "to take you away from here!"

She looked at the snowy white head in alarm.

"Whatever do you mean? I should not allow that!"

"Wouldn't you, my dear? I rather think you should." She stared at him uncomprehendingly.

"Go down into the garden, and you will see why," Mr Hooper said, smiling now with great satisfaction. "Go on. There is nothing to be afraid of. He is waiting for you, but he will not pursue you if you run away. He has only one leg and walks with crutches."

She knew then.

In the hall, she cast an anxious glance in the mirror as she passed by and did not like what she saw. Her face was white, her eyes still bright blue but fearful, her hair threaded through with the unwelcome grey. She was wearing a becoming dress (for her age) but thought she looked very faded. Her heart was in turmoil, and her mind in confusion. What could it mean? Why had he come? Had he found out about his son? Had someone told him? If they had, she would never forgive them.

He was waiting under the tree by the white garden table and chairs, in the exact place where she had first met Mr Hooper, standing in the lengthening shadows cast by the evening sun. He looked, she thought, with a rapid skip of the heart, extremely well. His hair was still sandy and thick, his figure straight. He no longer wore an Army uniform, of course, but a fine, well-cut suit of grey cloth, an embroidered waistcoat, and a silk cravat. He was older, of course, as she was, but still Hartley. Oh, but why had he come now, whilst she was in this vulnerable state?

He stretched out his hand for hers, took it and raised it to his lips. "Cait," he said simply as if he had never been away. "Let me look at you!"

"Hartley?" Her voice was weak.

"I know you didn't believe me that day on the station platform. That we could ever be together again. But I did. And now the time has come. Polly told me where you were."

He told her that Rosa had died six months ago. He would not have her believe he was glad of it because he wasn't. When she died, she looked more like eighty than sixty-seven. He had never told her about meeting Caitlin again. He had loved and respected her until the end, though she had never completely got over Johann's death and was never really able to enjoy their prosperity as a result. Still, the fact remained that after so long he was now free.

"But I am not!" she cried. "I could never leave Mr Hooper, who has been like a father to me in the last years of his life. Who would talk to him and read to him and comfort him then?"

But it was all arranged, said Hartley. He understood the situation. He had made a proposition to the old gentleman, which had been most gratefully accepted. Mr Hooper would be only too willing to sell up and come to live with them. He had said he was beginning to feel the upstate winters too much in his old bones. He had never lived anywhere else, it was true, but now it was time he did. His greatest wish was for Caitlin to be happy, and he felt that he and Hartley Senior could become great friends.

"But he would hate New York," said Caitlin. "I know he would!"

"Not in New York exactly," Hartley replied. "I have a house as large as this now on Long Island, looking out to sea. He said he would like to hear the sound of the sea. Will you not take me, Caitlin, after all this time?"

She reached out her arms for an answer, overwhelmed with emotions, and he embraced her. They stood together like that quietly for a long time.

Then, there was a shout of laughter from behind the trees. A group of young people had come out onto the terrace and in the midst of them was the fine, tall young man that was Hartley Shawcross Hooper and his fiancée. Hartley caught sight of him at once and stood there wondering, uncertain and unsure what to make of it all.

"Come," said Caitlin, extending her hand and smiling at him. "There is someone you must meet. He doesn't know it yet, but he has waited for this moment a very long time, and so have you."

EPILOGUE

They were married before Christmas and honeymooned at Niagara-on-the-Lake before returning to their extended family home on Long Island. At first, it seemed impossible to Caitlin that they could find such happiness again in their fifties, and yet it became evident it was all the stronger because of that. Where once they would have quickly found fault with each other, they now knew tolerance.

In 1895, ten years later, they were dispatched to visit Europe by their children, most tentative and fearful at the idea of the dreaded sea-crossing. But this time, they travelled on a steamship in first class. Their berth was a stateroom, and they dined in a saloon resplendent with chandeliers and inlaid mahogany. They were attended by smart waiters and serenaded by violins. They could not believe how much they enjoyed it.

They saw Paris, London and Rome and wondered if all of these places could have been there all of this while. There were other pilgrimages to make too: to Frankfurt, to Yorkshire, where they were cordially received by the stiff-necked Jeremiah Senior, who professed great delight in seeing them but was nonetheless relieved at their departure, to Liverpool, where Caitlin made a sadly fruitless attempt to find the descendants of Padraig and Bridget Murphy and finally to little Ballakenny in South-West Ireland.

It was a moist, drizzling, damp morning when they arrived there.

Hartley stood back and watched Caitlin lay the flowers on the grave of James. She stood for a long while before it with tears in her eyes, but when she turned back to him, he saw she was smiling and content.

"Is it done well?" he asked her with understanding in his voice.

"Yes, it is done well."

They sought refuge in the covered trap. He put his arm around her rain-dampened shoulders as the wheels bore them away, secure in their love for each other and bound once more for America.

"The greatest gift of all he gave me," said Caitlin, "was in teaching me to read."

"He stayed with me a long time," she continued. "Perhaps always, though not at all in the way I thought."

Hartley nodded. "You know," he said, equally pensive, looking out at the rather dismal grey-green countryside and the hills. "We should have brought the children to see all of this. When I left these isles, I only thought of myself at the time but looking back over the years, it is the children that it was all about. They should know something of this."

"No," she said. "No, Hartley, they shouldn't. Not this time. One day, they'll want to know, or maybe their children, our grandchildren, or great-grandchildren will. But not now. They have too much of life before them. They are Americans."

POSTSCRIPT

REUBEN KLEIST: Survived the Civil War and became a pianist and songwriter. For many years, he struggled to make a living and was supported patiently by Hartley. At the turn of the century, much to his elderly stepfather's astonishment, he suddenly became enormously successful as a composer of melodies for musical shows. He never married but had a secret, much-loved male partner.

RACHEL KLEIST: Was known as a great beauty in New York society and acted to much acclaim on the stage until her marriage to a man whom both she and Hartley found acceptable. Her life could not have been more different to her mother's.

FRIEDRICH KLEIST JUNIOR: Trained as a doctor and became an eminent surgeon in New York.

JEREMIAH SHAWCROSS: Was an uncertain, awkward boy who always felt somewhat at odds with his father but did eventually settle into the business career for which he was trained and continued the family business.

MARGARET SHAWCROSS: Married a farmer and moved to Wisconsin, against her father and especially her stepmother's wishes. Despite their fears, the farm was a success, and the family eventually bought into timber mills.

HARTLEY SHAWCROSS HOOPER: Gave up his business career and read law. Was much concerned with civil rights, entered politics, and ultimately became a United States Senator. His name was known throughout the country, and he was respected for his integrity and moral compass. During his long life, he was able to do much good, thereby fulfilling the prediction of the estimable Miss Caroline Cholmondeley.

And somewhere, in what used to be Kickapoo territory way out in the Mid-West, it is still claimed to this day there lives a colony of yellow singing birds, similar to canaries. But few folks have seen them so the locals who know better are not much believed. Nevertheless, they insist a half breed Indian man with a fine horse used to nurture them and was instrumental in their survival.

END

ACKNOWLEDGEMENTS

Passage to America: A History of Emigrants from Great Britain and Ireland to America in the Mid-Nineteenth Century by Terry Coleman
Published by Penguin Random House 1972
ISBN 10 0091104009

The Great Hunger: Ireland 1845-9
By Cecil Woodham Smith
Hamish Hamilton
ISBN 978-0140145151

Manhattan Manners: Architecture and Style
By Christine Boyer
Rizzoli International publications
ISBN 10 0847806508

The Civil War
By William C Davis
Published by Time Life books Inc. 1983
ISBN 0-8094-4704-5

American Notes
By Charles Dickens
Published by Chapman & Hall 1842
ISBN 9780140436495

Thank you also to the helpful guides at Llechwydd Slate Mine in Blaenau Ffestiniog, North Wales.

And with many thanks to Jeff W Goodwin at Arcanum Press and my helpful editor, Julie Cummings.

THE AUTHOR

Alison Harrop (alias Alice Mitchell) won a prestigious Betty Trask Book Award in 1985 for her first Novel 'Instead of Eden' which is about the lives of a grandmother, mother and daughter during the '60s and '70s in the North of England. More than thirty years later, after a rewarding career as a medical Doctor, she released her second work 'The Mortimer Affair - Joan de Joinville's Story' set in the turbulent reign of Edward II. After many years living in Merseyside, Chester and North Wales, Alison is now retired and has returned to Yorkshire. Her work of Historical Fiction 'The Golden Door' is a tale of 19th Century emigrants to America. Whilst initially struggling to make their way in New York, they are then embroiled in the lead up to the Civil War along the western frontiers of Kansas, and the battles of the Civil War itself.